LIONS AT NIGHT

ALSO BY RICHARD HIMMEL

The Twenty-Third Web

LIONS AT NIGHT

A NOVEL

RICHARD HIMMEL

DELACORTE PRESS/NEW YORK

Published by
Delacorte Press
1 Dag Hammarskjold Plaza
New York, N.Y. 10017

Manufactured in the United States of America
First printing

Designed by Jo Anne Bonnell

Library of Congress Cataloging in Publication Data

Himmel, Richard.
Lions at night.

I. Title.
PZ3.H575Li   [PS3515.I7147]   811'.5'4   79–592
ISBN 0–440–04980–6

Acknowledgment of gratitude does not constitute a diminution of indebtedness: I know that. But I am grateful to Sterling Lord who energized and implemented my renaissance as a writer and to Robb Land who ran ragged to document it and to Mitzi and Jim Magin who abetted research. But most of all, I am grateful to my wife who took the resultant confusion, all the disparate elements, and kneaded them smooth into the whole of our lives.

—R.H.

The lions of the night
are the lambs of the day.
An Ethiopian proverb

1978
AUGUST

TUESDAY

AN UNIDENTIFIED INSTALLATION NEAR WASHINGTON, D.C.

The undersecretary's eyes were focused on the younger man, still assessing him, trying to appraise the human characteristics concealed behind the expressionless face mask and the armor of rigid military posture. Lowell Callender had already made up his mind; he was searching for intellectual justification for his gut decision. Without redirecting his visual fix, his words were spoken to the older man. "There is no point in playing games, Colonel. As far as I'm concerned, all systems are *go*. The State Department officially sanctions the candidate." Now he turned and faced the colonel. "Approve the assignment now. Don't wait for the red tape to unwind. Urgency, Colonel. The key word is urgency. Don't get hung up on procedure." He gathered the dossier spread in front of him, stacked the documents together neatly, and inserted them into a folder which had been marked EYES ONLY, then crossed out and reclassified SECRET.

With practiced patience and restraint, Colonel Jack Kelly took the folder, put it in front of him, folded his hands over it. "Due respect, Mr. Secretary, but we have our own way of handling things out here. From where you sit, it might appear as though we spin a lot of unnecessary wheels but we've had long experience at this."

"Don't give me your CIA mumbo-jumbo, Colonel. This is a special task force directly responsible to the National Security Council. It was set up very deliberately to avoid getting bogged down in CIA mire and confusion."

"The chain of command may not be quite the same but it's still CIA no matter what initials you put on the operation." Purposefully, knowing the undersecretary's background, he pointed out, "We're all career men here. We haven't been plucked out of civilian life to suddenly take over jobs which require years of training, years of experience. We're seasoned professionals. Specialists. Our system of checks and balances is not a dilettante exercise to look impressive on an organizational chart. Lives are at stake, Mr. Secretary. National security. Those stakes are too big to take chances or to plunge into an operation without thoroughly investigating the qualifications of personnel." He leaned forward, spread his hands flat on the dossier. "I understand the urgency completely, sir. That's why I am being so careful. You do understand, don't you, that the final decision is ours?" He watched the undersecretary's face tighten in anger. "And the final responsibility is also ours. In other words, Mr. Callender, it's our ass that can wind up in a sling if anything goes wrong."

"I'm not worried about your ass, Colonel. I'm not worried about my own ass either. I'm worried about our President's ass. I'm worried about our country's ass."

Kelly retreated slightly, lowered the volume of his own voice, tried unsuccessfully to smile. "We're not trying to be difficult, only careful. As I said, we understand the urgency as well as the sensitivity of this project." He looked over at the younger man, still sitting ramrod straight, his face showing no reaction. "When we have completed our investigation and evaluation of Edgerton, we'll pass along our recommendation."

"Hasn't anything that I've said gotten through to you, Colonel? Why wait? You wouldn't have chased me all the way out here unless you were more than reasonably certain that Edgerton was the right man for the job." Now he, too, looked over at Edgerton. "Everyone else who has interrogated him agrees that he's the right man. I confirm it. Isn't that enough for you?"

"You haven't heard anything I've said, either, Mr. Secretary. Everything here goes through the chain of command. It must. Safeguards are built into our routine."

"This operation was conceived in my office in response to an imminent danger. Your job is to expedite and implement. If you procrastinate, your safeguards can defeat the very thing we're trying to accomplish. You don't know the total picture, Colonel.

Your range is limited to a tiny sector. This is a broader canvas than your usual cloak-and-dagger forays. The pressure for action starts at the top, all the way from the top." The drawl in his voice became more noticeable as he became angrier. "I realize that you professionals consider us the new boys in town. I can understand some of your resentment at the shake-ups in the Agency. But I think the blood baths have been justified. The presidential directives are clear-cut and precise. Things are moving in a straighter line these days. Faster. Even out here, you must have noticed that."

Terminating the meeting, the undersecretary stood up. Kelly and Edgerton rose at the same time, standing erect, not quite at military attention. Callender held out his hand to Edgerton: his whole structure softened, his smile was an indication of understanding between two men in the face of opposition, the lingering handshake was the secret grip of conspirators. "I am confident that everything will work out and that we will be seeing each other again very soon." He moved around the table, looked back. "Off the record, Edgerton— and I am aware of your personal reasons for secrecy as well as the official designation—but I can't resist my own observations. I can see very much of your real father in you. Now that I know the facts, I can see a very definite physical resemblance. It's amazing. I saw him on television only a few nights ago. You two could be taken for brothers." He smiled again, put his own hand on Edgerton's arm. "Southern country boys have an affinity for each other. We understand things that no Northerner can feel. That's why your father has always been a great favorite of mine. He's a bright star to follow. Good luck to you." He firmed the touch on Edgerton's arm into a squeeze. "God bless." He turned sharply, started out of the room. Kelly turned to Edgerton, signaled hopeless desperation, followed Callender out of the room.

When he was alone, Edgerton leaned against the table, relaxed his body tension. There was almost no distention of his stomach muscles now. He punched the hard wall of gut. Even if it all came to nothing, these three weeks of total immersion had put him back into physical shape, tightened the sags, and trimmed off the fat of years of easy living. He ran his hand over his face, feeling his own features, trying to find the resemblance which the undersecretary had seen. But there was no cleft in his chin, not the famous dimples nor the high cheekbones and straight nose. Maybe the eyes, he was thinking: there could be a sameness about the eyes or the expression around the eyes.

He stood straight again, shook his head to clear it, to make the fantasies stop.

Years ago, this had been a consuming part of his life, studying photographs in movie magazines, watching the man perform on television and in films, always searching for a reflection of himself in the face of the man whose sperm had fathered him. This quest for identification, the daydreams of the king finding the long-lost prince, had been destructive to him then: they would be even more destructive now. He blanked out his consciousness, stopped the flow of dreams.

He began pacing the small room, circling around the long table, gradually changing to a jog; his head down and his arms bent, each arm moving in a contrapunctal, semicircular motion at a coordinated cadence with his legs and breathing. When he felt the perspiration on his forehead, he stopped, took a handkerchief from his back pocket, blotted the wetness, and sat down again to wait for Jack Kelly.

Waiting.

It seemed that his whole life had been spent waiting until the waiting became a total existence by itself. When the awaited event happened or did not happen, the result was an anti-climax, a jolt to his physical and mental systems. In action, he was a stranger to himself; another man moving in his body, motivated by a different mentality. Only when it was over and he began to wait again, immersed in the familiar placenta of waiting, did he become himself again.

The dossier had been left on the table, the scarlet letters SECRET staring at him. Edgerton did not touch the folder, tried to mind-x-ray the contents, guess at all the documents which it contained. His entire record couldn't be all there: the folder was too thin. He had been recruited when he was nineteen years old. In fourteen years there would be many more documents, much more evidence of the long waiting periods and the short intervals of action; his successes, his failures. This file could only contain information relating to this immediate assignment. His master file would be buried somewhere else, probably at the CIA headquarters in Langley. But with all the changes there, he couldn't even be sure anymore that his covert identity still existed. The only evidence he had was that the money was still being deposited quarterly in his bank in Chicago. Once, his wife had questioned the source. The cover for the payment had been set up long before: a dividend check from a dummy stock issued by a dummy corporation. Edgerton was not certain how much Kelly knew about his background. Kelly was in charge of personnel evaluation, probably had no access to master files, particularly those of covert operations. In Vietnam, where they had first met, Kelly had thought Edgerton was just another soldier, another prisoner of war. Edgerton wondered if he had ever learned the truth.

Kelly burst back into the windowless room, slamming the door behind him. His face was red with the anger no longer kept under control. "That prick. That lousy, pompous prick. I don't know how I sleep at night knowing guys like that are running the country. God help us." He shook his head as he sat down, folded his hands on the dossier, unaware that he breached security by leaving it unattended. "This is a great country. We always muddle through in spite of the Lowell Callenders."

"He wasn't as bad as I thought he would be. You painted a much blacker picture."

"Don't be fooled by the way he looks or the way he talks. Those new Washington bastards are all alike: they look like Yale law school and talk like Amos and Andy. They say God bless when they mean fuck off."

"He's younger than I thought he would be. What do you guess, mid-forties?"

"About. Give or take a couple of years. There are two ways of looking at it: You can ask, how did a guy get to be such a mean bastard in only forty-odd years? Or you can ask how a guy can live forty odd years and still be such a dumb shit."

"You may be underestimating him, Jack. I've run into his kind before. Lineal thinkers. Single-minded purpose. The straight line . . . the shortest distance between two points."

"Lineal thinker, my ass. He's a jughead. Maybe an egghead, but also a jughead. Do you know what he asked me out there, after he got through chewing my ass out, do you know what he asked me? You won't believe this. I heard him and I can still hardly believe it. He asked me the name of some of the movies you've been in . . . just in case they come up on the late, late show. I mean you really turned that guy on. I thought he was going to send me back for your autograph. I didn't tell him that you also did some guest shots on *Star Trek*. That poor, little Southern boy would have gone bananas, freaked out." Kelly took off his jacket, loosened his tie, unbuttoned his shirt collar, sat down, untied his left shoe, took it off, and rubbed his stockinged foot. "As a matter of fact, Edgerton, and strictly off the record"—he was mimicking the soft, Southern sound of the undersecretary's voice—"I would like to permit a personal indulgence and ask you a few questions about your film career. You see, I took the prerogative of having a private screening of some of the movies you were in. My, but you were a pretty sight on all those beaches with your muscles hanging out." He looked up, talked in his own voice. "Tell me, did anyone ever actually fuck Annette Funicello?"

Edgerton laughed. "You're stalling, Jack. You're playing for time. Why don't you get to the point? If the answer is *no*, tell me. But don't shit me, don't string me along."

"The answer isn't *no*. It isn't *yes*, either."

"That leaves *maybe*."

"You want this assignment pretty bad, don't you?"

Edgerton nodded.

"Your marriage . . . it wasn't going right, was it?"

"Leave that out of this."

"I can't, Edge. I have a job to do. I can't recommend a man for a job just because he wants out of a marriage."

"You know me better than that."

"Do I? I've been thinking about that, wondering how well I really do know you." He rubbed the leather of his face and reached behind his glasses to massage his eyes. "We've known each other for a long, long time. We're damned good friends, wouldn't you say? Years go by and we don't see each other, but good friends are good friends no matter what." He looked straight at Edgerton for affirmation. There was no response. "That stinking POW camp in Vietnam . . . kind of a microcosm of the primitive world. You get to know a man pretty well when you grovel for food with him, sleep in dungeons together, shit in the same pits, fuck the same broads. Christ, you made me look like a fucking amateur when we got to that rest area. Guys always talk big about what kind of cocksmiths they are but I've seen you in action, Edge, and seeing is believing. I thought I knew everything about you." He slammed his hand on the dossier. "It turns out, I didn't know you at all."

Edgerton cocked his head toward the folder. "What did you find out in there that turned you off?"

The colonel sat up straight, put his elbows on the table, locked his hands, gnarled his fingers together. "I'm not turned off, Edge. I'm confused."

It was a narrow line for Edgerton. He was still unsure of how much information was in that dossier and how much other information Kelly had access to. "What are you confused about? Isn't it all in my record?"

"I've learned a lot about you in the last two weeks. Maybe more than I want to know about a friend and maybe not enough that I should know in the line of duty. In all that time together in Nam, I realized now that you told me very little about yourself, none of the important things anyway. By the time we got out of there, you knew as much about me as I knew about myself. I didn't know anything about you except that you were a kid from Tennessee whose mother had been a piano teacher. I didn't know that you had a whole movie career and blew it. My wife recognized you from that Polaroid shot the Red Cross gal took of us. She said, 'My God, that's Marc Polo.' And I told her she was out of her mind, it was just an ordinary guy named Ross Edgerton. One night we were watching the late show . . . son of a bitch, it was you. Ross Edgerton and Marc Polo were the same man. How come you never told me?"

"It didn't work out, the movie thing. I was no good at acting. I wanted to forget that part of my life."

"I thought you were an orphan. I felt sorry for a kid whose mother and father were both dead, a kid without anyone in the whole world who cared about him. Then last week, I find out that you're not an orphan at all. Your father is a big star . . . the hip-swinging rock idol of the nation. Now, why didn't you mention that in all those months in prison?"

"I've never seen my father. He's never seen me. It's something else that hurts to talk about." He hesitated. "It hurts now." Edgerton touched Kelly's arm. "We didn't know if we were going to live or die, Jack. All I thought about was getting out of there . . . trying to escape. All those other things didn't seem important then. Are they now?"

"Maybe each piece by itself isn't important. But when you put it all together, it's confusing. Nothing figures right. It's like doping football games pre-season. Every damn statistic points to a winner.

It's all down on paper. There's no disputing facts. You've picked an unbeatable team. Then the season starts and those bastards lose every game." He looked up. "Do you understand what I'm trying to say?"

Edgerton's face tightened; his eyes narrowed; he started to speak, changed his mind, said nothing.

"I know what you're thinking, Edge. Here I am calling you a loser when I should know better than any man in the world that you're a winner. At least once. I'm on this earth today because you were a winner at least once. Christ, do you think I'll ever forget that? That I'm still alive because another man had balls and brains. Bravery. Christ, that's an old-fashioned word. But that's what you were, Edge. Brave. In my book, you're a fucking hero."

"You've paid that back in many ways, Jack."

"Not in kind. I haven't paid it back in kind. It fucks me up, fucks up my thinking, living with unpayable debts to another man." He looked up at the ceiling, trying to penetrate it with his eyes, searching for an answer beyond it. "Maybe if I ax you for this job, I'll be paying you back. Maybe if I stamp DISAPPROVED on your application, I'll be saving your life. But I would never know for certain, would I?" He walked around the table, stood behind Edgerton, both hands on his shoulders, his thumbs kneading the base of Edgerton's neck. The same image was in both men's minds: six days crouched in a cave, forced by the confines into a fetal position, then the days of working the knots out of each other's muscles until they could hold their heads straight again. "I don't even know what this job is. I never know. I just get requisitions for personnel. I beat the bushes until I get the guy with the qualifications requested. I never know what he does, where he goes, whether he lives or dies. Sure, once in a while I read something in the newspapers and I can put two and two together but usually I never know. When you called me, right before you left your wife, it was the same day I got the requisition. Everything just seemed to fit together. The timing seemed predestined."

"Don't play with yourself, Jack. You're too disciplined to make a professional decision for emotional reasons."

"Am I?" He reached over, slammed his hand flat against the dossier. "There's a document missing from your file. I destroyed it. Tell me *that* isn't emotional."

"What document?"

"Three lousy pieces of paper, in a handwriting you could hardly read. How many psychiatric examinations have you had since you've been here?"

"Five. Maybe six. I didn't keep score."

"One guy, one wizened little guy who can hardly see through his thick glasses . . . he saw something no one else saw. *I* sure as hell never saw it." The colonel returned to the other side of the table, facing Edgerton directly again. "Go ahead, Edge, ask the question." Edgerton said nothing. "That shrink said that in his opinion you're a loser, a compulsive loser. He makes quite a case out of it. School. He compares your IQ with your achievement record. Loser. Tennis. Right at the threshold of big time. Crack-up. A loser again. Your stint in the movies . . . it's his theory, and he talked to some people in California, that you could have been big time but you walked away from it, purposely blew it. The same with every job you ever had, every personal relationship. Your marriage. He thinks you subconsciously sabotaged that. All in all, he makes quite a case for his theory."

"But it's still only a theory."

"Right. And his opinion is only one out of six. The other five thought you were dandy. A few minuses here and there but mostly pluses. None of the other shrinks even came close to recognizing this pattern. It never would have occurred to me. But once a case was made for it, I can't see anything else."

"Dr. Kaplan," Edgerton said.

"That's right. Dr. Kaplan. Little Dr. Kaplan who can't find his way to the men's room alone, doesn't know the Army from the Navy, can hardly speak English. That's the one."

"Bright guy," Edgerton said.

"Is he? Is he right about you?"

Edgerton shrugged his shoulders. "This is your bag, Jack. You're the personnel expert. You have the expertise to read the facts and make the judgments. Is he right about me?"

"You know what else he says, Edge? This one is a corker. He says that subconsciously you have made the ultimate choice of the compulsive loser. In spite of all your denials, he is convinced that you are sexually impotent . . . zero in the sack." The colonel's voice softened. "When did that happen, Edge?"

"Who said it happened?"

"Dr. Kaplan."

"It's only a theory."

"Damn it, Edgerton, answer the question."

"Does it make a difference in the job, Colonel? Does it?" The older man looked away, rubbed his eyes, slouched in the chair. Edgerton hammered his advantage. "Does getting a hard-on, getting my rocks off, make a difference? Use your famous mental discipline, Colonel. In the unique qualifications that you say this job requires, does getting a hard-on make the difference?"

His voice was hardly audible. "It might."

"For Christ's sake, Jack, are you sending me out to stud or to save the world?"

"According to this requisition it may be the same thing. Halfway down the list of requirements, after psychologically and physically able to kill, are two little words in lowercase type: genitally endowed." The Colonel grinned. "What do you suppose that means?"

"I've fucked for my country before," Edgerton said.

"And been fucked?"

Edgerton did not answer.

Kelly squinted at the document, the decision made. "You're hung like a horse, Edgerton." He scratched his initials in the approval box of the requisition. "You've got the job."

ENROUTE TO WASHINGTON, D.C.

His personal limousine was waiting in the parking lot, the driver half-asleep behind the wheel. When administration directives had tightened up expense spending, Callender had bought his own Cadillac limo, hired his own driver, charged only the fuel and maintenance to the government. He took the driver's salary and the depreciation of the automobile as a deduction on his individual tax return. He was in the back seat before the chauffeur could get out to open the door.

"Back to Washington, sir?"

"As fast as you can." Callender opened the window as the car began to move, inhaling fresh air after the airlessness of the interrogation room. He wondered about Edgerton, if he really was the right man at the right time. Edgerton had answered his questions minimally, revealing little of himself. There had been no way to get inside Edgerton's head to understand thought processes and feelings. Kelly had been an inhibiting factor in the questioning, acted as a buffer, a protective shield. There was a relationship between the two men which was not clear to Callender. It did not matter: once the assignment was approved, Kelly would be out of the picture, officially out of touch with Edgerton and, barring a security breach, Kelly could have no idea of the details or general nature of the operation.

Edgerton would make the sixth agent under special assignment to the Undersecretary of State, completing Callender's hand-picked operatives. The other agents would be CIA regulars, interrelating with those on this special assignment. But the hard-core six were personally important to Callender, a future source group for the implementation of his own motivations. Callender had been more thorough in the examination of the other five, estimating not only their skills for the specific mission, but their political and moral flexibility to adapt to a sudden superimposed plan. The blueprint for this master plan existed only in Callender's head. Evidence existed nowhere else: no incriminating documents in files, no confidants who could talk later. Each of the other five agents, Callender was certain of this, had a capability of turning, switching allegiances under properly motivated distress. In one way or another, they had been mishandled or misused by established authority and they were uncertain of their future because of the recent intelligence shake-ups in the NSA and CIA. They were afraid that the purge would continue, that the blood bath would reach them, wash them out of their careers. He did not have this certainty about Edgerton. Under the pressure of adhering to the time table, Callender had acted on instinct, not shoring up his instinctive reading of the man with enough hard facts. But it was done. Kelly would stamp his approval; taking his own time, trying to make his job appear more important than it really was. Callender had finally pinned him down to a five o'clock deadline. If he had not heard from Kelly by five after five, the ball-busting machinery would be put into action. The operation had to begin on schedule.

*   *   *

Lowell Callender was not a career diplomat, did not have the tenure in government which inured professionals to the frustrations of routine, structured procedures and to the snail-paced, circuitous channels of communication and command. Born rich, Callender had made himself super-rich in private life by destroying equivalent established structures in the financial world, straight-lining the fierce drive of his ambition from one goal to the next and each goal became not an end in itself but a stepping-stone to a higher goal. Money had never been the ultimate object: it was a cumulative by-product of winning. He had an Alexanderine passion to conquer, each new attack against a bigger army with lesser odds for success. Callender was not a man to analyze and dissect the source of his passions, endangering the possibility of diluting them in the process. He fueled his passions, always needing a greater energy source and supply.

None of these characteristics had surfaced while he was growing up in New Orleans, where he was born and bred. He was an obedient child, diffident, slightly bookish, rarely remonstrative against the pre-established way of his life. There had been four years at Annapolis, two years at Harvard Business School, and three years at the University of Virginia Law School. Secure with these credentials, he went into the family business, attacked it with a suddenly unleashed fury and in five years had turned an import-export firm into a public company on the New York Stock Exchange and in seven years into a major conglomerate diversified into real estate, banking, shipping, farm machinery, and weapons brokerage. His area of expertise was Central and South America, the Caribbean Islands. He developed markets in Latin America, created new markets where none had existed before. He used underdeveloped countries to mask enormous sales of merchandise to Iron Curtain countries and to the bludgeoning African continent, circumventing Federal trade restrictions by elaborate cover devices.

He had been sitting in his office one morning when, unannounced, his grandfather had been wheeled in by a black attendant almost as old as the old man. Cancer had reduced Lafayette Callender to a thin-skinned skeleton. No vestige remained of the physically powerful man he had once been. Only his eyes remained alive, still capable of penetrating and cutting down another man. The bony, gnarled hand pointed to the tall French doors overlooking the harbor and the old docks. "Put me over there," he directed the attendant, "and then haul ass."

Callender was forced to abandon the fortress of his antique, pa-per-laden desk, walk around, and pull over a chair close enough to hear the frail voice. "I'm near dying," his grandfather said. He put his hand on Callender's knee. "Now, don't you start counting my money yet. I've been near dying for ten years and I'm still here, crustier than I ever was."

"You'll probably last for another ten."

"Maybe. I hope not. But either way, you and me are going to have a talk right now. It's been on my mind a long time. Your daddy isn't man enough, or maybe he doesn't care enough to give you a talking to. I'm so old it doesn't matter what I say." Callender smiled at the old man, stretched his arms, surreptitiously looking at his watch, annoyed at the interruption of his schedule, calculating how many minutes he could allot to indulge his grandfather. "I'm looking at you, Lowell, and I'm seeing a quiet-looking man in one of those Haspel seersucker suits. With those horn-rimmed glasses and that peaceful expression, you look like a professor of some kind. You appear to be a gentle man, Lowell, like butter could melt in your mouth." He strained forward, trying to get closer to his grandson. "Now, we both know that isn't the truth, don't we, Lowell? We both know that you're really a mean son of a bitch."

"Get to the point, Grandpa."

"I'm old, Lowell, running out of time, yet I feel I've got all the time in the world. You're young and you don't have time for any-thing, not even a helpless old man."

Callender smiled at his grandfather. "And we both know that isn't true, either, don't we, Grandpa? You're still a tough, smart, old bastard."

"I hope you mean that, Lowell. I hope you really think that I am a smart, tough, old bastard because I'm going to give you some advice." He dropped the volume of his voice, smiled. "You going to listen like a good boy?"

"Go to it, Grandpa."

"The folks around here used to talk a lot about us, how the family started. That was long ago, before we became so respectable. They used to say that we started as pirates; raping, robbing, plundering. I think that's true. It's how come we have a history of trading with all those countries across the gulf. My ancestors were pirates but they were nothing compared to you, Lowell. Sitting there prim and proper, you're really the biggest pirate of them all."

"Thank you, Grandpa. Knowing your life history, I take that to be a commendation."

"I didn't mean it to be, Lowell. I meant it to smart just as if I'd whipped your backside raw. You have no excuse being a pirate. You already have more money than you and your children can ever spend. It seems to me you ought to be putting back, not taking out. I'm not saying that you shouldn't keep on making money . . . that's your nature. But there are ways of making money that's positive, not negative. Looking at your own country, seeing how the South is building up again, how this whole sunbelt is prospering, ripe to prosper even more . . . that's positive, Lowell. You put back here and you're going to profit twenty times." He tried to back off his wheelchair. "You're smart enough to understand that, aren't you, boy?" He looked at the impassive face. "Aren't you?"

The change in Lowell Callender had not been abrupt. His grandfather's words had not been a sudden revelation, turning a pirate into a missionary, changing the direction of his life. The words had begun a chain reaction of restlessness, a boredom of repetitive triumphs of equal magnitude. An emotional turn-on was missing: the achievements were hollow. He studied the potential growth pattern of his corporation, understood that the giant growth had already come in the last seven years. The indication of the next seven years was a more gradual curve, not always a straight ascent. He had structured the corporation so that the slow growth period would happen with or without him.

It was time to turn his eye to a bigger mountain.

Now, two years later, all of his holdings were in a trust which he did not directly control: Callender's commitment to the government was total, his sights aimed in another direction. In Washington, heading the Latin American desk of the State Department, he took hold quickly, solving problems almost instantly because he understood the Latin American mentality, could think like them, understood that most problems which appeared political were actually financial. Money was a universal language transcending everything else: it was a language Callender was fluent in. And Callender, through his business dealings, was directly in contact with hidden power structures operating in the area, the unofficial organizations of men which made things happen or not happen according to their personal needs. These men would never trust a career diplomat, would never expose themselves publicly. But they had dealt with Lowell Callender before: he was one of their kind and they trusted him, understood that no matter what mantle he was cloaked in, Callender was one of them.

When Callender was first warned of a possible Cuban invasion being planned by unknown perpetrators, other fragments of information and intelligence which had come across his desk made sense suddenly. Isolated bits and pieces fit together to give credence to the possibility of some kind of impending operation against Cuba. Circumventing State Department channels, he used his own network to test the feasibility, to see if there was further evidence available to substantiate the information he had. All the information fed back to him was negative: no symptoms anywhere. But Callender was still convinced that the story was true; some kind of an attack was being prepared.

The timing was right. In spite of the increasing threat of Cubans in Africa and an estimated 20,000 troops in Zaire, undercover normalization with Castro's government was proceeding with the State Department's other hand. If he were on the other side, Callender knew it would be time to throw in a monkey wrench, break down the reestablishment of U.S. and Cuban relations before they became a reality. Russia was using Castro as a front to gain deep African roots. Soviet-equipped Cubans were in Angola, Zaire, Ethiopia, Tanzania and ready to metastasize horizontally. At this point, a diversion in the form of an invasion of Cuban soil, particularly if it appeared to be sanctioned and implemented by the United States, was the excuse Castro needed to step up his military imperialism, draw in open Communist military support for the defense of his island. Callender examined the possibility that Castro himself was masterminding the plot but he rejected that thesis. Castro's geopolitical strategy was to play both ends against the middle, eventually be nourished and enriched by both sides of the opposite ideological worlds.

If the evidence was true, there was an imminent danger to world peace and an immediate personal danger to the President of the United States. Callender assumed the evidence was true, fabricated it in his own mind so that it would appear more than circumstantial. Then he contacted the White House.

In spite of the intimacy and mutual dependence which had existed between them during the campaign, Callender's direct contact with the President was infrequent after the election, his access to the Oval Office limited and restricted, appointments difficult to obtain through the echelon of honchos guarding him. Callender sat on the Cuban invasion threat information for three days before he was granted an appointment with the President and then the time was limited to twenty minutes.

"I have been involved often enough on the other side," he told the President, "to recognize the evidence, know that it's valid and be certain that it points to an insurrection or invasion of some kind. Whoever is planning this is planning it cleverly. Surplus arms are being bought up all over the world, never enough in one place to cause suspicion. Airplane parts, discarded and obsolete small aircraft are being shipped into various Caribbean islands, all the way from the Bahamas to Cozumel and as far down as San Andreas off the coast of Colombia. Somehow all this equipment disappears. Mercenary soldiers, some of them who have fought against Castro in the African insurrections, are being filtered out of Africa and appear briefly at one Caribbean port or another and then they, too, disappear, are never heard of again."

"How did you get on to all of this?"

"Through a man named Julio San Marco. The CIA recruited him for the Bay of Pigs invasion; he commanded one of the major thrusts on red beach, served directly under Artimè. San Marco and Castro grew up together, went to school together, were close friends all their lives. When Castro came down from the Sierra Maestra to take over Cuba, San Marco was at his side. He was a skilled intelligence officer, had been the key man in organizing the fifth column inside Havana itself." Callender studied the President's face, trying to assess how much background information was stored in the back of the President's head. But he was only allotted twenty minutes. "San Marco was one of the handful of intellectual idealists in Castro's original group. When Castro's brand of Communism, his ties with the Soviet Union, became clear, San Marco split with him, actually masterminded a counter-revolution which failed. Castro imprisoned him, tortured him. It was a very emotional time in Cuba. San Marco finally escaped to Florida. We found him, used him in the Bay of Pigs. Castro captured him again, tortured him, and finally used him as bait in the Donovan trade. San Marco has been living in New

England since then. We have given him cover and pension with no cost-of-living escalation provision."

The President looked at his watch.

"Now San Marco says that he's been contacted by some relatives living in Florida. He won't reveal their names. Obviously Cuban Nationals. But from what I can fathom they have brains and know-how in addition to fervor for a cause. They spoke in vague terms about an insurgence and an invasion plan, multi-forked thrusts to free Cuba, eliminate Castro. The details of the plan were sketchy, according to San Marco. Most of the conversation was theoretical, playing on San Marco's record of patriotism, prodding him with promises of personal glory and vindication; revenge on Castro. They tried to revive the emotion which had existed between the two men, a lifelong friendship that about-faced into a personal vendetta of opposing idealisms. They hinted at the possibility of high public office for San Marco under a new, free Cuba. His relatives were obviously pros. They knew all the recruitment tricks of a professional espionage team. But San Marco is no dummy. He had been through this kind of pressure before. He was smart enough to know that he was being used again, trussed up to be a sacrificial lamb again."

"How did San Marco get to you?"

"Through a television newscaster. Laurie Golding. Do you know her?" The President nodded, a slight smile cracking his stern face. "After San Marco was contacted, turned down the offer, he stewed for a while and then decided he ought to push the panic button. I'm not sure how he got to Laurie Golding. She seems to be the only person he still knew in Washington. She taped a three-hour interview with him: let him tell his own story and then riddled him with a long series of well-prepared questions. It's a dynamite interview. I hope it never gets on the air. The press would have a field day muckraking old mistakes, hidden intrigues, legal deviations by the CIA, the FBI, and the State Department. The Republicans would jump on it like we did Watergate."

"Do you have the tape?"

Callender shook his head. "Laurie Golding made it quite clear that I was seeing a copy. The original is well secured in a vault somewhere. She's using it as a bomb threat to prod us into action."

"Did you make a deal with her?"

"It's not that easy, sir. Laurie Golding is tough and with a mind of steel. She's going to use this for her own personal ambition. She has a long string of conditions." Callender smiled. "Miss Golding and I are currently negotiating the terms."

"Have you personally talked to San Marco?"

Callender shook his head. "That's one of the terms. No one is allowed to talk to San Marco directly. She coerced me to get the CIA to hide him out in a safe house. If anyone tries to get to him directly, she threatens to run the tape of the interview on her news broadcast. As I explained, she's tough: she would do it in a minute."

"I don't doubt it," the President said. "She is not friendly to this administration."

"The evidence, as I see it, is overwhelming. We must stop this plan before all hell breaks loose. And it must be kept secret. There is no way we can win diplomatically on this one. If there is an invasion in the guise of Cuban patriots, the world is going to think we backed it, financed it, implemented it. Our previous track record is going to condemn us regardless of facts. On the other hand, if we try to stop it, the whole Cuban population in this country will be up in arms. There's enough nuts rioting in Miami the way it is."

The President said, "I'm damned if I do and damned if I don't."

"Exactly," Callender said. "If any of this ever becomes public we lose either way. I'm concerned about your personal safety, sir. I'm worried that some crazed Cuban Nationals in this country are going to begin taking pot shots at you."

The President's face was grim. "That has already happened, Lowell. We hushed it up."

"Shit," Callender said. "I wish I had known. It would have been a lead, a thread to follow. I should have been informed."

"You're supposed to be a diplomat, Lowell, not a gunfighter."

"Where is the man now?"

"Dead."

Callender looked up. "Well, you're not dead and I intend personally to see that you stay alive." He held up his hand when the President started to speak. "Diplomatically," he assured him, "not as a gunfighter."

"As you know, Lowell, this is a very important area, probably never as important before as it is right now. Politically, and on the surface, we must maintain the status quo in Cuba. That is the official policy of this administration. It is an open secret that we are working undercover to normalize our relationship with the Castro government. We have teams working around the clock to do just that. I have given top priority to this project. The public knows that the tension is easing, that we are slowly and unofficially reestablishing communications, breaking down some of the restrictions which have been in effect for so long. It is a most important mission. It is imperative that the status quo remains while the negotiations proceed."

"If what San Marco says is true, if there is an attempted invasion, the whole thing will burst wide open."

"Exactly," the President said. "We cannot give any foreign power an excuse to occupy Cuba for its own protection or self-defense. As you know, Lowell, Castro has many operatives working in Panama. He's a very influential man in that whole third world down there. If there is any attempt on Castro's life, I fear for the Canal: I fear for world peace. The whole area is an unstable powder keg. The whole world is looking at the Mideast but my personal concern is right in this hemisphere. You understand that probably better than anyone else, Lowell: it's your world down there."

"Do you want to hear my gut reaction?"

"My experience with you is that your gut reactions are not based in your gut. You know more than you're telling me, Lowell."

Callender smiled. "Some foreign power wants another Bay of Pigs. Maybe it's Castro himself. Whoever it is, they want us to take the blame. We're being set up as a patsy."

"Knowing you so well, Lowell, and knowing your previous records of performance, I assumed you already had a plan." When Callender started to answer, the President interrupted him. "I don't want to know what it is, Lowell. I might find it unsavory." He locked his fingers together. "More than likely, I would find it unacceptable to this administration."

"I'm trying to protect your safety."

"I have God, the Secret Service, and the FBI."

"They didn't stop the assassination attempt."

"I'm still alive. Someone is watching out for me." He looked at the clock on his desk, pulled his chair closer. "I assume that this plan of yours needs some kind of executive implementation."

"All I need is your word, sir. All I need is your authority to go."

"I cannot do that officially, Lowell. You understand that. Personally and off the record, I can look the other way. I never doubt where your heart is. I have a quarrel sometimes with your methods."

"Then the signal is go?"

"With reservations. It is important that you do it by the book, do not ignore established procedure. I have heard rumblings about the Callender Commandos, your private task force in the State Department."

"It's legal."

"Being a lawyer like you are, Lowell, and being the cautious man I know you to be, I'm sure that it is legal. However, you cannot run this as a one-man operation. You must interrelate to the other agencies and departments involved."

"I want to work this through the NSA Coordination Committee. You've set it up so that they can function above the CIA too but the main thrust has to come from the top. The NSA has a limited paramilitary capability, I know that. But there will be a way to augment that if it's necessary."

"You don't want to work directly through Turner?"

"Things will move faster if I use the Coordination Committee apparatus. There are too many legal questions at the moment with the CIA. I'll coordinate with them, but I need less hog-tied vehicles for action."

The President nodded his agreement, looked at his watch. "No one questions your intentions, but there are questions as to your methods. In the beginning, it was my opinion that you were the man to handle the normalization process with Cuba, the perfect man to deal directly with Castro. But then it was pointed out to me your history of implementing insurrections in many countries, sometimes masterminding revolutions . . . creating them, so to speak . . . all of this for personal gain, to make a fortune for youself. I cannot be identified with that kind of behavior, cannot condone that kind of profiteering."

"You don't know all of it," Callender said. "Did your unimpeachable sources tell you that there were times when I personally fired guns, detonated bombs?"

"I already know more than I want to know, Lowell."

"Did you know all this about me, Mr. President, before I campaigned for you, before I was a major contributor to your election?"

"I consider that question impertinent."

"You realize that all these things you have learned about me make me the most qualified man in the country to deal directly with Castro."

"I know that you sold him guns. That disqualifies you." The President looked at his watch again. "I could find a more scrupulous man to stop this threat," he hesitated, smiled his toothy, calculated smile, "but I couldn't find a man as potentially effective as you might be. I'm giving you my off-the-record sanction, Lowell, but I'm warning you that I will tolerate no roughrider tactics. I don't want to hear the details of your plan. If this thing backfires, I want to be able to say in all honesty that I knew nothing about it." The President pulled his chair closer to the desk, lowered his head over a sheaf of documents. "God bless," he said.

The buzzing of the mobile phone in the limousine brought Callender to attention. He reached forward, pressed the button. "Callender," he said.

It was his secretary. "I've been trying to reach you for a half hour."

"We were out of range." He looked out the window trying to determine where he was, how close to Washington. "What's the problem?"

"Laurie Golding," she said. "She's frantic. Is it all right to talk?"

"Go ahead."

"She's been calling from her mobile phone every ten minutes. She says that it's imperative that she talk to you before her five o'clock telecast. She said that you would understand."

"Did you tell her where I was?"

"No way. Does she have your mobile phone number?"

"Probably. Or she can get it, knowing her." He thought for a moment. "When she calls again, give her this number. No, wait a minute. I need twenty minutes." He leaned forward, touched the driver's shoulder. "How much time before we hit Washington?"

"We're going to hit traffic. Another fifty or fifty-five minutes."

Back into the phone he instructed, "When she calls again, tell her to meet me at the Holiday Inn parking lot on Route two-ninety-four, right outside Bethesda. I should be there in thirty minutes. It will take her about the same time to get there from Washington."

"Okay. Holiday Inn, Route two-ninety-four outside Bethesda."

"Is Farnsworth in the office?"

"Somewhere."

"Find him. Get him in my office. I'm going to stop in about five minutes and call on my private line. Have Farnsworth there." When he replaced the instrument in the cradle, he leaned forward to the driver again. "Stop at the next phone booth on the highway." He leaned back in the seat, closed his eyes again.

His secretary had said frantic. Frantic was an unusual way to describe Laurie Golding. In all his experiences with her, she had always been outwardly calm, unruffled even under extreme stress and always soft-spoken, her voice still thinly honey-coated with her South Carolina origins. She was like that in bed; silently orgiastic. He had been warned in the beginning that Laurie Golding was a piranha, devouring every new boy in town, extremely disciplined and totally unprincipled in performing her job. The buzzer of the mobile phone sounded again, the red light blinking. This time Callender did not answer the phone, watched the red light blink on and off until it finally stopped. Frantic was an unusual way to describe Laurie Golding, he thought.

From the freeway phone booth, Callender called his private line. Farnsworth answered on the first ring. "Yes, sir?"

"Anything happening?"

"Not that I know of."

"Laurie Golding has been trying to reach me, any idea why?"

"Can't imagine."

"You haven't heard anything?"

"Not a word. All's quiet as far as I know. How did it go? Is Edgerton the man?"

"I think so. As far as I'm concerned we have YELLOWJACK."

"Great. I was hoping that was the reason you were calling. That's the last niche to be filled. Should I get things rolling now?"

"Not yet. Kelly hasn't officially cleared Edgerton. I tried to get him to do it on the spot but he's a tough one. I didn't want to press too hard. Those people insist on doing things in their own way and in their own time."

"Maybe it's just as well," Farnsworth said. "I think it looks better if the ultimate responsibility stays with them. Our necks are out far enough as it is. If anyone ever starts unraveling the irregularities, it could be trouble for us. They're nervous as hell upstairs. My powder room spy network reports the word came down from the Oval Office . . . guarded tolerance is the way they have been instructed to treat us."

"They can't stop us now," Callender said. "The Department is committed."

"What's Edgerton like? Is he what you expected?"

"Physically, he's perfect for that slot; well-built and no dummy. Kelly thinks he may be too cerebral for the job. Those Agency people distrust anyone capable of independent thinking. All they think the job requires is a pretty face masquerading as a dead-eye marksman. Edgerton is more than that. He can be made to understand urgency. He'll know how to circumvent channels in an emergency. For some reason, he has a personal loyalty to Jack Kelly but otherwise he seems to have no commitments to anyone."

"Well, once Edgerton is cleared, I'm ready to push the button, get it all in gear."

"I gave Kelly until five o'clock tonight for a definite answer. If he hasn't made contact by five-five, we'll put on the heat. As soon as he's cleared, you can push the button. It will probably be tonight. It means working late again."

"I'm getting used to it."

"Don't go back to your own desk. Stay in my office. I'm meeting Laurie Golding midway back to town. If there's trouble, I'll alert you."

The undersecretary's limousine waited in the filling station across the highway from the Holiday Inn until a similar limousine turned into the hotel parking lot, stopped at the far end. Callender touched the driver's shoulder, the car drove out, went around the clover-leaf exit and pulled in, leaving a one-space interval between the two limousines. Callender looked directly across to Laurie Golding. Neither of them moved to get out of the cars. She said something to her driver, who got out, walked across the blacktop and opened the door beside Callender. For a moment Callender did not move. Laurie Golding was looking straight ahead, not watching. Slowly Callender edged forward, stepped out, waited until the door closed behind him and the large black driver opened the door to the other limousine.

He felt the chilled air of the air conditioning and the faint aroma of lily of the valley which always clung to Laurie Golding. Each time he saw her, he was initially disarmed by the softness of her, the instant smile, the flowing hair, the ingenuous eyes reacting without apparent guile. But all this vapid prettiness was bait for the steel trap of her mind, the abrasive words she used as weapons to gun down public figures on prime time.

She did not bother with a greeting. "Julio San Marco has disappeared, vanished. Don't bother to ask obvious questions, I have already asked them all, investigated thoroughly. You promised me protection for him. What are you going to do about it?"

"I can't believe it. Did you check with the people at the safe house?"

"I told you not to ask obvious questions. I've checked with all the personnel. They didn't even know he was missing. Idiots. They're all idiots. I warned you that someone would try to get to him."

There was a three-screen Sony television built into the sound-proof divider between the back and front seats, a different picture on each screen, the sound mute. A small typewriter was bolted to a specially installed ledge, a sentence unfinished midway down the page. A tape recorder was bolted below the typewriter, the large spool unwinding slowly. Callender pointed to it. "I don't think it's wise," he said.

"Don't be paranoid, Lowell, you know I record everything. Those tapes will be history one day; they're well protected at all times."

"I'm amazed about San Marco. Who could have known he was there? I'll have to check with the Agency people."

"I turned him over to you, Lowell, not the Agency people. You promised protection for San Marco. I hold you personally responsible, not the Agency."

"You knew that I couldn't do it alone, you knew that I would need the Agency's help. I need it again to find him."

"It's probably too late. He's probably on his way to Moscow by now." She typed three words and an exclamation mark. "Or murdered," she said.

"You forget that San Marco knows all the tricks. He was a soldier . . . and a damn good one. He also masterminded Castro's intelligence operation. The CIA trained him for the Bay of Pigs. He knows his way around. He could have just walked out, maybe defected back to Cuba. Maybe he was just a decoy. Maybe Castro planted him here. I don't know. You would never let me talk to him. I could have gotten to the real truth in twenty minutes."

"I gave you the real truth. You saw the tape of my interview with him. Can you tell me that that wasn't an honest man? San Marco is sincere, he told me the truth. I'll stake my reputation on that."

"Disillusioned men do strange things."

"Do you blame him for being disillusioned? You're as responsible for that as anyone. He hung around the State Department and the CIA for two weeks trying to get someone to listen to his story. Nobody even remembered his name, let alone listened to him."

"It seems very contrived now that I think about it, just a little too coincidental, a little too pat."

"You're pure ice, Lowell. You've been rich and secure so long that you don't understand frustration. You don't understand desperation. There is San Marco in his hotel room, overflowing with a frightening story that no one will listen to. He sees me on television and remembers me from years ago, when I first interviewed him in the Super Bowl, the day that Kennedy did a tribute to the heroes of the Bay of Pigs. It's logical, Lowell. I can feel it."

"Too logical, maybe." He looked at his watch. "I can't accomplish anything here. I'll get back to Washington and see what I can do."

"That isn't good enough, Lowell. I want a definite commitment from you. I know how you think. You have a bloodless kind of pragmatism that I cannot accept. You're ready to abandon San Marco because you think you can't learn any more from him. You got what you wanted from him and now he's last week's laundry."

Callender smiled. "You have brass balls, Laurie, and up to a point your cunt compensates for it . . . but only up to a point."

"Which are you jealous of, Lowell, my brass balls or my cunt?"

He laughed, opened the door, started out of the car. "Call me at home tonight," she said. "Tell me what you've found out."

"I'll come over, tell you in person."

"Don't tell me your wife finally went back to New Orleans."

"I'll see you later."

"Don't. Call me. Don't come over. Is that clear?"

He turned back, laughed at her. "Yes, ma'am," he said.

1978
AUGUST

WEDNESDAY

A REMOTE FARMHOUSE NEAR CASILDA, CUBA

Even before they took off the blindfold, Julio San Marco knew that he was home. With the compensatory keenness of the blind, he was acutely aware of the sounds and the smells around him; the sea washing against the rocks, the slightly rancid smell of cooking oil filtering through from the kitchen, and the warm, moist air which recalled all his memories. He could feel and smell and taste it as he took breaths. He was certain that he had been brought home to die, to be killed, at last, for all the times he had been willing to die for his country. Death did not matter to him anymore. He was home.

At first he had been kept in a darkened room, allowing time for his one good eye to become adjusted to the light and his body to burn out and eliminate the effects of the drugs which had been used to sedate him after the kidnapping, on the long drive and then on the airplane coming back to Cuba. Had he been kidnapped or rescued? On the plane, there had been times when he had been awake, conscious enough to recognize that the muffled voices were speaking Spanish words, that these were his own people around him. Rescue, he decided: he was being rescued from an exile of living with strangers speaking another language in an unfamiliar climate. Even if they had kidnapped him to kill him, it was a rescue. And he was thinking that a man ought to die at home.

That morning, two uniformed soldiers had led him gently from the locked room and out to the porch on the back of the farmhouse. He sat on the kind of chair that had been on his porch when he was a boy: constructed of logs with the seat and back woven out of dried palm leaves. From here he could see the trees and the way the sky was blue and the motion of the sea as the waves crashed against the cliff. With his good hand he lifted his inert arm, rested it on the table, inhaled the aroma of the thick coffee emitting drifts of steam. He sipped the coffee. No other coffee tasted quite like it, had the same flavor. He thought again that home was the best place for a man to die.

The number of years he had lived said that he was too young to die. But when he looked in the mirror to shave, he saw an old man, not a forty-six-year-old face. Time and bad luck had taken it's toll on him. He bore all the wounds and scars of the emaciated body nailed to the cross. In the end, His essence had risen again to make men free. The day would come when all the battles which had been lost would be won.

San Marco lowered his head, made the sign of the cross as he heard the convoy of cars speeding up the driveway, the opening and slamming shut of doors, many footsteps grinding on the gravel path. Then there was only one pair of footsteps hitting the wooden steps with hard authority, continuing to clobber against the deck which circled the house and finally halting in front of him: dusty, well-worn boots and the familiar smell of the cigar. Slowly, uncertain of his future, San Marco raised his head and looked up into the face of Fidel Castro.

Before they had become enemies, these men had been boys together; dreamers and comrades together. That was in their minds now, those days when they had been friends, brothers in experience and ideology. For a moment, the last seventeen years that they had been apart did not exist. Each awkward, they smiled tentatively at each other, uncertain of the other's reaction. Using great effort, San Marco stood up, his limp arm fell to his side. Unsteady, still weakened by the drugs, he tottered. Castro caught him, engulfed him in a bear hug, held the frail body against his own, as though his strength were contagious, capable of reenergizing the other man. Tears came in San Marco's eyes. When Castro released his hold, stood back, reinserted the cigar in his mouth, he too rubbed his eyes, rubbed away the same instinctive tears.

"Old friends . . . brothers," Castro said. "Nothing changes that."

"Nothing," San Marco echoed. He felt the weakness in his legs, steadied himself against the table, then eased himself back into the chair. Shaking his head, he said, "Everything changes." He was looking up at the robust body overflowing with energy. "Once we were like brothers, the same age, the same past, and the same future. Now I am an old man and you are still young. How did that happen?"

"You were wrong, Julio. You must see that now."

"I did what I had to do."

"But you were wrong. We both wanted the same thing. In our hearts and in our heads, we were alike. Your way was wrong . . . impractical . . . too theoretical to make the revolution a success. The people were unprepared: they needed the leadership to be told how to become free, how to preserve that freedom against imperialism."

"Angola, Ethiopia, Zaire . . . that is not imperialism?"

"We are the success symbol to other revolutionaries. They look to us for leadership. We have a moral obligation to help other revolutionaries succeed. Cuba is free now, the people are happy. That's what we both wanted. Your way was impractical; there would not be enough years in our lives to accomplish it your way. I did the right thing. I made it happen quickly. You see that now, don't you?" He looked down for confirmation. San Marco dropped his shoulders, shrugged; weary of the dialectic he had carried on inside his mind these past years. Castro said, "The end justified the means, old friend. You must see that now."

"With only one eye. I see very little."

"Then I will make you see. I will be your other eye. I will make you see it all." He made a broad gesture with his arms. "In the next few days, you will see your country again. You will see what our revolution has done, you will see what we have accomplished and then you will know that my way was right." There was a sudden sound of a formation of jets flying overhead. Neither man looked up. Castro waited until the morning was quiet again. "When you see your country again, Julio, you will understand at last that my way was the only way that could make this happen."

"It is too late, Fidel. It is too late for me. Look at me, look at me closely. I am not the man I was in the mountains many years ago. You are still the same but I am not. I have only one eye and only one arm that works. In my mind there is an even greater disability to see and to act."

"Not too late. Never. You're home, Julio, back where you belong, back with the people who love you. You are still remembered here. They will know you again."

"The exiles in Florida, they remember me, they know who I am. I am still the symbol to them of what they wanted the revolution to be. But here, you have wiped out every trace of me, every evidence that I existed."

His voice was loud. "No matter what was in your heart, you were a traitor to the revolution."

"To your revolution, Fidel, not the people's." He held up his hand to stop the fury Castro was about to unleash at him. "We are like lovers who have quarreled and meet again after many years. In five minutes, we are fighting again, quarreling over the same things." He let his arm drop; his body slumped deeper into the chair. "I am good for nothing anymore. You have defeated me many times, why do you want to defeat me again? What purpose can I serve you this time, what will defeating me again accomplish for you?"

"How many times have you fought for Cuba? Twice. Right? Once for me and once for them. The number three is a magical number. The third time you will be a hero again; a hero by my side. The children will learn in school again about Julio San Marco, his patriotism to the revolution."

"How will the textbooks explain these other years? What will they say about the first counter-revolution I led against you? How will they explain the Bay of Pigs, the Army of Nationals I led in the invasion attempt?"

Castro grinned. Perfectly muscled, he lowered himself to the wooden floor, sat cross-legged at San Marco's feet. "I think of everything, Julio. You know that. When the time comes, I will tell the world how you have suffered for your country. You will take your place with Ché and me as the true heroes. Do you know what you have been doing all these years, Julio?" He smiled at his own cunning. "You have been a spy for Cuba in the United States. For all these years you have been sending me intelligence which has helped our fight against Yankee greed and imperialism. There is no greater hero than an undercover agent who has lost an eye and arm in the secret service of his country. It will read well in the school books, no?"

"Another lie, Fidel."

"No lie. This time it will be true. This time you will be a spy. The

Yankees know you, trust you. The exiled dogs living in Florida, feeding on Yankee dollars . . . you are still a hero to them. They will talk to you, tell you their secrets, trust you with their plans."

San Marco said, "I know nothing."

"You know that they will try to invade Cuba and that the CIA will help them. They asked you to be their leader. You have already made contact with the CIA. You have hidden in their house."

"There is more in your mind than you are telling me. You cannot trust me to go back to the United States. You would not be naive enough to think that I would not turn on you again."

"It is going too fast, Julio. Our reconciliation is moving too quickly. You need time to become nourished by your own soil, your own air again. Black bean soup. How long has it been since you've had real black bean soup? That will fill you out, make you strong again. And I will send you a woman."

"I am old, Fidel. The black bean soup sounds better than the woman."

"In a few days you will be strong again. My men will take you all over Cuba. You will see with your own eyes all the wonderful things that have happened since the revolution. You will see that I have made Cuba the country we dreamed about many years ago. It will not be necessary for you to have hostages for me to capture. When you see the miracle here, you will fight for Cuba again of your own free will. You will gladly become the man I have created for the history books . . . the greatest revolutionary of them all."

"The North Americans use the word charisma." He looked down at the upturned face of the leader. "I listen to you now and I forget what has happened; I only remember the way things were when we were young, when we were planning all of this. You make me forget all the terrible things which happened in between."

Without using his hands, Castro thrust himself straight up into a standing position, leaned over, and kissed San Marco on each cheek. "In three days we will meet in Havana. Then you will tell me that I was right, that I have made this the country we dreamed about. You will plead with me to let you fight again . . . against the Yankees and their CIA. You will find out what plans they are making now to invade Cuba and we will crush them again as we crushed them before. Three days, Julio. Three days will change your life. We will meet again like lovers but this time there will be no quarrel."

"Fidel, Fidel," he chanted to himself, the name becoming an

incantation as he listened to the heavy steps against the deck and then the grinding again against the gravel. The engines of the convoy of cars started up in unison, the loud screech of tires as they pulled away, and then the diminishing sounds as they drove away from the farmhouse.

San Marco was left alone again with the familiar smells, the reassuring rhythm of the sea against the rocks, and the nurturing, warm dampness of the air.

"Fidel, Fidel, Fidel."

HYATT REGENCY HOTEL, NEAR O'HARE AIRPORT, CHICAGO

The contact in Chicago was another anonymous face without any outstanding physical characteristics. Later, when Edgerton tried to reconstruct this meeting in his mind, the man was unfocused in his memory, a physical object without delineation or definition. Only the man's voice would remain distinct; soft-sounding and projecting empathetic understanding. Instinctively, Edgerton stiffened and strengthened his guard against the other agent, shored up his defenses against the seductive voice inviting a sharing of confidences, an exchange of mutual experiences, and in-common gripes against authority. In the past, he had played this other man's role; assigned to draw out another agent's weaknesses, sound-depth testing of fissures in the fiber of the other man.

Things had moved quickly after the meeting with Lowell Callender. Edgerton had been bussed into Washington, picked up an airline ticket and instructions from a pre-arranged drop at Dulles Airport. The ticket was one-way, economy class to Chicago. The only instruction was the name of the hotel. When he arrived at the registration desk, a reservation was being held for Marc Polo. He waited in the room until nine o'clock, watched television, ordered room service, and waited again. The contact did not appear until four o'clock in the morning.

This time there were no official papers on the table between them, no dossiers or documents. Edgerton felt the excitement. He was out of the classroom, into the field.

"Tell me," the man began, "how did you explain this to your wife?"

"Explain what?"

"Walking out. It was my understanding that when you were contacted, you just walked away from your marriage without any explanations." The man peered into the room service coffee pot. Edgerton had drained it. "I do have it right, don't I?"

"It wasn't like that. We were breaking up anyway. We both knew it was coming. Things weren't working out. This wasn't the first time. I established the pattern before." He thought for a moment, tried to see beyond the question. "She won't be suspicious of anything."

The other agent smiled: his eyes seemed to say that he had had a corresponding experience in his own life. "It's hard, isn't it, after living our kind of life to be satisfied with the lives most people lead? The humdrum is bearable when it's only a cover and you know that sooner or later the excitement will be happening again. Green grass is always somewhere else in our business. When you're in the field, sneaking through cities, fed up with dirty hotels and sleazy bars. . . . when you're up to your eyeballs in mumbo-jumbo and hocus-pocus. . . . home is the greener grass then." The man folded his hands behind his head, tilted back on the chair. "We lead lonely lives, don't we? It's hard to ever establish any kind of an enduring relationship with another person. Impossible, actually: there is always a part of yourself in reserve, cut off from sharing. And that's what human relationships are, aren't they . . . sharing?" The man leveled his chair, leaned toward Edgerton. "Didn't your wife ever know?"

When the man shot the question at him, Edgerton was aware that he had begun to let himself relax, unconsciously had begun to succumb to the seduction. "She never knew. There was no way of her knowing."

"How did you explain the other times? Twice in the last year, wasn't it? Once in Rio and once in La Paz? Do I have it straight?"

"They were short assignments. I faked arguments, provoked situations. I established the pattern of becoming sullen, walking out and disappearing."

He nodded, indicated that he understood more than Edgerton was saying. "You went back to her each time. Will you go back to her again?"

Edgerton considered the question: he did not answer it.

"In this business, it's hard to know what's real and what isn't. Sometimes our cover becomes us . . . or we become our cover. Either way, it's the same. After a while, it's impossible to differentiate yourself from the cover the Agency has given you." He thought for a moment. "Actually, your original cover identity is based on fact. Not only you . . . all of us. In the old days, the big guns in the Company were good at that, perceptive about personal characteristics. Your assigned identity was an extension of yourself, an enlargement of yourself. You were recruited during that period. You must understand what I mean."

Was he that, an enlargement of himself? Edgerton wondered if the funny psychiatrist had seen through his cover to the man underneath. Were both men compulsive losers, he and the man he pretended to be? Had he backed off from everything in his life because that was the covert identity which the government needed, or because he was really that kind of man? It was a circular dialogue he had conducted with himself many times before, never ending in a conclusion.

"I do have it right, don't I? It was fourteen years ago when you were first recruited?"

Fourteen years ago, Edgerton's world had collapsed. His mother, old enough to be his grandmother, lay dying. The piano never played anymore in the tiny room where she had given lessons to other people's children. The silence of death had replaced the music. The little dingy house became grayer and dustier, with his mother not able to care for it. Their isolation from the rest of the town was even more apparent now with no children coming to make repetitive discordant sounds on the upright piano. Only the doctor appeared every other day, shaking his head sadly, putting his hand on Edgerton's shoulder sympathetically, helpless against the incurable cancer.

Four days before she died, she confessed the lie her life had been; the lie he would inherit. "That picture on the dresser . . ." He looked over at it again, saw the handsome smiling soldier. "That isn't your father. The picture came with the frame. I bought it like that at

Penney's, just the way you see it. I made up the story about going to Atlanta and meeting a man and he goes off and gets himself killed in the second World War. I made up the name Edgerton. I read that name in a book somewhere. There was a wild boy in this town . . . a mean boy who ran wild. No one could control him." With great, deliberated effort, she said the name. "Billy Jarvis. Billy Erskin Jarvis."

The name was a face on a screen, a picture in a magazine; not a photograph on a dresser. The name was a legend. It had made the town famous. Edgerton was seeing it all and seeing the bronze figure in the park across from the bank: the idol of the fifties, with duck-tail hair, thrust pelvis, thick lips, and oversized guitar. There was that picture and there was the photograph of a stranger on his mother's dresser.

"He was the same age as you are now . . . even younger. But good looking like you are and full of life. Even then he had a feeling for music. He couldn't play the piano, didn't even want to learn. His folks made him come for lessons. He used to bring a guitar and sit on that chair in the corner, make me play church music and he'd make up words or just mumble sounds and follow along on the guitar. He was a seventeen-year-old boy and I was a forty-six-year-old spinster . . . an old maid. I don't know how it happened. It just happened. And it wasn't only one time. It was every week for three months. I was like a crazy lady. They should have locked me up, thrown away the key." She fought for breath through her eroded lungs. "When he found out I was pregnant, he ran away from home. Nashville first and then Hollywood, California. Look at him now . . . still a kid and everyone fussing over him and adoring him. And I'm a dying old lady." She touched his hand. "I feel sorry for you. That's the blood you have in you . . . a crazy old lady and a wild kid."

She died in March. In June, after he had graduated from high school, he sold the house, took that money, the insurance and savings, and went to Hollywood to find his father. He never saw him face-to-face, never got that close to him. He was buffered by his father's business agent who was gentle with him, tried to make him understand why it was impossible for his father to acknowledge him. "Look at you," he had said. "You're not a kid, you're a man. How old are you?"

"Almost nineteen."

"You look older. Christ, you look almost as old as he does. What do you think would happen to his career if all those screaming girls suddenly found out how old he really is, that he has a son older than most of his fans? You can see that, can't you? You can see how that would destroy him. You don't want to wreck his career, do you? He is a sex symbol to millions of teen-age girls, to the whole country. You can't destroy him."

"Does he know I exist?"

The agent looked away, out the window of his office. "Look, you've got everything going for you, you've got everything ahead of you." He reached into his desk, took out a large checkbook. "I'm going to give you some money, enough for you to go back to Tennessee and go to college, make something out of yourself." He filled in the date, then looked up. "What's your name again?"

"Does he know that I'm alive? Does he know that he has a son?"

He took a long time to answer, signed the check, and filled in the amount while he was thinking. "Yes. He knows that you exist. He knows that you are here in my office now. This is his money I'm giving you, not my own."

"How much?"

The man smiled, satisfied that he had been able to buy off trouble. "Five thousand dollars."

"It costs twenty thousand dollars to get through college."

"You blackmailing little snot."

"Add the five thousand that you were going to give me."

The agent threw down the pen. "Look, he's giving you the five thousand out of the goodness of his heart. He doesn't have to do it. You have no proof that he's really your father."

Edgerton stood up, turned and started out of the room.

"You're his kid, all right. The same balls, the same hillbilly chutz-pah. The nerve of Christ." He moved from behind his desk, grabbed Edgerton's arm as he was reaching for the doorknob. "Let me tell you something, son. The luckiest day of your life will be when you walk out of here and never see your father or even think about him again. He's a no-good son of a bitch. He hasn't one decent bone in his body. He's the biggest pain in the ass in the entire industry. Everyone idolizes him but the people who know him and work with him. They hate his guts. Including me. Maybe me most of all be-cause it's my job to clean up all the shit he leaves behind. I'm the one who has to bail him out of every dirty thing he does." He turned back, sat on the edge of his desk, looked out the window again. "If you were my kid, I wouldn't turn you away. I'd find a way to make it work, find a way to keep you around." He went back, sat in a chair, tore out the check he had started, crumbled it and tossed it in the wastebasket, started to write again. He looked up.

"Ross Edgerton." He spelled out his last name.

But he did not go back to Tennessee. He enrolled at UCLA, found a drama school with an evening curriculum, began hanging out in actors' bars, learning the language of actors, training the Tennessee twang out of his voice. His direction was clear: he was going to become a bigger star than his father, even more sought after. And when the roles would be reversed, when his father would come to find him, there would be no agent to shunt him off, buy him off.

Edgerton had been recruited that summer before he started at UCLA. A regular in one of the bars asked him one night, "Do you want to make a few extra bucks and get a trip to San Francisco in the bargain?" It had started that way; a simple drop in a bar in Los Angeles. When he was back in L.A. collecting the money, the man offered him another job, this time no further away than San Diego. When he went to collect his money after this drop, the man said he had some friends who would like to meet him, talk about a steadier job. Edgerton shook his head, pocketed the money. "I'm starting at UCLA in September."

"This won't interfere. As a matter of fact, it would work out fine."

"I'm going to acting school, too. There won't be time."

"Hell, this doesn't take much time. How much time have you spent so far? Not much and you've made two hundred bucks. Not bad for a few hours' work. Talk to my friends. I've set it up tomorrow at Cloud Nine about midnight."

"Why Cloud Nine? You can't hear yourself think in that place."

"Be there."

"You going to be there?"

The man shook his head.

"How will I know who they are?"

"They'll know who you are."

It had begun that night with two anonymous-looking strangers, shadowy figures no more easily identifiable than the man sitting opposite him now.

"Faked arguments with your wife," the agent was saying, "provoked situations . . . they always have a basis in fact. That's what makes a good agent, really. The good agents are always men who have the elements of the man they pretend to be. It gets so, after a while, you don't know what's real and what isn't real."

"This time," Edgerton said, "it's real."

"Then you're definitely not going back to your wife?"

"No."

"Then why did you call her from the airport?"

He had called from a public phone. How could they have known? "Who said that I called her?"

"You called her at seven-fifteen. There was no answer."

"I called her because I want her to start divorce proceedings." He studied the man, tried to read his purpose. "Why is my wife suddenly so important at this point? What does she have to do with this assignment?"

"Nothing. Absolutely nothing."

"You're too professional to be simply curious. What's in the back of your mind?"

The other agent smiled, kneaded his fingers. "The trouble with us is that we're trained to be suspicious. You and Colonel Kelly . . . you've come as close to friendship as men like us can. It's not like Kelly to be emotional about another man. I understand the debt he must feel to you but it goes beyond that. He seems so protective of you. It doesn't make sense. Of the two of you, you're far and away the stronger." He shrugged his shoulders, abandoned the analysis. "We chatted yesterday, Jack Kelly and I. You were probably still in the building. We talked informally, off the record. He's afraid that his concern for you as a person may have clouded his professional judgment."

"What did he tell you?"

"You mean, did he tell me about the psychiatric evaluation which he destroyed? No, he didn't tell me about it, but I already knew." He rocked his head back and forth, sadly. "Damn shame we have to grow old, isn't it? Jack's never been quite the same since Vietnam. We overestimated him, or at least we thought he would be the same man coming out as going in. That's why we sent you into the POW camp to rescue him. We thought he was too valuable to let him wither away. But we were wrong. His spirit was broken before you got to him." He smiled at Edgerton. "We almost wasted a good man to save a derelict."

"Jack isn't derelict."

"As far as we are concerned he is. This is no business for emotions. It's one thing in our private lives but emotions give us an unacceptable vulnerability in our professional lives. Unfortunately, there are few of us who can maintain a balance: we tend to turn off emotions at all times rather than take any risks."

"Is this what this meeting is about? Are you telling me that I'm off the assignment because of Jack Kelly?"

"I'm evaluating," the man said.

"For Christ's sake, how many times do I have to be tested?"

"This is the last time."

"What's the test? Let's get this shit over. Either I'm going to do the job or I'm not."

He waited until he answered, forming the words in his head before he spoke, then he asked, "When you took the tests, when you had the psychiatric interviews, who were you? Were you your cover or yourself?"

Edgerton took a long time before he answered. "I'd be lying if I answered that directly. The truth is, I don't know anymore. I don't know which is which. I've been at this for fourteen years, being the man you want me to be. I only know what I'm really like when I'm in the middle of action, when I am threatened. That record speaks for itself."

"Are you impotent?"

"Which man are you asking?"

The agent took a manila envelope bound with a rubber band from his inside pocket. "Your instructions are there and your airline tickets. Handle them in the usual way." He stood up, took out his handkerchief and wiped the handle and lid of the coffee pot and the edge of the table where his hands had rested.

"What about money?" Edgerton asked.

"There's a wad in there to cover expenses. Keep track. They're getting Aunt Nellie about expense accounts."

"I don't mean that. I mean what about pay?"

"As I understand it, that has been set up for a long time. It's automatic, isn't it?"

"It's the same amount it has been for the last seven years. Do you realize how much the cost of living has gone up in seven years?"

"You get paid whether you work or not. You get paid for a full year even if you only work a day. And you've always made money in the process of acting out your cover. It's my understanding that your father-in-law's business pays you eighty thousand a year plus bonus."

"That's over now. Besides, it's irrelevant. When you recruit a new covert man, you have to pay him according to today's standards. No one is going to work for bird feed."

"The patriots do; the ones who believe in this country and believe in keeping it free. They do."

"I'm a professional. I want professional pay."

He nodded. "I'll plead your case in Langley. I'm not sure they'll be receptive. Their budget has been cut to ribbons."

"They'll find a way; they always do for the covert stuff."

"I'll try."

"Will I see you again?"

The man shrugged and using his handkerchief on the knob, opened the door and went out.

Edgerton took the rubber band off the envelope, slipped it on his wrist and then broke the wax seal on the flap. He was booked on the noon flight to Denver. He checked his watch. He could sleep for three hours.

LAURIE GOLDING'S APARTMENT, CONNECTICUT AVENUE, WASHINGTON, D.C.

The young man taking off his clothes was short, heavily muscled, built square, his hair a bubble of sandy-colored, tight curls. He was eating an apple, juggling it from hand to hand as he undressed, clenching it in his teeth when he needed both hands. Stretched out on her bed, Laurie Golding was talking on the telephone, watching every movement, her face expressionless. The recording machine next to her bed was taping the conversation. The picture was on all three television sets built into the bedroom wall. She held the remote control in her right hand, her thumb ready to reactivate the sound.

"Really, Lowell, it's been a full day. It's impossible not to have some information if what you tell me is true. Between the State Department, the FBI, and the CIA someone must have come up with some lead." She listened while he repeated his excuses. "What about the Cubans themselves? Have you considered that possibility? How much do we know about Cuban intelligence in the United States?" The man was naked now, standing at the side of the bed, the apple reduced to almost the core. "It seems to me that as far as Castro is concerned, this would be an awkward time for Julio San Marco to resurface. He is an underground legend in Cuba. Tell the Agency to try that line. You must find him." The man pulled up her long nightgown, tried to insert the apple core between her legs. She hit his hand with the remote control, her expression never changing. "I am not threatening you, Lowell. I don't threaten; I do what I say I'll do. I'll run that San Marco interview Tuesday unless you give me proof of his safety before that." The man threw the apple core on the carpet, pulled up her nightgown higher, exposing her flattened breasts, the large coral nipples erect. "Don't talk to me about national security, Lowell, unless you're not telling me everything. If you're worried about national security then you haven't told me the whole operation." The man was bending over her: he opened his mouth, enveloped her clitoris. She closed her eyes at his wet impact. "Hold on a minute, Lowell," she said, dropping the remote control. She covered the mouthpiece with her hand. "Guido, you're an animal."

He looked up, grinned, and wiped the wetness from his mouth with the back of his hand. "Cunt and apples taste good together."

She dropped the phone, grabbed the bubble of his hair, pulled his mouth against her mouth, tasting herself and the apple and smelling the musk of oregano and garlic on his breath. Silently she mouthed the words, *You're an animal.* She smiled at him as she picked up the phone again. "Lowell, if you expect me to keep this off the air you'd better tell me everything. I'm not some congressional investigator who's dumb enough to settle for half-truths." As the undersecretary was answering, the man sat on the bed and ran his hand over the soft silk of her pubic hair, then took one strand and violently jerked it from her body. Her eyes closed at the sudden pain, she bit her lip to keep from screaming. "Look, Lowell, we'd better meet in the morning. I'll be in front of your house at seven." He explained his schedule. "Well, cancel your seven thirty. You can still make your eight o'clock. This won't wait." She hung up before he could answer, picked up the phone again, and started to dial.

"When are you going to get off the fucking phone?"

"I just have two calls, then I'm through. I promise."

He walked over to the dresser, opened her purse, took out her wallet and thumbed through the bills inside.

"Change in plans," she said into the phone. "I'll be downstairs at six thirty. Pick up some coffee." She hung up again.

"I thought you were going to bring me money. I told you I needed some dough."

"I didn't have time to go to the bank. I'll do it tomorrow." She started dialing again. "Open the first drawer, Guido. There's a present for you." He held the tiny box tied with a large pink ribbon and slowly turned to her. She motioned to him, patted the bed beside her. He walked toward her slowly, holding the box as though it would explode. "Sam," she said into the phone, "it's Laurie. I just spoke to Lowell. He's not telling me everything. My gut instinct tells me this is a bigger operation than he's letting on. He's feeding us just enough to make his position plausible but there is much more he's not telling us." She indicated the box with her head and smiled. The man pulled the pink ribbon, tore off the wrapping, and looked at the square black velvet box, still not opening it. "You haven't picked up any trace of San Marco yet, have you?" She took the box from him, opened the cover, removed the protective cotton layer and handed it back to him. "You know it's entirely possible that Agency people themselves may have San Marco. They've done stranger things than that. Maybe Lowell doesn't even know. I don't know why it didn't occur to me before. It makes sense for the Agency to kidnap him and hide him out. Work on it, will you, Sam?" The man took the large ring from the jeweler's box, the circle of gold coiled into a snake shape, the band carved with scales. The head of the snake protruded, tiny emerald eyes caught the light of the room. "You'd better put another man on Lowell and that man in his office . . . what's his name? . . . that's right. You'd better put surveillance on Farnsworth, too. I'll talk to you in the morning after I meet with Lowell."

He turned the ring, examining the unending circle.

"Do you like it?"

"How come so big?" He put it over three fingers; it was still loose.

She took the ring, gently eased it over one of his testicles, then the other. She forced his penis through the remaining diameter, adjusted the snake head so that it was exactly centered. "It's not too big," she said. "It fits perfectly."

1978
AUGUST

THURSDAY

A COMMAND TRAINING ROOM, LOWERY AIR FORCE BASE, DENVER, COLORADO

All during the night-long briefing session, the wall of glass had been a black mirror reflecting the small group of men huddled in the center of the huge room. Now daylight was beginning, the sky had turned a luminous gray and the mountains loomed large, almost touchable, outside the window. There was a perspective of ascending shapes, gradations of purple-brown and purple-black contrasting against the snowcapped farthest peaks, an eye-compelling panorama diverting the men's attention from the nondimensional charts and maps projected on the other three walls of the briefing room.

The man at the control console pressed a lever and the draperies began to close over the view; the hum of the motor and the metallic clang of the carriers sliding over the tracks stopped conversation. The man to the left of the console lighted a cigarette, stretched his legs in front of him, and yawned as he expelled the first mouthful of smoke. The other two men stood up briefly and stretched. One of them reached inside his pants, adjusted his underwear.

There was a group of twenty swivel chairs facing the console, each one equipped with a writing board, a pencil well, a carafe of water, and an ashtray. Edgerton sat alone here, the empty chairs an ominous bodyguard around him.

With the dawn and the mountains blanked out by the draperies, the charts became prominent again, demanding attention. The largest projection was of the island of Cuba. The other charts were smaller, of equal size to each other, and identified by code names.

YELLOWJACK was centered on Andros Island, the largest of the Bahamian group, with dots of the other islands stringing out to form the Antilles, a chain to the east running north and south. The coast of Cuba was at the bottom of the chart, surprisingly close to the western shore of Andros.

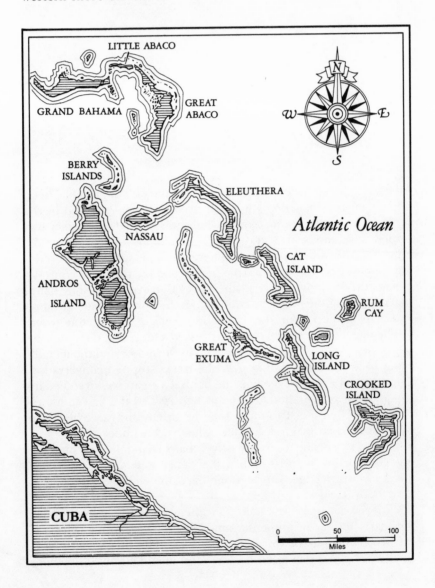

BARRACUDA covered the area from the bulge of Mexico on the Gulf, split between the Yucatan and Quintana Roo provinces, showing the island of Cozumel and the western tip of Cuba as far as Havana.

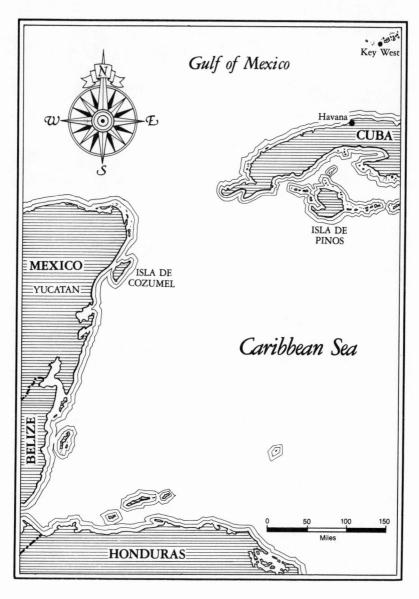

STINGRAY focused on the two tiny Cayman Islands, the Isle of Pines off the Cuban coast to the north and Honduras and Nicaragua to the south.

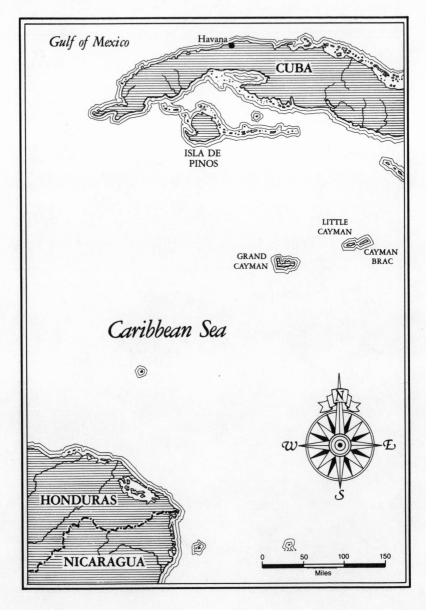

SAILFISH was the tight area centered on the Windward Passage between Cuba and Haiti, showing the Santiago tip of Cuba including the United States base at Guantanamo. Jamaica lay at the bottom of this chart.

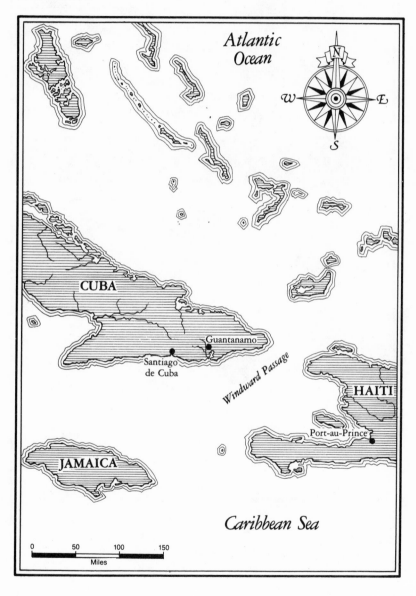

MARLIN was a horizontal projection showing Miami, the Florida Keys, and the Tortugas lying directly over the north coast of Cuba.

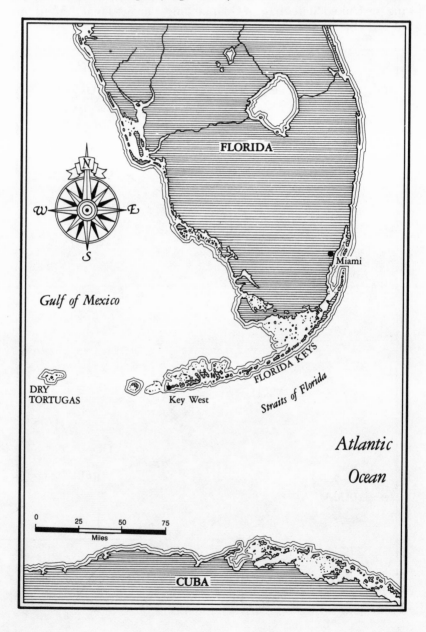

WAHOO centered on the Turks and Caicos Islands with Great
Inagua within sixty miles of the Cuban coast.

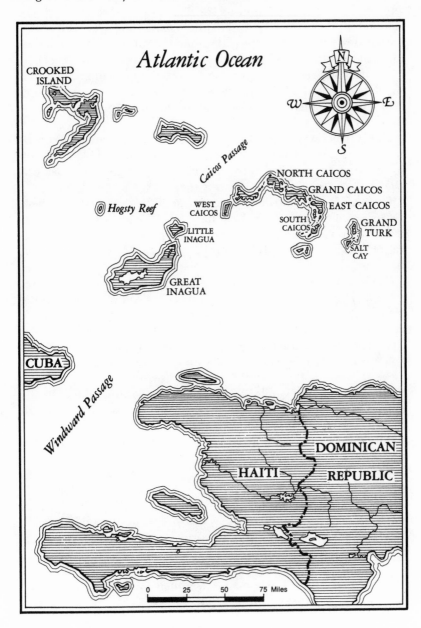

For thirty-six hours Edgerton's attention had been rapt to this geography, the charts committed to memory, the mileage tables by rote, all distances in relation to Havana. The men instructing him spanned the expertise required to understand this part of the world, always stressing proximities, air hours between places, nautical miles, navigable waters. All of the information was apolitical; technical information relating to geography, topography, and oceanography. He absorbed all the instructions as an actor learning a script, a student cramming for an exam, but he could not personally relate to any of it.

The instructions droned on for another hour, constant repetitions of the same facts. Then the geographer said, "That winds up my end of it." He looked at the other two men. "Anything to add?" They shook their heads. "That's it then."

The man at the control console activated the draperies and there was bright sunlight now, a slight haze over the mountains. All four of the other men stood up, gathered their papers, and left the room without acknowledging Edgerton in any way. Their job was over, the candidate ceased to exist.

Alone, Edgerton went to the window, looked down to the foreground of grassy slopes, densities of trees, a sliver of a river coming down from the mountains, hooking to the right and disappearing from view. Everything outside was crisp and cool, restrained by the cyclical winter elements from becoming a jungle. What did Colorado have to do with him or with Cuba or with the size of his cock?

There was a men's toilet through one of the three doors at the far end of the room. He had used it earlier but forgot now which door it was. (And how many nautical miles from Havana?) The middle door was locked; he tried the door to the left and this led into the toilet. He turned on the light, looked into the mirror and studied his face as though it was terrain. The rigorous exercise and Spartan diet had been good for him. There was even color in his face, his jawline was tight, and the slight pouches had disappeared under his eyes. He splashed cold water on his face, wiped it dry with the rough paper towel, went to the urinal and studied the arc of his penis as he waited to urinate.

"Stop playing with yourself," she had said. "I'm frustrated enough. Stop playing with yourself. It's obscene." His wife was watching him through the makeshift mirror over her dressing table as she brushed her hair.

He lay naked on the bed, flicking his limp penis back and forth with his index finger, making a mental list of all the things he did not like about her, aggregating petty things into an abrasive whole, abrasive enough to get him out of bed, out of the house, and out of this life. The big room was empty except for the king-sized box spring and mattress propped off the floor with books and for the girlish dressing table she had brought from her parent's house. Packing cartons were improvised as night tables: thrift shop lamps sat precariously on top of them. Sheets were taped over the glass slidewall, blocking out the view of the newly seeded lawn and straggly shrubs, still in shock after being transplanted. Wallpaper samples were pinned to bare drywall and discarded fabric samples were heaped on the floor.

"Don't forget that your tee-off time is ten-ten," she said. "You're playing with the buyers from Sears, in case you've forgotten. Daddy is having breakfast with them at nine-fifteen in the grillroom. He said for you to join them."

"I'm not hungry."

"Honestly, Edge, you can be so difficult sometimes. It isn't a question of whether you're hungry or not. You never will understand business, will you?"

That was another one of the things he did not like about her, her father's business. When they were first married, and even now when they met new people, she would link her arm through his possessively, "Isn't he divine? I found him in my father's underwear." With younger people she would add, "I couldn't wait to find out if that was all him in Daddy's cotton-nylon briefs." There was no need for further explanations; everyone in Chicago knew that Harry Samuels was a manufacturer of men's underwear.

It was a period when there was a long time between missions. It had been eight months since he had had any contact at all and then it had only been a short directive requiring him to reestablish a New York base. He tried several modeling agencies, found one that remembered Marc Polo and he began to get modeling jobs again. He had assumed his cover completely, hung out in out-of-the-way bars with other models and aspiring actors, lived more frugally then he needed to.

Doing the catalogue shots for the Superjock Division of Samuels

Mills guaranteed three weeks work, enough money to carry him through three months. On the first day of the shooting, Harry Samuels himself came to the photographer's studio with the agency people, introduced himself to Edgerton during a break. "You look damn familiar to me. Where would I know you from?"

"Maybe ads. I've done some TV commercials."

Samuels shifted his curved pipe to the other side of his mouth. "Something to do with sports. That's it. Sports. Were you ever on the golf circuit?"

"I played tennis for a while. Nothing serious. That was a long time ago."

Then he remembered. "You were the kid from UCLA playing in a tournament at the Racquet Club in Palm Springs. When was it? 1962?"

"Could be," Edgerton said.

"I offered to stake you if you wanted to turn pro." He took the pipe, tapped the dead ashes against the heel of his shoes, ground them out on the studio floor. "You could have been one of the great ones. Do you play at all anymore?"

He shook his head again remembering that he had been a no-show in the finals, had spent that afternoon and every afternoon for a week in a motel with Harry Samuel's wife, living for two months off the money she stuffed into his tennis racket case.

"Never forget a face," Samuels said. He put a man-to-man hand on Edgerton's bare arm. "I have an idea. I'll be back tomorrow. We'll talk about it then."

He came back the next afternoon while they were photographing a locker room shot. Edgerton was posed in white briefs, banded in red and blue, one foot on the wooden bench, the locker door opened behind him, a towel slung over the door. From the darkness behind the camera he heard Samuels call out to the photographer. "My daughter has a great idea. Prop a tennis racket against the door."

The photographer came out from behind the cover of the camera. "Are you selling underwear or tennis rackets?"

"Maybe both. Try it. If the shot doesn't work, it's my fault." His voice lowered. "I am paying for this," he said.

Edgerton put on a robe and walked out of the heat of the lights while the prop people tried to find a tennis racket.

"You do a lot for my father's underwear."

She was slightly taller than he, thin but big boned. Her black hair was cut very short, highly styled, a carefully coiffed replica of a photograph in a beauty salon window. Her eyes were almond-shaped, heavily made up to give them a Cleopatra look, greasy green lines on her lids. One arm was covered by a coiled snake bracelet that came to her elbow. Edgerton remembered the dinner with the Samuels family but could not picture the face of the daughter.

"My father is impressed and everyone knows that Harry Samuels does not impress easily."

"Do you work for your father?"

"I might. I've been the one pushing him to manufacture tennis clothes. I might even take up tennis."

"I don't play anymore," Edgerton said, and walked away.

Even while it was happening, he wondered why he was letting it happen. Marybeth and Harry Samuels were obvious and relentless in their temptations; fancy lunches every day, dinner every night, theater parties, brunches, weekends in warm climates winged to in their private jet. They dangled all the symbols of the rich life in front of him. It had been ten months since he had had any contact with the Agency. He had just turned thirty, needed to soften the trauma of that milestone. He took stock of himself, trying to determine his own destination. All the things he could have become, the successes he could have been that had been thwarted, cut off by his CIA commitment either because they would not let him succeed or because an assignment pulled him away on the brink of success. Or would he have failed anyway? That was a question he had always had to ask himself.

He heard enough stories from other agents about being discarded when their active usefulness was over; nailed to a desk job at a reduced income and finally retired with a meager pension. There were no rich men in his profession. None of them lived the good life.

There was no one at the CIA to contact, to ask permission, or to discuss the advisability of getting married. There was no one to even submit a resignation to. He was a covert operator. They contacted him when they were ready.

At no time did he think about love. In retrospect, there had never been a time when he thought about love; the climate of his life had never been right for it. Sex was getting his rocks off, an animal act without tenderness. Or sex was a tool of his profession, like a gun or knife to be used in accomplishing a mission. Marybeth was his match, needed sex as he needed it and as often as he needed it. There were no preliminaries, no soft caresses or whispered words. They mated without thought to each other, using each other only to achieve explosive orgasms and then separated without clinging together in the afterglow of love.

In considering the package deal of Samuel Mills and Marybeth, he knew the sex part would be good. That was important to him.

And Chicago seemed a remote place, peaceful, out of the turbulent mainstream of both coasts. He would slip effortlessly into a predestined pattern of ascension in the Samuel Mills operation, a special slot reserved for a son-in-law. This was the chance to live a warm, full life out of the cold uncertainty of government service.

In the end, after countless dialogues with himself, he took that chance, reaching for what appeared to be the good life.

For a year and a half, Edgerton was convinced that he had made the right decision. There was never a contact from the Agency. His quarterly check continued to arrive promptly, forwarded from New York. He felt secure, rarely missed the excitement of the infrequent missions.

"My tennis match is at nine. I'm just in the mood to clobber Freddy Shore."

That was one of the things he did not like about her. She had taken up tennis right after they were married, played it like a man: a powerful game with an emasculating serve. When she got too good, when he really had to play hard to beat her, he had retreated to the golf course but never really enjoyed playing.

And there was the tuft of hair that grew at the base of her spine. That was on the list.

"Edge, would you please stop playing with yourself." She turned from the dressing table, the hairbrush in her hand. "You're driving me bananas."

He put his hands behind his head, studied his inert penis. He blamed her for what had happened to him. When he listened to the psychiatrists, the medical doctors, endless explanations by therapists including the Masters and Johnson staff in St. Louis, he understood that his impotence was not her fault but he blamed her nonetheless.

Edgerton had always taken his sexuality as an integral part of physical functioning; always there, performing automatically without forethought, without complication. When it stopped, when the complicated mechanism of sexuality failed, a short in the circuit of psycho-physical power lines, sexuality became the prime focus of his life. He acted out the trauma, plunging deeper into despair when every attempt at coupling failed, when every mechanical device, sexual toy, and nutritional supplement proved to be a quackery, noneffective.

The surface reasons seemed obvious, the lowering graph from sexuality to impotency beginning one morning when Marybeth said, "I meant to tell you last night, I've been to a doctor to take some tests. The results came back yesterday. I'm as fertile as hell. It must be you."

"What are you talking about?"

"I've been off the pill for six months. I should be pregnant."

"Off the pill? I thought we decided to wait."

"*You* decided to wait, *I* didn't. I made an appointment for you this afternoon."

"For what?"

"A fertility test."

"You're out of your mind."

"Your appointment is at two o'clock with Dr. Finnegan. He's supposed to be the best in the city. Daddy got his name from Mayo's."

"You've discussed this whole thing with your father without consulting me?"

"You're pigheaded about it. I'll never understand why you don't want children, you're absolutely marvelous with other people's children, they all adore you. I'll never understand why you don't want your own." He turned away from her. "Two o'clock," she said. "I've already given your secretary the time and the doctor's address."

He constrained his anger, controlled his voice to a low register. "I'm not going."

She touched his arm gently, he felt the breath of her words as she spoke. "Do it for me, Edge. It's so God-awful important. Do it for me. Just find out for sure, then we'll talk about it. I promise."

"I do everything for you or for your father. When is it my turn?"

"Just this one time. Do it for me. Please."

He had, of course, gone to the specialist and taken the tests which were conclusive: he was fertile. There was no physical reason why they could not conceive. For three months they experimented under a doctor's direction, trying different positions, keeping a temperature chart for Marybeth on the theory that when her temperature was highest, she was most likely to conceive. She would call him any time at the office, demand he race home, that the time was right. When before they had met each other with equal heat, equal intensity, his wife now lay inert on her back, not wanting pleasure, demanding conception.

The first time he could not get an erection he lashed back with anger. "It serves you right, it serves all of you right. You're trying to make a stud horse out of me. That's all I'm good for in your tight little lives, a fucking stud horse. Your father, too. He shows me off to his friends in the locker room . . . as though he were saying, look at the stud I bought my daughter. I'm sick of it."

"It is true," she said. "He did buy you. Or maybe you sold out."

That is when he had left her for the first time, slamming out of the house her father had built for them, running to the anonymity of a downtown hotel room, dissecting his life, examining his identity, knowing the truths about himself. Later that night in the hotel bar, he selected a small, diffident appearing hooker, took her up to his room, and charged at her with fury. But it was no different. As she tucked the money into her brassiere her voice was soothing, understanding. "Don't fret, honey, it happens lots of times, even to guys as good-looking as you, hung like you are. You must have had a fight with your wife. That's usually the case. Some guys get so mad they come three times, tear a girl apart. Then there are other guys who are so mad they can't get it up at all."

But it was not a temporary condition. He had gone back to his wife, resumed his life, experimented with other women, tried to masturbate: none of it worked.

When he finished urinating he zipped up his fly, washed his hands, and went back into the briefing room. A man with a beard sat there, dressed in civilian clothes, his legs crossed, heavy-framed glasses pushed up on the top of his head. Edgerton hesitated at the men's room door until the man smiled. "It's political science

time. Are you too brainwashed by now to absorb anything more?"

"I'm okay. Try me."

"You look familiar to me," the man said.

Edgerton sat down. "I have that kind of face."

The other man shook his head. "No, it's not that. It's like I've known you before." He studied Edgerton closer. "I suppose it would help if I knew your name." He held up his hand. "Don't tell me. I'm not supposed to know. It's against the rules. You are only a candidate number as far as I'm concerned. It seems silly but they must know what they're doing."

"Let's get on with it."

He pressed the button to close the draperies again; the room gradually darkened. "How much do you know about Cuba politically?"

"Zero."

"I'll assume you know who Castro is and that momentarily we have no diplomatic relations with Cuba." Edgerton nodded in the darkness. "This exercise is done from the new Cuban point of view, done through Castro's eyes. Someone thinks it's important that you understand how Castro thinks." He activated the projection equipment. Names, in different style lettering, began to flash on the three walls of the room. Edgerton swiveled from one wall to another.

The names all disappeared at once and before another image appeared, a recorded voice, high-pitched and frantic, came over the recording system; Spanish words spoken with fury. Then a close-up of Castro's face, his mouth twisting out the venomous words, the English translation on the bottom of the screen. Slowly the camera panned back, revealing the full figure of the man, punctuating his words with violent gestures, the camera moving back slowly, showing the endless shirt-sleeve crowd standing in the hot sun, perspiring heavily, listening silently, erupting suddenly in a rolling thunder of applause.

The film cut off abruptly, the lights went on.

"I knew I recognized you," the man said. "You're Marc Polo, aren't you?"

Edgerton did not answer.

"You don't have to answer. It's been bugging me. I know you're Marc Polo. In a lot of ways you look the same." He looked down, away from Edgerton. "You were kind of a cult to some of my friends and me. I even wrote to your studio for an autographed picture of you in your famous leopard bikini. I even remember the movie you wore it in, *Beach Party Bingo.*"

Edgerton cut him off. "I don't know what you're talking about. Let's get back to political science."

1978
AUGUST

4

FRIDAY

VILLA LES PENSÉES, CAP FERRAT, FRANCE

From the tall French doors leading off her bedroom, Contessa Marla Rinaldi looked down on the pool deck of her villa, an oval of blue water cantilevered over the cliff, half of it suspended over the Mediterranean. Her son and his newest friend were splashing at each other in the water, shouting vile names in several languages; grown men playing like children. It was always a shock to her when she saw her son for the first time each day, surprise followed by revulsion that any creature so obese and ugly could have been conceived and nurtured inside her own body.

Not even her son's father had been this physically repelling. There had been a hard maleness which had made her husband's ugliness sensual, a macho fiber which had made his softness seductive. And he had been rich, very rich as only the Cubans could be in those days of Batista. The son had inherited none of his father's virility, none of the brains, none of the shrewd cunning which should have been part of the parental heritage. Even the money he should have inherited was gone, secreted under rocks on the Cuban coast or discovered by now and confiscated by the revolutionaries. He had inherited nothing from her; not her bone structure, not her beauty, and not her talent for elegant survival. She had emerged from each disaster in her life into the spotlight of a greater triumph; more fame, more wealth, more adulation.

Tired of the child's play, her son climbed up the ladder and stood at the edge of the pool, fat rolling and hanging over the too-tight band of his bikini, wetness matting the black hair of his body against his skin like black tar from the sea. She felt the slight shudder of revulsion, consoled herself that she was seeing less of him these days; he was away more often and for longer periods of time. He was involved in some kind of project which she did not question, grateful that whatever it was, it kept him away from her most of the time. He had taken over their plantation in Great Guana Cay off Eleuthera Island. She could not imagine why anyone would want to be in the Bahamas at this time of year and particularly when they had this villa on the Riviera. In her world, everything which happened in the summer happened on the Côte d'Azur or at least no farther away than Sardinia.

There would only be today and tonight. Tomorrow he was going back to the Bahamas. If she could only live through tonight. He was insisting on going to the gala at Cannes with them, insisting on bringing the young man with him. There would be talk and questions among their friends. It was awkward for her to have a son twenty-six years old. It required so many explanations, caused further speculations on her own true age. If he kept insisting, she would find some excuse not to go that evening, not to be embarrassed by the presence of her son.

When she looked into the mirror, she saw herself through the scrim cameramen used to photograph her; the wrinkles, the lines, the slight sags became nonexistent, invisible. Twice she had had plastic surgery, both times a face lift, and the last time cosmetic surgery to raise her breasts. She had done all of this just in case of a financial emergency. She had no real desire to make another film. There were still offers from America, mostly cameo roles in major productions. Producers were still trying to entice her out of retirement with flattery but not much money. She had never liked working, never enjoyed the craft of acting. Being a star had been a means to an end for her, not a way of life. But if it ever became necessary to go back to acting she would be ready. She was keeping herself young looking, her body trim and firm. Their mutual friends gossiped and compared Princess Grace and Contessa Rinaldi. She turned from the view of the Mediterranean, admired herself in the mirror, the young girl's body, the perfect posture, the unblemished skin. Grace, she thought, had let herself go, become matronly looking. And Grace was younger than she.

If anything happened to the Count, she would go back to films.

In the final analysis, she reasoned, her own real security was her face and figure plus the jewels in her safe. Neither Italian law nor her husband's family acknowledged her legal status as wife or countess. Italian divorce laws were so antiquated, she explained to her American friends, and then assured them that they had been very properly married and by American law, everything was ironclad and binding. Yet she knew that if Aldo died, there would be legal confusions. He was an Italian citizen and his family, who had never acknowledged her, would fight her claims to the estate. Nothing was in her name. There was some money in a Swiss account but not nearly enough to maintain her life-style. Once before she had existed in what she had considered insulated security, never imagining that anything could happen to penetrate that insulation, interrupt the unending supply of wealth at her fingertips. Then Castro began his descent from the mountains, marching toward Havana and a nightmare had begun.

Raoul Ramirez was officially Secretary of the Cuban Treasury when she married him, a close personal friend of Batista and the number-two strong man in the government. Ramirez was the creative financial genius who continually found new ways of producing income for the régime and devious ways of diverting those monies from the treasury directly into personal wealth for Batista and his inner circle. Ramirez's greatest coup had been the unprecedented deal with the Mafia to let them take over all gambling in Cuba, skimming thirty percent off of the top of the take and funneling it directly into his own and Batista's pockets. While it lasted, the cash inflow was enormous, an unending geyser.

The career of Maria Worth had already skyrocketed from an exotic sex symbol to superstardom when she met Ramirez. Through the studio, an attaché of the Cuban government had approached her, presented her with a velvet box containing a four-inch diamond-and-emerald bracelet. On the back of the officially engraved card, in his crude handwriting Ramirez had written a message in Spanish. "I don't understand this," she said to the attaché. "I didn't order anything. Are you trying to sell me this bracelet?"

"It is a gift," the man explained. "A conditional gift."

She looked at the card, her fingers fondling the heavy engraving. "I don't know any Raoul Ramirez." She turned the card over. "And I don't read Spanish."

"If I may." The attaché held out his hand; she gave him the card. He read the message silently, smiled slightly. "Mr. Ramirez says that the quickest way to a lady's bed is through her jewel box."

She grabbed the card angrily, began to tear it, was distracted by the dazzle of the diamonds, and laughed. "I don't know who Mr. Ramirez is," she told the attaché, "but he is direct, isn't he?"

The courtship which followed was handled with the same skill and cunning Ramirez had used to bargain with the Mafia. There were no dialogues of love. From the beginning, it had been a unilateral trade, her beauty for his money. It was only a question of how much money. Once that agreement was made, their marriage worked well; neither stinted on the bargain which had been made.

Huge sums of cash were always available to her in any currency. When they built a house in the Miramar section outside Havana, Ramirez had installed a bank-size vault on the second floor, an eight by ten room lined with steel boxes, each box filled with currency or negotiable securities. One section was specially equipped with velvet-lined trays for her jewels.

Until Castro was in Havana and the revolution won, Ramirez had insisted that there was no real danger, that the revolution could not possibly succeed. Then suddenly it was beginning to happen all around them, their friends fleeing, some of them caught, some executed. Possessions were being confiscated, property nationalized.

There had been only time to pack one small bag, jammed full of dollars and as much jewelry as she could take. With her son, she escaped during the night to a small boat hidden in the rocks behind their estate, a treacherous crossing on choppy water, the boy crying, thrown against the side of the boat by the turbulence time and time again. She sat huddled against the boat, clutching the bag, not letting go of it to hold or to comfort her son.

Ramirez had stayed behind, still not believing that what was happening around him could happen to him. Three days later he was arrested, tortured brutally when they found the vault empty, the contents secreted somewhere. For a week every form of torture was used but Ramirez never broke, never revealed the hiding place. The bodies of the two gardeners who had dug up the rocks on the cliff and hidden the steel boxes of money and jewels under Ramirez's direction washed up on shore eight days later, bloated and partially mauled by sharks. By then, Ramirez had been executed, the fortune never discovered.

It was over a year before she knew anything of this or that Ramirez had been executed. He had entrusted a letter to a nephew, a last will and testament, together with a map showing the exact location where the steel boxes of currency and jewels had been hidden in the rocks. It had taken the nephew a year to escape from Cuba. When he delivered the letter, she was back in films, starting a second career, catapulted back into the limelight by her hazardous escape from Cuba, her continuing public denunciations of Castro.

She was on holiday at St. Moritz, resting between films, when she met Rinaldi. He had a vague association with his family's jewelry business in Rome, an independent and unending supply of money, the source of which she could guess at but never confirm. She saw the opportunity, through Rinaldi, to return to the kind of life she had lived in Cuba, become again the international beauty, the international hostess but this time with social acceptance, regain the title of Contessa and access to the royalty of the world.

Three years after their marriage, the Contessa finally confessed to her husband that she had a son living in Utah with her parents. The young man was brought to Rome. From the beginning, her son had resented Rinaldi, fought the man's offer of fatherhood, would not even accept friendship. The boy was loyal to a father he did not remember, to a country to which he could never return, germinating vengeance against the people who had deprived him of his heritage. The vengeance was undisciplined, fragmented into futile daydreams until his twenty-fifth birthday when his mother gave him the letter from Ramirez bequeathing half the hidden fortune to him.

The sound of the other young man's voice, hollering Italian obscenities from the water, brought the Contessa's attention back to the swimming pool. Her son was laughing, waving the other man's swimming trunks in the air, finally tossing them over the cliff. The younger man raised himself out of the pool, the muscles in his arms and back contracting, his wet, smooth skin glistening in the sunlight. The Contessa felt the slight chill at the base of her neck, the warning signal of lust. Twice before she had had affairs with her son's friends. Both times it had been costly, but worth it. She watched this one closely now, completely out of the pool, his back to her, his buttocks bright white against the golden color of his skin. This one, she decided, had to be from Northern Italy, his skin was very fair and he had curly, blondish hair that fit his head like a bubble. Last night, she had taken inventory of him, was fascinated by the animal body straining against his clothes, the transparent hazel color of his eyes. When he turned around, was full-face toward her, she caught the dazzle of sunlight reflecting off something metallic on his naked body. She reached for her eyeglasses on the dressing table, held them in front of her without putting them on. There was something gold around his penis. Her son had seen it too. He touched the gold ring, tried to twist it. They spoke in low voices to each other, laughed and walked off to the cabana, out of her sight.

If it was going to happen, the Contessa decided, it would have to happen this afternoon. Tonight was the gala and tomorrow the man would be off with her son for the Bahamas. If she could create a crisis, insist that her husband have a long talk with her son, she could go to the young man's room. She saw herself as though she were on the screen, her long white peignoir filmy over her nakedness, the young man lying on the bed, not surprised, expecting her, wanting her. She would sit on the edge of the bed, smile the half-smile she was famous for, touch the gold ring around his penis. She saw all of it happening, projected through the hazy, ethereal scrim over the eye of the camera.

The cabana was under the swimming pool, carved into the rocky cliff, protected overhead by the cantilevered, concrete mass. There was a sheer drop from the deck of the cabana down to the sea. Roger Ramirez sat cross-legged at the unprotected ledge, his arms folded against his chest, staring out into space. The young Italian was drying himself in the shadows near the door to the sauna room. "You look like a buddha, Roger. You dream like a buddha. What are you dreaming about?"

"I don't dream: I plan."

Playfully, Guido flayed his towel at Ramirez, snapped it short of hitting the back of his neck. "If you're not dreaming, then what are you planning?"

"It must look like this," Ramirez said. "The place we lived in Cuba must look like this. My mother says that there was not such a sharp drop to the water but my mother is very nearsighted. She is not a good judge of distance or time. Beautiful women don't have to bother with things like that. Beautiful women have no loyalty. They live only for the moment."

"It was seventeen years ago. What do you expect?"

"I was ten years old. I should remember. But I can remember nothing except that little boat and being thrown against the side of it in the rough storm. And crying." He turned slightly to look behind him. "I cannot remember my father's face. She didn't even take his picture with her when we escaped. Nothing. I have no evidence of the first ten years of my life."

Guido sat beside him, put his arm around Ramirez's fat shoulders. "It won't be long. You will have the jewels and the money. That is better than memories." He squeezed Ramirez's shoulder. "Think of what we can do with all that money, all the places we can go, all the fun we can have. There will be enough for all of our lives. We will never have to work, never have to beg for money." He put his mouth over Ramirez's ear, darted his tongue into the orifice, felt the result-ant action in a shiver through Ramirez's body. "We can tell the whole world to go to hell. You won't need your mother. You won't need Aldo."

"You understand," Ramirez said, "that you will always need me."

"You're a goof, baby. You think all I want is the money." He put his mouth over Ramirez's ear again, inserted his tongue. "Do you think I do to you what I do just for money?" He shook his head. "No way."

They had not heard Aldo Rinaldi coming down the stone steps. The Count was barefoot, dressed in crisp white shorts, an unbut-toned white silk shirt tied at his waist. "I want to talk to you, Roger." He looked at Guido, motioned for him to leave. Guido stood up, adjusted the gold cock ring, winked at Rinaldi behind Ramirez's back, started to go into the dressing room.

"Guido can stay," Ramirez said. "He knows everything anyway. We are partners in this."

"I want to talk to you alone, Roger. You can tell Guido what you want him to know later." He turned to the young Italian man. "Put something on," he directed, "and go back to the house."

Rinaldi waited until Guido was gone. "Turn around, Roger. I like to look at a man when I talk to him."

Ramirez stood up, wrapped a towel around his waist, sat in one of the aluminum chairs. "You don't like Guido."

He shook his head. "I do not sit in judgment, Roger. You know that. Guido is your friend. I do not like him and I do not dislike him."

"You disapprove."

"We are what we are. You are what circumstances have made you. I don't approve and I don't disapprove. I accept what is inevitable." He sat opposite his wife's son. "It is inevitable that I will never have a son. I would have liked you to be that son. I gave up on that many years ago. But I still have concern for you. I still have . . ." he fumbled for a word. "It is difficult for an Italian man to explain his Italian emotions in English. It is better we speak Italian."

"You are concerned for me because of my mother."

Rinaldi shook his head. "No, it is not because of your mother. She is impenetrable. I have no control over what she feels. I have a concern for you as one man has for another and because I have known you and loved you since you were twelve years old." He gestured with his hands. "That is not unnatural, is it? Why can't you accept that?"

He ignored the question, shied away from the offer of intimacy. "I know what Guido is," he said. "Guido thinks he is using me to get to the money. I am actually using him for my own purposes. I tell him just enough to keep him with me and not enough so that he can take the money without me."

"I don't want to see you hurt, Roger."

"I told you that I know about Guido."

Slowly, afraid of the answer, Rinaldi asked, "What do you know about him?"

"He's a whore, a hustler. He pretends feelings for me for his purposes and I pretend feelings for him for my own purposes. There are no real emotions involved." He looked across to Rinaldi. "Does that reassure you?"

"I hope that you recover your father's wealth, Roger. I think that once you have been successful at that there will be a chance for us to become real friends."

"Half of it goes to you and your associates."

"You couldn't do this without them. I don't personally have the kind of money this takes. My friends are investors. They have the resources and they have the connections and professional advice you need."

"They treat me like dirt," Ramirez said. "I planned this whole thing. It was my idea. You know that, Aldo. You know that I had it all planned out before I came to you. Now they treat me like dirt. The men at Great Guana hardly talk to me. They have just taken over as though I don't exist. They're like Guido . . . whores."

"Mercenaries are a very special breed of men."

"Whores. Like Guido." He smiled. "They think that they are using me. In the end, they will understand that I am using them."

"I warn you, Roger, for your own safety, do not play games with my friends, do not try to outsmart them. They have invested a lot of money in this project. They take their investments very seriously."

"I can take care of myself."

"Not with them. I warn you, do not try to outsmart them. The bottom of the ocean is filled with bodies of men who tried."

"When will I get the final payment? I must have the money tomorrow if I am to keep on schedule."

"That's what I have come to tell you. There is a meeting tonight. Victor Castle has come to Cannes. There is a meeting at midnight. I will tell them then that you are ready for the final payment."

"They must do it, Aldo. You must make them see that it is imperative that I get the money at once."

"All I can do is tell them, Roger. They will understand."

"You would like out of this, wouldn't you, Aldo?"

The Count thought a moment, stretched his legs in front of him. "I have made the commitment. My life will never be any different." Then, he said, "Yes, I would like to back out but I know that it is impossible. So I accept it as I accept myself and you."

"And Mother?"

"Yes. I accept your mother, too, just as she is."

"Are you ever going to tell her about the money?"

"If you're successful, you should be the one to tell her. It is not my place to. Rightfully, according to your father's bequest, half the money belongs to her."

"She has no right to it. She has no loyalty to my father's memory. It is as though my father never existed in her life."

"Nevertheless, half of the money belongs to her. It was your father's wish. It is not your privilege to change the specific instructions of a dead man."

"I have the only proof and I can destroy that easily."

"You cannot destroy what you know, what your mother knows, and what I know." He put his hand on Ramirez's arm. "In the end you will do what is right, Roger. You know that, no matter what you say, I know that, too."

"It had better be a big piece of pie. Half goes to you and your friends and then I have to split the other half with my mother. And I'm the one taking all the risks."

Rinaldi shrugged his shoulders. "What if there is nothing there? What if Castro has found the vaults? It's been seventeen years, Roger. Many things could have happened. If there is nothing there, my friends will have lost their investment. A million dollars is quite a risk."

"Not against thirty or forty million."

"A million dollars is still a major risk. If they lose their investment they will not hold it against you. They understand that failure is possible. As long as you don't try to cheat them or outsmart them, you will be perfectly safe even if you fail."

"I will never fail."

"I can give you only one piece of advice, Roger. I do not know what is in your mind, but do not underestimate my friends. Use judgment." Rinaldi looked beyond the young man, out to the sea. He wished that he did not know all the things he knew. He wished that he did not feel this compassion for his wife's son.

THE PALM BEACH CASINO, CANNES, FRANCE

Standing behind the players, Aldo Rinaldi was watching the young woman play roulette at the fifty-franc table. His jeweler's eye appraised the masses of diamonds and emeralds she wore: his man's lust was alive to the excitement there would be in the almost-ripe body, imagining the taste of the taut, tanned flesh in his mouth. Daydreams, he was thinking. He brought himself back to the reality of this moment; look but do not touch. The young woman belonged to Victor Castle and Castle flashed her at his friends and business associates, tempting and taunting them, daring them with unspoken threats of emasculation. This woman, the way he used her, was another symbol of the don supremacy.

As she played roulette her long fingers caressed the pearlized plaques before she dropped them on the green felt table. The smaller denominations were round discs, the larger denominations rectangular, increasing in size and changing in color from the red, five-thousand francs to the white, hundred-thousand francs. Each number played on the board, she played to the legal limit; the large plaques *en plein*, the smaller chips stacked *en carré* and *au cheval*. Rinaldi estimated that the pear-shaped diamond on her left hand weighed between twenty-three and twenty-four carats, the color and brilliance of the highest quality, knew that it had been purchased in Geneva where Castle now maintained legal residence. The alternating bracelets of diamonds and emeralds were typically Van Cleef; no other jeweler had quite mastered this kind of workmanship so skillfully. The earrings, a farrago of different shaped stones at the lobe supporting pear-shaped drops at least fifteen carats each, were probably also Van Cleef; slightly vulgar, exquisitely crafted. The large flower pendant in the cleavage between her breasts was from his own firm, a classic example of their design: stem and leaves paved with emeralds supporting a large flower of canary diamonds, each petal of the flower individually sculpted and at the center of the blossom, a clustered stamen of diamonds mounted on invisible springs, shivering and shimmering as the woman moved, refracting sparkles of light on the other gamblers. This pendant alone had cost four hundred and twenty million lire. Victor Castle had paid for it in cash. American dollars.

Number 17 hit. "*Dix-sept*," the croupier muttered. Her face was the same mask, winning or losing. One of the croupiers raked the other chips off the table and then with his stick, touched the stack directly on and around number 17. She acknowledged her winning with a slight incline of her head. The croupier, preparing the pay-off from the table bank, fanned the plaques in straight lines, each stack beginning with a red, fifty-thousand chit and ending with stacks of round hundred-franc discs. With his rake, muttering as he added, the croupier counted out her winnings, restacked them neatly, pushed the huge piles in front of her. She was already playing the numbers for the next roll of the wheel, did not look down at the fortune shoved in front of her. As she leaned across the table, placing her bets, the dangling pendant brushed against the stack of chips still on 17, toppling them. Her eyes met Rinaldi's. He inclined his head slightly, smiled. She did not acknowledge the tribute. When she was seated again, her fingers ran through the stacks of her last winnings, counting the chips without looking at them, stack by stack. Not turning around, she handed them to a young man standing behind her who stuffed them in the pockets of his dinner jacket. His face, like her face, was immobile, registering no emotion.

Rinaldi turned from the table, moved across the room, shouldered his way through the noisy Americans at the crap table and went to the bar where his wife's son was standing, dressed in a white jacket that was too tight for him, sipping a soft drink, monitoring the room, his head moving as though he were watching a slow-motion tennis match. "Any signs?" Rinaldi asked.

"American FBI," he said. "They know that there will be a meeting. And Italian income-tax agents. They're always here. I can identify no one else."

"What happened to your young friend?"

"Guido?" He turned back to the bar, put down his glass. "Guido said he was tired. Bored. He felt constrained in a jacket and tie. You cannot shackle a wild animal forever. He went back to the villa."

Rinaldi smiled, knowing that soon his wife would be in the young man's bed. It did not matter anymore, she was still useful to him and he loved her just enough to feel no jealousy, to take a small delight in her fulfillments. "There is no point in your waiting here for me, Roger. This meeting may go on all night. There will be other business to talk about as well. You might as well go home. If the meeting lasts too late, I'll stay at the apartment in the Carleton overnight and come back early in the morning. We can have breakfast together. I'll tell you what happened then."

"I'll wait. I want to know what happens tonight. I must have another two hundred thousand dollars to take back with me."

"You will have it. I promise. There will be no problem."

"Remember, I leave for the Bahamas tomorrow. The timetable is desperate. You said that yourself. You said that timing was the most important thing."

"I promise, Roger. The funds will be in Nassau by the time you get there."

"The same procedure?"

"I am not certain. That will be Victor's decision. He knows best about these things. So far his judgment has been flawless. We must continue to trust him."

Roger swallowed the remainder of his drink, lowered his voice, switched from Italian to English. "Fifteen days, Aldo. In fifteen days I will be standing on my own soil again, on my own land."

"God willing," Rinaldi said. "Your friend Guido, does he go back to Washington?"

"He flies there directly from Paris on the *Concorde.* He will do what he has to do in Washington and then meet me at Great Guana."

"Is there news yet of San Marco?" His stepson shook his head. "San Marco could be dangerous. You must find him, eliminate him."

"San Marco knows nothing, no details. He's an old man. When I had my cousin contact him, I stressed that San Marco was to be told no specifics. I trust my cousin."

"It is dangerous enough that he knows something is happening. I don't like not being able to keep track of San Marco. What about the television woman?"

"Laurie Golding?" Ramirez shrugged his shoulders. "Guido can handle her."

"One way or the other?"

Ramirez laughed. "If he doesn't kill her with his cock, he'll do it with his bare hands. Don't worry about Guido. It's not his first time out."

Rinaldi looked at his wife's son, felt a compassion for his innocence. Guido was Victor Castle's man, hand-picked and directly accountable to the don. Young Ramirez did not know that, took credit for recruiting Guido. What appeared to be an accidental pickup at a bar in Rome, Guido hustling Ramirez, was actually a carefully planned maneuver which Rinaldi had implemented. Guido insured Castle of constant surveillance and instant information. In the end, Rinaldi hoped that young Ramirez would not have to be sacrificed. Eliminating Roger would probably be part of Castle's master plan. Rinaldi did not dare question Castle about what would happen to his stepson. Regardless, he would be powerless to stop it if Castle had destined his death. He put his hand on the young man's arm. "Take care of yourself, Roger."

"Because my mother worries about me?" Ramirez laughed. "She would like me to be dead. I am an embarrassment to her, I know that. First she would like my father's money and then she would like me dead. Don't try to tell me that my mother worries about me. We both know better than that."

"I worry," Rinaldi said. "I worry enough for both your mother and me."

The mocking defensiveness disappeared for a moment as Ramirez looked at his stepfather, saw the genuine concern in the other man's face. Then he recovered, tried to button his jacket, touched Rinaldi tentatively. "Ciao, Aldo."

"Yes, Roger. Ciao."

Victor Castle sat at the empty chemin-de-fer table in the *salon privé*, the plaited pink lampshade casting a rosy glow on his pale face and white hair. Age had mellowed him, refined his looks so that he fit that part he now played to the public. At first sight, he may well have been a private Swiss banker. But when he spoke, the physical illusion evaporated. His heritage was still in his voice, his choice of words. He was still Vittorio Casteleone, a Sicilian immigrant working the Boston docks.

His current exile from the United States was self-imposed, technically not an exile. His business interests and sphere of operation had become international. With the developments in the Mideast, partnerships with Arab conglomerates, Geneva was now more central to him than New York. There were tax advantages to Swiss residency and some protection of his privacy from the relentless predators and observers of various agencies of the United States government. Even now, wherever he was, there was constant surveillance on him. There would be men downstairs, at this moment, agents with hidden cameras, photographing the men coming upstairs to the private meeting. The surveillance was an harassment to Castle rather than a danger. He had always been too clever for them, too careful to cover his tracks, no crime or malfeasance directly traceable to him.

He looked at his watch. His own men would be outside the door now, a few minutes before the appointed time. Although he could hear nothing through the insulated door, he knew that they would be there, shuffling silently, not daring to speak to each other yet or to the guards protecting the room.

At sixty-eight years old, Castle was still hard as a rock, as virile as he had been at forty. The young woman attested to that, was a symbol of it. Twice a year he spent three days in the clinic at Montreaux, took animal injections, drank foul-tasting concoctions prepared by the doctors and believed these doctors when they told him that, with his physical constitution, he would live forever. Castle reasoned that if a man was going to live forever, he needed enough money to last forever. He was determined to amass more money than any other single individual ever had.

In the corridor outside, the assembled men parted to let the young woman through. The guard opened the door quickly so that she would not have to hesitate, break her stride. She walked directly to the table, stood behind Castle, leaning over to kiss the top of his head, then pulled a chair as close to him as she could, took off her left earring, tossed it on the green baize, massaged the empty ear lobe, kicked off her shoes, and dug her bare feet into the thick carpet.

"Did you win?"

The woman answered in Italian. "I always win. It would not be proper for the woman of Vittorio Casteleone not to win." Then in unaccented English, "I killed them at the roulette table and lost some of it back at the crap table. Not much. An American crapped out three times in a row."

Castle groped under the table, pressed a buzzer. Almost immediately the men outside filed into the room, took their places facing Castle. The young man in the tuxedo, who had stood behind her at the roulette table, stood behind the young woman again. Two additional guards placed themselves outside the arc of pink light, keeping a vigilance on the five men confronting Castle.

The oldest man in this inner circle was Julius Schwartz; for some reason, which no one now remembered, he had been nicknamed Hotdog. He sat with his hands in his lap, his fists clenched to hide the scarred, disfigured fingers without fingernails. His face had a blank look, thin scars where his eyebrows had been, and vapid eyes, unframed by lashes which had been plucked out and never grown back.

For a brief period in the early Fifties, he had become notorious during the televised hearings of the Kefauver Committee investigating organized crime in the United States and interstate violations of laws controlling gambling, narcotics, and prostitution. The main thrust of the hearings was to link crime directly to the Mafia. Witness after witness was called up, each man pleading the fifth amendment, giving no information.

It had been Lucky Luciano's idea to throw Hotdog at the committee, use him as a diversion from the real issues. It was Luciano's concept to have it appear as though Hotdog were defecting, offering evidence in return for protection. "So you get a couple of years," he had told Schwartz. "We'll make it up to you. In spades, Hotdog. We'll make it up to you in spades."

Enjoying the hot lights and cameras, the little hoodlum had sat at the hearings, nattily dressed, his shirt pocket embroidered with his symbol, a big red hotdog, and his tie hand painted with a long link of the sausages, his cufflinks solid gold hotdogs. He became the comic relief of the hearings, using his low humor to avoid some of the direct questions, making plausible lies to divert the investigation from the truth. In the end he had been accused of perjury, made guest appearances on television while he awaited his trial, was sentenced to five years in prison, got off in three, and was rewarded with the top post when the Mafia took control of gambling in Cuba. He became a local celebrity in Havana, the can-do man. Whatever his friends wanted and whenever they wanted it, Hotdog produced it. But behind his genial host façade, behind his puns and wisecracks, Schwartz ran a tight operation, produced tremendous profits, avoided political problems. Luciano had looked at Schwartz's records, pleased with his choice. "Four years of college and a little class," he had told an associate, "and that little Yid could have been Bernard Baruch."

Castle spoke to him first. "Long time, Hotdog."

"Lots of water, Victor. Lots of bridges."

"You look good. You must be as old as me. We both look good."

"You look better. You got more gelt. Makes a man look better." Schwartz looked at the woman. "Buys him better things."

"You got complaints?"

"No use," he said. "Morocco ain't bad except for the fucking Arabs who live there. I don't contribute no money to Israel but I make Arabs eat a lot of shit. Same thing, I guess."

"Are you sure of all your information? It's been a long time. My memory isn't so good sometimes either. You're sure of everything you told us?"

"Victor, a man don't forget six million bucks, he don't forget where he hid it. I took care of it like it was my own dough. Every time those spick bastards pulled out a fingernail"—he looked down at his scarred fingers—"I remember it even better."

"The money first, Hotdog. Remember that. The money first.

Then you can go after the bastards that did it to you. We take no responsibility. Once you give us the money you're on your own. Nobody's going to wait for you. We're in and out in an hour."

"I know, I know."

"What good is it going to do you, Hotdog? What good? You still think like an old Jew, an eye for an eye. What good?" He leaned forward, put his hand on the table, reaching for Schwartz. "You don't need it. Ten percent of the dough is yours, right off the top. A lot of dough, Hotdog. You can make a lot of people eat a lot of shit for that kind of dough. What good is an eye for an eye?"

Schwartz smiled, put his maimed hand out to touch Castle's hand. "I got a psychological problem, Victor. Imagine an old fart like me with a psychological problem. My psychological problem is that I want to murder those mother fuckers. Catharsis. A dame taught me that word. I need catharsis and no fucking Ex-Lax is going to work. It's going to take a big catharsis to solve my psychological problem . . . like murdering the biggest Cuban mother fucker of them all." He pulled his hand away. "You got to understand human psychology, Victor." He leaned back. "I go in with the raid or the whole deal is off."

"You're going to get yourself killed."

Schwartz smiled. "Then that's going to solve my deep-seated psychological problem. Right? Either way I win, Victor. Either way."

When their business was concluded the men stood up, nodded reverentially at Castle and then to the woman at his side, and began filing out of the *salon privé*. Castle motioned to Rinaldi to wait, took a bundle of French francs from his jacket pocket, set it on the green baize in front of the woman. "Go break the bank."

"I want to stay," she said.

"Get your ass out of here before I kick it out."

"I know everything anyway, why can't I stay?"

"You know just as much as I want you to know." He took the wad of money, shoved it roughly down the front of her dress. "You don't know shit."

She looked directly at Rinaldi, deliberately provoking him, but her words taunted Castle. "I know enough to put both of you in jail for the rest of your lives. I know that much. I might as well know it all."

With an open hand, Castle whacked her across the face with

enough force to knock her out of the chair and knock the chair to the floor. She got up slowly, rubbing the side of her face. Tears brimmed her eyes: stubbornly she held them back. Reaching over, she took the earring, put it on, then groped under the table to recover her shoes, slipped into them as she bent over, letting her breasts fall out of the halter of her dress. The money fell to the floor. She clutched it in her hand, walked slowly out of the room.

"Good kid," Castle said. "Lots of spunk. I've always been a sucker for broads with balls." He rubbed his face. "She's never going to live to be an old lady." Castle leaned across the table to be closer to Rinaldi. "If I go before you do, make sure she don't live to be an old lady."

"You'll outlive me, Victor. You'll probably outlive all of us."

"Probably. But just in case, get rid of her, will you?"

Silently, the two men put their elbows on the table, grasped, and shook hands. Then Castle leaned back. "You look tired, Aldo. Tough trip, huh? When did you get back from Moscow?"

"Yesterday morning. I flew to Paris and then down here."

"You made the deal?"

All the tension of three days of negotiation with the KGB in Russia was reflected in Rinaldi's face as he nodded; the in-fighting, the money haggling, the wary machinations of trading information, estimating the extent of the other side's intelligence information.

Castle had begun the crack of a smile. "They bought it *as is?*"

"Except the money. The ten million they agreed to, but not in Swiss francs. American dollars. They're loaded with dollars."

"Shit." Castle thought for a moment. "The way the dollar is, it's like skimming a million bucks off the top."

Rinaldi was the contact man, the negotiator, and the buffer in dealings with undercover agencies of governments in Victor Castle's sphere of operation; Europe, North America, the Mideast. He also dealt with terrorist groups and insurgents in this territory. Castle had overlord counterparts in Central South America, and Africa and access to an older, more structured organization in the Far East. Rinaldi functioned as liaison with these other groups.

As an Italian count, a representative of one of the most prestigious jewelers in Europe, Rinaldi moved easily around the world, deliberately keeping a high-profile exposure so that he was accessible to established echelons needing contact with the underground power structure. He had continuing lines of communication with the CIA, the KGB, Interpol. He was also covered in France, East Germany, West Germany, Egypt, Lebanon, Syria, and Iran as well as the secret arms of the dissident Arab countries.

While the overt agencies were trying to track down Castle, break down his network of drug traffic, gambling, and prostitution, the covert agencies of these same governments were buying his services, protecting him as a source of information, using his thugs and assassins.

The CIA, hog-tied by legalities and ethics, had been Castle's prime customer. When Roger Ramirez had come to his stepfather with a scheme to recapture the jewels and money hidden on the Cuban coast, and presented a military plan using a mock commando raid as a diversionary screen for the recovery, Rinaldi had at once seen the possibilities for an even larger operation. The geopolitical implications could mean a big payoff from one side or the other. His first inclination was to go to the CIA but the shake-up under the Carter administration was making the Agency run scared, not being aggressive in covert operations. The whole organization was cut back at the moment to minimal function. Rinaldi decided that the KGB was a less complicated prospective buyer. When he presented Ramirez's plan, Castle had agreed instantly to finance the operation and concurred with Rinaldi on giving the Russians first shot at using it for political purposes.

"The Russians ought to be worth ten million," Castle told Rinaldi. "You say that the kid thinks there's maybe twenty or thirty mil in cash and jewelry buried in Cuba. That's forty." He was quiet then, thinking back. "You remember a hood named Hotdog Schwartz?" Rinaldi nodded. "Find him. When we had to pull out of Havana, Lansky left Schwartz behind with a lot of dough. Schwartz got beat up by Castro. They pulled out all his fingernails . . . that kind of stuff. But that little Yid wouldn't break. He never told them where the dough was hid. If we get that, that's maybe five or six more. It adds up."

"The Ramirez stuff may be worth more," Rinaldi explained. "The jewelry market has more than doubled in seventeen years."

"What do you think it will cost?"

"Not more than two."

"Do it," Castle said.

1801 CENTURY PARK EAST, CENTURY CITY, LOS ANGELES, CALIFORNIA

Edgerton arrived in the lobby of the office building five minutes early: Carroll Coulter was already waiting. For a minute, the two men did not recognize each other. They shook hands, mumbled each other's name, and moved to a corner of the lobby. Coulter had not changed, Edgerton decided, he was just an extension of the man he had been when they first met. Now, he had that desperate has-been appearance of past-prime, cosmetic attempts to appear youthful, which made him look older. His hair was bleached blond, augmented with a cheap toupee over the center bald spot. His face and neck were coated with a bronzing gel which did not quite cover the inherent pallor of his complexion and which contrasted with his white hands, veined and freckled with age. He had gained a lot of weight, corseted it under the standard Hollywood uniform: expensive jeans, Gucci loafers, gold-buttoned blazer, open shirt, and the status gold chain exposed on his bare chest. Coulter had added a silk handkerchief, carefully knotted to appear casual in order to cover the deep crease at the base of his sagging neck.

When Edgerton was still at UCLA and had had a few bit parts in films, Coulter was a big-time Hollywood talent agent, the status agent specializing in young bodies, mostly men, who looked good in bathing suits. To supply the demand for beach and surfer films, he had a permanent table in the Polo Lounge of the Beverly Hills Hotel and was always surrounded by the harem of talent he represented, holding court like a queen surrounded by chamberlains. At one of the sessions he created Edgerton's name. He began introductions by saying, "We were sitting in the Polo Lounge and I said to myself, why not? I was so sick of the Tabs and the Rocks and Rips. And don't you think he looks like Marc Polo? Don't you just wish Marc Polo looked this handsome?" Coulter was riding high on the crest of youth-oriented scripts. Edgerton had suffered through the induction into Coulter's stable: the wild drug parties in his Bel-Air home and fending him off at the weekend alone with him at his Malibu Beach house.

Carroll Coulter had been on the skids for the last five years. The climate of the industry had changed, a new kind of hero required:

tough, ugly, macho, and preferably Italian names were in. The tight assed, clean-cut beach boys were out.

"You look marvelous, Edge, simply marvelous. Age has done a lot for you, given you charisma. It's going to be a whole new career for you. This spread in *Playgirl* will make you a star. I know it. When they get a look at your cock in living color, every woman in America is going to go ape. Trust me, Edge. I know what the talent market is and you've got it . . . exactly the right thing at the right time. I told the people upstairs that you were perfect for the story. Believe me it took some convincing. First they thought about Tab. Well, you know what happened to Tab. I haven't represented him in years because of it. They went through a whole list but I kept plugging for you. The timing is so right."

Edgerton played along with the charade. "I'm not crazy about taking my clothes off in front of a camera. Do you really think it will lead to something?"

"They'll be pounding down the doors. Every producer in town is going to want you. Look what it did for Burt. It's not that you're just another pretty face. You can act. I mean, hell, you're a real actor. Do you know how confident I am? The day that the magazine appears on the newsstands, I'm changing back to an unlisted telephone number. That phone will be ringing off the wall."

"What's this meeting about?" He looked at his watch. "We'd better be getting upstairs."

As they walked to the elevators, Coulter explained, "They want to get background stuff mostly. It's a full-scale editorial meeting; they'll all be there. They will show their layouts and give you a feel of what kind of story they're doing. I think you're the whole issue, front to back. They've never done that before."

"I've never seen the magazine."

"*Playgirl* was the first magazine to break the ice with frontal male nudes. They're the only ones who have been able to survive. I don't think there is a gay person in Los Angeles who doesn't absolutely devour it. They won't release a breakdown of their circulation. They try to make everyone think it's mostly liberated women who read it but let me tell you, it's read in a lot of closets."

They were off the elevator, walking toward the big double doors at the end of the corridor. "Where are you staying, Edge? I have room at my place." He smiled tentatively, testing. "It will kind of be like old times."

"I'm flying out to Miami right after the meeting. I have to be on location in the Bahamas by Monday. Sooner if I can."

At the reception desk, Coulter gave his own name to the young man at the switchboard, did not give Edgerton's. He waited at the counter while he was being announced.

Or what if the miracle did happen? What if this elaborate cover the Agency had created with *Playgirl* really did relaunch his film career and this time he worked at it, made it succeed?

Coulter said, "It will be a couple of minutes." Edgerton noticed that Coulter was perspiring heavily, shaking as though he had a fever. "One of them will come out to get us." He sat down on the bench, took a handkerchief from his sleeve, and wiped his face. Edgerton put his hand on Coulter's shoulder, a silent offer of reassurance.

A man in a *Playgirl* T-shirt and jeans, carrying a lucite clipboard, came through the swinging doors from the office, walked directly up to Edgerton. "All ready for you, Mr. Polo," he said. "We're set up in the conference room." He looked down at Coulter. "It won't be necessary for you to stay." Coulter could not hide his disappointment. "This is an editorial meeting. All we need is Mr. Polo." He turned back toward the doors. Edgerton exhanged glances with Coulter. There was no way he could save face for the man, no way to protect him.

In the conference room, instead of a center table, eight leather lounge chairs formed a semicircle facing a blank, wood paneled wall, each chair equipped with an arm-attached writing surface, complete with a recessed pencil holder, a fresh pad of note paper and an ashtray. At the far end of the room, five people were standing clustered around a built-in bar, drinking coffee from *Playgirl* inscribed cups. "This is Marc Polo, kids," the man with the clipboard said. With a vague, indicative gesture he reeled off the names. "Ed. Nancy. Monica. Jim and Cynthia." They all smiled and mumbled to acknowledge the introduction. One of the women handed Edgerton a mug of coffee. He shook his head.

"We're waiting for Roy," she said. "He's finishing up a conference call with New York." Casually, she sauntered away from the group. Edgerton followed her. "I'm Cynthia," she said. "I'm the editor." She looked him up and down carefully. "I thought I ought to give you the game plan so that we don't waste any time. We've a tough deadline, a lot of work to do." She sank in one of the deep chairs, stretched her legs in front of her, rested her head on the back of the chair. "You're not going to find much enthusiasm in the editorial staff for this project. Nothing personal, you understand. It's not you, it's the idea. None of us like it. As a matter of fact, we think it's the pits. I don't believe that our readers are going to like one whole issue devoted to one man: I don't care how gorgeous his prick is. But Gabe wants to do it and we do what Gabe wants. It's his money."

"Who's Gabe?"

She looked surprised. "Gabe is the publisher. I thought you knew him, I thought you were friends." She watched Edgerton shake his head. "That's a surprise. I owe him a mental apology. I accused him of all kinds of devious motives." She lighted a cigarette, shook out the match, let it drop on the carpet. "If it isn't Gabe who's railroading this through, then who the hell is it?"

"I don't know what you're talking about."

"Someone is ramming this issue down our throats. The logical assumption is that you're the reason. Either somebody high up is fucking you and wants to stop, this issue being the pay-off; or somebody is fucking you and doesn't want to stop. Those are logical assumptions, aren't they?"

"The only thing I know is that my agent set this up. I did a new composite and did the test nude shots and here I am."

"Your agent had nothing to do with this. We had to find him, fish him out of the gutter." She mashed out the cigarette in the ashtray. "It's done and maybe the rest of us are crazy, maybe the women of the world are ready to fall in love with a clean-cut, mature man. It's too late anyway. I have a whole crew on location doing the background stuff." She reached for the phone next to her, punched two buttons, waited for a moment, then shouted, "Where the fuck is Roy?" She hung up, hollered across the room. "Places everybody. Roy is on his way in."

When Roy came in, he went directly up to Edgerton, started talking without introduction formalities. "This won't take long. We'll show the layouts, give you the game plan, give you the feel of the story, what our thinking is. There'll be an in-depth interview but we're getting a free-lancer to handle that on location." He looked at his watch. "You're booked on the eleven-forty to New York. We're going to do the cover shot in the studio. Skrebneski has agreed to work tonight. It's a tricky shot. It has to be perfect. Don't worry about a suntan. We'll use makeup for this one shot." He studied Edgerton's face. "How long does it take you to grow a moustache?"

"Never tried."

"Start. They'll fake it on location until your own grows in. It'll take a couple of days to tan your body anyway. The makeup crew is already down there. They know what to do. We've got a late start on this. The costs are going to be tremendous. We have a full crew on location for almost a week."

"Couldn't be helped," Edgerton said.

Roy raised the volume of his voice. "Okay, kids, let's go to it. Somebody turn down the lights and start the projector."

As the lights dimmed, the wooden wall separated, the first picture appeared on the screen controlled from a remote source. It was a dummy cover of the magazine, a close-up of a nude, male torso in macro-scale, running at a sharp diagonal from the upper-left corner to the lower right. The head, most of the neck and shoulders were bled off the page and the body was cut just above the groin, a thin line of hair extending from the navel and beginning to fan wider just as the cover ended. The name *Playgirl* had been superimposed across the top of the photograph and the lead teaser had been roughly lettered in the lower right-hand corner.

BEACH-BOY IDOL OF THE SIXTIES
MARC POLO REDISCOVERED

"Because of the time element, we considered using a stand-in for this shot but some nutty broad is going to start counting pubic hairs and write us an irate letter if we tried to fake it. So that's going to be you, Polo; the first shot they'll get of you. We figure that over ninety-five percent of our readers won't recognize your name so we're going to tease them into buying the magazine so that they can see what's above and below on the cover." He pressed a button; the picture changed to a double-page layout headline: WHAT HAP-PENED TO ALL THE BOYS ON THE BEACH? "We're going to print some old stills of Fabian, Tab Hunter . . . all those guys who were big in those films in the late Fifties and early Sixties. We've got a couple of you which are pretty good." He flicked to the next picture. "Then we'll do another double-page spread of what they look like now, what they're doing." He pressed the switch quickly five times, changing the pictures instantly. "We run the gamut of our regular features." He focused the sixth picture, a dummy of the lead story: HOW OUR HEROES HAVE CHANGED. There was a picture of Sylvester Stallone on one side and Marc Polo on the other side. "No nudes in this spread; hard-nose copy about women's taste in men. Cynthia is writing it herself, using the hero and the anti-hero as a symbol of a deeper sociological thing. It's really going to be a dynamite story. We're all excited about this one." He changed the picture. "Now begins the in-depth interview. We're still working on the questions but they'll be keyed to the hero/anti-hero theme." When the next picture came on he said, "Why don't you take over, Ed? This is your department."

"We're going to do a big fashion section this time. We've got two other male models down there and three girls. The idea is to show the return of romanticism in fashion . . . long flowing stuff; fluffy, feminine styles. We're going to interface them with you guys doing the bare-ass scruffy look. The lady and the pirate. Get it? We're going to show resort wear too. Lots of bathing suits. In some of those shots you guys are going to be wearing some regular stuff. The wardrobe girls have it all down there. Wear what fits. It's not important who wears what. The photographer knows to keep you in the forefront, keep you in focus. It's not a bad layout, really. It may just catch on. They're going to have a problem with height. I did all this before somebody got around to telling me that you're only five-nine. Shit, I think two of those broads are six feet tall. Anyway, I think the photographer can handle it. I wish to hell we'd used somebody we were sure of. This is the first time out for this photographer. I'd better cable him today and warn him about your height. It's almost impossible to get a phone call through to those islands."

The pictures changed in quick succession, stopped at a sketched figure, the page bannered MARC POLO: A PICTORIAL POR-TRAIT OF A MAN AND HIS BODY. "Normally, we only run six pages of this," Roy said, "but Gabe insists we increase it to twelve for this issue. I don't think we can sustain twelve pages. A man has only so many parts to his body. That's going to be the project director's worry. They may have to shoot you bun by bun, ball by ball. Karen is down there. She'll figure out how to do it." He flicked the next group of pictures quickly, stopped at the horoscope section. "I don't know when your birthday is, Polo, but from now on you're our man for November. There's only going to be one big shot of you in this. We'll mix it up with some other guys." He activated the lights. "That's it. Does anyone have any specific instructions for Polo?" He looked around the staff.

Cynthia waited until she was sure that no one else wanted to speak. "You don't have to be a genius to pose for these shots, Polo. Our crew down there knows what they're doing. But maybe it would help if you understood that the only way this issue has a chance is if we can communicate the new romanticism to our readers. Your body is going to say what it has to say. You can't make your navel smile. But your face ought to reflect the romantic shit. Errol Flynn. Nobody ever believed that he would really rape a virgin on the silver screen. What he did in his private life was something else. But on the screen he playacted at being a rapacious pirate. He was always too clean . . . like the boy next door done up for Halloween." She stood up, walked to face him. "I see you the other way: you're the real pirate. You'd rape a virgin or make a whore scream. You're the pirate dressed up to look like the boy next door. That's going to be hard to do because most of the time you're not going to be dressed at all. You have to do it with your face and your eyes and the positioning of your body. If you feel it, you'll project it. Do you understand what I'm trying to establish?" Edgerton nodded, said nothing. Cynthia looked disgusted. "God save us from the strong, silent type."

Roy checked his watch, turned to Edgerton. "You have about an hour before you leave for the airport. Monica is going to stay here and get some vital statistics about you."

None of the editorial staff stopped to say good-bye to Edgerton. They emptied out of the room quickly. Edgerton was left alone with the woman named Monica.

She seemed out of place in Los Angeles, particularly out of place with the other women on the staff of this magazine. She reminded Edgerton of the women his wife had gone to school with and of the women who sometimes surfaced in their social life or when they traveled; quietly pretty, radiating an understated elegance and self-assured quality which only a lifetime of money could produce. Tarantulas in tweed is the way his wife referred to her prep-school friends. "They do everything in the world to keep themselves from looking like sexual women. It's as though they're ashamed of it. Even when they get dressed up to go to a ball, they still look like they're in their station wagons on the way to the local supermarket."

Monica was like those women: sun-streaked hair tied at the back of her head with a small yellow ribbon, wearing a skirt and sweater with a string of pearls . . . no other jewelry. Her fingernails were long and well manicured but colorless. His wife was wrong about women like Monica. They were confident and assured of their own sexuality. They did not have to flaunt it. He smiled at her, attempting to establish a rapport between them, trying to indicate that he understood how really feminine she was. "Not the friendliest group I ever met," Edgerton said. "Well, I don't believe in long good-byes anyway."

"You only have an hour, Mr. Polo. I need quite a bit of information." She poised her pen.

"To begin with, my name is not Marc Polo. My name is Ross Edgerton. I am called Edge by everyone who knows me."

"I'm interviewing Marc Polo."

"Marc Polo is an invention of my agent's imagination. Polo doesn't exist. He has no statistics."

"Where and when were you born?"

"Heeley, Tennessee. Two *ees*, not an *a*." He looked over, watched her cross it out, rewrite it. "In September of nineteen forty-four."

"Exact date?"

"September third."

"Parents' names?"

"Look"—he put his hand on her pad to stop the writing—"you don't know enough about me to know whether I'm a bad guy or not. Everybody around here seems to have a bug up their ass about me. I don't know what the hell I did." He walked over to the bar, reached over to the coffee pot. "Do you want some coffee?"

"No, thank you."

"You look different from the others. I thought maybe you'd at least be civil to me. I'm not a leper. Why is everyone's back bristling? What's going on?"

"This is my first week on this job. I'm not up-to-date on office gossip but I assume there has been a great deal of talk about you. This story is being forced on the staff by someone high up. They resent the intrusion on their editorial independence and integrity just because somebody wants to promote his lover's career."

"I take it that I am the loved one."

"Aren't you?"

He wanted the woman to like him but he had to retain his cover, be the man they thought he was. "So what? There's some historical precedence for the press being used to further someone's career."

"I'm sure that there are many historical precedences but none of the people involved were very nice people, were they? Not the kind of people you would want for friends necessarily and, thank God, one still has that prerogative; choosing one's own friends."

"I give up. Ask your questions."

She hesitated, picked up her pen, put it down again. "I told you that this is my first week here. I don't know the ins and outs of the office gossip. If you're being treated unfairly, I'm sorry."

"What did you do before this?"

"Des Moines, Iowa. *Better Homes & Gardens.* I did features there."

"Busted magazine or busted marriage?"

"The magazine is still doing well."

"Join the busted-marriage group."

"We have less than an hour, Mr. Polo."

"That's too bad, isn't it?"

At last her smile broke through. "Maybe and maybe not." She picked up her pen. "Now about your parents; what were their names?"

It was time for Edgerton to start lying again.

An hour later, the male musk still lingered in the cubicle. The symptoms of her confusion were a vulva awareness, the pleasure-pain of naked nipples in friction against her silky blouse and the imagined sensation of a tongue darting in and out of her ear. Monica Webster stared at the typewriter, a sentence started on the summary of Marc Polo's life, left dangling on the white paper. She was thinking about her own life, summarizing it, playing both parts —the interviewer and the subject of the interview—knowing the questions. Not knowing the answers.

Polo/Edgerton would not stay pigeonholed in the slot the editorial staff had niched for him. He was not a smart-assed opportunist. He was not a stud for hire by anyone for anything. She had no evidence for this; no words he had said or not said. She only knew that, guarded as she was, he made her feel like a woman again, tempting her into the vulnerable dream of total immersion in a man and the total immersion of a man in her.

This would not be only a coupling of genitals. Her marriage had been that: a man consumed by his law practice and a high concentration on the fitness of his body for the purpose of competing against other men at every game. Basically, he lived in a man's world, abandoning it only to satisfy his physical needs.

Working was an attempt to fill the hollow in her life, create a woman-world as all-absorbing as her husband's man-world. But after a year, the excitement of her career had degenerated into tedium, sameness, a limited future horizon. The fulfillment was temporary, the fullness draining out to leave a void again. In the course of the experiment, she and her husband had drawn even farther apart, their alienation seemed irreconcilable.

Now she wondered if she had tried hard enough to make the marriage work, if walking out had been a selfish rather than a self-fulfilling action. The male musk of Edgerton was strong in her senses even after it had evaporated from the air. What had been rigidly clear and concise when she left Des Moines was blurred and confused. Why? Because of a man she had talked to for an hour? What kind of a man was he?

Marc Polo was . . .

The sentence dangled in her mind, the same unfinished words which were on the carriage of the typewriter.

1978
AUGUST

5

SATURDAY

THE AIRPORT, KEY WEST, FLORIDA

Changing planes in Miami, Edgerton had been vaguely aware of the oppressive mugginess and wet heat seeping through the air conditioning of the terminal. Now, the moment he stepped off the DC-3 in Key West the tropical climate totally engulfed him, constricting his breathing, clogging his senses with the dank smell of the sea, the musty odor of moist plaster, decaying wood, and rotting vegetation. He squinted toward the bright sun. Storm clouds were forming to the east. He thought of the times his life had started again, new chances in new places. Had there been omens then; bright sun, black clouds?

He blurred into the line of deplaning passengers, another figure in ragged cut-offs and a sweat-marked T-shirt, bare feet shoved into worn leather sandals. There was a duffel slung over his shoulder, a brown paper bag in his free hand. He was unrecognizable from the spit-and-polish man being interrogated by the undersecretary, from the candidate being briefed on Cuba. His hair was different, the sandy color sun-streaked, ruffled now, and unkempt. He had a moustache, blonder than his hair, thick and untrimmed.

A woman burst through the small group waiting at the gate, rushed to Edgerton, kissed him full on the mouth before he was aware of her. He was surprised at how young she was. She looked like a runaway teen-ager with frizzy hair and a body still misshapen by baby fat, too much rump straining at her shorts, incomplete breasts outlined through a thin halter top.

There had been no specifics of his initial contact in Key West. "You haul ass down there," the man in Washington had instructed him, handing him a folder of airline tickets. "They'll take over from there."

She took the brown paper bag from him. "Did you bring me a present?"

"No. I bought some paperbacks and magazines at the airport." She seemed disappointed, as though she was actually expecting something. "Where are we going?" he asked.

"My place. Where else?" Her voice told him nothing.

This terminal was wide open to elements, not even an attempt to air-condition the structure. The people milling around and sitting on the hard wooden benches were markedly divided, very young or very old; no middle. Some of the young were baby-faced naval personnel, short haircuts, wrinkled uniforms. Others were derelict-looking young people, too much hair and too little clothing. The older people had come here to retire: their faces and bodies were burned too many times by the sun, weathered and beaten by years of exposure to the elements. The young people seemed all hair and bare feet, the older people prominent blue veins, sagging flesh.

Near the exit was an abandoned counter, an electric sign above it, HAVANA SIGHTSEEING. It had been disconnected and the dusty cord dangled near the plug.

The car was a bright orange VW convertible, the dents and scrapes heavy with rust. A large red dog was tied in the back seat, panting heavily in the direct sun, drooling a continuous stream of saliva. It wagged its entire hindquarters, tugged at the rope when they approached the car. Edgerton threw his duffel into the back seat, patted the dog, walked around and sat on the hot vinyl uphol-stery next to the girl. The radio blasted as soon as she started the car; screeching rock filled the quiet day. When they were on the main highway he reached over and turned down the volume. "What happens now?"

"You've got until seven o'clock. Sundown time. They're very big here on sundown time. Everybody stops resting and starts drinking at sundown."

"Then what?"

"You go to Sloppy Joe's. Everybody goes to Sloppy Joe's. Not the Conches. They know better. Tourists mostly. Some of us when we get tired of looking at each other."

"What happens at Sloppy Joe's?"

"You wait. Order beer and wait. You get used to waiting here. It gets so that it no longer becomes waiting—you find that out. It's a way of living."

"What's your name?"

"Peggy. Ruth. Wendy. Your choice. What name do you like?"

"You're pretty young to be as disillusioned as you seem."

"Illusion is luxury for the old," she said. "When they discover they can't beat the system they cop out, surrender. Their illusion is that everything is just nifty the way it is. Except us. We're shit in their fan."

"I guess I'm at an awkward age."

"How come you didn't ask what a nice girl like me is doing in a place like this?"

"Do you have a shower at your place?"

"Why? You want to fuck?"

"What's that got to do with it?"

"You older guys always want to take a shower before you fuck." He laughed.

"Well, do you?"

"Take a shower?"

"No. Fuck."

He wondered if it would be different now, starting this new life. He wondered if it could happen like this, with a smelly kid in ball-breaking heat. "I don't think so," he said, then added, "Nothing personal." He turned the volume back up on the radio and leaned back against the seat. The dog nuzzled his hair, wetting it with saliva.

SLOPPY JOE'S BAR, KEY WEST, FLORIDA

The floor of Sloppy Joe's bar was a mosaic of tiny colored tiles, intricately laid to form a Turkish rug design. A labor of Cuban craftsmanship many years before. The floor was cracked now, the brilliance of color dulled by dirt and time. Edgerton, on his third beer, studied the tracery of little pieces forming the endlessly repeating pattern, looking up from time to time as new bodies wandered into the bar, which was completely open to the street. No one moved quickly or spoke in a loud voice; mostly men drifting aimlessly, a few young women sitting at the large bar, their long hair blowing softly under the slowly rotating blades of the ceiling fans. Everyone seemed to have abandoned his direction to the elements, moving with the wind, staying stagnant with the calm.

"Hi, Edge. Long time." The man sat at the barstool next to him, signaled the bartender, pointed at the beer, and held up two fingers. "You look different."

"Older, maybe. A little heavier." Edgerton studied the younger man, trying to remember him. If he had known him before he would have remembered his eyes, a strange watery blue, almost transparent.

The other man asked, "What are you up to?"

"Down here?" Edgerton asked. The man nodded. "Not much. Trying to kill a summer cold mostly. Restless. Lots of things at loose ends. Why not?"

"Join the group. We're all like that in one way or another. It gets in your blood after a while. I've been here for eight months; I came for a weekend. Drifting becomes a way of life down here."

"Do you do anything? Work?"

He shook his head, took a long swallow of the cold beer. "Not much. Hustle mostly. It's quiet now but during the season every rich fag in New York seems to show up here. Fire Island revisited." He finished the beer, pushed the glass away. "Not the worst life. You interested?"

Edgerton shook his head.

The man stood up. "I guess I'll wander over to the Pier House and see what the action is. Listen, if you change your mind . . ."

"I won't," Edgerton said.

"You may." He signaled the bartender again, took the pencil

from his shirt pocket, opened a matchbook lying on the counter, wrote an address on the inside cover, and handed it to Edgerton. "Just for kicks," he said. "I never take money from old friends." He left a two-dollar bill on the bar. "See you around, Edge. Keep loose."

Edgerton pocketed the match folder, sipped the beer slowly. He watched the man move through the bar and out to the street where the darkness had already descended.

The address was three blocks from the bar, still in the old section of Key West. A narrow street lined with gingerbread houses built in the early 1900s by ship carpenters for traders and sea captains. The foliage around them was dense, overgrown, hiding most of the architecture. A few houses had been restored, painted garish pastel colors, electrified ship lanterns flanking entrances. Blue and amber lights were hidden in trees, new picket fences enclosed the properties, shiny brass plaques on the gateposts. They were engraved with street numbers and contrived names recalling ancient ships, pirates, and smugglers: *Windlass IV, Chateau du Chêne, Casa Bluebeard*, precious conconctions of the Northerners who were establishing a colony here.

The house itself was one of those which had not been restored. The clapboard was weathered gray, in disrepair, the fence broken and only one of the gateposts was still standing. Two metal numbers were still in place, the other numbers legible only by faded outlines. There was no light near the door, only the spillover from the streetlamps filtered by the dense vegetation. Edgerton could not find a doorbell, the clapper of the door-knocker was missing. He tried the knob. The door was unlocked. He pushed it open with his foot and looked into an empty hall, dimly lit, an intricate, curved staircase directly ahead. He stepped inside cautiously, closing the door behind him. To his left, framed by intricate fretwork, was a tiny room, dark except for the reflected, colored light of a television set.

It took a moment to adjust his eyes, then he looked around the tiny, stuffy room. A fat, black woman, her head wrapped in a turban, sat on a dilapidated sofa, holding a broom. Her eyes never left the television set. "You come early, man. The boys is mostly out. Maybe some here and maybe not here." Her voice had a sing-song quality, a calypso rhythm. "You go out back there. If any boys is here they'll be out back there."

Edgerton was not certain now; the man in the bar might have
known him before, he might have really been a hustler. If he had
misinterpreted, he would have missed the contact at Sloppy Joe's.
"You go ahead back out there," the woman said. "Maybe boys is out
there. Else you come back later. Lots of boys then."

Through a narrow passage beside the stairs, Edgerton walked
toward the rear of the house, passing through a dirty kitchen
which smelled of fish and rancid grease. There was a porch beyond the kitchen with screens torn and broken, the door off the
spring. The back yard was completely enclosed by foliage, a
dense, impenetrable wall of snarled, lush green. One tree had
electrified Japanese lanterns hanging from it, strange lighted fruit.
A makeshift bar had been set up under a palm tree. At a nearby
table, three bare-chested men sat around a rusted iron table and
as the wind moved softly, swaying the lanterns, there was a faint
cloying musk of perfume. The largest man, heavily muscled, had
his legs stretched out, propped on an empty chair. He wore low-
rise, black leather pants, was barefoot, a barbed, manacled dog
collar around his left ankle. There was a complicated tattoo on his
left forearm. One of the other men was black, his head shaved as
smooth as his hairless body, a large gold hoop earring in one ear,
his long legs shining black through thin, white harem pants. The
other man was much younger, a boy really, with long yellow hair
which hung to his shoulders. He wore only a sling pouch, held in
place with a gold chain hugging his hips.

The big man swung his legs off the chair and sat up straighter.
"You want a drink?" Edgerton shook his head. The big man
shrugged his shoulders, his face did not change expression. "Did
you set up with Angelina?" Edgerton shook his head again.

The boy said, "When that black bitch watches *Name That Tune* she
don't give a shit for business."

"You got hot rocks or you want to wait until some of the other
guys get here?" The boy stood up, adjusted his pouch. "We don't
usually see a trick this early."

"Sit down, punk," the big man said. "This dude's looking for
heavier action. You don't want a punk, do you, man?" He stood up,
moved closer to Edgerton, gave the boy a sharp slap on his bare
buttocks. "Take off, punk."

The boy rubbed the red spot on his backside, turned to Edgerton.
"Don't you want to kiss it and make it well, mister?" He stuck his

tongue out at the big man, went back into the shadows to sit with the black man.

"What are you up to in Key West?"

Edgerton shrugged his shoulders. "Nothing really. Trying to kill a summer cold. Seemed as good a place as any."

He pulled out a chair at a nearby table, nodded to Edgerton and then sat down in another chair. "It all starts like that," he said. "We all show up here at one time or another for one reason or another. In a way, it's like San Francisco used to be; a third world to live in. Only it's better here. Nothing ever happens. No pressure."

Edgerton looked around. "It's quiet around here."

"Off season," the man explained, "and too early for action." He leaned forward. "What kind of action are you looking for?" Edgerton shrugged his shoulders, did not say anything. "You didn't want the punk, did you?"

"Not particularly."

"I sized you up for a man that can handle some heavy stuff." He inclined his head toward the back of the yard. "This dump is mostly a front. Back there, across the alley, we have a bigger house for the heavy hitters. Fun and game machines," he explained. "You interested?"

Edgerton was unsure. He had given both this man and the man in Sloppy Joe's his identification when he told them he had come to Key West to kill a summer cold. The man in Washington had not explained if the Key West contacts would give a counter-identification. He examined the man's face for some signal. There was nothing there. "I don't know," Edgerton said. "Maybe it's a little early. Maybe I ought to have a drink."

"You trying to tell me that the big stuff isn't your bag?" He shook his head. "I don't believe you, baby. I've been at this too long not to know a heavy hitter when I see one." He stood up, pressing his arms on the table as he did, expanding the muscles in his arms. The key on the chain around his neck swung as he moved. He grabbed Edgerton's hand, yanked him to his feet. "Even if you never tried it, you're going to like it." He released the hard grip, laced his fingers through Edgerton's fingers caressingly. "You say that you're trying to kill a summer cold?" He smiled. "I'm going to sweat it out of you."

Edgerton's body yielded before his mind did, let himself be led, hand-in-hand to the back of the yard where a wall of oleander blocked their passage. The big man unwound his fingers from Edgerton, held back the bushes, revealing a wooden gate in a brick wall. He leaned over, used the key around his neck to unlock the door. Gently, he touched Edgerton's shoulder, moving him forward. They were in a dark, dirty alleyway, only the faint light from second floors of houses illuminating it. The big man made sure that the gate was locked behind him and then with the same key opened the rear gate of the house directly across the alley, held it open and signaled for Edgerton to precede him.

The back yard was immaculate, the entire area paved in old brick with wells for pruned trees. Aluminum furniture was placed around the area. The house had been freshly painted white, the shutters a bright yellow and the colonnade of columns around the back porch, shiny black. A candle burned on the porch, an odor of citronella filling the air. There was a man sitting on a chair. He turned to face them at the sound of their footsteps on the wooden deck.

The undersecretary said, "I wouldn't have recognized you, Edgerton. You look just right."

He shook hands. "It's good to see you again, Mr. Secretary."

"We can be off guard here. Lowell," he said. "Call me Lowell."

The man in the black leather pants hesitated at the kitchen door. "Signal when you're ready, sir." The undersecretary nodded acknowledgment.

"Sit down, Edge. Relax. We can talk freely here." Edgerton sat down. "First names always sound better in a whore house. Beginning tomorrow you're going to be Marc Polo again. You'll learn about that later. Maybe I should call you Marc, get you accustomed to hearing that name again."

Callender stood up, touched Edgerton's arm, led him off the porch, stopped under one of the lighted trees. "This place is a safe house, no bugs. They tell me it's clean as a whistle. But I always wonder, when they talk about safe houses . . . safe from whom? Safe from what?" Callender sat down on the brick ledge around the well of the tree, motioned for Edgerton to sit beside him. He looked up into the night. "I grew up in a climate like this; cloying, heavy nights like this with no air conditioning to escape to. I lived in my grandfather's house and he didn't believe in creature comforts like air conditioning." He looked over at Edgerton, waiting for him to say something. Edgerton's face was expressionless. "There's ten years difference between us, that's not a whole lot except for the times we grew up in. That makes the big difference between us. I still have hang-ups. Instinctively my back bristles in a place like this . . . men fucking each other, torturing each other in sex games . . . men kissing each other. All this goes against every concept of manliness I was brought up to believe in. That ten years between us makes the difference; you accept it all calmly, without feeling threatened. You can take it or leave it; you don't feel the obligation to destroy it."

"Are you telling me all this because it's important for the job you want me to do?"

Callender smiled, looked away from Edgerton, looked down to the brick paving. "I think my instincts about you were right," he said. "In your own way, you're a tough one. Noncommittal. It's hard to tell what you're thinking. That's good. My grandfather used to say that a man who can handle himself at a poker table can handle himself anywhere in the world, under any circumstances." He looked back at Edgerton. "If I were a stranger, if I didn't know your background and the job you have been assigned . . ." He thought for a moment. "If I didn't know all these things, I would have a hard time figuring you out. The difference between us is obviously not a generation gap. You probably are more a part of my world than the group younger than you. But looking at you here, in this kind of place, I'd take you for a part of the hippie generation. You look like some of the others around here, hippies who just never grew out of it, never grew up. A man like me never understands what kind of standards those people have, what makes them drop out of the fight."

"What fight?"

Callender laughed. "That may be the capsule of it, Edge. What fight?" He shook his head. "To a man like me everything is a fight, everything is a challenge. Nothing comes easily. Drifting with the current is not my nature."

"I can't tell about you," Edgerton said. "I know your reputation. It doesn't fit with the way you are now."

"You're right. I'm out of character. A man like me doesn't allow himself self-doubts. Maybe it's Key West. Maybe it's because I can feel a storm coming." He looked up at the sky, then faced Edgerton again. "But mostly it's because I want you to understand me, to understand my motives. I want you to see that there is another dimension to my character. I'm not all blood and guts. It's important that the two of us be able to communicate on a one-to-one basis."

"I don't understand," Edgerton said. "My instructions are specific; the chain of command is well defined."

Callender shook his head. "Nothing about this operation is specific or well defined. If you think that, then you won't be able to do the kind of job I think that you are capable of doing. Nothing about this job is routine. Men who do not understand expediencies, who are not capable of meeting extraordinary circumstances, armor themselves with routine. Routine becomes the end in itself, not the means for action. What you are going to be involved in is an unusual action, not the usual Agency routine. My being down here, talking to you like this, is in itself, unusual." He straightened his body, adjusted his glasses. "You will find that the people down here as well as the people in Washington do not approve of me or my methods. They're professionals and they consider me a hotheaded, bungling amateur. They dismiss me as an egghead from the State Department, out of his depth in this kind of an operation." He smiled at Edgerton. "Now that we have established a one-to-one basis, I want to warn you not to make that same mistake about me."

He waited but Edgerton did not answer.

"The Agency and the State Department working together is a shotgun marriage. The President of the United States is holding the gun. Neither one of us likes the marriage."

"Am I working for you or for them?"

"Me. Don't ever forget that. They think you're working for them and ostensibly and according to organizational charts, you are working for them. But I made this trip down here and we're having this talk so that you understand that you're really working for me."

"Jack Kelly warned me that this might happen."

"And if it did happen, what were his instructions?"

"Play it safe, stay with organized chain of commands."

"And what are you going to do?"

"Listen a little more."

Callender put his hand on Edgerton's knee, drew it away quickly. "Good man," he said. "Hear me out."

"I'm listening."

"Actually, we all want the same thing, it's just that my way is faster, it eliminates time-consuming routine procedure. You must understand urgency. Tomorrow morning these so-called professionals take over; they'll brief you on the details all the way down the line, they'll give you all the spy mumbo-jumbo which is their bag." Callender stood up, looked at the sky again, wiped the dampness from the palms of his hands on his seersucker pants. "You've been through the briefings, you understand the sensitive geographical location of Cuba, you understand Cuba's expanding involvement in the world . . . Angola, Zaire, Ethiopia, Uganda, Panama, Jamaica. Cuba is about to become another Middle East, another powder keg." He pointed into the black, still night. "A powder keg right off our shore there. Frightening, isn't it? Right across the gulf. We have American military personnel on that island, all huddled at Guantanamo with no contact at all with the rest of the island. We have to shuttle the people back and forth from Jamaica or Haiti and God knows what kind of diplomatic games Castro is playing with those countries. As an American and particularly as a Southerner, I'm frightened, aren't you?"

"I'm still listening," Edgerton said.

"At the moment we want to maintain a surface status quo in Cuba. I want you to understand that for many reasons we want everything to stay exactly as it is at the present moment. This point is germane to all our thinking. Status quo. It gives us the time to work on normalization of relations; it keeps the Russians, the Chinese, and the Arabs, if not out of there, at least working under minimum effectiveness. You're going to ask me why, how come we want a Communist country right over there, a thorn in our underbelly?" He sat down again. "Well, we don't like it at all. But it's there and we're pragmatic in the Department. We face global realities every hour. And what we like even less than a Communist Cuba is the alternative . . . whatever it is. If anything happens to Castro, no matter who does it, the United States is going to get the blame. The Russians and the Chinese and God knows who else would like nothing better than to be able to accuse us of interfering with the legal government of Cuba. It is our policy to coexist. The Department has made mistakes in the past. Vietnam was one of them. Chile another. Maybe Jamaica is going to come out the same way. Regardless, we can't afford to let anything happen to Cuba. We're going to get the blame regardless if it's our responsibility or not. Am I going too fast for you?"

"Go ahead."

"Listen, we get word all the time that some other country is trying to set us up as pigeons in Cuba. That's the Communist mentality. They're not above creating a situation just so it will look like we did it, that we're interfering in other governments again. That's basically what this exercise is all about. I give you my word that as far as I know, our government is not interfering. We have a hands-off policy. But somebody is up to something, the Agency boys will fill you in on that. All I know is that whoever it is, or whoever *they* are, we've got to stop them. Lots of people are going to try to prevent us from stopping them. It's not going to be easy. These people here"—the undersecretary gestured toward the house—"will give you only pieces of the total picture, a narrow dimension, only as it relates to you. They know what they're doing, I suppose, but I think a man does a better job if he understands concept. I've spent a lot of time equipping this operation with men like you, Edge. Men who just won't shoot at the first thing that moves in a shadow." He tapped his head. "You have to think, you have to understand."

"What exactly is my assignment?"

"They're going to tell you that in their own way and in their own time. They're also going to tell you that I'm full of shit"—he made the word sound as though it had two syllables—"and that you're supposed to do what they tell you. Nothing more, nothing less." He handed Edgerton a slip of paper. "You memorize that number on that piece of paper. You tell anyone who answers that phone that you want me. They'll find me wherever I am. Understand?"

"Yes, sir."

"You destroy that piece of paper. Right away before they take it from you. They don't like me any better than I like them but we are necessary evils to each other."

"Do I do it now?"

The undersecretary shook his head. "They're watching us right this minute. The important thing is to memorize the number. Do it in your own time and in your own way."

Callender led Edgerton back toward the porch where the light was stronger. He took a photograph of Julio San Marco from his pocket. "Remember this man, Edge. He has one eye, and one arm is paralyzed. If ever you see him anywhere at any time, phone me instantly. Do not report him to anyone else. Is that clear? His name is Julio San Marco. Most likely if you do see him, he will be using another name." Callender secreted the photograph back in his pocket.

A figure appeared in the doorway holding a suit jacket and attaché case. "They've phoned from the airbase, sir. The weather is closing in over Atlanta. They'd like to start back as soon as possible."

The man helped the undersecretary with his jacket, never looked at Edgerton. He handed the attaché case to Callender who was looking up into the night. "It's no wonder all the trouble in the world seems to be in these tropical climates. It makes men restless, gets to something inside of a man that makes him mean and ornery." He went through the door without looking back, the other man directly at his heels.

In that split second, Edgerton committed the number to memory, dropped the wad of paper into the candle on the table; the flame flickered lower and then burned more brightly as it consumed the paper.

There was a distant sound of thunder; black clouds moved over the moon, obscuring most of the stars. There was an excitement in his body which he had not felt for a long time, a coming alive of his physical senses. Far to the south, flashes of lightning, like a blinking sign, lighted the sky behind the clouds. He touched his crotch, felt the excitement translated there. A sudden hot wind bent the trees, filled the air with even more moisture.

"Is a beer okay?"

The big man was in the kitchen doorway, wrapped in a thin black robe, carrying two glasses. His hair was still wet from the shower, combed straight back over his head. The chain and key were still around his neck but the manacle was gone from his ankle, the power of his body less menacing under the cover of the robe. He sat down, handed Edgerton the beer. "This is no climate for the black leather scene. I'm going to get jock itch from those damn pants." He crossed his legs and rubbed his ankle. "My skin is raw from sweating under all that hardware."

The beer was a cold line going down his throat to his stomach. It did not dissipate the heat in his body.

"We've got a lot of time before we go back. You're supposed to be getting the hundred-dollar shot, usually takes about two hours."

"Do you really have all the S and M stuff in there?"

"The Agency is thorough. Does that stuff turn you on?"

"I don't know, I never tried it. I don't think so. What about you?"

The man smiled, the fierceness gone from his face. "I am by nature a pussycat: clean white sheets, soft music, and vintage champagne." He swung his legs up on the table, toppling the candle. Edgerton set it straight. "Not that I'm not good at the S and M thing. I can make those guys scream like they never screamed before, come more times and in more ways than they thought possible." He wet his lips with his tongue "Well, what about it?"

"What about what?"

"We don't have to do the S and M stuff, if you don't want to. We could fuck regular. I like it best fucking regular." His hand touched Edgerton's leg. His voice was caressing, husky. "Hell, we've nothing else to do. You're not due to report back here until eight in the morning. Why not?" Edgerton did not answer. The man kept pressing. "There's a lot of time. What can be safer than a safe house? It's going to storm like crazy. There's nothing to do in a storm but stay out of the rain and fuck." He stood up. His robe fell open. "Christ, look at me. I'm ready."

Edgerton looked away.

He felt himself being pulled off the chair, aware of the feral force of the other man, counterpointed by the gentle way he was being enveloped in the strong arms, the tenderness as the man took hold of Edgerton's face, raised it toward his own.

With sudden strength, Edgerton pushed him away. The man staggered back against the wall of the house. Edgerton backed up, wondered why his own reaction had not been instantaneous, why he had let it go this far. The same question: was it the man he was or the man he pretended to be who had momentarily yielded?

The sounds of the storm were directly above them now. Edgerton felt the first cold drops of rain.

1978
AUGUST

SUNDAY

DUVAL STREET SAFE HOUSE, KEY WEST, FLORIDA

"First off, Edgerton, forget all that shit the undersecretary handed you last night. You're old time Company: you know better than to play games with other agencies. I know everything is supposed to be different now, I know that we're supposed to interrelate but this reorganization fuck-up is the brainchild of a lot of amateurs who don't know the intelligence business, don't understand how to make it work. So this operation is like old times, Edgerton: I'm the boss and you're going to do exactly what I tell you to do. Starting right this minute, I am in control. You follow instructions exactly. Nothing more, nothing less. I give you the contact. You follow established lines of communication. Under no conditions—I repeat, under no conditions or circumstances—are you to contact the undersecretary directly. Is that clear?" The man with the face of a defeated boxer drummed his fingers against the table, staring Edgerton into submission. "You've been given a cover identity. Be that man, nothing more and nothing less. You're another pretty face, Edgerton. That's your function: you're bait to attract big fish. But I am the fisherman. Remember that. A bait is never the hero, the fisherman is. Don't try to save the world single-handed."

He cleared his throat, a rasping gravel sound. "Is that clear?" Edgerton nodded. "This is a team effort. Don't try to be a one-man army. You won't be alone out there." He stopped the drumming of his fingers, took off his dark glasses, put them on the table. There was a scar in the corner of his right eye which pulled it out of shape.

"The word is out on this operation: play safe, don't take unnecessary chances. Do you know how I read that? I read that to mean that no one believes there is any real threat, that this whole thing may be a figment of someone's imagination: i.e. Lowell Callender. If anything was really happening out there, we would have known it through our normal channels."

He stood up, reached inside his pants, adjusted his underwear, sat down again. "My personal prognosis is that nothing is going to happen but we have to play it straight." From the drawer of his desk, he took a large unidentified envelope, broke open the seal, took out a stack of photostats. Edgerton recognized the copies of the *Playgirl* layout he had seen in Los Angeles. "All that really is going to happen is that you're going on vacation. You're going to get your bare ass and big prick photographed all over the Caribbean. You're going to be a big movie star when this is all over and the magazine is published. Won't that be nifty? Cunts and asses all over the world are going to be dreaming of your prick." He lowered the volume of his voice to a hoarse whisper. "But that isn't what you're out there for. Remember what I said: you are the bait. So wiggle that bare ass and pump that big prick until some son of a bitch finds you or you find some son of a bitch and that's the son of a bitch that we're after. Am I getting through to you?"

Edgerton nodded.

"Like I said, maybe there's no one out there. Maybe this whole operation is Lowell Callender's wet dream but you have to play it as though the whole KGB is gunning for you. Don't have such a good time wiggling your ass and pumping your prick that you forget the reason that you're there. You're looking for military installations, you're looking for a nut who's trying to invade Cuba. Maybe he's not a nut. Maybe he's the smartest guy in the world. Maybe he isn't even a he; maybe it's a she. You were briefed on all this earlier this morning. You know what you're looking for. My job is to tell you to watch out for Lowell Callender. He may be Undersecretary of State but in our book he's a bungling amateur. You know what happens to bungling amateurs when they start thinking that they can out-fox the big boys? They get killed. They get their ass shot off or their head blown open. The word is out on Callender: he's a hothead and a fuck-up. He talks like butter would melt in his mouth but he has a short fuse and guys with short fuses are dangerous in our business.

"Play it like you want to come out of this alive, Edgerton. Forget you ever saw Lowell Callender. Forget you ever heard of him. Forget the shit he handed you about being a one-man army. Pretty face. Big prick. Bare ass. That's your trinity, Edgerton." He leaned forward, studied Edgerton closely. "Somehow I don't think I'm getting through to you. You haven't said a fucking word."

Edgerton said, "I'm good at my cover."

The man in control laughed.

BELLE RIVAGE PLANTATION, NEW ORLEANS, LOUISIANA

Lowell Callender studied the disguised photograph of himself in the forged passport, comparing it to his own face reflected in the mirror. When he heard the knock on his bedroom door, he swept the passport, a wallet, and three unmarked envelopes into the top drawer, locked it, stood motionless, and waited for the knock to be repeated. Then there was his wife's voice through the partially louvered door. "Don't be a child, Lowell. I know you're there. I want to talk to you."

Callender unlocked the door without opening it, turned his back, walked across his bedroom, through the tall French doors and out onto the veranda which completely encircled the second floor of the old plantation house. The night was noisy with sounds of insects and night predators, the stiff resistence of magnolia leaves to the soft breeze. For a moment he was a sixteen-year-old again, plotting a sixteen-year-old's escape from the prison of the house and the prison wall of the dense vegetation where cotton had once grown.

"Has our marriage deteriorated to the point where I have to learn from the servants when you're home?" When he looked at her, he saw what he always saw, what he had seen the first time that he had seen her: an icy perfection, a cubist sculpture of the female form, abstracted to lines and planes, polished surfaces of unblemished beauty. She stood beside him at the cast-iron railing, looking out into the nothingness of the night, seeing different things than Callender was seeing.

"I'm only here until the morning. I needed some documents. I didn't want to interrupt your life."

She laughed. "What life, Lowell? What kind of life do you think it is here all alone?"

"The children," he said. "You made that choice a long time ago."

"The children have their own lives now, they don't need me anymore."

"You could always come to Washington. Other women in the administration do it, pick up roots, move families, live the required life."

"I married you to get away from that. There are no roots in Washington, only living from election to election, from administration to administration. I grew up like that. I won't have it happen to my children. They belong here." She turned to him. "You do too, Lowell. You belong here."

"It's not enough anymore. You know that."

"Will anything ever be enough for you?" He did not answer, not her question nor the same damn question he asked himself in unguarded moments of introspection. She turned, touched his arm. "Let me go, Lowell. Let me get a divorce."

"We've already said what there is to say about that."

"But it's different now. The children aren't babies anymore. There's no point in this for either of us." She took her hand away, faced the night again. "I've met someone, Lowell." She waited for a sign from him. There was nothing. "I've met a man, Lowell. He's in love with me, he wants to live with me, grow old with me. Do you understand?"

"How *is* Ralph?"

"I should have known that you already knew it. Your spy system is still intact." Now she took his arm, tried to pull him to face her. "Ralph is fine, Lowell. He's a marvelous lover. He's gentle and passionate and he cares about me. He cares what happens to me in bed. I feel like a woman with him, not a brood mare. Are you insanely jealous? Let me go, Lowell. I want to marry Ralph."

"You are married to me"—his voice was quiet, constrained—"and you will stay married to me as long as it suits my purpose."

"Your father has a theory," she said. "He understands you better than you think. His theory about you is based on your boyhood fascination for Teddy Roosevelt. He told me that when you were young you read everything there was to read about him, hero-worshipped the man. Your father's theory is that you've become a Rough Rider in a Brooks Brothers suit, masquerading behind horn-rimmed glasses."

"My father's theories do not interest me, they never have."

"Why do you hang on to me, Lowell? What good can I possibly do you at this point in our lives? Let me marry Ralph. Let me have some kind of life to live."

"Keep sleeping with him, if that's what you want. As long as you're discreet, I'll look the other way."

"Do you want to be President, Lowell, is that it? Are you so much in love with power that you want to be President?" Callender turned, walked back into the bedroom. His wife followed him, sat on the edge of the big four-poster bed which had been Callender's since his childhood. "Answer me, Lowell. Do you want to be President?"

"Is that my father's theory or did you dream this one up all alone?"

"Answer me."

"The question does not deserve an answer."

She lay back, the slowly revolving ceiling fan casting moving shadows on her face. "Lowell Callender for President. He's the man the people want." She laughed. "How are you going to do it?" He did not answer. He had taken an old, worn suitcase from the closet, opened it on the bed next to his wife. "I'll go to the library in New Orleans tomorrow, read about your hero, find out how Teddy Roosevelt did it, how he became President. He had to start a war, didn't he, to make himself a public hero?" She sat up. "Do you have a particular war in mind or will any old war in the world suit your purpose?"

She got up from the bed, straightened her dressing gown, smoothed her swept-back hair. "My father would have understood all this, he would have understood your kind of mind. Don't be flattered into thinking that you're at all like him, Lowell. He limited his acquisition of power. Being a senator was enough for him. His ambition was not for himself but for the people he represented."

"Bullshit."

"We've had this very discussion before. It's true, we've already said everything to each other that we're going to say. From now on it's rehash; dreary, pointless repetition." She walked to the door, put her hand on the knob. "You're better with words than I am. You put it so well. From now on everything we have to say to each other is bullshit."

"Remember," he warned, "that Ralph is vulnerable."

She turned back to him. "We're all vulnerable in one way or another, aren't we, Lowell?"

1978
AUGUST

MONDAY

NICOLLSTOWN, ANDROS ISLAND, BAHAMAS, WEST INDIES

It was a one-hour flight to Andros Island in the twin-engine Seneca. Edgerton sat next to the pilot, looking down over the water, asking questions about tiny islands and cays as they flew over them.

"You must be part of that magazine crew who have taken over the Andros Beach Club," the pilot said. "You've got to be one of the models." Edgerton nodded. "You have some catching up to do. Every one of them have been over there for a week stretched out on the beach, naked as jaybirds, getting suntans all over. You're going to look mighty pale."

"What's it like on Andros?"

"Better if you're black. Andros never did have any tourist business, no history of getting along with the whites. They're fiercely Bahamian; they take their independence seriously. There's a big agricultural program going on over there. I've been flying a lot of farming experts over for the last year. Andros is the largest of the Bahamian group, enough land to do some farming. A few years ago one of the big United States corporations stripped the island pretty bare, cutting a lot of wood for pulp. There're some trees left; kind of funny looking pines, thin and straggly . . . not much green. Anyway, the land is cleared enough for farming. Where most of the other islands have geared up for tourists, resorts, and condominiums, this one has a lot of industrial action; constructing an irrigation system, road building, warehouses . . . some heavy stuff. I can't figure out why the magazine picked Andros, there are so many

prettier islands. This one has almost nothing but huts and warehouses."

"Good beaches?"

"Beautiful beaches, pretty good fishing but no fancy marina like
some of the islands. Your magazine has the biggest damn catamaran
I've ever seen, never saw a yacht like it. But they have to anchor it
off shore, use a dinghy. We'll make a circle before we land in Nicollstown, you'll be able to get a good look at the layout."

The catamaran lay at anchor off the shore; they flew low enough
to read the freshly painted letters, PLAYGIRL, on the life preserv-
ers. The Andros Beach Club was one small building with eight,
separate, tiny cottages, four on each side, a crescent of civilization
conforming to the shape of the inlet. There were five women on the
beach; three waved at the low flying plane. Two men lay at the far
end of the beach, face down on the sand.

As he approached the short runway, the pilot warned, "You're
going to have to go through customs and immigration. It's a real
Mickey Mouse operation. These guys are going to go through every
piece of paper in your wallet and I'm not sure they can read. They
take all this very seriously. Got the picture? Play it straight."

The woman waiting in the Jeep wore a *Playgirl* T-shirt, denim
cut-offs, and was barefoot. Her long, black hair was pulled tight, tied
with a colorful scarf. She had been watching Edgerton during the
long ritual with the customs and immigration officials but now
turned away and looked straight ahead as he walked toward the car.
He threw his bag in the back seat, climbed in beside her. "Hi."

"Hi."

"How did you know I was coming?"

"Heard the plane. We've been waiting for the star." She looked
over at him briefly, her pony tail bouncing on the rough road. "I
wouldn't pick you out in a crowded room." She smiled. "But I guess
the makeup department and the right camera angle can make a star
out of you." Her face was unevenly sunburned, there were freckles
on her cheekbones, and her nose was peeling.

"What's your name?"

"Lindsay."

"Lindsay what?"

"Lindsay Stavapolis and no corny Greek jokes." She turned off
sharply to a dirt road. "I am Greek by injection only. Née Rosen-

berg. The Greek injections have stopped. I am the ex Mrs. Stavapolis. I thought of taking back my maiden name but there's not much of a choice between Rosenberg and Stavapolis." She looked at him again. "I'm looking for a man with a nonethnic name. Are you one of the boys?"

Edgerton laughed, did not answer.

"There's a five buck lottery going on you: straight, gay, or both. Do you want to buy in?"

"Where did you put your money?"

"I'd like to change my bet. My vibes seem to be sending me a different signal." She laughed a little. "It'd be a shame if you turned out to be gay: that gorgeous hunk of meat going to waste." When he looked surprised, she explained. "I don't have X-ray eyes. I've seen your portfolio, the nude shots of you. It's part of my job, remember? I'm a professional appraiser of men's bodies. Limited experience, I grant you, but young and eager to learn. My job takes gonads, not a hell of a lot of intellect."

"What kind of message are your gonads sending you?"

"I almost always look messy but right now I care. I should have showered and washed my hair and shaved under my arms and worn my living, eighteen-hour bra." She looked over at him, smiled. "Does that give you a rough idea?"

"It may be the nicest thing a lady has ever said to me." He gripped the door handle as she made a sharp turn on the road. "What's your official capacity with *Playgirl?*"

"Technically and on the masthead, assistant art director. In actuality, housemother to this ark of freaks, keeper of everything from Tampax to K-Y jelly." She gripped the steering wheel with both hands as the Jeep ran over a deep rut in the road. "I'm also a damned yo-yo, back and forth to the airport. This is my second trip today."

"Who else?"

"Some new broad from the California office. Jesus, she looked like she was coming to cover a harpsichord recital for *The Christian Science Monitor.* Peck and Peck ten years ago. Little white gloves. Would you believe that? She must have thought she was coming to one of the Hamptons."

"What's her name?"

"Monica something or other. She's going to do the interview with you. They had a free-lancer set up from New York but something happened and she bugged out the last minute. She must have known what it's like in this hell hole with this assemblage of kooks."

"Who do I bunk with?"

"One Russell Langston. He's second banana. There are three male models altogether." She looked over at him. "I can't swear to your compatibility. Rusty is quite a character."

"Meaning a weirdo?"

"Depends what you call weird. Let's say he's eccentric. I've used him in layouts before. He's unique. He used to teach at St. John's College in Annapolis. He was one of the great books boys, up to his ass in Aristotle and that kind of jazz. He worked on the Syntopicon with Mortimer Alder. I guess it was enough to freak anyone out. He did an about-face, shaved off his beard, threw out his boxer shorts, and burned ninety-nine out of the hundred great books." She stopped him before he could ask the question. "I don't know which one he kept. I suppose if I did, I could understand him better."

"You sound involved."

"We've had a go or two at each other in New York. It didn't mean anything. Nothing seems to mean anything to Rusty anymore. Except fucking. He manages to mount any moving thing that hesitates."

There was a large sign with an arrow, some of the letters missing, the wood background beginning to rot. SAN ANDROS BEACH CLUB. She swung into the driveway, headed toward the beach. "You're in cottage number one. The water works erratically but you can drink it. The plumbing works seldom. The mosquitoes work all the time." She slammed the brakes; the Jeep jolted, stopped. "I'll send over the makeup girl to oil you up, then get bare-assed into the sun. Telltale bikini lines are against editorial policy at the moment."

The cottage was one big room, two double beds, a driftwood cocktail table, two lounge chairs, a dresser, and a cracked mirror. The closet indicated that his roommate was tall, size 32 waist, 10 1/2 shoe, partial to white drip-dry shirts and white jeans. Everything hung neatly in a line. The bathroom further confirmed the other man's sense of order, his limited toiletries lined up with precision, in order of use, the only deviation being both a spray and a stick deodorant. There were no books or magazines in the room, no clue to the man's personality.

Edgerton self-consciously lined up his toiletries on his side of the gear shelf, wondering what to do about his packages of Alka-Seltzer, the small container of Valium, and the large bottle of vitamin E pills. He left them in his toilet kit, went back into the bedroom and put the kit in the bottom drawer. Except for one pair of swimming trunks, the other drawers were empty.

The woman came into the room through the terrace doors, carrying a large cosmetic case. She was heavyset, with short grayish hair and heavy black fuzz on her forearms. "So the star finally arrived," she said, dropping the case on the bed. She put her hands on her hips, studied Edgerton. "I didn't think you'd be this straight looking. Maybe a scar in the corner of your mouth would help." She opened the case, took out a quart vodka bottle, shook the contents vigorously. "This sun is treacherous. All you have to do is get a base, I can handle the rest with makeup. After I grease you up I'm going to put some stuff on your hair, the sun will react to it, give you some highlights. What's your image supposed to be . . . rugged?" She shook her head. "I'll never be able to do it. You're always going to wind up looking like the boy next door."

"Sorry."

"You can't help it. We are what we are." She went into the bathroom, came back with two towels, spread them on the bed. "Take your clothes off and lie down." Edgerton took off his shirt, threw it on a chair, kicked off his shoes, turned his back and took off his jeans, folding them neatly, self-consciously stalling for time. When he turned around the woman appraised him. "Not bad," she said. "It makes up for a lot of things. Your fan mail is going to be staggering." She motioned to the bed. "Face down first."

The initial impact of the oil was cold on his back and against each buttock. The woman worked the oil into his body with the experienced hands of a masseuse. "You can relax," she told Edgerton. "I'm not going to rape you. As a matter of fact, I'm not at all interested. Different strokes for different folks."

She wiped the excess oil from her hands against her blouse. "Get your ass on the beach. Watch yourself. Better safe than sorry."

Edgerton deliberately walked in the other direction, away from the nameless bodies on the beach. He needed time by himself to think out the new life which was beginning now. The wet sand was white and soft as he edged the shoreline, letting the lazy surf roll against his legs, feeling the warmth of the water, holding his head toward the sun, willing his consciousness to become void, aware only of the nourishment of the tropical elements recharging his strength. He walked around a cove, waded in water up to his knees, past a growth of dense vegetation, then into another inlet completely hidden from the San Andros Club beach. He spread his towel on the immaculate sand, took off his robe, lay on his back, his eyes closed, consciouslessly not squinting, not wrinkling the corners of his eyes against the intense sun.

There was no way he could keep his mind a vacuum: this was the day he was being born again, a resurrection to another life. He was remembering all the other times of new beginnings, other resurrections. There was the running away from Tennessee and beginning in Hollywood, running away from that life to New York and from that life to Marybeth and her mogul father.

He lay on his back for almost an hour, rigid, at attention to the sun's tanning rays. Perspiration was breaking through the heavy coat of oil. The water was enticing but he maintained his discipline for becoming sunburned. Before he changed positions to lie on his back, he allowed himself to go to the water's edge, wading in only up to his ankles. He dipped his hands into the sea, splashed his face with the cooling wetness from his hands. The view was infinity from here, only the water extending to the horizon, no interruption of islands, no man-made obstacles in the way.

At first he thought it might be a fish, the movement at right angle to the current. Then he identified the black end of a snorkel moving inches above the water. It stopped, turned, and began moving toward the shore. Edgerton backed out of the water, felt the sharp impact of a rock under his foot, continued backing off toward the beach, always keeping the snorkel in focus. It moved slowly, at a constant pace, but headed directly toward him. He reached behind him, diverting his vigilance for only a moment, picked up his robe, covered himself, and waited.

Fifty yards off shore, the wake of the snorkel stopped, the black tip hovered in the water. The head appeared first, black hooded, large black goggles, turning in arc, monitoring the water to the north, south, and east. Then one arm appeared, black and shining, sheathed in a sleeve of a wet suit, holding a spear gun. In a quick movement the other arm appeared, pushing the underwater goggles back on the helmet of the wet suit. Finally the man himself appeared, the water just below his waist, every part of him protected with the black plastic armor. Only his face was white, uncovered. He held the spear gun slightly over his head, his eyes continuing the arc of surveillance. When the water was to his knees, he stopped, reached under the water, took off one flipper, hurled it to the shore, then the other. He started walking again in direct line to Edgerton.

There was no reason to run, no basis for fear, but Edgerton calculated the range of the spear gun, already had reconnoitered the protective cover of the vegetation behind him.

A few steps on the sand, bending from the knees, the snorkler reached down, arranged his fins side by side, unzipped the top of his wet suit and each sleeve to the elbow, placed his helmet and goggles beside the flippers. He smiled toward Edgerton, walked slowly through the hot sand. "Beautiful day," he said. "Welcome to the zoo." He put the gun on Edgerton's towel, twisted his legs, lowered himself into a sitting position, his legs crossed. "I'm getting a little old for this kind of work. My lungs don't work the way they used to."

"You're part of the *Playgirl* group?"

The man looked surprised. "The photographer," he said, adding, "also your contact in case that didn't occur to you."

"Contact for what?"

"Oh, my God, you play it by the rules. I always feel like such a horse's ass when I have to go through the rigamarole of establishing contact. It's kind of like a fraternity with secret grips and passwords." He straightened his legs, wiggled his toes. "YELLOW-JACK," he said. He looked up at Edgerton. "Satisfied?"

Edgerton moved the gun to the edge of the towel, took off his robe and lay face down, his back exposed to the sun.

The man said, "Watch the bottom of your feet. That sun is treacherous. My assistant almost got his cock burned off." He scooped up some sand, packed it against the bottom of Edgerton's feet. "Tomorrow morning you and I are going off alone to take some test shots in a couple of locations I think will do well for the story. Unfortunately, the pilot of the plane will be along and I suppose I have to keep up appearances and take my assistant along. We won't be able to talk freely; it's why I wanted to brief you first. I've been doing some scouting this week under the guise of looking for locations. It's not easy to hide an army on these islands. I suspect that they have the operation diversified, bits and pieces strung out throughout the area so that nothing looks suspicious. A few things look possible to me."

He lay in the sand beside Edgerton, talked in a low voice directly into Edgerton's ear. "There are some guys over on Norman's Cay restoring an antique brigantine . . . a big mother, must have been built at the turn of the century. There are some nice, clean-cut-looking kids working on deck and some ugly-looking guys working below. Seems to be a lot of action for restoring an old brigantine. They've got it staked out like Fort Knox. The security looks off-hand but it's still stiff as hell. We've tried shoving the girls at them, suggesting we just take a few pictures . . . even offered some money to use the ship for the photographs. No way. There is no way they'll even let you up the gangplank."

"What do you think?"

"I think when they get her all rigged up, the square riggers and mainsails, she's going to be a beauty. I think she could make the little jaunt to Cuba and not look like anything more than a restored classic, an innocent bit of sailing history, but I also think she'll have guns below and plenty of men hidden in the hold."

"Any reports of anything else like it on any of the other islands? Could be they may be trying to put together an enormous ship operation."

"I've fed the information through channels to Key West. Asked for confirmation of similar boats. So far no answer. We haven't spotted anything like it on the other islands we've seen."

"What else looks suspicious?"

"This island is going through a building boom, big agricultural stuff going on. They're building roads and warehouses and irrigation trenches all over the place. There's lots of equipment coming in at the south end of the island, ships from all over. It's hard to get a lead on exactly what's in all those containers. I'll tell you this much, some of those warehouses are big enough to hide a few planes. They're big enough to hide anything, as a matter of fact. Doesn't do any good to talk to the natives down there. Close-mouthed. They don't like whites in any shape or form. I've asked the Key West headquarters to try to get some laborers to infiltrate some of the installations. I don't think they can. The natives of Andros are a people all to themselves, different enough from the other Bahamians so they won't be fooled. They're jealous of outside labor, covet every job. It's a tough one."

"Any foreigner around who could be running the show? I noticed some big houses when we flew over. Any idea of who lives in them?"

"There are three of them at this end of the island, two of them above Morgan's Cove. When Owens-Illinois was here, some executives lived up there but no one lives there now. There's another one . . . more isolated, that is in the midst of a reconstruction job, supposedly to be turned into a resort of some kind. Doesn't make sense why anyone would try a resort on this island. It's not pretty enough and there's no direct flight from the States."

"Any way to get a closer look at the house?"

"We can try. We'll fly over everything tomorrow."

"What about the cast of characters?" Edgerton asked. "Anyone poking around trying to get friendly? Any press interested?"

"There are so few people around here. I haven't noticed anybody in particular. The local press seems to consist of a mimeographed sheet put out by the local high school. There sure aren't any tourists on the island. No one seems the least bit interested. The staff at the hotel takes us for granted." He stood up. "My hunch is that something may be happening around here but that this is not the center, it's not the headquarters of the operation. I'm staying up at the other hotel . . . or what they laughingly call a hotel. It's near the airport. There are two or three guys staying there, all of them Americans. Nothing suspicious. They're farm experts and they behave like farm experts, early to bed and early to rise. I've fed their names to Key West and Key West says forget them, they're clean."

"It's got to be frustrating, sitting here waiting for something to happen."

"You get used to it. Make up your mind, Edgerton, that this is a rocking-chair operation. Someone else is going to be the hero, not us. Enjoy the sun, enjoy the view." He stood up, zipped up his sleeves, the top of his wet suit. "I'll see you at dinner. Pretend like you never saw me before." He looked up at the cloudless sky, the unobstructed sun. "Don't get your asshole burned, Edgerton. You may need it before this is all over."

SAN ANDROS BEACH CLUB, ANDROS ISLAND, BAHAMAS, WEST INDIES

Two women lay naked, side-by-side, asleep on top of one of the beds. Edgerton looked around the anonymity of the hotel room, back at the number on the door, the number on the plaque of the key, identified his suitcase where he had placed it. This was the right room. Both women's bodies seemed identical, long and bony, breasts flattened, nipples distended, pubic patches trimmed to perfect V's; both burned by the sun to the same reddish-brown; both heads bound with identical scarves, no hair visible, imperfect faces. Stripped of makeup, their eyes were naked looking. The bed was rumpled, one pillow on the floor, the other squashed under one of the women's buttocks. They seemed to scarcely breathe, the movement of air intake and output almost imperceptible.

Until it stopped, Edgerton had not been aware of the sound of the shower running behind the closed bathroom door. He threw his towel on the chair, bound his robe tighter, still did not move. The man who strode through the bathroom door was wet from the shower, the water dripping from his hair, forming rivulets down the topography of his body, puddling on the shaggy, dirty carpet. He shook his head and body to dry himself, the movement of an animal emerging from water. He was taller than Edgerton, his hair cropped close to his head, square cut on top, a short velvety nap with the gleam of scalp showing through, a model for Marine Corps recruiting posters in World War II. His body was smooth, no definition of musculature until he moved, then, like a race horse, the powerful ripples showed through the sleek coat.

When he saw Edgerton he smiled, showed no concern for the women on the bed, for his own nakedness. "Hi," he said. "Welcome to the armpit of the world." Edgerton didn't answer, looked toward the bed. "You can talk," the other man said. "They're so stoned they won't wake up for hours. Did you have a good trip down?"

"I don't know your name," Edgerton said.

"Rusty is what everyone calls me. Real name, Russell Langston." With his hand, he wiped the wetness from his body, fondling himself as he did. "What can I say to make you feel less awkward?" Edgerton

looked toward the bed. "I thought you Hollywood guys were used
to all kinds of action," Langston said. "This is no place for a scout-
master." He rubbed his head, a spray of water coming from the
bushlike bristles.

"Sorry," Edgerton said. "I'm not disapproving, just surprised."

"There's not much else to do here. I'm not much for booze or
funny cigarettes. An innocent three-way helps kill a dull afternoon.
You'll get used to it."

"I'm going to take a shower."

"O.K."

"Any way to get those women out of here?"

He shrugged his shoulders. "What for? I told you that they'd be
out for a couple of hours. They won't bother you." On his way past
him, Langston touched Edgerton's arm, stopped him. "Tell me,
now. Are you going to play the star bit?"

"It was a long trip," Edgerton said. "I need a shower."

"That bed gets a lot of action. You're welcome to join in, turn
your back, or go for a walk on the beach. But censors I don't need.
It's fun and games, Polo. Everybody gets fucked. Nobody gets hurt.
Those are the ground rules. You don't have to play but nobody
wants a prig sitting in judgment."

Edgerton did not answer, walked into the bathroom, took a long,
tepid shower, dried himself thoroughly, and put on his robe before
he went back into the bedroom. Langston, still naked, lay on the
edge of the bed beside the two women who were now face-to-face,
clutching each other, sleeping soundly. Edgerton pulled the spread
off his own bed, folded it carefully, fully, placed it on top of the
dresser, and then flopped on top of the bed. Through the window
he watched the sun as it began to set, the day still bright, the water
bright blue.

"We got off to a bad start," Langston said. When Edgerton did
not answer, he continued, "That was in the way of an apology."

"You don't have to apologize. Maybe I should. I've been out of
it for a while. Give me time." He closed his eyes. "That's in the way
of an apology," he said.

Sleep came slowly, even as tired as he was. There was always the
sound of three other people breathing in the room. There was the
resolve that a new life was beginning for him this day. There was
everything he had been up to this day which must be eradicated
from his consciousness. Start over. But nothing in his past would

leave him. He turned on his stomach, away from the light, willed himself into the unconsciousness of sleep.

He awoke to the sound of a woman screaming. He looked toward the other bed. Langston lay on his back, his hands behind his head, his eyes open, his face expressionless. One of the women was straddling him, riding him with an orgastic fury. The other woman sat in the chair at the far end of the room reading a magazine.

Edgerton tried looking away but his eyes were magnetized to the action in the next bed: the animal abandon of the woman, using the man under her like a dildo. Langston was rigid, consciously constraining his own power to erupt, his face without expression or emotion. Then the power broke through the constraint: his pelvis arched, thrusting the woman up off the bed. She reached into the air, grabbed at empty space, and screamed. His eyes closed, his face still a mask.

In the other bed, Edgerton waited for the relay of excitement to trigger a reaction in his own body. He touched himself, felt nothing. He looked away, beyond the woman sitting in the chair, still reading a magazine. Outside, the red ball of the sun was almost touching the water.

BACATA HOTEL, BOGOTA, COLOMBIA

The man who was Lowell Callender was known to these other men as Luis Kunz. The face matched the photograph in the Panamanian passport; bushy eyebrows, gray-streaked, unruly hair, thick moustache, and metal-framed, dark-lensed glasses. Sometime in the past his credentials had been established with these men. Luis Kunz was of German descent. His father had been a second-string statesman in Nazi Germany, had escaped to Argentina, changed his identity, and assimilated into the South American culture. Officially the designated occupation in his passport was a broker. For fifteen years Kunz had surfaced in this world periodically, without a prescribed pattern. These men accepted Kunz at face, considered him as one of their own. No longer were there any questions of genesis; no motivations had to be explicated or probed. Kunz was a man to be trusted without trial. He paid for what he wanted in hard currency of any country, never disputed a price.

These nine men dealt in the pragmatic means of terror and violence to the end result of power and the end commodity of money. They functioned according to their own morality, unregulated by man-made or God-made laws of conduct. Yet their own intraethical code, their loyalty to each other, was rigid, unyielding. Deviation from the unwritten ethic was a death sentence, always executed— never a pardon given. No one had ever crossed this group and was able to hide out forever. They used the same skills to eliminate their own as they used in accomplishing their missions.

From the beginning, Callender had known that these men were only a task force for a higher echelon. He had never tried to probe the source: that was part of the ethic. It was enough to know that they would do for him as occasionally he was requisitioned to do for them. No questions were ever asked. Regardless of their nationalities, they spoke to each other in unaccented Spanish, using short sentences, communicating ideas and information quickly, using nods of heads, few words. They were men accustomed to doing business together.

Smoke hung heavily in the large hotel room, stayed suspended in the thin air of Bogota's high altitude. Cigarettes burned slowly. Ashtrays were spilling over with butts. Tables were cluttered with cardboard coffee containers, Coke bottles, and beer cans. There was a stale smell in the room, sweating men too long contained in inadequate air conditioning.

The charts taped to the walls were reduced replicas of the same charts Edgerton had studied in Denver. Code names had been translated to their Spanish counterparts; otherwise, no changes had been made. Callender stood against the wall, his finger pointed at the island of Cozumel. "Here, Nando. You strike here. Do you remember the raid we once did at Talcahuano?" The man Nando nodded. "It will be like that: in and out like that. You understand?" The small man acknowledged with an almost imperceptible movement of his eyes.

The oldest man in the room interrupted Callender before he could continue. "You must tell us what is to be done, not how to do it. We will accomplish what you want but we will do it in our own way. The tactics of Talcahuano will not work in Cozumel. You must leave it to us to decide the best way."

"You can do what you want," Callender answered, "as long as there is no bloodshed. That is important."

The old man shook his head. "We cannot promise that." He smiled. "You have changed, Luis. What has happened that you now faint at the sight of blood?"

"These units"—his hand indicated the charts along the wall—"belong to me. I have created them for my own use. The attacks against them are being arranged for another purpose, not to destroy them. Is that clear?"

"No, it is not clear but it does not matter. If you wish to terrorize your own personnel, the reason for it is your own business, not ours. It is not important that we understand."

"It is why I do not want bloodshed."

"We promise nothing, Luis. Nothing."

Callender moved to the third chart. "We strike here at the same time. It is important that the first actions occur within a twelve-hour period. The timing is desperate, you understand that?" He looked over at a big man, a stubble of gray beard on the man's face, waiting for the man to acknowledge. He moved to the next chart, put his finger directly on Nicollstown, Andros Island. "This is one of the two delayed actions. You strike here on Wednesday, not before." He moved to the STINGRAY map. "This is also to happen Wednesday."

When he was through outlining all the action, he started again at the first chart, repeating his instructions, stressing the timetable. The oldest man stood up, walked to the wall of charts, pulled each one down, crumbled them in his hand, threw them on the floor. "Your memory is short," he said to Kunz. "You tell us once and that is enough. We are not American innocents." He cocked his head toward the discarded papers on the floor. One of the other men picked them up, wadded them in his pants pocket. "We agree to everything but the woman in Washington. We will not confiscate the tapes. The information as to where the tapes are hidden is meager. To bungle in Washington is too dangerous now, there is too much to be lost. In Washington we must depend on other people, not only our own. We have had this experience before." The man held up his hand to silence him before Callender could speak. "It is not the money, it is the danger. We risk other imminent plans if we attempt this and do not succeed. The other operation is much more important than this. Perhaps later, when the other mission has been accomplished, the other contracts executed, we can discuss this again."

Kunz considered for a moment, realized that there would be no way to change the man's mind. Laurie Golding and her tapes would have to remain a calculated risk. "Agreed," he said.

The leader turned to one of the other men. "How will Fidel react?"

"CIA," the man answered. "That is the way he always reacts. He is paranoid about the CIA. It would even be good if we make him deliberately believe that it is the CIA. He will become so enraged he will not probe behind this."

Callender smiled. "Good idea," he said. "The CIA raiding the CIA will be believable to him. The right hand does not know what the left is doing. Fidel will believe that."

The older man studied Callender, disapproving of the man, not the concept. "It is, in a sense, true, is it not?"

The conversation was interrupted by three sharp knuckle raps at the door. The older man opened it. A young, blond, blue-eyed man entered the room. This man, too, in spite of his Aryan origin, spoke in unaccented Spanish. "It is confirmed. Julio San Marco is in Cuba. He is being held in a house near Cienfuegos."

"Then Fidel must know of the proposed raid," the oldest man said. He looked at Callender. "How does that change your thinking, how does it change your plans?"

Kunz said, "San Marco may not tell him anything."

"You are naive if you think that Fidel will not get information from San Marco. To begin with, San Marco is like an old man, beaten and defeated so many times, he has no more resistance. And even if he were young and strong"—the man made a fist, stiffened his arm—"if he was like iron, Fidel would get the information. He would first overwhelm San Marco with his warmth and fervor. I have seen him do it. Fidel can be spellbinding. He is not number one in Cuba for no reason. When he turns on his personality, men lose their ability to think. And if this does not work with San Marco, if San Marco knows him too well for this to be effective, then Fidel has other ways of making men give him the information he requires." He looked directly at Kunz. "Do not be like your other countrymen. Do not be naive."

"If we can get to San Marco before Fidel does." Kunz's eyes questioned the leader, testing the idea. "Is it possible?"

"We will try. I guarantee nothing. It is difficult in Cuba as you well know." He looked at the blond man who was still standing. The young man nodded, left the room. Back to Kunz he said, "You have told us much, you have not told us everything. There may be an adjustment later in the price. You understand that this could happen?"

"I understand," Kunz answered. "I think you will find everything as I have explained it. If there is more, then it is worth more. That will be between you and me."

When he was alone, the men gone to begin the operation, he stood in front of the mirror, pulled off the moustache, peeled off the wig, rubbed his head. There was an exhilaration back in his body, dormant fibers excited again. The picture of his wife standing opposite him on the balcony came into his mind. He saw her tangled in bed with Ralph, acting out a passion he had never known in her. He was introspective enough and astute enough to recognize the behavioral pattern of his own psyche, the direct relationship of sexual drive to clandestine maneuvers and physical danger. He accepted this in himself without guilt. Lowell Callender was a cold mechanism. Luis Kunz was a passionate man.

It was ten minutes before he heard the light rap on the bedroom door. Startled, Callender replaced the wig on his head, pasted the moustache into place, checked his image in the mirror, and opened the door. A young, smiling girl stood there; the old man who had been at the meeting was directly behind her. He pushed her into the room. "We speak English," he said to Callender. "She don't understand nothing."

"You look troubled, Miguel. What is it?"

"We will do as you say. I have given my word."

"But what?"

"Always, before this, I have understood what you are doing even though you don't explain it. This I do not understand. It makes no sense to kill your own people."

"I said, no killing."

"You know better, Luis. You know it cannot be done without death. You tell us that so the deaths will not be on your conscience but you know that men will die." The girl was at the far end of the room taking off her clothes. "You must tell me the reason."

"It's complicated. Are you sure that you want to know?"

"I must know."

"These attacks are taking place against CIA intelligence teams. They will be caught off guard. Do you understand?"

The old man nodded. "I begin to understand."

"If the CIA does not have the capability to be forewarned of an attack on their own personnel, who will trust them with a larger mission? This plan will discredit the CIA, force the President to turn to another source for intelligence and protection."

"You have said enough. I understand." He smiled. "Like old wine, Luis. Better with age." He held up his finger. "But not wine as old as I. It turns sour by then."

"Not you, Miguel. You'll go on forever."

Callender turned to the young girl.

ON THE BEACH, SAN ANDROS BEACH CLUB, ANDROS ISLAND, BAHAMAS, WEST INDIES

The scrim of black clouds moved away from the moon, the night became bright again, reflecting on the white coral sand, coating the beach with a luminous glow, the breaking white caps with phosphorescence. Behind him, from the bar, came the loud sound and incessant beat of the calypso band, the music distorted by the noise of the old generator pumping power to the cluster of cottages. The sea moved silently, no sound to the ebb and flow; the surf breaking softly, mute. The anchored catamaran bobbed slightly, the twin white hulls glowing in the night. Edgerton ground his bare feet into the coarse sand, feeling the cool, damp sublayer of the beach. He sat down, facing the sea, hunched forward, his arms straddling his bent knees. The picture of the man, Carroll Coulter, had become preserved in his mind, a continuing reminder of the frailty of his own future. The interior dialogue began again, another ingredient added to fuel the fire: when was a man at his prime and did any man ever admit he was past it? There was no future for the man the CIA had created Edgerton to be; he would just keep drifting, passing from person to person, used to satiate appetites, and left with the carrion; discarded, a prey for jackals.

He saw her standing in front of him; had not heard her coming across the beach. His face reflected nothing of what he was feeling, an excitement at seeing her again, her softness lighted by the night, the sea in the background. Her long hair hung loose, partially covering her face, flowing to her shoulders. Her body was covered in a long, flowing, white caftan which gave no definition to the form underneath the thin cloth. Yet barefoot, without makeup, she had naked vulnerability.

Edgerton said, "You're a long way from Des Moines."

"Farther from Los Angeles."

"What happened?"

"I fell instantly in love with you, forced myself at the editor, made him give me this assignment."

"What really happened?"

"The woman in New York, the free-lancer, chickened out for some reason. Roy decided to use in-house talent." She crossed her legs, lowered herself to the sand opposite him. "I drew the short straw."

"Sorry."

She picked up a handful of cool sand, let it sift through her fingers. "It's not your fault." She looked up at him. "I've been watching you for a while. You seem so caught up in yourself. You can tell me the truth. Would you rather be alone?"

He shook his head, could not say what he wanted to say.

"I finally caught up with jet lag. It's murder coming all the way from California. When I woke up it was too late for dinner. Everyone was in the bar. I don't know how they can stand it in there. The music is loud and it never stops. It's funny to watch them. No one talks to anyone in there, no communication. They just sit there, bombed or stoned, staring into space. Vacant faces. Beautiful bodies with vacant faces." She waved her hand in front of Edgerton's eyes. "You're as bad as they are. Have you heard a word I've said or are you another beautiful body with a vacant face?"

"I'm sorry. It's a funny night. My mind was millions of miles away." When she started to get up, Edgerton put out his hand, held her back. "I like you sitting here," he said. "Sometimes people can communicate without saying anything."

"Not strangers. Strangers need to talk to each other, become friends or lovers before they can communicate silently." She saw the startled look on Edgerton's face, the beginning of a smile. "People do make love in Des Moines," she said. "Iowans come equipped with all standard parts."

"I'm glad."

"I wouldn't have bothered you but I owe you an apology for my silent thoughts."

"Forgiven."

"Without knowing what my silent thoughts were?"

"I can guess."

In spite of what he was feeling, Edgerton considered the alternatives, decided that this was a good time to project his cover identity, spread the illusion of the man he was supposed to be. "A man does what he has to do. I don't know why other people have to sit in judgment. This is a last chance for me. I'm thirty-three years old. If I can't make it this time, when can I make it?" He shook his head. Never.

"What do you want to be when you grow up?"

"A great big movie star."

"No matter how?"

"I won't be the first person who's fucked his way to get the break he needed. There's a lot of documented precedents. Besides, what's so special about fucking?" He lay back, his hands behind his head. "A man does what he has to do."

"You're talking to a girl fresh out of Des Moines, reared on Ann Landers. I was brought up to believe that there is something very special about fucking. I was brought up to believe that it's a sacred act of love; skyrockets shooting out in the night."

"You were married. Is that the way it was?" She looked down, shook her head. "You see, you can't believe what Ann Landers tells you. Fucking is basically a body function."

She laughed. "My luck," she said, looking up now into the sky. "How could anything be more romantic than this? Deserted beach, starry night, music in the background, gentle surf, handsome man, anxious lady?" Again she laughed, an edge of bitterness now to the laughter. "I wind up with a man who thinks that making love is nothing more than another bodily function." Monica leaned over, bent down to look into his face, her long hair brushing against him.

He asked himself, why isn't your cock standing straight up? Why isn't it busting out of your pants? You can smell her, you can feel her, you can taste her. This is different. This isn't like the other times. This is no cunt to be banged and forgotten. Get it up, you fucker. Get it up.

But his penis would not respond to his brain.

She ran her fingers through her hair, combing it straight back so that it did not touch him. Her voice was as soft as the breeze. "You know something? I don't believe that you mean what you're saying. You're a complicated man, aren't you, Marc Polo? You look so together, so self-assured, so confident of . . ." Her voice trailed off. She did not say the other words. "What's Ross Edgerton like?"

"More of the same," he answered.

"I don't believe that about either of you." She lay back next to him, careful not to touch his body with her own. "Do you want to talk about it?"

"No."

"I do. Not talk about you. Talk about me. Is it all right?"

"I'm not Ann Landers."

"Maybe it's the way the night is. Or this island. Or those kooks in the bar. Everything seems different. I'm not as sure of myself as I was in Des Moines. I'm not even as sure of myself as I was in Los Angeles." She seemed chilled in spite of the warm night, crossed her arms over her chest, hunched her shoulders forward. "It's the first time I've been on my own really, the first time there hasn't been a man to . . . fall back on, I guess. I know it isn't very chic to need someone but . . ." Her voice trailed off. "Damn it," she said, and although he could not hear the sounds or see the tears, Edgerton knew that she was crying. He stayed motionless, knew there was no point in starting something he was incapable of completing. She was asking for love and Edgerton-the-agent should respond; it was part of his cover, but Edgerton-the-man was remembering the repetitive failures with his wife and those after. The other times—the easy times—of his sexuality would not come into focus in his mind. Monica had stood up, looked down at him for a moment, saw that he made no move toward her, and walked slowly across the sand toward the water. At the edge of the sea, she took off her caftan. The soft fabric fell into a puddle around her feet. She stepped over it and waded into the water. Turning her head, she looked back at Edgerton. He was sitting up, watching her. All of his sensory network was responding to the frail, naked body so alone and defenseless in the huge night. His breathing was accelerated, his groin ached, and he was feeling a kind of tenderness which was new to him. He touched himself; not even a half-hardness there.

Monica walked slowly into the surf, her fragile body disappearing into the sea and then emerging again as she walked on a sand bar. Now the pale body took on a voluptuousness, a shimmering quality as the lights of the night refracted on her wet skin.

Edgerton watched her disappear into the water again, swimming now, her body disappearing and then surfacing again. She swam well, completely in control but, nonetheless, he was feeling an anxiety about her safety. Never letting his vigilance stop, he took off his watch, stuffed it into his pants pocket, unbuttoned his shirt, took it off, folded it neatly, and set it on the sand. Edgerton unfastened his belt, unzipped his pants and without getting up, took them off, folded them, and placed them on top of his shirt.

Monica was swimming now in a straight line back toward the shore. Edgerton walked slowly toward the water's edge to wait for her. She had stopped swimming, stood up, the water to her waist, wading slowly, her arms outstretched, her fingertips skimming the surface of the sea. Her small, firm breasts hardly moved as she walked. She made no attempt to cover her nakedness as her body gradually emerged from the water. Edgerton waded in until the water was to his knees and waited for her. When he held out his arms, Monica stopped completely, studied him openly and then with a sudden surge, ran to him, pressed her wetness against him, clutched him, dug her nails into his back.

Edgerton felt the taut nipples against his chest, the soft body hair thrust against his penis, was charged with the physical urgency transmitting from her. Their mouths were opened to each other when they kissed. Another mechanism took over Edgerton, an animal unconsciousness rising above deliberated thought. Her arms moved up, tied around his neck. He stood straight, unbending, as she hoisted herself up, her legs winding around his waist, a tightening tourniquet around his body, humping and rubbing against him. Supporting her, his hands gripping her buttocks, Edgerton backed up until he felt the sand of the beach under his feet. He pulled his mouth away from the suction of her mouth, was aware of the pleasure/pain her teeth left in the fleshy interior of his lips. She loosened the pressure of her arms and legs, slid down his body, her face against him, her extended tongue tasting each part of him, lingering at the tip of his penis, mouthing the sac below it for a moment. She was sitting on the sand, looking up at him, her eyes bewildered, her mouth about to question him. He threw himself beside her, covered her mouth with his own before any words came out. He intercepted her hand as she reached between their bodies, groping for him and put his own hand between her legs, holding it firm as she tried to pull away from him. He manipulated her slowly and gently, persistently maintaining a rhythm as she struggled to get away from his touch. Then at last she abandoned herself, grinded in counterpoint to the motion of his hand, climaxing quickly, a diminuendo of tremors racking her body as Edgerton held his fingers thrust inside her.

When it all subsided, her pattern of breathing nearly normal again, she pushed him away; first his arm with fingers extended into her, then her body. She sat up, looked down at him and then into his face. The tears dammed up in her, broke free, streaked down her face, mixing with the sweat and the seawater, the tears as soundless as the surf. With clenched fists, a now unleased fury, she pummeled his chest with all her strength, pounding out her frustration, punishing his weakness. Edgerton absorbed the shock of the onslaught without flinching. Then it was over as suddenly as it began. Edgerton rolled over, face down, his head cradled in his crossed arms, aware now only of the changing tide washing back and forth under him. In this new life, which had begun this day, everything was exactly the same.

Later, walking back to his room, he saw the black storm clouds moving in from the west.

The storm came suddenly while Edgerton was asleep. He was aware of the sounds of it in a dream-drugged semiconsciousness, felt the sudden airlessness of the room, the moist heat building in intensity. With his eyes still closed, his body curved in a fetal position, he heard the thunder in the distance, the fury of the wind against the windows, the spray of the surf pelleting against the glass and the rain relentless against the roof. His mind was assembling the ingredients of the storm, putting the sounds together. In a fright, fully awake, he was sitting up in bed seeing nothing in the darkness. He reached for the light between the beds, groped for the switch at the base, turned it and heard it click, but there was no light.

The voice from the darkness said, "The storm has knocked out all the power." Edgerton saw the glow of a cigarette in the next bed, an instant of a naked body as lightning ignited behind the black clouds, flashing a moment of blue-white light into the room. Reality came into focus: the hotel room, the man in the next bed, the island, his mission. "I was beginning to think that you could sleep through anything."

With the edge of the damp sheet, Edgerton wiped the moisture from his face. "It's hotter than hell in here. When did the storm begin?"

"Twenty minutes, maybe more like thirty minutes ago. It came up out of nowhere. When I was a kid I used to be afraid of storms like this. My dog and I used to turn on the light in the closet and hide there until it was over. There's no fucking door on the closet in this room."

Edgerton said, "I feel like I'm suffocating. I have to have some air."

"No power, no air conditioning."

He got out of bed, felt his way toward the bathroom, cranked open the glass louvers of the little window there, felt the direct power of the wind, the wet of the rain mixed with the salt spray of the sea. He turned, lifted the toilet seat, urinated, his aim guided by sound. When he was through, he pushed the lever but the toilet did not flush. He turned the handles on the sink. There was a trickle of water and then nothing. When he turned back, his feet were in a puddle of water on the cracked tile floor. The wind was forcing the rain through the opened window. He cranked the louvers closed, tried to mop up the floor with a damp towel. Useless. He left the towel wadded on the floor.

When he came back into the bedroom, there was a thin flame of candlelight, Langston sitting in a chair beside it. "I remembered seeing the emergency candle in the drawer," he explained. "There's usually a candle in a place like this. Power gets knocked out a lot." Edgerton sat on the edge of his own bed, his eyes staring at the thin flame, deliberately looking away and then drawn back by the hypnotic power of it. Langston asked, "Did you know that Ernest Hemingway and Napoleon were both afraid of the dark? I suspect that Alexander the Great was afraid too. I did a lot of reading once but I couldn't come up with any conclusive evidence. I was into fear of the dark once . . . read everything I could about it. There's even a medical name for it. Nyctophobia. Did you know that? I was going to write a book about all the famous men in history who were afflicted by it. It is technically an affliction. I thought it would make a great book. There's always comfort in knowing that you're not alone, that there are brave men, productive men who have the same affliction. It surprised me to find out that there were brave men who were cowards, afraid of things that a coward is afraid of . . . like the dark."

"Are you still afraid?" Edgerton asked. Langston inclined his head, blew out the candle. The darkness was total again. "How did you get over it?"

"I worked at it," Langston said. "For a long time I believed in the power of the mind to control the body. I was into positive thinking until I decided that that was crap when the pressure was really on. Then I was into analytical things, psychoanalysis. Probing all the time, probing my own mind and having my mind probed by professionals. I spent a long time at it, a lot of money, and then I found out that that was shit, too. There's a basic problem with the mind. The mind sees images but the images are translated into words and words are the real problem. The problem with words is that I choose them, subconsciously or not, I still choose them. I choose the words I say to other people and I choose the words I say to myself. Words lie. I told lies to myself in words and I lied to people trying to help me. I'm using words now, I'm lying with words now. I'm using words like cowards who whistle in the dark. My mind is still afraid of the dark. My body isn't. I'm into that now, the power of the body over the mind. I believe in the superiority of the body—natural instincts and natural functions undirected by the mind. I know that if you take that theory to its logical extension it becomes ridiculous but most things become ridiculous when you take them to their logical extension. Most of the time however—not now, not with this storm, this time is an exception—but most of the time I behave only with my body, let my body make physical decisions, physical choices, function by natural instinct, not by man-made words which can lie. Do you see what I mean?"

"You're still whistling in the dark," Edgerton said. "Go ahead, light the candle. You don't have to put on a show of bravery for me."

"I don't need the candle. I can handle it now. I can handle the dark. The thing is, I thought maybe you were like that, that you had the same kind of phobia. I watched you sleeping. Your body seemed frightened. You were moaning in your sleep. You were curled up defensively. You had your hands cupping your cock, like it was in danger.''

"Sorry. I didn't mean to disturb you."

"Your body doesn't know fear, only your mind does. You must have been dreaming."

There was no let-up in the sounds or the velocity of the storm. The airlessness of the room had become heavier, more oppressive. "Look," Edgerton said, "light the candle. You'll feel better." He hesitated. "We'll both feel better." When it was lighted, he could see the other man's face, connect the voice to the face, establish the reality that this was not an internal dialogue in a dream. Langston's face was dry, calm, not twisted with emotion. He was smiling toward the darkness that obscured Edgerton. "Maybe I read you wrong," Edgerton spoke softly. "This afternoon I didn't figure you this way."

"It's part of the picture. My body was doing what it wanted to do. It was not shackled by words."

"Lindsay said you used to be an egghead, that you taught at St. John's, were wrapped up in the Great Books."

"I wasted three years of my life in a dialectic process of proving the existence of angels."

"How did you make out?"

"I never believed in Divine Revelation but it happened to me. A lighted Presence appeared in my study one night while I was reading Aquinas for the thirty-third time. It was weird. There was this body of light, a neon outline of a human form filled in with a phosphorescent glow. I knelt before it like I was in some kind of damn church, waited for the Word to be passed to me, saw myself as becoming some kind of a saint. But the Presence never said the Word . . . any word. Instead the glowing light refracted into my awareness. I saw myself as though I were standing in front of an X-ray machine. I saw myself stripped of delusions, stripped of illusions. I saw myself as I really was: a grown man playing with himself, using words and ideas to masturbate his mind, to hide from the reality of human contact. The experience literally scared the shit out of me, the shit out of my mind."

The flame of the candle became a flickering presence to Edgerton. He tried to see himself in it, use Langston's discipline of an X-ray machine. But the X ray he saw was an X ray of a ghost; a reflection of nothing.

Langston went on talking, looking at Edgerton, but not seeing him. "At that moment," he said, "I gave up everything to do with the intellect, with any intellectual processes or procedures. I started, that minute, to restructure myself, to recycle my life to be what I am now. There are no words anymore: when I work there is my body and the camera. My body says all there is to say to the camera. The picture the camera communicates is of my physical being only. There are no words, there are no lies which words tell. I am what I am. Stephen Dedalus. My little dog knows me."

Edgerton was transfixed, his mind split. He was assessing the man as a kook, a psychotic fanatic. Yet, at the same time, he was turned on and responding to the other man, not understanding the words or allusions but sharing an undefined emotional experience and an exhilaration of a buried part of his own being.

"It's hot in here. I can hardly breathe."

"Anguish. You have to get rid of the anguish. Anguish is destroying you."

"Somehow I have to get fresh air. I can't breathe in this mugginess. That isn't my mind. That isn't just words. My body is suffocating."

"Then do what your body wants to do this minute. If you had no mind to regulate your body, what would your body do right this minute to sustain itself? Do it, man," Langston urged. "Don't think about it. Do what your body needs to do in order to stay alive. Don't suffocate it with words. Be an animal. Have the dignity to be an animal. Survive. For God's sake, survive. Your natural instinct is to survive."

Edgerton ran to the glass doors, slid one open, fought his way through the pressure of the wind, the pummeling rain. At last he broke free on the beach, ran on the sand, his eyes closed to direction, until he stumbled and fell, lying on the sand, his nakedness exposed to the storm. Slowly his breathing returned to a normal pace, the cold rain and his body were one temperature. The thunder continued and lightning was visible even though his eyes were closed. He was surviving. The elements pounded at him and he was feeling nothing. He was pitting himself against the force of the storm and surviving it. He opened his eyes. Earlier in the night this had all been calm, a seductive serenity in the water and the sky. Now it was all chaos, the sea and the trees churned by the wind, the sky dark and light, changing color with the movements of the black clouds. In the chaos, he was finding a calm.

And the erection of his penis was an existing thing, not artificially aroused or caressed into tumescence. It was a big, hard, hot thing as real as the storm, strong enough to stay stiff against the pounding rain. He stood up, began running again toward the cottage. Nothing was labored, not the rhythm of his body, the cadence of his breathing nor the sustaining hardness of his erection.

In the flash of lightning, he thought he saw a body standing motionless ahead of him, hands on hips, legs spread apart. When he was closer, Edgerton identified Langston blocking his path, smiling into the night. He stopped, was aware that his penis was still erect; it did not shrivel when Langston reached for him as it had done in the garden in Key West. At the first touch of Langston's hand, Edgerton pushed his arms away gently, without rancor.

"Fucking is fucking, man. Don't fight it."

Edgerton sidestepped, started to pass the firmly rooted body. Langston made the countermove. The two men collided. Langston put his arms around Edgerton. Roughly this time, Edgerton pushed him away. The other model's body was a rock. The force did not even seem to shake him. "I can handle a little rough action, get the juices going."

The thunder and lightning continued. The velocity of the wind and the force of the rain seemed to subside as the men struggled on the beach. Edgerton knew that he could fell Langston with one sharp karate blow but reminded himself that he should maintain his cover, be the man the CIA had created, not a deadly agent. So he fought back, not using any of the skills of hand-to-hand that he had mastered. Would his covert identity lose this fight, succumb to the other man's power? What would Edgerton do? What would Marc Polo do? Which man was he now, at this moment?

He lost his footing, distracted by the internal dialogue, fell face forward on the sand. Langston was instantly on top of him, straddling him and grabbing his arm, twisting it behind his back. He struggled to get out of the vise of Langston's spread-eagle legs. Langston increased the twisting pressure on Edgerton's arm, inflicted ascending pain.

Enough was enough. Even for the sake of his cover, Edgerton was unwilling to lose the fight, submit his body to the consequences of defeat. With his free hand he raised his upper torso slightly off the sand, bent his legs up enough to give him leverage, then hammered his heels into Langston's back with force enough to stun him, for a split second knock out his wind, and in that split second, Edgerton freed himself from the pincerhold, thrust the surprised Langston supine, pressed his thumbs against the arteries at the base of Langston's neck. When the eyes staring up at him turned from surprise to terror, Edgerton released his hold, elevated himself into a standing position, backed off still on guard, remembered other men he had killed, let that instinct ebb, and then walked away.

The storm had lost its potency, the clouds thinning out to let through the light of the night.

1978
AUGUST

8

TUESDAY

MIAMI AIRPORT, MIAMI, FLORIDA

Laurie Golding stayed huddled in the seat, her face hidden by a floppy, black straw hat. The other passengers stood up, gathered their belongings and, still sleepy-eyed from the night flight, began filing off the plane. All the crew were forward as the passengers deplaned, hurrying them through to the jetway. Miami based, as sleepy-eyed as the passengers after a turn-around flight, the stewardesses and pilots were anxious to get home and were performing perfunctorily, seeing a blur of people, not individual faces. The instructions to Laurie Golding had been explicit; the rationale behind the prescribed procedure was abstruse. Flying economy class from Washington, she had used the name Felicia Hernandez, had checked no luggage, was carrying only the oversized, overloaded handbag stowed under the seat in front of her. All her cosmetics and pills had been dumped in the case plus her tape recorder and twelve two-hour reels.

When the rear cabin was almost empty, she reached down, wrested the handbag from under the seat, went into the toilet at the rear of the plane, being careful not to lock the door which would have automatically illuminated the occupied sign. Because the locking mechanism also activated the interior light, she was forced to wait in the darkness. She unzipped the bag, groped for a smaller cosmetic case, found it, and fumbled for her lipstick. Accustomed to doing this during commercial breaks on her television broadcasts, she applied the lipstick in the dark, without a mirror. She kept one hand on the door latch so that if she was discovered, it would appear as though she were just leaving the toilet.

She waited twenty minutes in the airlessness there. With the engines shut off, the ventilating system did not work, the heat from outside penetrating the plane. Then there was a slight pressure against the door, a contact of another hand on the outside knob. Quickly, she pushed the door open and strode forward. A big-hipped, dark-haired woman blocked her way. The woman was dressed in powder-blue slacks accentuating the girth of her body. A basket of cleaning equipment was hooked over her arm. She looked up and down, measuring Laurie Golding carefully, mentally matching description to person. Satisfied, she nodded her head and motioned for Laurie Golding to follow her. The other women cleaning the plane did not look up as they hurried down the aisle. The service door at the midsection galley was open, a mobile service scaffold parked alongside it. The woman pushed her through the galley, out on to the catwalk, and closed the door behind her. Laurie, thrown off balance by the heavy handbag, clutched the rail, began walking down the narrow, open-tred staircase, feeling the swaying movement of the steel stairs, watching each step, looking neither up nor out. On the ground, she set down the bag and for the first time was aware of the labor of her breathing, the extent of her fear. When the accelerated rate of her respiration began to ease, she looked back, up the steep incline of the stairs to the closed aluminum door. There was no retreat from her commitment.

A black, unmarked station wagon, its headlights unlighted, pulled up on the runway and stopped fifty yards in front of her. There was a moment of light as one of the rear doors of the wagon opened and shut again in one continuous movement. She looked both ways into the abandoned darkness, picked up her bag and walked slowly toward the vehicle. Twice she had stopped, held on to her hat as rushes of hot air swept across the field. Standing at the side of the wagon, she could make out the undistinguishable bulks of figures, two in the front seat and one in the back, but she could not see any individual characteristics. When she opened the door and the automatic light went on, the faces were turned away from her. There was a chain-link barrier between the backseat and the rear deck. A large, sleek Doberman pinscher was frozen at point directly facing her, the only movement a sliver of saliva dribbling from the dog's mouth. She lifted the bag, put it on the seat, pushed it over toward the huddled figure, and then squeezed in next to him. Now she could feel the hot breath of the dog in the cold air of the station wagon. She closed the door, did not hear the contact of the lock, opened it again, and exerted strength in closing it this time. The wagon began to move instantly, not switching on the headlights, leaving the dashboard dark. The driver maintained a median speed, making sharp turns and following a definite route. He was a man obviously familiar with the intricate traffic patterns of the huge field.

As her eyes adjusted to the darkness and as her professionalism overcame her fear, Laurie Golding examined the men around her. She moved a little, tried to see the face of the driver through the rearview mirror but the angle was wrong and there was not enough light. She studied the profile of the man beside the driver: medium age, medium size, medium-toned skin, medium-sized moustache. The figure next to her was turned in the seat so that three-quarters of his back was toward her. She touched the black-shirted arm, felt the quicksilver muscular reaction producing the dark metal gleam of an automatic.

Her voice was television calm. "Where are you taking me?"

Without turning, the man's voice answered her. The accent was Spanish. "No questions. You follow instructions. Understand?"

She turned her head, was face-to-face with the guard dog. The animal snarled, quivered, but did not move. She noticed then that the gate holding the dog back was unlocked: the opened padlock hung on one of the links of the barrier. Only a voice command and a sudden leap was keeping the dog from her throat.

The station wagon kept at a constant speed, cutting across runways, bisecting white demarcation lines, sometimes weaving between the prehistoric shapes of jumbo jets parked in the darkness. There was no activity at this hour. The silhouettes of the aircraft, the hangars, and the mechanical equipment were in ominous shadow. The car was headed east. She could tell direction from a thin edge of light as the day was beginning ahead of them, the light brightening rheostat-slow in the distance. The driver made a sharp turn off a runway. The wagon bounced as it cut across a stretch of grass covering a rough terrain, speeded toward some lights straight ahead.

He braked the wagon to an abrupt stop in front of a long row of wooden, one-story buildings, huts lined up with only the width of a path separating them. A single exposed light bulb hung over each alike door, minimal illumination, not casting a large arc. She reached over for the door handle but the driver's hand was quick, restraining her. A mechanic came to the driver's window. The two men spoke to each other in Spanish, then the car took off again, circling the long row of buildings and heading back in the direction from which they had come. They stopped suddenly on a runway; the driver pulled out the lever and pushed it in again to blink the headlights, turned the key, killed the ignition, rolled down the window, lighted a cigarette. He held it in his hand hanging out the window, smoking it just enough to keep a glow on the tip, using it as a signal. There was a muffled sound on the runway behind them. Laurie turned to look through the rear deck. The Doberman had turned, standing guard at the tailgate, looking out the back window. A Jeep-like vehicle was towing a small jet painted nonreflective black, only the decorative lines and the identification numbers were in white. The jet stopped parallel to the station wagon, the driver of the tow vehicle jumped out, disengaged the connecting rod, drove away quickly. The figure beside Laurie grabbed her arm, pulled her across the seat as the door opened. She resisted, groped for her bag, then let herself be pulled out of the car.

The man who had been sitting beside her, and was still holding her arm firmly, reached up with his free hand and tapped on the bottom edge of the jet door. It opened quickly. The cabin inside was dark but a white-jacketed figure knelt down and reached out. Laurie handed him her bag. The man on the ground put his hands around Laurie's waist and started to lift her into the cabin. The large hat fell off, her long hair flowed down to her shoulders. She clutched for the hat but the man above grabbed both her hands and was pulling her up as the man on the ground was hoisting her from the waist. When she was in the cabin, the cartwheel Frisbeed through the door just as it was closing. Lights went on inside and outside of the small jet as the engines started. The big wooshing sound was startling. This last hour of her life had been lived in silence.

The white-coated attendant was Japanese. He smiled at Laurie, spoke perfect English. "Please sit down," he said, "anywhere. You are the only passenger. Fasten the seat belt. You may smoke as soon as we are airborne." He opened the door to the cockpit. The two pilots were uniformed in white shirts with épaulets and caps. One of them was talking into the headset of the radio. The young Japanese man hollered over the sounds of the engines, "Up, up, and away, men." He closed the door again, sat in the narrow seat paralleling the length of the aircraft, opposite the galley/bar. He strapped himself in, looked over at Laurie, smiled again, his narrow eyes almost closing. "Once we're up in the air, what'll it be, coffee, tea, or milk?"

"I want a double Jack Daniel's," Laurie said, "and I want it now, not when the plane is at cruising altitude."

"No can do," he said, shrugging. "FAA regulations, you know."

"Fuck the FAA," she said. "I want the drink and I want it now. Is that clear?"

"You're one tough lady."

"You bet your little yellow prick that I'm one tough lady. Now get me that drink."

When she heard her own words, the tight sound of her own voice, she realized how frightened she really had been, still was. Before, on other assignments, she had been awed by the people she was sent to interview, the movers and the shakers of the world. But it had been a different species of fright, frightened, not afraid of physical harm. Before, only the answers to her prepared questions had been the unknown quantity. Now as the plane ascended into daylight, even the destination was unknown.

Julio San Marco was unrecognizable from the cowering man she had befriended in Washington. Only the withered arm and the patched eye were the same. He seemed taller, younger, harder muscled; a man in the prime of being alive, challenging life. He was dressed in a white shirt, opened far down toward his waist, exposing a thick gold chain and a large gold medallion. Olive-drab trousers were tucked into shining black leather combat boots. The early morning was bright outside the window behind him. The two men who had escorted her into the room released the pressure on each of her arms, then turned around and left her alone with San Marco.

Consciously, she had to remember where she was, who and what San Marco had been the last time she had seen him. She had to remind herself that Laurie Golding was always in control. She slung her handbag on the table between her and San Marco. "Where's the toilet, Julio? I have to pee and fix my face."

"That is all you can say?" He held out his good arm. "You have no questions about the man I have become again?"

"First things first, Julio. Where's the toilet?"

She took a long time in the bathroom. From the window she could see trees and patches of sea between the trees. There were no other buildings in her sight lines, nothing to identify or establish where she was. The Japanese attendant on the plane had blindfolded her as they made the descent to another airport and they had kept her blindfolded until she was in a car driving down a country highway. She had been to Cuba twice before, once to tape a documentary called *Cuba: Ten Years of Castro,* which had won an Emmy, and the last time to do an in-depth interview with the Cuban president which was aired two successive nights on prime time. When the blindfold had been removed and she readjusted her eyes to the brightness, she studied the terrain carefully, trying to identify crops, or any road signs which would give her at least some indication of what part of the island she was in. It was not Havana, not near it. There were no trucks bringing produce to the city, no buses laden with workers going to the city.

She had to consider Julio San Marco and what had happened to him. Or had anything happened to him? Was the miserable man she had interviewed in Washington a hoax, was his story of trying to be recruited for an invasion of Cuba a deliberate plot of Castro's? She never underestimated Castro, not his cunning, not his nerve, and not his intelligence. She understood that underneath the arm-waving crowd-rouser was a steel trap of a mind, a man skilled in geopolitical economics, sophisticated in government. If San Marco had been a bait, a trap sprung on her, what was the reason, what was the purpose? While she washed her face, reapplied all her makeup, combed her hair, she kept the dialogues of whys and why-nots going in her head, coming to no resolution, no insight as to what had happened or what would be happening now. Right before she went back into the room, she reloaded her tape recorder, turned it to full volume to pick up voices through the leather bag. She threw the bag back on the desk again as San Marco stood up.

"All right, Julio, what's happening?"

"You are my friend. You were a friend to me when no one else would be my friend. I will never forget that. I am always grateful for that. You must believe this. It is important to me that you understand."

"That sounds like what someone says before they pull a knife on you. This isn't my first time out, Julio. I have covered myself. If anything happens to me, the whole story will come out. Name for name, date for date."

"No, no, no. That is not the way I meant it. You are safe here, more safe than in Washington. This I guarantee." He sat down again, seeming winded. The appearance of strength was a veneer over the innate physical weakness. "I want you to understand that when I came to you in Washington, what I told you in Washington . . . all of this is true. There is an invasion force being assembled. There will be a military attempt against Cuba. Perhaps to try and assassinate Fidel. None of that has changed. The dangers are still all there."

"Then what has changed, Julio, what's different now?"

"I was wrong about my own country. I asked you for protection. I was afraid for my life, afraid that there were still old scores to settle, that old grievances had not been forgotten. You understand?"

"I understand perfectly. For example, I understand that the room we are sitting in is bugged, that our conversation is being recorded and what we say will eventually be heard by Fidel. That I understand. I can't figure out if you were a shield for Castro or simply a stupid innocent. I believed you in Washington. Maybe you were smart enough to dupe me or dumb enough to let Castro turn around your ideology. Either way, he's used you again, Julio. He's turned you around for his own purposes, for his own needs."

"I agree. I am not afraid to say it in this room, with other voices listening again. Fidel has turned me around, he is using me for his own needs." He leaned forward, enunciated his words clearly so that they would be audible and distinct on the bugging device. "What I understand now and what I did not understand then is that Fidel's needs and Cuba's needs are one thing, they are the same. By serving Fidel—being used by him as you would say—I am also serving my country."

"Bullshit," Laurie Golding said.

"It has been a long time since I have been in Cuba. I know what it was like when I left. I have seen the miracle that Fidel has begun since I've returned. You would not believe how much better the people are, what schools there are now, what hospitals. There are not the slums, there are not people living like animals. In my dreams I did not think this would happen. Fidel was right. His ideas were right. I was wrong. I have been made to see that now."

"I wish I knew the Cuban word for bullshit," she said.

San Marco supplied the word. *"Mentiras."*

She repeated the word. *"Mentiras."* She stood up, walked to the center of the room, stood under the chandelier. "I would guess that Russian intelligence personnel are employed to bug rooms in Cuba. In the spy films, Russians always conceal the microphone in the chandelier." She raised her head toward the fixture, spoke up into the center of it. "I accepted to come to this meeting under the condition that I would be back in Washington for my five o'clock news broadcast. If I'm not there, if no one knows where I am or where to find me, there will be an international incident, I promise you that. I suggest that if there is going to be a high-level meeting in this room that it take place promptly." Then back to San Marco, "You and I have nothing to say to each other, Julio. I thought you were one thing and Castro has made you another. You are not a man controlled by destiny as I thought you were. You are a man who is so weak he defeats himself. Do you really believe that when Fidel is through using you that you won't be discarded again, tossed into a rubbage heap with other obsolete weapons?"

He was not cowered by her, not hurt by her words. "You do not understand. We want you to understand. We want to make you understand."

"Tell me one thing, Julio. Was it all a lie? Did you make up the story about the invasion?"

He shook his head. "Everything I told you was true. I am, perhaps, guilty of weakness but I am not a liar."

They sat in silence then, waiting; Laurie Golding drumming her long fingernails in a staccato rhythm against the table, San Marco smiling benignly at her.

When Castro strode into the room, she stood up and faced him, felt a hollow in the pit of her stomach. She held out her hand. He ignored it, put his large hands on her shoulders, pulled her toward him, kissed her on each cheek and then bear-hugged her to him. Her body went limp, melted when surrounded by the maleness of him, momentarily overcome by the heat of his body, the mixed aroma of cigars, cologne, and sweat. Then she tightened up, pulled away. Without taking his eyes off her, he spoke to San Marco in Spanish. "Tell her, Julio, old friends . . . old comrades. Tell her nothing changes that."

Laurie Golding said, "I understand what you say, Mr. President."

She smoothed her hair. "But if I remember correctly, your English is much better than my Spanish." She gave him her prime-time network smile. "We're not on camera now. You don't have to be self-conscious with your English."

He laughed, turned around, sat on the desk, his back to San Marco, absentmindedly fumbling with the strap of her handbag. In English, he said, "Your language is better for ideas. My language is better for expression of the heart." He had picked up the bag, put it on his lap. "You agree, yes?"

"You're a disconcerting man, Mr. President."

"What does this mean . . . disconcerting?" He looked over his shoulder to San Marco. "Say it in Spanish, Julio." He opened Laurie Golding's purse while San Marco translated the word in Spanish, took out the tape recorder, held it in his big hand, studied it, found the control button, and turned it off. He looked back at Laurie Golding. "How am I *desconcertar?*"

"I think of you as a certain kind of man, a representative of a certain ideology. I read about you in the newspapers, what you say and what you do. I think of you that way, but when I see you *cara-a-cara* you are suddenly a man quite different . . . more a man than a president or a premier. Do you understand what I mean?"

He had removed the back of the machine, found the rewind button, watched the spool as it spun backwards. "I feel what you mean," he said. "The words I do not always understand." He removed the tape, put it in his shirt pocket, replaced the back of the recorder and put it back into the handbag. "There are many things I do not understand about you and your country."

She sat in the chair near the President, crossed her legs carefully. "We have had this discussion before, Mr. President. We have explored our opposing political views. The interview we did together was successful in the United States. I won an award for it. Did you see it?"

He nodded, smiled, stretched his legs, and examined his dusty boots. "I do not see myself often," he said. He touched his beard. "I do not shave. I do not see my face in the mirror when I shave . . . not as other men do." He jumped up suddenly, went behind the table, touched San Marco's withered arm tenderly. "We are no longer the young bulls, Julio. When I see myself on your television program, I see an older man. I feel like a young man. I do not know how old I am until I see my face on your television." He kissed the top of San Marco's head. "But old bulls can still fight, is that not so, Julio?" He walked around the table, stood over Laurie. "You wave the red flag and old bulls still fight. Is that not so, Miss Golding?" She looked away; Castro slammed his hand against the table, a show of power and strength. "Why does the CIA plan this invasion of my island?" He did not expect an answer, kept talking. "Has not your CIA learned its lesson often enough, have I not defeated them often enough? Do they want the world at war, is that why they do it? There will be war, the world will be at war. All because of your CIA. Your president talks from both sides of the mouth. To me he sends messages of peace . . . what does he call it?" He turned to San Marco, asked in Spanish. "What does he call this, this word which means *diplomatico relacion?*"

"Normalization, Fidel."

He slammed his hand against the table again, shouted the word. "Normalization." He spat on the floor. "I give back prisoners. I talk to tours of your capitalist businessmen who come to see how they can bleed my people again. Let us be friends again, your President says out of one side of the mouth and from the other he tells the CIA to kill Castro. Kill Castro. Invade Cuba."

Everything about Castro softened then, the rigidity of his body, the volume of his voice. He spoke now in almost a whisper. There seemed to be tears in his eyes. "Men will die," he said. "Good men will die. My people . . . your people. What for? Do you know that answer, Miss Golding?"

"I know nothing, Mr. President. I don't know what you mean."

"It is difficult when a pretty woman lies." He touched her face, holding her chin in his hand. "A pretty woman lies, it is one thing. A president lies, it is another thing." He pulled his hand away, her chin dropped. "I want to know why."

"I cannot answer for the President," she said. "I have no evidence that what you say is true."

He pointed back at San Marco without looking at him. "You heard the story. He tells you what your CIA tells him. There is going to be another invasion, another Bay of Pigs. You believe that. You know they tried to get Julio to lead that invasion."

"I know only what Julio told me, Mr. President. His story may or may not be true. I don't know what to believe anymore."

"It is true, it is true. I know that it is true. I know where the troops are, I know where the invasion will be. I know everything but I do not know *why*. That is what I do not know. I do not know *why*. Tell me *why*, Miss Golding."

"What evidence do you have, Mr. President?"

"I have told you. I have all the evidence, everything. Tell me *why*."

"You arranged this whole meeting to find out from me?" She smiled, tossed her head so that her long hair fell away from her face. "I am a television reporter, Mr. President, not an official of our government. I know nothing. I know what Julio told me and I know what you are telling me."

"It was you who arranged for Julio to be hidden by the CIA. We know that. You arranged this by contacting Lowell Callender. We know that too. We have intelligence in your country. Do you think we are . . ." He fumbled for the word, turned to San Marco.

"Naive, Fidel." He repeated the word in Spanish. *"Candido."*

"We know how to spy like your CIA. Better. Much better. They hide Julio." He laughed and spat in one gesture. "We find him and now *they* cannot find him. We are better spies. Is it not so?"

"It is true," she said, keeping her voice calm. "I did contact Mr. Callender to ask for his help in protecting Julio. Mr. Callender is Undersecretary of State, he is also a friend of mine. He was a logical person for me to turn to."

"And a lover." Castro waved his finger at her, smiled salaciously. "And a lover. We know that too. We have spies. I told you. Bad girl." He continued shaking his finger at her. "Bad girl."

"The last time we met, Mr. President, we both decided that we were people with normal human emotions. You understand what I am saying?" He nodded, still smiling. "You may spy on my bedroom all you like. I am responsible to no one but myself."

He stood up, clasped his hands behind his back, strode around the room. "You tell your lover, Mr. Callender, that I know him. I know what he is now and I know what he used to be. You tell him that Fidel knows all these things."

"Then you must certainly know that Lowell Callender has nothing to do with this. He was only doing me a favor in helping to protect Julio, keep him safe."

"I do not believe that," Castro said. "A man like Callender never changes."

"If you know everything, why did you call me here? What good can I possibly do you?"

"You can tell your President that if he wants to avoid a total war, he must call off his CIA. Today." He stopped, shouted the word. "Today." He continued pacing. "Unless he stops this invasion today there will be trouble. The world will know the imperialism of your country, the . . ." He turned to San Marco. *"Qué es* la traición *en inglés?"*

"Treachery."

"Yes, the treachery of the capitalist giant invading the defenseless island."

Laurie Golding laughed. "You are not defenseless, Mr. President. That has been established. You have already told me that you will crush this so-called invasion if it would occur. And you are not naive, as you admit. You do understand very well that it is against the best interests of the United States to have Cuba taken over by anyone. Not by us, not Russia, not China. You don't seriously believe that we would plan or sanction any kind of an invasion."

"The CIA. Always the CIA. Your President maybe does not know. Your President always pretends he does not know. Tell him," Castro shouted. "Tell him."

"I have no access to the President. I cannot simply call him on the telephone. I am a journalist, nothing more."

"Then whisper into the ear of your lover. Callender will tell the President."

"There is no evidence. I can give no one any evidence. I won't even be able to prove that I have been here, you made certain of that. There will be no record of my leaving or reentering the United States. I will have no credibility." She saw that Castro did not quite understand. She looked to San Marco.

"Estimable," he said.

"Do you understand, Mr. President? I will have no credibility. Why would anyone believe me? You have shown me no evidence that this invasion is being planned or how it is being planned or where or when it will occur."

He stopped pacing, grabbed her handbag from the table, drew out the tape recorder, threw it into her lap, fumbled for a spool of tape, tossed it at her. He jerked his head toward the machine. "This will be your *estimable."*

Slowly, deliberately, not rushing, Laurie Golding loaded the recorder, tested it, then settled back in the chair. She spoke softly. "This is Laurie Golding reporting. The date is August eighth. The time is ten-fourteen, Eastern Daylight Time. I am somewhere in

Cuba, in a room in an unidentified building with Julio San Marco and the President of Cuba, Fidel Castro. Mr. Castro has a message which he would like for me to deliver to the President of the United States."

She held up the machine, nodded to Castro. He cleared his throat and began talking in Spanish.

GREAT GUANA CAY, THE EXUMA CHAIN, BAHAMAS, WEST INDIES

The small plane began another low circle over the tiny cay. The details of the huge house and grounds were more visible now. A woman had appeared on the roof deck and was waving to them, clutching her robe around her fat body. Lindsay, sitting in the middle row of seats next to Edgerton, spoke for the first time since they had taken off from Andros. "What kind of a spook do you suppose that is?"

The photographer, next to the pilot, was using a small camera, shooting quickly, contorting his body to get as many different shots as possible. "I've seen pictures of that house in some magazine," he said. "I'm sure that it was designed by a famous architect. It's either Yamaski or Pei, I can't remember which. Maybe *Architectural Digest* ran it." He turned back to the window, looked down again, began clicking the camera. "That's the best location spot that I've seen since we've been here. Great backgrounds for the fashion shots, don't you think?" He turned back to Lindsay. "Wouldn't you like to see your little group run bare-assed through that joint?"

"I don't know. We're not a rich-kids' magazine. Maybe the layout is too swell for us simple, working girls. We're supposed to be able to relate." She looked down. "Girls in Buffalo and Butte would have a tough time identifying with that spread." The woman was still waving to them.

"It would make a dynamite setting."

"I suppose we could raunch it up a little, give it that after-a-weekend Club Med look. Maybe it would work. It's worth a try. I wonder how we get to it?"

The pilot said, "They have a private landing strip. See it down there? They have a hangar somewhere. It's hidden by trees. Rich folks like to camouflage their basic necessities."

"Who lives there?" the photographer asked.

"Some Italians. They don't use it much. The only times that I have seen action down there is for a week or two in February and March. How would you like to have that kind of bread; have a spread like that and only use it a month or so a year?" He banked the plane. "It doesn't look it, but there's a deep harbor there. I've seen six or seven big yachts anchored at one time, parties going full blast on all of them as well as in the house."

"Do you know the Italians' name?"

The pilot shook his head. "It's a prince or a count or something. But I don't know the name."

"It's not Mafia," Lindsay said. "They wouldn't live that far from a carry-out pizza joint."

"Do you have radio equipment? Could you contact them by radio?"

"They have a ton of equipment down there. Every time I fly over I get jammed. They have enough power to reach the North Pole."

"Try to contact them."

The pilot put on his headset, turned on the radio, immediately moved the ear receivers. The static was so loud they could hear it. He adjusted the speaking tube in front of his mouth. "Calling Great Guana Cay. This is 742-607N, calling Great Guana Cay. Do you read me?" The static continued. "Great Guana Cay. Calling Great Guana Cay. If you read me, come in, please." They all waited but there was no answer. The pilot shrugged his shoulders, turned off the radio. "Either they have their equipment shut off or they're not interested in idle conversation."

"We'll check it out later. Maybe the manager of the Andros Beach Club knows who lives there. We'll find a way to contact them." The plane straightened out, headed west. The photographer looked at his watch. "Hey, it's still early. We have time. Why don't we turn around and go into Cape Eleuthera?" He turned back to Lindsay, his words meant for Edgerton. "Do you remember I told you about that old brigantine that some kids are restoring?" She nodded. "I think we could get some great shots there; neat spot for male nudes. Super macho backgrounds."

"I thought you told me that the natives weren't very friendly there," Lindsay said. "Didn't you tell me that they wouldn't let you on board?"

"Maybe we can tempt them with the blonde bomber back there." The model, her head bound in a scarf, was stretched out across the rear seats, snoring faintly. "Wake her up, will you, Lindsay? Make her comb her hair and loosen her halter."

The plane had turned, gained altitude and the pilot leveled off, adjusted his instruments to a northeast course. "It's about a twenty- to thirty-minute run. There are head winds. It will probably storm later on."

Edgerton reasoned that there would be some place in Cape Eleuthera where the photographer could make contact with control in Key West. He knew that as deserted looking and tranquil as Great Guana appeared, it was a possible installation point. The location of the cay, the deep harbor, the landing strip, and the radio equipment made a formidable combination for any military thrust. Edgerton estimated that the distance to Cuba was a little over a hundred and fifty miles. Although they had not spoken directly to each other, pretended to meet for the first time that morning at the airport, Edgerton understood that most of the photographer's conversation with the pilot had been directed to him, alerting him to the investigative strategy. It was the photographer's job to communicate with Key West, get the information on the cay, find out the name of the owner of the villa and check all credentials.

Edgerton had memorized the skinny worm shape of Eleuthera from the briefing charts he had studied at Denver. It was different now as the plane flew low, approaching it. Surfaced with green vegetation, edged with white coral sand, and surrounded by spectrums of bright blue water, the skinny worm shape of the island was obliterated. The aerial picture was a postcard to send home from a winter vacation.

The photographer said, "Buzz the marina at the Cape Eleuthera Club. I'd like Lindsay to take a look at that brigantine."

"Would you mind explaining," Lindsay asked, "to a landlocked girl from upper New York State exactly what a brigantine is?"

"I don't know exactly. The kids working on it said it was a brigantine." He turned to Edgerton. "Do you know what the technical definition is?"

"Pirates used them mostly or least that's how I know about them. I was brought up on Errol Flynn movies. It's a two-masted sailing ship, square rigged. There's something different about the mast. I think it's rigged fore and aft."

"Like some of the people I know," Lindsay said.

The pilot nosed the plane down over the harbor. "It's not there. She's gone."

"What's that out there?" The photographer was squinting into the distance. He pointed at a white object on the water to the southeast. "That could be her. Fly over it, let's take a look-see."

The white blur took the shape of sails as they came nearer to it. "That's her. I didn't think she was this close to being ready." The plane was almost directly over the boat. "What a beauty. They've really got her in condition. That deck looks like you could ice skate on it. They must be out on a test run." The photographer had taken out his camera as he was talking, taking pictures now in quick succession.

"How do you know," Edgerton asked, "that she isn't being moved to another port?"

"It doesn't matter. We can always find her. She stands out like Raquel Welch in a convent." He nudged the pilot, indicated for him to turn around, fly over the brigantine again, continued taking pictures. "We ought to land in Eleuthera anyway. Somebody around the dock will know what's going on."

The pilot had his headset in place, was communicating with the airport on Eleuthera. He moved the speaking tube away. "The control guy at the airport said he thought they were getting the boat ready to use in a movie that is going to be filmed in the Caicos Islands. He doesn't know if they're out on a test run or if they're heading for the Providenciales now. They're sailing in that direction. Do you want to land here anyway?"

"Let's see what we can find out on Eleuthera. We can always go on to the Caicos. How long a flight is it?"

"About two hours," the pilot said.

"If the boat is going there it won't get there until late. We can always fly to the Caicos tomorrow."

"Sooner or later we have to take some pictures, Herbie. We do have a vague kind of deadline but, nevertheless, I'd like to get some shots of Marc before his social security checks start arriving." Lindsay smiled at him. "And before his abdominal muscles droop." She looked at him closely. "God, you look terrible, Edge. Couldn't you sleep or wouldn't The Humper let you?"

Edgerton smiled to cover the hangover of terror remembered from the night before.

GREAT GUANA CAY, THE EXHUMA CHAIN, BAHAMAS, WEST INDIES

Roger Ramirez was standing on the wooden deck off his mother's bedroom looking northwest across the Caribbean, searching the sky for a shimmering speck which would materialize into an airplane bringing Guido back from Washington, D.C. But there was nothing in that direction except endless blue water, endless blue sky. According to plan, Guido should have been back at Great Guana yesterday. They had programmed the Laurie Golding assignment for two days maximum. Guido, in spite of all his erratic behavior, had always adhered to timetables, followed the regimen set up by Ramirez and the mercenary commander. Something must have gone wrong in Washington to throw him off schedule. Unless the radio operators were lying, there had been no communication from Guido directly or through established secondary channels. Ramirez had reminded him before they separated in Paris to keep in contact. Timing was becoming desperate as the countdown day came nearer.

There was a double edge to Ramirez's concern. He was lonely here. He needed the tough body of the Italian to fulfill the needs of his own body and he needed the tough, street-smart mentality of the Italian to cope with the unexpected developments here.

In the six days that he had been absent from Great Guana, Ramirez had lost complete control of his own project. Major changes had been made without consulting him: new authorities had been established, his own authority deteriorated to the zero point. Another eight-man team had been added to the twelve mercenaries who were on his original staff, directing and coordinating operations. All the servants had been dismissed, shipped off the cay, sent back to Eleuthera. Ramirez could imagine his mother's rage if she saw the pigpen the soldiers had made of the villa; unmade beds; empty whiskey bottles; leopard spots of cigar ashes on her white rugs; rotting, half-eaten sandwiches turned blue-green with mildew and buzzed over by swarms of insects.

In the beginning, they had arrived two-by-two, according to the master plan to implement the operation of Ramirez's scheme. These were tough men, toughened in wars around the world, seasoned to creature-discomfort, at ease with each other and accustomed to living together as a pride of animals in a jungle. They were men of various nationalities who spoke English, had private jokes, mutual experiences, and related pasts. At first they accepted Ramirez's authority, followed his instructions and did their job well. But other than work, they contained themselves in a tight circle, did not let Ramirez penetrate that circle.

The change had begun with the arrival of the last two men of the original twelve. Wordlessly, a new authority had taken over, displacing Ramirez. Of the last two men, the shorter man seemed in command. Without calling him sir and without saluting him, he was given the deference of a general. His opinion and his instructions were never questioned. He was a soft-spoken man, about fifty, almost bald and physically slight. Ramirez's first reaction had been that they send an accountant instead of a field marshal to conduct this war. Ramirez had fought the changes that this man had immediately begun to make in the organization. The command post was moved out of the cabana into the loggia of the main house between the living and dining rooms. The swimming pool had been drained of water for no apparent reason. A giant hole had been dug in the center of a mass of trees. Again for no apparent reason. Ramirez tried to countermand the orders, argued with the leader, screamed at the men in every language he knew. He was shunted off, ignored. Not one of them even bothered to match his rage, return his anger.

One morning he had gone down to the study, which Count Rinaldi used as an office and which Ramirez had taken over as his own base of command. Every one of his possessions had been removed; all his papers and files, the framed snapshots he had taken of Guido on the beach, all his books on commando tactics. Tables had been moved in from the pool deck, set up as work stations. The big desk was taken over by the leader who had brought in a straight kitchen chair, shoved the luxurious leather swivel chair into a corner, its back to the room. Ramirez stood in the doorway, surveying what had happened, ready to erupt and explode. But not one of the men turned to look at him. He rushed to his desk, started to reach out for the man sitting behind it. His thrust was cut off with a karate chop against his forearm. The man had not even looked up, had executed the counterthrust automatically, with no more deliberation than brushing off a fly.

By the time he returned from Cap Ferrat, the takeover had been completed. Everything he owned had been moved to his mother's bedroom. An old refrigerator had been brought up, stocked with meager provisions. His clothes were heaped on the floor. All his files, books, and personal papers were dumped on the bed. The snapshots of Guido were carefully arranged around the lip of the bidet in the bathroom.

The command post in the loggia had been cordoned off with hastily erected chain-link fences, a gate at each end with huge padlocks. Some kind of a computer system had been installed, television information screens dotting the area. The radio communicating center had been tripled in size and capacity. The bottom of the swimming pool had been painted bright blue up to the former waterline. A network of fine wire had been laced over the pool. The hole dug in the clearing of trees now housed a huge generator which must have been transported and dropped in place by a helicopter.

No attempt was made to conceal any of these installations from Ramirez. They were open in their defection from his authority. Ramirez was not even important enough for deception. When he asked questions, they ignored him. Six new maps had been added to the original three, designating his original staging areas. There was no written identification on these charts, only code numbers programmed into the computer.

There were twenty men now. They worked around the clock, no longer took time to joke with each other, reminisce with each other or drink beer in the shade of the cluster of palms on the patio. Everything else may have changed, expanded, but it appeared to Ramirez that the target date was the same, the countdown was nearing. He could feel the urgency in the men, see it reflected in the pace of their movements and in the shorthand words they used to communicate.

But from here, from the deck off his mother's bedroom, there was no indication of the activity below. The sun reflected off the criss-cross of silver wires over the pool, making it seem as though it was still filled with water. The huge generator was hidden by the other trees, the constant humming sound of it partially muffled by the fan-shaped leaves. The staff of mercenaries kept hidden inside the house, protected from aerial detection by the wide overhangs of the flat roof.

These men, even the leaders, misinterpreted Ramirez's accept-ance of the new authority as a capitulation, underestimated the man's cunning, misread his sudden docility as weakness. Nor did they understand that Ramirez had the innate pragmatism to adjust to a tactical situation. He was his father's son: he would prove that to them. He faced away from Washington, turned southwest toward Cuba which was only a hundred and fifty miles away. He stood straight, smiled as though his father were watching him. His father would understand, be proud of his son's brilliance. Rinaldi did not understand. Rinaldi had warned him not to try to outsmart his friends. But in the end, he would outsmart all of them; all the soldiers who excluded him from their macho world, including Aldo. Even Victor Castle himself. He said the words out loud, "Even the great Victor Castle himself." They had not considered that a mind capable of creating this plan was also capable of creating fail-safe devices for his own protection. They could go through all the mo-tions of triumph but at the zero hour he would be holding the trump card. He had told no one, not even Guido.

He turned northwest again. When he thought about Guido, he felt the restlessness return; the need for sexual outlet became stronger. The hot sun always made him horny. He went back into his mother's bedroom, stood in front of the tall mirror over her dressing table, lighted the strips of bare bulbs that flanked the mirror, took off his robe, and examined his own nakedness, repelled by his own image. Only Guido seemed to be capable of ignoring the gross, flabby flesh and the gorillalike matting of hair. He closed his eyes and saw Guido fondling him, caressing his body as though it was the hairless, soft skin of a young girl. Guido would pretend that the fat points of his chest were a woman's breasts; licking them, kissing them, and nipping at the dark nipples. Guido could make him feel beautiful. Guido could make him feel as his mother must feel when millions of men react to her image on a movie screen. Guido made him feel like that. Only Guido. He repeated the name, an endless incantation, a verbal foreplay to masturbation.

He opened the drawer of the dressing table, took a comb and arranged his hair, first down over his face, then parted in the middle and with his hands swept it back to form two black dips over his forehead. From another drawer he took a lipstick, and with practiced skill smeared it over his lips, making them larger, outlining a cupid's bow. Then he worked the green eye shadow, his mother's trademark, boldly over each eye. He went into her closet, selected a pale green flowing chiffon robe with a matching caribou collar and cuffs, put it on, clutched it at the neck to hide his body. In front of the mirror again, standing close, almost kissing his own reflection, Ramirez pursed his lips, arched his eyebrows, bloused the robe above his waist, giving himself the illusion of breasts. With his free hand he began to induce an erection, pressing his lipsticked lips against the cold mirror, opening his mouth, and pointing the tip of his tongue against the glass.

In the distance there was the sound of an airplane, the sound becoming louder as it flew directly overhead and then diminished as the plane was beyond the cay. At first, the identification and meaning of the sound did not penetrate through the ritual of Ramirez's sexual fantasies. Unconsciously, the movement of his hand became faster as the sound became louder, slower as the plane flew away. But the plane had circled over the water, was returning at a lower altitude. This time the sound had meaning. Ramirez let go of himself and ran out to the deck again just as the twin-engine plane was making a circle over the villa. It was not Guido. It was not the same kind of plane. This plane was low enough so that he could make out figures in the cabin; the pilot, two men, and a woman. He leaned over the rail, looked down toward the loggia. All the men were lined up, out of sight, looking up at the plane. One of them spotted Ramirez, signalled to the other men, pointed up to where he was standing. They all stared at the sight of him; their faces showed no expression. Ramirez clutched the robe around him, held it with one hand, stood at the edge of the deck, waved wildly at the people in the plane. He could see them looking at him but no one returned his greeting. The plane gained altitude and flew away again in the direction of Eleuthera.

The same plane had flown over the villa the day before. Ramirez had seen it, reported it to one of the mercenaries. Yesterday there had only been two men besides the pilot. Ramirez was not sure that this time it was the same two men. He was certain, however, that the surveillance was deliberate. The men below would not slough him off this time. He would demand an explanation and a thorough investigation.

He scrubbed the makeup from his face, showered quickly, put on a clean pair of white shorts, and went down to the control room. The men looked at him when he appeared, turned away, their faces showing disgust. The man controlling the air support section was named Randolph, was one of the original staff. Ramirez stood over him but before he could speak the man said, "Get out of here. You make me sick."

"It was quick thinking, wasn't it?" Ramirez said. "I put on my mother's robe, tried to make them think that there was a woman living alone here. I think I fooled them."

"You don't fool anybody," the man answered.

"That was the same plane which flew over here yesterday. They're looking for something."

"Don't bother me. Get out of my sight."

The other men were watching the interchange. Ramirez walked through the dining room, out into the gallery and into the room which had been his office. The man behind the desk looked up and then down again at the chart he had been studying. Ramirez modulated his voice, lowered the register of it. "What are you going to do about that plane?" he asked. "It was the same one that circled here yesterday."

"I checked it out. There's a bunch of nuts over on Andros; some magazine people shooting fashion layouts. They're looking for locations, nothing sinister about that. I had our people investigate. They're all up at the north end of the island, nowhere near our installation. They're no trouble."

"I don't like it."

"Tough," the man said. "I'm satisfied with the explanation. They couldn't see anything anyway. The only thing they saw was a drag queen on a roof deck. It probably turned their stomachs but they couldn't see anything else out of the ordinary." He stood up, came in front of his desk, sat on the edge of it. "They told me that you would be like this; nervous as a girl when the countdown got close.

Relax, Ramirez. We're pros at this. We know what we're doing. Just relax and stay out of our way and everything will be fine."

"I still don't like it. The plane coming over here twice can't be accidental."

"I told you they're looking for locations. This is a flashy spread. Maybe they want to photograph here. Forget the whole thing. Go out and play somewhere." He turned, went back to his chair. "Where's your little Italian friend? When is he going to show up? You need another little boy to play with and stay out of grown men's ways. We have work to do."

Ramirez said, "I am going over to Andros. I'm going to look around."

"Bully for you, Ramirez. And how are you going to get there? Water wings?"

"You are going to get the pilot to fly me to Nicollstown."

"No way," the man said. "You're grounded. In case you hadn't noticed, you're not much more than a prisoner here now."

"Tell the pilot that from Nicollstown, I will be going on to Nassau."

"I told you Ramirez, you're not going anywhere."

"The money is in Nassau. I left it there in a safety deposit box. It can only be released on my signature. I made certain of that. I'm not quite as stupid as you think." The man did not reply. "I will be at *my* landing strip in thirty minutes. Have *my* plane completely gassed and ready to go. Have one of your men pick up *my* suitcase in twenty-five minutes. I'm going to spend the night in Nassau." He left the room before the man could answer.

SAN ANDROS BEACH CLUB, ANDROS ISLAND, BAHAMAS, WEST INDIES

Edgerton lay in a hammock that had been slung between two palm trees on the beach. They had photographed earlier in the afternoon on the catamaran. He had forgotten how physically tiring photographic modeling could be. He was posed now so that one leg was over the side of the hammock almost touching the sand. His head was propped up with pillows and he held a can of beer in his right hand. The tall model, Maryellen, was posed behind him, her bare back toward the camera, a large straw hat on her head. The photographer had rigged the camera for an up-angle shot, burying the legs of the tripod deep in the sand, lying on his belly, trying to focus through the lens. His assistant held a black umbrella over the photographer's head to block out the sun. "How does it look?"

"Gorgeous," the photographer said. "From this angle his cock looks five yards long."

Edgerton, although he looked relaxed, was uncomfortable. "What's going on?" he called over.

Danny shouted back. "Herbie says your cock looks five yards long."

Lindsay was standing nearby, clutching an assortment of straw hats, wearing three of them. "He doesn't need help from camera angles. Let's get this going. His body makeup is going to start running in this heat."

Now the photographer was ready. He raised the upper part of his body, hitting his head against the umbrella. "For Christ's sakes, Danny, watch me, not him." He was up on his knees then, holding the shutter cable. "Ready everybody. Get ready." Edgerton froze his position, raised the beer can a little. The makeup woman came over, scanned him, walked away. "It's a lazy day; you're just lying around thinking about fucking. Think about it, Marc. Think about what it feels like." He turned to his assistant. "Keep that umbrella over my head before I burn up." He held up the shutter cable, poised to press the release. "Get that creep out of there," he shouted. "For Christ's sake, isn't anybody watching this set? Lindsay, get that creep out of there."

They all turned to look at Roger Ramirez, standing on the beach within range of the camera, staring at the naked Edgerton. Lindsay ran forward, dropping the collection of hats, pulled him away. It took another ten minutes for everyone to get back into position and for the photographer to readjust his exposure for the diminishing light. He took twelve shots of the same position, talking to Edgerton all the time, coaxing him to the expression he wanted on his face.

When it was over, everyone moved quickly out of the way, out of the heat. Maryellen dug her bikini top out of the sand where she had hidden it from the camera, tied it over her breasts. "I don't know why I'm covering myself up," she said. "That creep is more interested in your cock than my boobs."

Lindsay came over and handed Edgerton his robe. "Who's the creep?" he asked.

"Haven't the foggiest. He just showed up out of nowhere. Some kind of a Peeping Tom. I've done these location shots before. All kinds of spooks materialize out of the blue. Get used to it. That's show biz."

"Are we through for the day?"

"You are. I have bits and pieces to pick up and put together."

He debated, then decided. "I'll wait for you in the bar, buy you a drink."

She stared at him openly as he stood up, covering himself with the robe. "Sorry, Buster. I'll take a raincheck but you can't make it. You have another date."

"I have?"

She nodded. "Her royal highness from *The Christian Science Monitor* requests your presence at the very same saloon as soon as you've put your body and soul into shape. She deigned to talk to me so that I could relay the message."

"The interview?"

"I don't think Miss Frigid Tits is looking for an assignation." She began picking up discarded props. "Don't forget the raincheck on the drink."

The other end of the beach was deserted now. Edgerton walked around a shallow cove, took off his robe, ran into the water, and swam out toward the coral shoal at an easy pace, coordinating his strokes and breathing, enjoying the cool of the water, the decreasing heat of the day. When he swam back, came near the shore, he saw a figure on the beach. When he got closer, he realized it was the creep who interfered with the shooting. The man was sitting on Edgerton's robe staring toward him. Edgerton beaconed the beach in both directions. There was no one else in sight. He stood up, walked straight ahead; with his fingers he combed his hair back, out of his eyes. He ignored the man, reached down and pulled at his robe. The weight of the man held it fast. "Get up."

Roger Ramirez smiled, raised his body so that the robe came free, watched while Edgerton put it on. "You are modest for a man who does this for a living."

"I don't like Peeping Toms."

"Then why do this for a living? Why expose yourself to millions of people? A man like you could make a hundred times as much money without exposing himself to all those people."

"He can? I've never figured out how to do it."

"Maybe I can teach you."

Edgerton looked at him deliberately, trying to appear provocative. "You can't teach me anything," he said. "Now why don't you get your fat ass out of here before there's real trouble."

"You don't want to be rich?"

Edgerton sensed the possibility, kept up the interchange. "Everybody wants to be rich. I want to be rich but I also want to be left alone. Do you understand?"

"I can make you rich."

"How?"

"By not leaving you alone." Ramirez smiled the way he had seen his mother smile in a film.

"Not for sale," Edgerton said.

"Everyone has a price," he said. "That's why you're still standing here. If you didn't have a price you would have walked away or hit me."

"I still may," Edgerton said. "Probably slug you."

"Only if you don't agree to the price."

Edgerton laughed. "What kind of a creep are you, anyway? What are you doing here? How did you get in here?"

"My own plane. I heard you were all here. I came to see what kind of people you are."

"Freaks. But we're our own kind of freaks, we have respect for each other. This is a closed corporation. Strangers aren't welcome."

"When do we negotiate the price?"

Edgerton started walking toward his cabin. The man on the beach did not try to follow him, did not even get up. Edgerton had been trained to regard everyone with suspicion, to be suspect of what appeared to be accidental. The man would follow him, he knew that. He had to play him just right. He remembered what the CIA man in Key West had told him. You are the bait, he had said. At the moment he was the bait without a fisherman controlling the line. The bait had to be the bait and the fisherman too: not too fast to pull away, not too slow to be swallowed, paced just right to continue the taunting. He looked back before he made the turn toward the cabin. Roger Ramirez was still sitting there looking out to the sea.

When he came into the cabin, Langston was asleep. Edgerton showered, put on a tank top, a pair of cut-offs and went out, crossed the grass, went around the pool and into the bar. Monica was on her way out, did not look up, tried to get past him.

"Hey, hold on. Where are you going?"

"I wanted to start the interview but it's too late now. Maybe tomorrow."

"We can still have a drink."

"I don't think it's a good idea." She looked up at him, not able to hide the hurt and confusion she was feeling. Her face was still puffy from last night's tears. He grabbed her arm, turned her around, and led her into the dark, empty room. The bar was being tended by a big, black woman in a *Playgirl* T-shirt that one of the crew had given her. The black skin and distended nipples of her floppy breasts showed through the thin, white knit. Listening to a small radio behind the bar, humming with the music, she watched them come in, gave them no greeting, made no effort to serve them. Monica had started to sit on a stool.

Edgerton said, "Let's sit over in the corner."

"I'd rather stay here."

"I want to talk." He saw her stiffen and added, "Please."

She slipped off the stool, started toward a booth in a dark corner. Edgerton called after her, "What do you want to drink?"

"Just a Coke."

He brought the two drinks over to the table, sat across from her. "Maybe it's just as well we start the interview tomorrow. I had a big day, forgot how tough modeling can be. It went pretty well, though. Did you watch any of it?" She shook her head. "Funny, we spent all morning looking for locations and wound up shooting right in our own back yard, the catamaran and the beach." She was looking down into the depths of her Coke, hardly hearing his words.

"I don't think we ought to talk now," she said, starting to get up. "Tomorrow when it's broad daylight or in a brightly lighted room." He felt the shiver in her body as he put out his hand to restrain her. "Don't," she said.

"Don't walk out on me. Sooner or later we're going to have to say what there is to say to each other."

She shook her head. "No, we're not." For the first time, she looked up at him. "That's why I wanted to meet you." Lowering her head again, she explained. "I spoke to Los Angeles this morning. I quit my job. They're going to try to find someone else to do the in-depth on you."

"Because of last night? Don't blame yourself for that."

"Because of a lot of things. As you might guess, I didn't do a lot of sleeping last night. I didn't think about you, I thought about me: what I really am versus what I think I am. I thought about all the mistakes I've made. I thought a lot about my husband for the first time since I've been divorced. Maybe I didn't try hard enough to make my marriage work. Maybe editing food articles for *Better Homes & Gardens* is all the depth I can handle. I wasn't afraid in Des Moines. I'm scared to death out here. I feel so damned alone."

"You're a hell of a woman, Monica. Don't let me, these freaks, or this island blow a hole in your confidence and self-respect."

"Do you think I have any since last night? Either confidence or self-respect?"

The room seemed brighter as night descended outside the windows. Two natives had come in, drank beer silently at the bar. "Last night was my problem," Edgerton said, "not yours."

Monica shook her head. "I tried that salve but it doesn't work. The truth is that I threw myself at you. I admit it. I wanted you to make love to me. I was shameless. You felt sorry for me. You tried to make love to me because you felt sorry for me. But a man can't fake it when a woman turns him off, no matter how much compassion he feels. When a woman feels sorry for a man, when she goes to bed with him out of sympathy, all she has to do is breathe hard, scream a little, dig her nails in his back. A woman can pretend; a man can't."

"It wasn't like that. It's more complicated." He took a deep breath. "I wanted you as much as you wanted me. Maybe more."

For a moment, she let down her guard, believing his words, then her defenses stiffened again. "Nice try, Edge, but no go. I appreciate the gesture."

Softly, not sure that he could continue, he said, "It's my problem, not yours." When she started to talk, he put his fingers against her lips. "Don't ask any questions. I really don't want to talk about it. I just don't want you to blame yourself for something that is my problem."

"Are you a homosexual?"

"No."

"What is it, then?"

"Forget it. Please. Just don't torture yourself for no reason. You picked a dud, that's all. A week from now or when the story is done, you'll forget it. When the issue comes out and you see my picture you'll remember again and be able to laugh it off."

"You think it's going to be that easy to get over this?" She shook her head. "I don't." She reached across the table and touched his hand. "I'd be dumb to fall in love with you, wouldn't I?"

"Very dumb. No future."

"What if I can't help myself?"

"You'll get hurt again. Besides, love is a very old-fashioned word, an old-fashioned emotion. I'm bunking with a guy here named Rusty Langston, one of the models. They call him The Humper. When he isn't humping someone he's a philosopher. Life, he says, is all body; subjugate the mind to the body; subjugate the emotions to the body. Let the body do its own thing. Let the animal loose. Carried to its logical conclusion, the message is: Fuck, don't love."

Slowly, testing the words as she said them, Monica asked, "Where does that leave you?"

Instead of crying, screaming out, Edgerton laughed. "Nowhere," he said. "In a perpetual, extended, and eternal state of limbo."

"Love could change that?"

"Could it?"

"It's a question," she said. "Could it?"

Out of the corner of his eye, Edgerton saw Danny, the photographer's assistant, come into the bar with Roger Ramirez. Danny was being skittish, giggling, flirting with the Cuban. Edgerton was back on guard, wary of the creep and half falling in love with the girl. "I'm fucked up, Monica. Save your own skin while there's still time."

She said something to him which he did not quite hear. He was listening to the conversation at the bar, Ramirez talking to the woman behind it in Spanish. "Talk English, Mon. Don't understand."

"Champagne."

"We got rum. We got rum and whiskey."

"Two whiskeys."

Danny was at the jukebox pressing a series of levers. Ramirez, waiting for the drinks to be poured, looked over to the corner where Edgerton and Monica were sitting. Monica was still talking softly about love. When the music started, the calypso sound blaring and filling the room, Danny started to dance by himself, mimicking the native dance movements, wiggling his hips, deliberately trying to attract Ramirez's attention and provoke him.

Then it happened, without warning: the sound of the explosion shook the building. A wave covered the beach, flooded the pool, and there were seismic splashings against the windows of the bar. And beyond the wetness, a pillar of fire on the water, exploding debris catapulted upward and falling in a blazing shower.

At first, none of them moved, frozen by the shock, unable to locate the source. The movement of the building triggered the jukebox. There was a scratching sound and then the rhythm began again. Then they all ran at once to the door. The huge sheet of water was receding back over the pool and beach.

The *Playgirl* catamaran was nothing but a bier of flames on the water. People came running from all directions. Monica ran out with Edgerton, held his shirt when he stripped it off, and watched Edgerton hit the water and start swimming toward the burning wreck. In spite of the havoc, she was still thinking about love, saying to herself the words she had not finished saying to him. The disaster on the water was a picture on a television screen while she was reading a book. It was five minutes before the reality penetrated her introspection. Then she realized that Edgerton was in the water swimming out to the burning wreckage. She screamed his name, clutched his shirt, began to cry.

Halfway to the burning hulk, Edgerton looked up, saw the twin hulls disappear under the water. He still kept swimming, aware of her screams coming from the beach. Up ahead, there was no sound, no movement in the water. It was futile, nothing could have lived through the force of the explosion. He swam forward, around the area where the yacht had sunk. There were bits of debris, a floating life preserver, but no signs of life. He floated on his back for a moment, rested to regain his wind, then started back toward the shore. Someone had found a small boat, rowed out toward the wreckage, stopped to pick up Edgerton, hoisted him on board. It was Russell Langston and the other male model. "Anything?" Langston asked. Edgerton shook his head. "That was a damn fool thing to do, swim out there. There could have been more explosions."

Breathing hard, Edgerton replied, "There could have been someone still alive."

Langston was smiling, pulled off his sweatshirt, handed it to Edgerton. "I knew you were straight as an arrow, but I didn't know I had a damn-fool hero for a roommate."

LAURIE GOLDING'S APARTMENT, CONNECTICUT AVENUE, WASHINGTON, D.C.

Laurie Golding was back in her apartment a few minutes before five o'clock. She immediately switched on the television screens in her bedroom, activated the sound on her own channel, waited for the news to come on as she dialed Lowell Callender's office from the phone beside her bed. She took off her large hat, threw it on the bed, noticed for the first time that the bed had been turned back, slept in. She looked around the room, saw other evidences: a man's shirt thrown over the back of her dressing-table chair, jeans stepped out of, left on the floor, a rotting apple core on the dresser. In the excitement she had forgotten that Guido was due back from Italy. She wondered how he had gotten into the apartment. There was no answer at Callender's office. Damn it, she thought, those damn government people jump before the five o'clock gun. The news came on, she heard her own name, and her anchor explained that she was on assignment, would be back the next day. She deactivated the sound, took off her dark glasses, kicked off her shoes, fumbled in the night-table drawer for her personal telephone directory, found Callender's home number, dialed it, reached under her skirt, and began pulling down her panty hose. A woman's voice answered the phone. "Mr. Callender, please. This is Laurie Golding calling."

"Oh, Miss Golding. How nice. This is Adele Callender. We've never met. I've heard so much about you. Lowell and I were just sitting here having a drink, listening to the news. They said you were off on assignment."

"I am," she said, "that's why I'm calling Lowell. I need some information."

"I'll put him on. It was nice talking to you."

She pigeonholed the fact that Lowell Callender's wife had come back to Washington for later consideration. She knew that Adele hated it here, had continuously refused to establish any kind of base for Lowell's career.

"Where are you?" Callender asked.

"In my apartment but no one is supposed to know that. I must see you right away. This is hot."

"I can't. Adele just came in this afternoon. I scarcely had time to say hello to her."

"This is hot, Lowell. I don't cry wolf, you know that."

"Jesus, Laurie, I don't know how . . ."

She cut him off. "Be here fast. I'll leave the door on the latch. Walk right in."

"Give me an hour, anyway."

"The world can be lost in an hour."

"I'll be there in an hour."

Laurie sat on the edge of the bed, peeled the panty hose off her legs, went into the bathroom, ran the water into the tub. Guido's shaving gear was strung out over the sink counter. She put the cover back on the can of shaving cream, rinsed out the razor and put it neatly beside the can, arranged his brush and comb, put the cap back on the toothpaste. He had used her toothbrush. She ran it under the hot water, shook it out, put it back on the rack. She squeezed some liquid into the tub, watched the bubbles and foam appear, removed the rest of her clothes, remembered she had not left the door on the latch, returned to the living room, adjusted the lock, tried the handle to make sure it was on the latch, returned to the bathroom, settled into the tub. She heard the phone ring, began to reach for it in the alcove behind her, decided not to answer it, closed her eyes, and succumbed to the hot, fragrant water.

She was not aware that she had dozed off until she felt the movement of the water, the weight of Guido on top of her, her own head starting to submerge. She sat up, pushed him back. "You animal. Look what you've done to my hair."

He sat back at the other end of the large tub, grinned his boyish grin. "Where the fuck you been? I've been waiting all day."

"I forgot you were coming. I had to be out of town on an assignment." Then suddenly remembering, "What time is it? I'm expecting someone." She looked over to the clock, realized that she had only slept for ten minutes, settled back in the tub. Guido's foot was between her legs, his toes moving against her. She pushed him away, stood up, got out of the tub. "Get out of here," she said. "Go play in traffic for a while. I have important things to do. Come back later tonight."

She grabbed the towel, wrapped herself in it, examined her hair in the mirror, took a smaller towel, and tried to dry the ends of her hair which had become wet in the tub.

"I got no place to go," Guido said. "Besides, I'm hot as hell. I got to get my rocks off. Nothing's more important than that."

"Go rape somebody. I don't have time now. I have a million things to do, a million things to think about. This isn't the time for oversexed little boys."

He ripped the towel from her; she kept drying her hair. He took the small towel, threw it on the floor, put his arm around her gently, engulfing her opened mouth with his, pressing her to him with increasing force, his hand sliding down her back, forcing her legs open. In one coordinating, simultaneous second, he bit her, pinched her, and jammed his erect penis into her. She screamed and tried to push him away. He let loose of her suddenly. She toppled against the sink. Blood came from the corner of her mouth; there was a red mark bright against her pink skin. Guido laughed, thrust his pelvis forward. "You love it," he said. "You love oversexed little boys." She bent forward, started to pick up the small towel. He grabbed her hair, pulled at it, twisted it so that her neck jerked back. She screamed again. "Go on, say it," Guido commanded, "say you love it. Say you love it."

The words were hard to get out through the pressure of the pain. "I love it," she whispered.

He released her hair. Her head hit the cabinet below the sink. There were tears in her eyes, no sound of crying. Guido laughed again. "You remember who Guido is, huh? You remember what a man feels like inside you. A man." The words were a snarl of language and emotion, neither defined. "You need a man, not an oversexed little boy. You need a man so bad you can't think straight. You can feel nothing but Guido between your legs. That's no boy. That's a man. Guido is a man." He started out of the bathroom, hesitated at the door, his back to her, not turning his head. "One hour. I'm back in one hour. No more. You be here and you be alone." She stayed on the floor, bruised and bleeding, until she heard his heavy stride through the carpeted bedroom and his hard sounds against the wood floor of the living room and finally, the front door slamming. Her face twisted with pain, she pulled herself up to the sink, looked at herself in the mirror, took a washcloth and wiped the blood from her face, washed the cloth out in cold water, touched the cold cloth against the puffiness which had appeared below each eye. There was physical pain as she began to comb her hair, awareness of the root of each hair pulling at the pressure of the comb. From the medicine cabinet, she took a bottle of lotion, squeezed the milky liquid over her fingers, rubbed it against the raw bruises his hands had inflicted, wincing at the first cold, biting contact, then gently massaged the lotion into her skin. She squeezed more lotion on her fingers, put her hands between her legs, winced again at the cold and the pain, then closed her eyes as the pleasure began.

The spool kept turning after the Castro tape was played, the loose end of the cartridge flicking as it turned. Laurie Golding was huddled in one corner of the sofa, her legs curled under her, her body completely covered in a turtleneck, long sleeve, dressing gown. Lowell Callender stood up, walked over to the machine, squinted at the identification label on the knobs, found the right one, turned it off.

"Now," she said, "you can understand why it's urgent that I see the President at once. Arrange it, Lowell. There is no time to be lost."

"It's not that easy, Laurie. The President is not always that accessible. Not to me anyway. You must have heard that scuttlebutt. He thinks I'm after his job."

"Aren't you?"

"I know my own limitations," Callender answered.

"And I know you, Lowell. You believe your limitations are slightly this side of God." She shifted her body, tried to relieve the pain between her legs. "From time to time, I have made the mistake of underestimating both your ambition and your ability to achieve that ambition. I've smartened up, Lowell. I know that nothing is beneath you and nothing is too far beyond you." She lighted a cigarette, put out the match between her fingertips. "Pick up the phone, Lowell, and call the President."

He walked over to the phone, put his hand on the receiver, changed his mind, and paced the room. "Castro is bluffing. He

doesn't know any more than we know." Callender pointed at the
tape. "He's lying when he says that he knows who is doing this and
where they are and when they'll strike. If he knows it, we would
know it. I've seen to that."

"You had better tell me everything, Lowell, and tell it to me
straight, without lies and without omissions." He seemed not to
have heard her, kept pacing, his face tight in concentration. "Lowell!" She screamed his name. The sound of her voice stopped him,
snapped him out of his concentration. "Julio San Marco's story is
true then, isn't it? There is going to be a Cuban invasion."

Damn the red tape, he was thinking. Damn the tortuous routes of
government. He still had no evidence, no reports from any of the
intelligence teams combing the area trying to confirm San Marco's
story. There had been reports of possible staging areas for the
invasion. A very definite possibility from STINGRAY working out
of Grand Cayman Island. But nothing definite. If he had been doing
this privately, using his own sources, his own methods, he would
know facts by now, not these conjectures and reasonable possibilities. He would know hard facts, know how to move quickly and
decisively.

Laurie Golding had stood up, placed a new spool on the tape
recorder, pushed the recording button. "There is going to be a
Cuban invasion, isn't there, Lowell?"

He shut off the machine. "I don't know, Laurie. That's the truth.
Castro is bluffing when he says he has confirmed documentation.
He's going on San Marco's story just as we are. It's a bluff. We are
combing every inch of the Caribbean and the Gulf, looking for some
kind of a military buildup, some kind of staging area where this
could be happening. So far zero, not a shred of evidence, not even
a possibility. That's the truth."

"Castro says the CIA is behind it."

"Castro sees the CIA under every bed in Cuba. He's paranoid
about the Agency. This is not the CIA or even CIA inspired. I
guarantee that. I know that for a fact."

"You said that if Castro has evidence, then you would have it too.
Do you have agents in Havana?"

"I can't answer that."

"Off the record?"

"Not even off the record."

"Why not?"

"I cannot answer that question without endangering my source."

"Now you're bluffing, Lowell." She smiled, sat down again, curling her legs under her. "You and Castro are not that much unalike now that I think about it. He's so gruff and you're so smooth, it puts me off. He's all black and grizzly and you're all blond and finely honed. But you're both smart and you're both bastards."

"I'm smarter," Callender said. "He does what he does for intellectual and sociological reasons."

She laughed. "You're probably right, Lowell, you are smarter than he."

"Right now he's being maniacal because everything is unknown to him. He doesn't know any more than we do. I am certain that this tape is a diplomatic bluff. He's going on unofficial record to pin the blame on the United States no matter what happens." He touched the recorder, ran his finger around the tape. "If there is going to be an invasion, for whatever reason the invasion is being planned, we're playing into their hands. This is exactly what they want. They want the United States to be the villain. We keep getting closer to normalization with Cuba. Somebody is trying to blow that up. It has to be political. It can't be economic. Cuba isn't a big enough market for any country, any group to get rich. We've sounded that out very carefully. The President has sent mission after mission of businessmen over there, financial wizards to survey the market. All reports have been negative. The President didn't have to go to all that trouble, send over all those missions; he could have asked me. I would have told him in one sentence that Cuba is small potatoes as a potential market, not worth the bother. This is geopolitics. Maybe you were right. Maybe it is Russia. They've poured billions down that Cuban drain and they're nowhere. Maybe they're forcing a showdown so that they have an excuse to take over completely, be in real control, get rid of Castro as a dominant figure." He began pacing again. "If I were Russia, if I were plotting this, that's what I'd do. I'd make it look like a bunch of Cuban exiles were trying to recapture their homeland, invading the island under CIA sanction. There's historical documentation for this. In the process of the attack, the invaders are repelled, defeated but not until they've managed to assassinate Castro. Russia would be the savior then. They would have to protect the island, avenge Castro's death. They would be the good guys in white hats and we would be the villains whether it was the true story or not. Russia wouldn't have to sit on that expensive fence anymore. They could burrow in and take over the country. There's historical documentation for doing this, too." He thought for a moment. "If I was charting the game plan, that's the way I would do it."

"If you really believe that, Lowell, for God's sake call the President. Every minute is important."

"There's one great flaw in my theory. The CIA is not in this. They're helping me smoke it out, stop it."

"But they can make it appear as if the CIA is behind it. All they need is an excuse. By the time the truth comes out, it will be too late. Castro will be dead and the Russian government entrenched there. We can't let that happen. Call the President."

Callender's hand touched the instrument. "Have you checked the phone for taps? Is it clean?"

She concealed the fact that when he began dialing, the call would automatically be taped by the machine in her bedroom. "Why would anyone want to tap my phone?" She shook her head disgustedly. "Of course it's clean. Please hurry, Lowell." She had also to consider that Guido would return soon. There was no point in confronting Guido with Callender. There would be too many questions that she would rather not answer. She watched while he dialed. It was not the official White House number, but she assumed that he would have a more direct route to the Oval Office. He held the phone for a long time before someone answered. She heard him say, "This is Lowell Callender. This is an emergency. I would like to talk to the President." He looked over at Laurie while he waited. Their looks conveyed nothing to each other. "Hello, Barney. This is Lowell Callender. Can I get through to the President? This is an emergency . . . I can't wait until the day after tomorrow. This is hot . . . there's no time to go through channels . . . I'd rather not. This is for his ears only. Tell him that. He'll know what it's about . . . well, call him there." Callender looked at his watch. "He doesn't go to bed this early, not even on the farm . . . well, interrupt the Goddamn softball game, I told you that this was an emergency . . . all right, Barney, do it your way. This call is on record. If the damn situation blows up through the night, it's on your head, not mine. I tried." Callender hung up, turned to Laurie, shrugged his shoulders. "That's how the democratic form of government functions," he said. "Softball at twilight down on the farm."

"Can't you do anything?"

"Evidently not until tomorrow. I'll make a few calls, put some pressure on our surveillance teams, try to dig up something. The President is going to throw it back at me anyway. It's my ball to carry."

"Where will you be?"

"In my suite at the Madison." He picked up the Cuban tape. "I'd better take this for safekeeping." He slipped it into his pocket. She jumped up, lunged at him, tried to take the spool from his pocket.

"That tape is mine. I risked my life for that." She was struggling against him, scratching him.

Callender stood firm, avoiding her attack, holding hard to the tape. "Be reasonable, Laurie. What if the President calls through the night? What if he wants to hear the tape?"

"Then call me. I'll give it to you then."

With his free hand, he was able to push her away. He started for the door. She ran after him, catching his arm, using all her force to hold him back. They were struggling like this when Guido noise-lessly opened the door, his squat wall of a body blocking the exit. Laurie let go of Callender instantly, smoothed her dressing gown and then her hair. She turned her back, started toward the living room, hesitated. "Guido," she said, "this man has a spool of tape in his pocket which belongs to me. Ask him for it nicely. If he refuses, beat the shit out of him and take it away." Then, almost as an afterthought, she said, "Then kick him in the balls, spoil the romantic reunion with his wife."

The two men stood face-to-face. Guido held out his hand. Callender shook his head, took off his glasses, slipped them into his pocket, and with an unexpected lurch tried to burrow through the young Italian barricading the door. Guido, caught by surprise, yielded momentarily, then stiffened his body and grinned at Callender. "You like to play rough? Me too." Head down, shoulders forward, he charged at Callender, knocking him back into the living room, crashing a table and lamp to the floor. Callender wavered, managed to remain on his feet. When Guido charged again, he sidestepped, only caught a shoulder impact as the Italian lunged past him. Callender ran toward the door, was outside the apartment before Guido caught up with him, put a stranglehold arm around his neck, brought up his knee with great force into the base of Callender's spine, dragged him back into the apartment, released the vise of his arm. Callender fell to the floor, turned over, and was on his hands and knees looking up into the salacious grin of the Italian. Guido motioned with his hands, urging Callender up. "Come on, baby. Come on, baby." Callender feigned a movement; Guido reacted, was caught by surprise when Callender, after a delayed second, sprung from a crouched position and with his head, bucked against the hard wall of Guido's abdomen, got to his feet as Guido staggered from the impact. They were squared off, face-to-face again.

Casually, Laurie Golding walked into the bedroom, closed the door against the sounds of the fight in the living room. She unzipped her dressing gown, hung it in the closet, put her slippers carefully lined up side-by-side on a shelf in the shoe closet, went back and lay on the bed, listening to the sounds of glass breaking and furniture being knocked over as the fight continued. On an impulse, she walked naked to the wall cabinet which housed her televisions and recording equipment, took a headset from a drawer, plugged it into the receiver, pushed the rewind on the recorder and stopped at what she thought would be the beginning of Lowell Callender's telephone call to the White House. She had rewound too far, heard the end of her own earlier conversation with Callender. She heard the cut-off of the telephone ending that call, a period of silence and then the dial tone, the clicking sounds of the number being dialed, the regular sound of the number ringing, and then a woman's voice caught in the middle of a sentence. ". . . exactly seven twenty-three and one half." A pause, then a tone sound. "At the sound of the tone, the time will be . . ."

She said it out loud. "That son of a bitch." Callender was her most direct route to the President but she did have secondary sources. There was no doubt in her mind that Guido would recover the Castro tape.

Guido came back into the room as Laurie Golding was checking a telephone number in her private file. He was breathing heavily, blood oozing from the side of his mouth. One hand was completely bloodied. The other hand held the retrieved tape. His erection was outlined under the worn denim. "That fucker fights pretty good for an old fart." She reached for the tape, he put his hand behind his back, the tape out of her reach.

"Don't be cute, Guido, give it to me."

He looked at the blood on his hand, dripping down his fingers. He turned his fingers, inserted the index finger into his mouth, sucked it clean. "It's your boyfriend's blood." He extended his center finger toward her mouth. "Taste." She turned her head away. "Suck it." When she did not move, kept her eyes closed, Guido lowered his voice, a husky sound through his heavy breathing. "You want the tape? Suck it." Slowly, open mouthed, she went down on the extended finger, closing her lips and drawing back. Her stomach retched at the taste of Callender's warm blood. "Suck it. Suck." She bobbed her head back and forth on the rigid finger. Guido slipped the tape into his back pocket, zipped down his fly, freed himself from the confines of his jeans. He coated the remaining blood on his penis, grabbed Laurie Golding's head with both hands, forced her mouth toward him. "Lick it off. Lick it. Lick it." With the point of her tongue, she touched the blood, began to lap it up. She felt the hot moisture between her legs, was aware of her own female musk, the pain around her nipples. She opened her mouth, sucked him into it until she felt the cold gold of the cock ring she had given him. She moved her head back and forth, the sound of the suction bursting her ears. Then with all her force, she bit him. He screamed and hit her across the face with his open hand. She fell back on the bed, blood gushing from her nose. Guido rubbed his hand in her blood, smeared in on her left breast, licked it clean, alternating the lapping with sharp bites.

He slid down, forced his head between her, the sticky wetness coating his temples. He turned his mouth from the inside of one leg to the other, drinking the juices. He inserted his tongue into her, wiggling it. In spite of her pain, Laurie Golding responded to him, thrusting her pelvis toward him. His hands went up the length of her body, squeezed the taut nipples and continued to her shoulders, his thumbs extended toward her neck. When he bit into the soft flesh, felt it come loose in his mouth, he pressed his thumbs against her throat, stifling her scream, cutting off her breath, holding hard as she struggled against him. Her blood was oozing out over his face. His mouth dug deeper, spitting out tender pieces of flesh. His hands were around her neck, suffocating the last breath of air. Her body was motionless.

Guido fell back, his bloodstained face pointed toward the ceiling, grabbed himself as he ejaculated a high geyser of semen. When it was over and the tremors stopped and the hot viscous fluid flowed down his body, he smiled.

SAN ANDROS BEACH CLUB, ANDROS ISLAND, BAHAMAS, WEST INDIES

The beach at midnight was exactly as it had been the night before. But now, as Edgerton looked over the water, there were no mooring lights bobbing in the sea, no white hulls reflecting the moonlight. The Tongue-of-the-Ocean had swallowed the debris of the *Playgirl,* digested it and the surface was tranquil again, as though nothing had happened.

Edgerton sat alone on the sand, coldly assessing the tragedy, plotting his own actions, appraising his chances for completing his mission. The photographer was dead, destroyed in the explosion with the captain and one member of the crew. He had been his only direct contact with the control center at Key West. There was no way of communicating the disaster back to control center or to receive alternate instructions. The cause of the explosion was unknown. Rumors and theories ran through the group like a virulent, contagious disease. Edgerton knew too much to accept any explanation of an accidental explosion. The *Playgirl* had been destroyed deliberately, he was certain of that. The photographer had been the target; that was the only reasonable explanation. Were they that close to the source of the invasion task force? Edgerton had to answer yes to his question, otherwise why would Herbie have had to be eliminated? If they were that close, where was the source? The brigantine harbored in Eleuthera? The strange house with the waving woman on Great Guana Cay? Or the creep? He had to examine the interrelationships of the unexplained appearance of the creep and the murder of the photographer. He could not accept that timing as accidental.

Or was it someone in the *Playgirl* group? The man he slept next to? The woman he had begun to feel an undefined love for? When there were spies there were counterspies. It could be any one of the stone-faced models or any of the silent, black Bahamians moving noiselessly around them. Edgerton knew that he was close to the source. What was he blind to? It was there but he could not see it. Again he ran each detail of his experiences on Andros through his mind, looking for a clue, a nuance or detail which might have escaped him.

The status of the *Playgirl* story was also up in the air. The whole cover which had been created to mask the CIA investigation might have to be scrapped. Lindsay and Danny were in the Club office now, trying to get through to Los Angeles for direction. The telephone system on the island was primitive, the Bahamian operators not accustomed to urgency. The islanders had seen yachts explode before, other ships sink: they shrugged their shoulders to the inevitability of man against the sea, never changing the expressions on their faces or speeding up the pace of their movements.

At some point—he could not pinpoint the exact time—Edgerton had made the unconscious decision to function according to the Agency directives, ignore the drama of direct contact with the undersecretary. Lowell Callender had made him uncomfortable that night in the garden at Key West. There was a familiarity in the soft-spoken, Southern sound of the undersecretary's words. It had reminded Edgerton of other times, other places when someone wanted to use him or get an undisclosed gratification from him, but never considered him as a person but only as an object, a body. The Agency had admitted that they were using him as an object, a deliberate bait. Callender had dangled a bait to the bait; a direct, incisive action offered the temptation to be a man, not a male object. Somehow, without knowing him, Callender seemed to know too much about him, had a radar perception of Edgerton's inner needs.

202-657-0798.

Edgerton reasoned that if he called that number now, the resultant action would be immediate. Callender would act instantly. If he waited for procedure, Key West would eventually contact him through some source. But by then, it might be too late. The murder of the photographer was a desperation move. The invasion had to be imminent.

202-657-0798.

And if they knew about the photographer, why would they not know about him, destroy him, too?

202-657-0798.

There would be no way to get through to Callender until morning. The *Playgirl* crew were all in the office around the phone in the hotel. They were having problems getting through to Los Angeles. He had until daylight to make the decision.

Edgerton found the creep by the side of the pool, lying on a sun chaise, covered with torn beach towels, his eyes open, staring into the night. The calypso music was still coming from the bar; the whole area was quiet and surface calm. The lights were on the pool reflecting murky, green water. Neither Edgerton nor Ramirez acknowledged each other's presence. Edgerton slipped out of his shoes, pulled the sweatshirt over his head, stripped off his jeans. There was a cool undercurrent to the warm wind against his naked skin. He walked slowly around the pool, past Ramirez, climbed the ladder, stood on the balls of his feet at the end of the diving board, his body muscles rigid so that when he swung up and down at the tip of the board, only his penis moved in counterpoint to the action. He dove into the water smoothly, reemerged toward the shallow end of the pool, lay on his back and floated with his arms outstretched, every once in a while propelling himself back toward the other end of the pool, turning and doing another lap at the same time. Ramirez watched every move.

When Edgerton hoisted himself out of the pool, he walked around, pulled off one of the towels covering Ramirez, began drying himself, first his head and hair, then his chest and under his arms, putting one leg at a time on the end of the sun chaise, drying his feet. He discarded the wet towel on the deck and took a dry towel off Ramirez, tied it around his waist, and faced Ramirez directly.

Ramirez sat up, his voice low-pitched, almost a whisper. He said, "I see that you have made the decision." He swung his legs over the edge of the chaise, folded his hands over his chest. "I like the way you negotiate price. You didn't really have to go to all that trouble. I was already aware of the quality of the merchandise." His hand gripped the back of Edgerton's calf: Edgerton did not draw away.

"Who are you?"

"My name is Roger Ramirez. I already know your name. The sissy photographer told me all about you and everyone else around here."

"Where do you live? Where do you come from?"

"I live all over the world. Right now I am staying in my house on Great Guana Cay."

"Do you live in that big modern house? We flew over it earlier, Herbie—he was the photographer who was killed in the accident—was trying to find out who lived there. He wanted to use it for fashion shots. It's quite a layout. What do you do for a living?"

"One thing or another," Ramirez said.

"Oil?" Edgerton asked.

"Because I look like an Arab?"

Edgerton shrugged his shoulders. "You don't particularly look like one thing or another. From your name, I guess you could be South American but you don't talk with any accent."

"I'm Cuban. I'm a real Cuban. Pure Spanish blood, not one of those half-black Bolsheviks that call themselves Cubans now."

"I don't know anything about politics. I don't care about politics."

"What do you care about?"

"What does anyone care about?" He shrugged his shoulders, looked away from Ramirez. "Surviving, I guess."

"Is that why you're doing this cheap thing, posing for a cheap magazine, letting frustrated women and fags get their kicks by looking at your cock? Is that how you survive?"

"One way," Edgerton said. "It doesn't matter how, survival is the important thing."

"We are alike. That's how I live my life. Surviving. But our standards are different. Surviving to me is having places to live all over the world with servants to wait on me and a private jet to take me from place to place. Survival is a basic instinct. The quality is different depending on what you are born to."

"And you were born to private jets and houses on Great Guana Cay and God knows where else?"

"It is my heritage," Ramirez said. "I have the Spanish instinct for destiny."

Edgerton laughed. "My instincts are all-American. It's called getting from one day to the next. My destiny is to hang in there until my chin sags and gut pops, then worry about tomorrow."

"You could learn a lot from me."

"I bet." He looked the fat young man up and down. "But I don't think I'm having any. Thanks very much but no thanks."

"Name the price."

"Sorry, it's not my thing."

Ramirez took a large roll of American dollars from his pocket. He tossed the roll to Edgerton. Edgerton's reaction was automatic. He raised his arm, caught the money in midair. "There's five thousand dollars there. How long does it take you to make five thousand dollars?"

Edgerton's hand caressed the roll of money, then tossed it back to Ramirez. "A long time. A lot of hot lights and back-breaking poses."

"There's a lot more where this came from." Ramirez touched the money which had landed beside him on the pool deck, did not pick it up. "I'm working on a business deal now." He picked up the money, threw it back to Edgerton who caught it again. "That five thousand dollars will be everyday pocket money."

"How did you get over to Andros from Great Guana?" Edgerton came over to the chaise, sat at the foot of it, placed the money on the discarded towel beside Ramirez.

"My own plane."

"Where is the plane?"

"Here. In Nicollstown. It's at the airport waiting for me."

"Tonight?"

Ramirez shook his head. "It's a two-engine prop. It can't fly at night around here. We'll fly back at daylight."

"How about flying me to Miami in the morning?"

"What for?"

"Nobody knows what's going to happen here. We don't know if they're going to scrap the whole story or send down another photographic crew. Either way there's going to be a couple of days to kill. The thing is that I gave up a good television job to take this assignment. If you could fly me to Miami, I could call my agent and let him see if the TV job is still open." He touched the roll of money with the tips of his fingers. "I took this job for the money. Frankly, I need it. If this washes up, I could be in trouble. If I contact my agent, he can get busy lining me up, if not for that particular TV show, something else. How about it?"

"If you took the five thousand dollars, you wouldn't have any problems at all."

"When I get involved, it's for a lot of reasons," Edgerton said, "but none of the reasons are money. Now what do you say about Miami?"

Ramirez shook his head. "It's difficult. I travel on an Italian passport. I didn't bring it with me. I don't know about the pilot. There's too many government formalities."

"What about your island, could I call from there?"

"No telephone, only radio contact. It would be difficult."

"What about Nassau?"

"That would work out. I could do that."

"Will you?" Edgerton put his hand out, touched the other man's leg. "No strings. Just to help out a guy in trouble."

"It's a one-way deal. I'm too good a businessman to make one-way deals."

"I told you before, when I get involved it's never for money, it's for a lot of other reasons."

"How do I know that you're not the world's greatest hustler?"

Edgerton laughed, stood up. The towel came loose from his waist. Slowly, he bent down, picked it up, slung it over his shoulder. "Maybe I am. Maybe we both play for big stakes. It's a gamble. What kind of a gambler are you?"

"What time does the sun come up?"

Edgerton tied the towel back around his waist. "About six."

"Be at the runway at six-thirty." He picked up his money, put it in his pocket, stood up, adjusted his cut-offs over his belly.

202-657-0798.

Edgerton went back to his room. Langston was gone. He redressed, walked to the small manager's office where everyone had been crowded, waited around the telephone. The office was empty now, locked up. He crossed the outdoor lobby, went into the bar. The voices were loud, frantic sounds of nervous reactions, triggered by liquor and fear. He found Lindsay, pulled her away from the cluster of people. "What happened?"

"Basically nothing," she said. "This telephone system is about as effective as two Dixie cups and a piece of string. By the time we got a call through, the office was closed. We finally tracked down the editor at home and after she got over the shock, she just said to hang on, that she couldn't make any decisions until tomorrow morning." She looked over to the jam of people. "So, we're all hanging in there the only way we know how. Booze."

"What did the police say?"

"These people have been controlled by fate so long that all they can do is shrug their shoulders and accept what happens, never question it. They'll never find out what happened to the boat. Everything is down there on the bottom, blown to bits probably. Somebody had the bright idea of doing the scuba bit in the morning, see what we could find. The manager warned us that if there are pieces of human flesh down there, sharks will be around and that canceled that expedition."

She rattled the ice in her empty glass, pushed her way to the bar.

Edgerton wondered about Monica. The tragedy had put an end to their talking about love. Better leave well enough alone, he decided.

202-657-0798
First things first.

HOTEL DE PARIS, MONTE CARLO

Aldo Rinaldi unfastened the clasp of his wife's diamond necklace, held the cold ice of it in his hand, feeling the sensuality of the stones being physically transmitted through the network of his body to lodge in his groin. He leaned over, kissed the back of her neck, looked up and saw both their reflections in the dressing-table mirror. He removed one of her earrings, kissed the naked lobe, palmed the shower of diamonds and then repeated the ritual on the other ear. "I have never seen you more dazzling than you were tonight." He whispered the words into her ear, kissing it as he talked.

"I can't believe how frumpy Grace looked."

"You were the princess, darling. Of all the princesses, you were the only real princess." He walked around, leaned against the dressing table, took her hand and kissed it, then inserted her third finger in his mouth, sucking the square-cut diamond loose. He held it in his mouth while she slowly withdrew her finger. He kept the diamond in his mouth, forced the tip of his tongue through the platinum circle. He opened the hand which held the jewels in front of his lips, spat out the ring, closed his hand and kneaded the jewels together in the lubricant of the saliva.

"I feel so marvelous." She smiled at him. "I feel so wicked sleeping in a hotel only twenty minutes from home. Doesn't it feel as though we're not married, that we're doing something very sinful?"

He placed her arm flat, palm up, along his leg, unfastening the
diamond bracelets with his free hand. "Every man envied me because I would be the one to be with you all night, make love to you."
He ran his tongue up the inside of her arm. He released the handful
of jewels inside his jacket pocket. "Even the young men at New
Jimmyz envied me, wanted you."

"I danced so much. I can't ever remember dancing so much. All
those wild bodies on the dance floor."

He slipped one strap from her shoulder, kissed it. "Your body was
as wild as any of them. Wilder." He walked behind her, zipped down
the back of her dress. One side fell, exposing a young girl's breast.
She cupped the breast in her own hand, studied it in the mirror. He
leaned around and put his mouth against the nipple. She grabbed
his head, pressed it hard against her. "I wish there were a gala every
night. And dancing at New Jimmyz every night. I'd never tire of it.
Never, never, never." She pulled his head away. "I feel so guilty,
Aldo."

"Why guilty?"

"When Roger left . . ." She did not say any more.

"What about Roger?"

"It was as though a whole weight was lifted off my head when he
was gone. I felt so free. Unburdened." She stood up, slipped off the
other shoulder strap, let the long gown slither down her naked body
to the floor. She stepped out of the dress, stood closer to the mirror.
"I should love him, Aldo. I should love my own son."

The count's voice was gentle. "I love him, darling. Like my own
son. Does that help?"

"I know you love him even though he's so horrid to you."

"No longer. Roger and I have come to understand each other. We
get along very well now. His life has been confused and with many
traumas. You must have patience with him."

"He's so ugly. I know he can't help that but why does he have to
be so fat?"

"Would you love him if he were not ugly, if he were not fat?"
She shook her head. "I did not love his father."

"But he is part of you, too."

"I know that. I want to love him. I want to feel a mother's instinct
for love. I know how that should feel. I've played those parts in
films. I know how a mother should feel but I can't feel that way about
Roger."

He kissed her navel, then each nipple. "Tomorrow, darling. We can talk about Roger tomorrow. Let's not spoil tonight."

She took the end of his bow tie, pulled it loose. "Hurry, Aldo."

"First I must put your jewels in the vault." He retied his tie. "Don't fall asleep. I will only be a little while."

Reluctantly, fingering them as he did, he relinquished the handful of diamonds to the steel box in the vault behind the cashier's cage in the lobby. He waited impatiently while the night cashier locked both locks and handed Rinaldi back one of the keys.

The man appeared from the shadows of the empty lobby as Rinaldi started toward the lift. When he saw him, he turned, walked through the lobby, down the wide steps outside the hotel, across the square and sat on one of the benches in the minipark. The man followed in a few minutes, sat next to Rinaldi. "The arrangements are complete." He spoke in a guttural French, not his native language. "I have brought the money." He took four large bank envelopes from his pocket which were bound together with heavy rubberbands.

Rinaldi kept his hands folded in his lap. "Why me? Why now? The arrangements should be completed in Geneva." He pushed the envelopes away. "The money must go directly to Mr. Castle."

The man shook his head. "Not possible. The United States government watches Mr. Castle too closely. We cannot take the slightest chance of discovery. If there is any indication or suspicion of any kind which could link us to this operation, the remaining monies due Mr. Castle will never be delivered. My people and Mr. Castle have a continuing business relationship. We are both very careful that nothing jeopardizes that. It was Mr. Castle's suggestion that this particular transaction be conducted through you."

"That means that I must go to Geneva tonight."

"Today," the man said, looking up into the sky. "The day will begin soon."

"What about the documents? Where are they?"

The man looked around the square, unzipped the edge of the inside lining of his jacket, extracted from a hidden compartment a large, malleable leather folder, and handed it to Rinaldi. "Go ahead, open it. Check the documents. I think you will find them to be superior work." He zipped up the lining.

The pouch contained forged documents, letters, and identification for Roger Ramirez and Julius Schwartz which, easily traced, would establish them as agents of the United States Central Intelligence Agency.

The man said, "Perfect forgeries. Not even the CIA will believe that they are not genuine."

"It's Castro who must be convinced."

"Castro would believe that they were CIA involved without any identification. But when he presents this evidence to the United Nations, these documents will be flawless. I guarantee that."

Rinaldi was now certain that Castle intended to kill Roger as well as Hotdog Schwartz. The bodies would be found after the invasion, inviolable proof that the CIA was directing the operation and sanctioned by the United States government. Rinaldi picked up the bank envelopes from the bench, weighed them in his hand. "Five million dollars front money. I will not count it," he said. "Partners must trust each other." He now stood up. All the lust, which he had so carefully, through the night, nurtured in his body, was gone. He looked up to the hotel, wondered if his wife would still be awake and if she was, how he would explain the delay. He stuffed the bank envelopes in the same pocket where the jewels had been and walked across the square without looking back at the Russian agent.

1978
AUGUST

WEDNESDAY

MADISON HOTEL, 1177 15th STREET, N.W., WASHINGTON, D.C.

Yesterday when his wife had come up from New Orleans, Lowell Callender had moved some of his clothes and his toilet articles into the small room off the suite which he normally used as a study. The bed was pulled out of a convertible sofa, the mattress lumpy and thin. He had not slept well, physically aching with the beating he had taken from the young man in Laurie Golding's apartment. The bruises on his face and body were painful. He had churned all night in a half-sleep, his mind swiveling from possible lines of action with Laurie Golding's interview with Castro. Also, there were the explanations he would have to make to his wife for the bruises on his face which could not be concealed. There would be no way to avoid a showdown with Adele. She would insist on it. The bruises from last night's beating put him at a disadvantage. Any explanation, including the truth, would be inept, not believed.

She was already in the living room, sitting at the room-service table, drinking orange juice, and reading the newspaper. He tightened the belt on his robe, went to the table, sat opposite her without saying anything.

When she looked up at him, there was an uncontrolled moment when there was compassion in her face, hurt for his hurt. Then her face hardened. "She must have put up quite a fight."

"You're paranoid about me and other women. You hallucinate," he said. "I was mugged in Lafayette Park. A couple of kids. Just for kicks. They didn't take anything. Just beat the hell out of me."

She turned the newspaper toward him. He read the bold black banner twice before the meaning of it registered in his brain or before the face in the photograph took definition. LAURIE GOLD-ING FOUND DEAD. He read beyond—the three line sub-headline. TV PERSONALITY MURDERED, APARTMENT RANSACKED, POLICE FIND NO CLUES. Callender could not read any further —the sudden surge of nausea was uncontrollable. He ran from the table and vomited on the bathroom floor before he could raise the toilet seat. The wretching never stopped, even after his stomach was emptied; the dry heaving continued, tearing him apart. That was the only awareness, the gasping for air between the wracking of his body, the pain of his bruises, the ache of his muscles. The reality of the headline could not resurface through the torture of his body.

It was twenty minutes before he could pull himself back together, clean up the bathroom, wash his face, comb his hair, and be certain that the nausea reaction was over. He went back into the living room, capable now of facing the truth, anxious to read the details of the story.

His wife was standing up, the newspaper folded, held in her hand as though she was going to use it to swat a fly. "Why, Lowell? Why?"

He grabbed the newspaper. She tried to hold on to it. He wrenched it free, partially tearing the front page. "Why, what?" His glasses were in the bedroom. He went back for them. She followed him.

"Why did you have to kill her?"

He put on his glasses, walked to the window for better light, began to read the small print. His eyes were riveted on the words . . . strangled . . . sexually abused.

She tore the newspaper away from his face. "Why did you have to kill her?"

"That doesn't deserve an answer," he said, holding the newspaper up again. The tapes would be gone: the Castro tape and all the others. The news story said that a vault, secreted behind a mirror, had been blown open and all the contents were missing.

"It does change everything, doesn't it, Lowell? I may be free at last." She sat on the rumpled sofa bed. "A murderer can't possibly be President, can he?" She propped up the pillows and lay down. I'll play it just fine, Lowell, you can count on me. The perfect Southern lady. I'll play it just the way Daddy taught me." She laughed, laughter on the verge of hysteria. "I'll get my way in the end. I'll be free of you, Lowell, and I'll have all the money. Won't that be a joy. I'll be free to do what I want, marry Ralph if I want to. But maybe I won't marry Ralph. I can marry whoever I like now. Or not marry. For the first time in my life, I'll be free to do exactly what I want to do. No Daddy. No Lowell. Only me." The laughter started, immediately turning to tears.

Callender was reading carefully, had not heard his wife, was only vaguely aware of the sound of her crying. As he read, he tried to reconstruct his own movements, coming into Laurie's apartment and leaving it. Who had seen him? Who knew he was there? He looked over at his wife. "Shut up, will you? I have enough to contend with without an hysterical woman." No one. As far as he could remember no one had seen him. He had walked to the apartment not passing anyone he knew. He had walked right up, the door was on the latch, he had walked right in. Fingerprints, he thought. But the place had been wiped clean, the newspaper said. If the young Italian had destroyed his own tracks he would have had to destroy the evidence of Callender being there.

The neighbors had heard nothing until the sound of the explosion, the blowing open of the safe. They had not immediately traced the sound to Laurie's apartment, thinking there might be some connection of the sound with the subway construction close by where there were always strange sounds in the night, unexpected happenings, and delays in the construction caused by accidents. By the time the source of the explosion had been located, the apartment was empty except for the corpse, all evidence obliterated.

Fleetingly, the thought crossed his mind: Go to the police, report the truth, give a description of the young Italian, aid in the apprehension of the killer. He had the thought but never the intent. Sooner or later, the police would uncover Laurie Golding's private life, the young toughs she picked up and used for her sexual pleasure, and the big Washington names she slept with, sometimes for pleasure and sometimes for information. His own name might even crop up. But like the other big names, the interrogations by the police would be discreet, the information withheld by gentleman's agreement from the press. Unless there were wise-ass young newsmen inflicted with the Woodward-Bernstein disease that would keep prying. He would have to chance that.

No, there was nothing to be accomplished by going to the police and telling what he knew. It would not bring Laurie back to life. It would only destroy his plans, imminent and future. Nothing would be accomplished except possibly a murderer brought to justice.

But who was the young Italian? She called him Guido. There could be ten million Italians named Guido. He was north Italian, probably somewhere around the Como region, close to Switzerland. Callender's trained ear could detect that, understand the colloquial obscenities shouted at him while he was being pummeled. One thing he was not: he was not just another young tough she had picked up on the street. If he had been only that, the tapes would not have been stolen or the evidence destroyed. A hopped-up, S and M, bent-psyche man would not be that professional, not that thorough. The man she had called Guido was a skilled, trained agent.

Who was Guido; who did he work for? How did he fit into the ever complicating pattern of the Cuban invasion?

No matter where Callender started the dialectic, he always ended at the same "no conclusion." The solution was constant. Finding the task force, finding the source of the invasion.

He picked up his private phone next to the sofa bed, for a moment allowed himself to look down on his sobbing wife. "Put me through to Farnsworth," he said to his secretary. When Farnsworth answered, Callender said, "What's happening?"

"Fireworks. All hell has broken loose. The chief upstairs, the CIA, even the President's office has been ringing the phone off the hook."

"Why didn't you call me?"

There was a silence, a clearing of his throat before Farnsworth answered. "I read about Laurie Golding. I thought maybe you wouldn't be in any shape to . . . well, I mean, I know how you felt about her. I mean there was . . ."

Callender interrupted. "Don't try to second-guess me, Farnsworth. Not ever. Give it to me straight, one at a time."

"Somebody is on to our intelligence teams in the Caribbean. Wait a minute." Callender heard the sound of paper being torn out of the Teletype. "I have written down all the decoding that's come in but what it reads like is that every damn team has had what appears to be an accident or a direct attack. Two guys in SAILFISH were gunned down by a power launch while they were out fishing. Three people were attacked by sharks off Cozumel and no sharks have been reported that close in for months. The leader there expects foul play. The damn boat we chartered for YELLOWJACK exploded off Andros Island. Cause unknown."

"Anyone hurt?"

"I don't think so. They were all onshore doing some photographing. Maybe one of the crew. I told you I haven't had time to accurately decode all this stuff yet."

"What about the President's office?"

"Don't you want to hear about the other teams? Something has happened to every damn one of them. We must be close as hell to whatever is happening down there."

"Did it ever occur to you to question the source, how it could happen? There's a very large leak at the CIA. Someone is double agenting there. It has to be Langley. No one else would know the whole structure, no one else would know all the teams, all the dispositions of all the teams. It has to be Langley."

"There is you and me," Farnsworth said.

"Are you confessing, Farnsworth, or making a rotten joke?"

"I'm sorry, sir. I guess I'm getting punchy from everything happening at once."

"Who called from the President's office?"

"Jud Server. Al Payton. Selma Feinberg."

Callender mentally catalogued the departments they represented; none of them would be a direct route to the President. "Listen, Farnsworth," Callender started. Farnsworth did not answer. "Farnsworth, are you there?"

"Yes, sir."

"Listen, Farnsworth, I didn't mean to fly off like that. You're right about Laurie Golding. It has knocked me cold. That's strictly between you and me. Understand?" He went on talking without waiting for an answer. "As a matter of fact, I'm not up to facing anything yet. Juggle the calls, even if the President himself calls. Tell him . . . tell everyone that I'm away. You don't know where. Understand?"

"Yes, sir."

"Start putting the screws on Langley. Keep screaming about a security leak. Leave the big guy to me. I'll give him a going over. You'd better stay on the phone all day and night. Keep the scrambler on. I'll be in constant touch. But you don't know where I am. Is that clear?"

"It's the truth, sir. I don't know where you are."

"Keep it like that. I'll stay in touch." He started to hang up. "Farnsworth, are you still there?"

"Yes, sir."

"What about San Marco? Any word?"

"No, sir."

"And no directs from any of our own people? Edgerton, maybe?"

"No, sir. Everyone keeps reporting what's happening to them but everything still winds up with a big zero in the information department. No one has located anything remotely suspicious yet."

"Okay, Farnsworth. Keep at it."

When he hung up the phone, he noticed that his wife was sitting up; her crying had stopped. "You don't love her, do you?" She corrected herself, "You didn't love her. You were just using her for some scheme of yours, the way you use everybody in the final analysis."

"I didn't love her and I didn't kill her. So don't see yourself playing the faithful wife while her husband is tried for murder. Nothing is any different from the way it was. You still will do exactly as I tell you. We are staying married. You may keep sleeping with Ralph as long as you are discreet. You can stay in Washington or go back to the plantation, whichever you choose. If you stay in Washington, please call housekeeping and order me a regular bed for this room. I cannot spend another night on that piece of junk."

She smiled. "Not quite the same, Lowell. You've forgotten a very important detail." She stood up, walked to the center of the room, held out her arms, the full sleeves of her robe appearing as butterfly wings, twirled around, a gesture of defiance and freedom. "Maybe you didn't kill Laurie Golding. But you did go to see her last night. I know that. Maybe I'm the only person who knows that you went to see her last night. And I know that you woke up this morning bruised and beaten, as though someone had fought you off." She stopped, put down her arms. "You see, Lowell, you're wrong for once. Things are not exactly the same as they were before. I can implicate you. That's one of your tenets of power, isn't it? Holding something over someone's head. I'm beginning to learn."

Softly, the drawl less pronounced now, he said to his wife, "I said that I did not kill Laurie Golding. I did not say that I was not capable of murder."

VICTOR CASTLE'S VILLA, GENEVA, SWITZERLAND

From this view, through the large windows facing east, Guido could see the range of mountains still snowcapped in August. He was bone-weary, exhausted. He had caught the Washington-to-London flight, connected to the flight to Geneva, slept all of the way, not even eating. Nonetheless, every muscle seemed to ache and when he moved too quickly, the pain inflicted by Laurie Golding's teeth was a reminder. He looked out of Victor Castle's chalet again, at the snow in the distance, then closed his eyes and could feel the cold against his skin as he would be skiing down the tortuous slopes, the downhill exhilaration, the wind biting at his face, the hollow of excitement in his groin, the complete freedom. His body would be in control over the elements, his skill harnessing the gravitational force and making it work for him. And up there he would be out of this summer heat, away from the lazy warmth inside Victor Castle's house. He would not be aware of the musk of Castle's woman, the scentless lure of a bitch-animal in heat.

She had not taken her eyes off him since he had arrived. Silently, without expression, watching him, watching every movement he made, measuring him, appraising him with invisible loupes of a woman's eye. Boldly now he went over to her, took a bunch of plump, green grapes from the fruit bowl, stood straight in front of her, his pelvis thrust forward and one by one plucked a grape, forced it with his fingers through his closed lips. He rolled the grape in his mouth to soften the skin, forced it out between his lips, took it in his fingers, his teeth nipping at it to break the skin, his tongue darting out to taste the juices that flowed out of it.

When they heard Victor Castle enter the room, Guido put the remaining bunch of grapes back in the bowl.

Castle hugged Guido, his mouth touching one cheek and then the other. "You're a good boy, Guido. You did well. Very well."

At the London airport, between planes, Guido had bought a tape recorder and three blank tapes, listened at random to some of the tapes he had stolen from Laurie Golding's vault. He recorded the tape which he had fought the other man for. He had no political awareness, only the fox's instinct for survival. Castro was nothing more to him than a name. The fact that Laurie Golding had died for that tape, that Lowell Callender had fought for it, and now, that Victor Castle had kissed him for it, made it important. He had recorded the original tape, secreted it, knowing that it was a weapon for survival.

"You work clean," Castle told him. "I have talked twice already to the United States. You work clean, not a clue."

"I told you," Guido said, grinning like a boy scout receiving a merit award.

"You're not hot, that's important. No one is looking for you."

"The only one who saw me is the guy I had to fight with. What if he talks?"

Castle shook his head. "He won't talk. I know who the man is. He will not risk exposing himself." He picked up a pear from the fruit bowl, fingered it, put it back. "I am taking every precaution. You can forget about him. Don't worry. You did good, Guido. We don't forget boys who do good."

Guido kept grinning, did not say anything. The woman spoke. "Teach him how to say thank you, Victor. He is like an animal, he does not say thank you."

"He will learn, *cara*. He will learn." Castle looked out the window, toward the mountains. "We all learn in the end. We all learn what suits us best." He touched the young man's shoulder. "You will learn, won't you, Guido?" Without waiting for an answer, he continued. "You will learn to say thank you and you will learn to respect your elders, not only with the mouth. You understand, Guido?" The young man nodded. "Now, go upstairs and get some sleep. Take a shower. You smell."

He knew better than to ask Victor Castle what he would be doing next. He was hoping he would not have to go back to Great Guana Cay and to the fat ass of the Cuban man. His own flesh cringed at the thought of touching Roger Ramirez again, having to play tender games. This woman was what he wanted, to penetrate the hard, cold steel of her, make that steel molten. That was his style. But he understood the structure of this world: the woman he could not touch and the man he must fuck if they instructed him to do it. He took a bunch of grapes before he left the room.

"That one is trouble, Victor," the woman said.

"When I was his age, I was trouble, too. The good ones start like that." He ran his hand over her bare legs, stooped over, and kissed her foot. "You like him, huh?"

"I am a woman," she said.

"My woman." He went back to his study to reassess the information on the tapes, readjust his plans to take full advantage of the information.

He sat at the big desk, alone in the big room, felt suddenly tired, weakened. He thumbed through the calendar on his desk. Three weeks from Tuesday he was scheduled to go to the clinic at Montreaux. They would revitalize him again. He pressed a button next to his phone, rubbed his eyes until a woman answered the summons and came into the room. She was in her mid-fifties, overweight, wore a tweed skirt and sweater, flat laced shoes. "Frau Kline," he said, "that young man brought a suitcase full of tapes from the United States." He opened the side drawer of his desk. "I have kept three of them. The others are in the closet. Take them to the computer. All the information is to be programmed by individual names and subjects, you understand?" She nodded with one determined movement. "When the work has been completed, you, personally"—he pointed a finger at her—"are to destroy the tapes and every evidence of them. This is delicate. You must do it personally. You understand?" She nodded again, started to leave the room. "I must talk at once to Count Rinaldi and then to Anselmo in Miami. Stand close. There will be other calls. It will be a busy day." She nodded again, started to leave the room. "And Frau Kline . . ." he thought for a moment, wavering a decision. "The young man upstairs . . . he is in one of the guest rooms . . . do you know which young man it is?" She nodded. "Lock his door from the outside," Castle instructed her, "and bring me the key."

When he was alone, he checked the complicated chronometer on his desk, pressed a series of buttons. It was seven o'clock in the morning in Miami. It would be the same time at Great Guana Cay. If he let Guido sleep for an hour, there would still be time to get him back to the island before dark. He picked up the phone, squinted, and dialed. "Let me talk to Kurt," he said. The man answered quickly. "Is the G-2 ready?" Castle asked. "You're leaving for Miami in one hour and twenty minutes. One more passenger only. Tell Rinaldi he has company. Carry maximum fuel. Radio ahead. Have a plane ready in Miami to fly them directly to Great Guana Cay."

GREAT GUANA CAY, THE EXHUMA CHAIN, BAHAMAS, WEST INDIES

Edgerton had made the decision to stay with Roger Ramirez, go back to Great Guana with him. He questioned that decision now as the small plane circled the tiny island in the early evening, preparing to land. Ramirez put his hand on Edgerton's knee. Edgerton ignored it, continued to look out the window, studying the topographical details of the cay, the oceanography of the water around it. When he had called Lowell Callender from Nassau, another man's voice had answered the telephone and had tried to probe him for the information. If his Key West contact had not been blown up in the *Playgirl* explosion, Edgerton knew that he would not have contacted Callender directly or in any other way deviated from explicit instructions. But the death of the photographer forced him to be on his own, make his own decisions.

There had been only one chance to lose Ramirez in Nassau. When they had gone to the bank, Ramirez had to go into a vault. The guard refused to let Edgerton enter with him. He was only out of the Cuban's sight for a few minutes but that had been enough time to get away. His instincts were dichotomous as he waited outside the vault. Key West had warned him that he was the bait, not the fisherman. Callender had shimmered the temptation to be his own man, act on his own judgment. He weighed one possibility against the other; remained immobilized by his own dialectic. Then the opportunity was gone. Ramirez was back at his side clutching a thick bank envelope in his sweaty hand.

The plane made a wide circle. There was the sound of the landing gear being lowered. The pilot said, "Fasten up, girls." The descent was steep. Edgerton could see no runway, only a long expanse of grass. The plane touched down at the edge of a cliff, the tail section still over the water when it landed. It was a hard impact, a rough taxi over the rocky ground. The pilot made a sharp ninety-degree turn, headed straight for a density of trees, turned sharply again thirty feet in front of the trees, and cut the engines quickly.

They had stopped on a concrete landing painted grass-green. The hangar was directly ahead, inserted into a forest of lush, thick trees. Even the roof was overgrown with tropical vegetation. The abrupt braking had whiplashed them forward and back. Edgerton felt a muscle pull in the back of his neck. The pilot opened the small window on his left, had his radio active, was whispering into the speaking tube. Another man had appeared on the ground and was putting blocks under the wheels. Ramirez and Edgerton unfastened their seat belts, waited for the pilot to get out and open the door. The heat inside the cabin built up instantly. Ramirez leaned forward, bending the seat in front of him, reached for the release on the starboard door. The pilot, with a sharp blow from the side of his hand, jackknifed Ramirez's arm away from the lever. "My instructions are that you are going to sit right there until somebody comes from the house."

"This is my island," Ramirez shouted. "This is my plane."

"Don't get your cunt in an uproar," the pilot said. "In any man's army an order is an order."

"This is my army." In anger, he took a handful of U.S. hundred dollar bills from his pocket, waved them in front of the pilot. "I pay for this army. You want to get paid? Open that door."

The pilot looked at the money, slapped it out of Ramirez's hand. "Chicken feed," he said. "Chicken shit."

Two men had appeared at the side of the plane while this was happening. Edgerton saw them before Ramirez did. Ramirez was picking up the scattered money. One man was young, heavily muscled, curly light hair, wearing low-rise cut-offs. The other man older, graying hair, dressed in immaculate white shorts and a starched white shirt. The pilot looked to the older man for instructions. The man pointed at Ramirez. "Okay, Fatso, out you go." The pilot turned to Edgerton. "You stay here."

Ramirez grabbed Edgerton's arm, tried to pull him up. "He comes with me."

The pilot raised his hand, threatened to chop at Ramirez's arm again. Ramirez released his hold, bent his head, turned around, and backed out of the plane.

"What's going on?"

The pilot did not answer Edgerton. He followed Ramirez out of the plane, locked the cabin door behind him. Edgerton watched the discussion with Ramirez and the two men. They were not close enough for him to hear what they were saying. The pilot had disappeared into the shadowy darkness inside the hangar. Edgerton could see that there were two other planes parked directly inside the entrance. One was an amphibian with fore and aft engines mounted back-to-back high over the wing. The men, as they talked, glanced over at Edgerton. The young man was talking excitedly, touching Ramirez as he spoke, not letting Ramirez finish a sentence. The older man seemed calm, more in control. Ramirez was gesturing wildly, pointed back to Edgerton several times. Whatever the younger man was saying seemed to slowly calm him, the fondling hands finally subduing Ramirez's frenetic gestures. Reluctantly, the Cuban capitulated to the young man who had locked fingers with Ramirez and began to lead him away. Ramirez turned again to look at Edgerton, made one halfhearted tug to draw away from the man's grip, and then walked side-by-side with him away from the hangar, out of Edgerton's view. The older man waited until the pilot reappeared, said a few words to him, and followed him to the plane, waited while the door was unlocked, climbed into the cabin, sat down, and faced Edgerton.

"I am Roger's father," the man said. "There has been a misunderstanding." He held out his hand. "What is your name?"

Deliberately he let his hand be limp when he shook hands. "My name is Marc Polo," he said. "What's the matter? What's going on here?"

"There has been a misunderstanding." He sighed, held up his hands in a gesture of despair. "My son has times of great emotional distress. He is not always completely rational in his behavior. You understand?"

"He seemed fine to me. We were going to have a great time."

"Did he offer you money?"

Edgerton hesitated. "Yes."

"How much?"

"He didn't say. It wasn't like that. He said there was lots of money. He even showed me a bundle of it."

Edgerton noticed that there was currency from three or four countries as the man thumbed through the bills in his wallet. He handed Edgerton a U.S. hundred-dollar bill. Edgerton made no move to take it. "I told you he said there was going to be a lot of money."

"What do you call a lot?"

He nodded at the bill. "I think five of those is a lot of money." Without hesitating, four more bills were counted out. "Who was the little guy Roger went off with?"

He fumbled for an explanation. "A kind of companion. He gives my son therapy." He signaled to the pilot to open the door.

Edgerton said, "Where am I going?"

"Back to Andros. Roger said he picked you up there. That's right, isn't it?"

"If I'm going all the way back to Andros, I have to pee first."

"In the hangar, toward the back." He turned to the pilot still standing on the ground next to the opened door. "This young man has to use the toilet. Show him where it is. Stay with him."

The pilot followed Edgerton into the hangar, walked with him to the rear. It was a much larger structure than it had appeared from the plane. There were two larger, old passenger planes at the far end, freshly painted, an airline insignia stenciled on the tail which he could not identify. Edgerton realized that they would have had to have been assembled on the ground. There was no way a plane of that size could land on the runway. It would have had to be specially engineered with equipment to be able to take off in a short distance. The pilot went into the tiny enclosure with him.

Edgerton took careful inventory of the hangar as he walked back through. A large cement-block square enclosure had recently been built into one of the front corners, the gray rectangles and the mortar joints still fresh and new looking. The room was entered through a steel overhead door which was closed now, padlocked at each side and at the bottom. Heavy horizontal timbers, stacked vertically, barricaded the door. Two large, unopened packing cases had been dropped in front of the door. The crating was new. PRODUCT OF ALBANIA had been stenciled across the crates in several places.

Outside, back in the sun, as they walked toward the plane, Edgerton said, "Boy, I never saw a spread like this. These people must be rich as hell. I sure would have liked some of the action. How about letting me get a look around?" He stopped but the pilot pushed him forward again. Edgerton let his body be weak, easily maneuvered. He had measured the potential strength of this other man, knew that he could handle him with one calculated karate chop. The element of surprise would be working for him. Edgerton's hand tightened as he thought about it. He assessed the alternatives. But the man in Key West had cautioned him not to be a one-man army. It was more important to communicate limited reconnaissance than to gain further information and not have the facility to communicate it. He let himself be pushed and shoved to the plane, waited while the pilot was unlocking the door. The moment for physical action was there. His hand raised itself to a strike position. He thought better of it. The pilot turned his head. The split second of opportunity was gone. Edgerton climbed into the second row of seats, fastened his seat belt. The pilot took his position, opened the side window, started the engines, adjusted his headset and mouthpiece, began speaking into the tube. After a few minutes, a man came running out of the hangar, removed the blocks from under the wheels, and with hand signals, directed the pilot through the difficult maneuver of turning the plane around in the constricted area. The pilot made the two difficult turns, taxied to the clearing, and then waited. He looked at his watch, leaned across the seat, pushed open the cabin door, let the churned air wash through.

Five minutes later the young man came around from the villa. He was still wearing the cut-offs but had put on a Carlos and Charlie Acapulco T-shirt, black canvas rope-sole shoes, and was carrying a small, leather, zippered bag. He pushed the front seat forward, indicated for Edgerton to move over, sat beside him. The pilot closed the door and the small ventilator, gunned the engines, and took off at a steep incline, the wheels just above the water at the shore line. Edgerton looked down, catalogued the swimming pool without water, the partially hidden antenna tower. Seven men were eating lunch around a round table and Roger Ramirez was on the roof deck, looking up at the plane.

When the wheels were retracted and the plane was at cruising altitude, the young man unfastened the safety belt, opened the leather case, took out a cigarette paper, filled it from a cloth pouch, rolled it with one hand, lighted it, inhaled deeply, holding the smoke in his mouth, and then passed it to Edgerton who repeated the process, gave it back to the man.

"Roger says that there is lots of puss on Andros."

Edgerton nodded, took another drag on the joint which had been passed back to him.

"Roger also says that you've got a cock that never stops."

Edgerton shrugged his shoulders, did not flinch when the man reached over to hand measure him.

"I'm going to like it on Andros." He settled back, smoked again. The acrid smell had begun to permeate the cabin.

Edgerton took another deep drag of the joint, pretended stony silence. Actually, he was feeling some of it; the euphoria and the anesthetizing of reality.

SAN ANDROS BEACH CLUB, ANDROS ISLAND, BAHAMAS, WEST INDIES

This time when the telephone call finally went through, there was no answer at all, not even the assurance of another voice contact. Callender had told him that he would always be available through this phone. Edgerton repeated the number to the Bahamian operator, heard her relay it to the Washington operator. The number was rung again. Edgerton could hear interruptive clicking sounds in the steady, repetitive rings, but dismissed them as mechanical problems. Still no answer. It had been six hours since he had placed the first call to Callender from Nassau. An hour ago he had been in touching distance to the vertex of the plot. That close. He had made a deliberate choice: the wrong choice. Now he had the information but was powerless to use it, not wired in to any channel of communication.

Lindsay burst into the manager's office carrying a clipboard stacked with schedules and photostatic layouts. "Where were you?"

"Around."

"Are you all right, Edge? You look funny."

Edgerton felt the heaviness in his eyes, tried to fight through the weariness in his body and the stoned, sluggishness of his mind. "I'm okay. What's going on?"

She sat on the desk, rested her hand on the telephone. "The show," she said. "The show must go on." She picked up the phone, gave the operator a New York number and then the number of the club, hung up to wait. "God knows how long this call will take."

"Is another photographic crew coming in?"

"Tomorrow. They're flying to Miami and our little plane is going to pick them up." Lindsay studied him. "You don't seem pleased, Edge. What's the matter? I fought like a tiger to keep this story alive. I know how much it will mean to your career. It'll be a whole new start for you. Isn't that what you want?"

He shrugged his shoulders. "I guess so. I guess that's what I want. Mostly, I need the money . . . enough money to keep me going until I do know what I want."

"You look awful, Edge. You ought to get some sleep. I'm Jewish-mothering you."

"I said that I'm all right." He meant for his voice to snap at her but the sound came out muffled, lethargic.

Edgerton stood up as the phone rang, let Lindsay answer it.

Monica was in the restaurant, sitting at a table, stirring her iced tea, staring vacantly into the space ahead of her. What he was feeling, what he felt each time that he saw her, was new to Edgerton; a mixture of lust and tenderness. There was an undefined need to be fulfilled with her, a latent strength and a latent weakness. It was the wrong time to be thinking about love. But they were both thinking about it now.

She recoiled when he sat opposite her, sipped her tea from the tall glass.

"What's the matter?"

"Nothing."

"I just saw Lindsay. She told me that the show must go on. What did you decide to do?"

"I didn't decide anything. Los Angeles made the decision for me. They couldn't get a free-lancer at the last minute. I promised to stick it out. The staff is preparing all the questions for the interview. All I have to do is read them off a piece of paper, turn on the tape recorder, and listen to your answers. Somebody in L.A. will do the rewrite, put it together. I haven't changed my mind; I'm still going back to Des Moines."

"And your husband?"

She shook her head. "That can never be good anymore. I don't know what I'll do."

"Maybe it's for the best."

"Is it? Is that what you want me to do?"

"You know my problem."

"I'm not sure that I do. I know what you told me but I don't know the truth." He did not say anything. "Where were you today? Everyone was looking for you."

"Including you?"

"Yes. Including me. We were on the edge of talking straight to each other when the accident happened. We were close to how we feel about each other. You don't know the terror I went through when I saw you swimming out toward that blazing boat. I was afraid for you and afraid for myself." She lowered her head. "You didn't even see me when you got back to the beach: you walked right by me. As though I didn't exist."

"I'm sorry." He did not explain further.

"It's not a question of being sorry, it's forgetting that I was alive. I excused you last night because of the excitement and confusion and I knew you must have been exhausted. But when you didn't come around all day today . . ."

"I'm here now."

"It's too late," she said, stood up, took her straw bag, and left him alone at the table.

Cutting across the pool deck, distracted, not looking where he was going, Edgerton collided with Danny as he headed back to his room. "Sorry, Danny."

"Loved it."

"Are you going to stay on the story?"

"I guess so. I hope so. Nothing will be exciting after this."

"I'm sure sorry about Herbie. Did you work together a long time?"

He shook his head. "First time out with him." He lowered his voice. "I've worked with some of the big ones. Frankly, I don't know how good Herbie really was. I never saw any of his stuff."

"Tomorrow the hard work starts again."

"So let's live it up today, huh?"

"You seemed to be living it up last night." Edgerton hesitated, tried to focus on the expression on Danny's face. "What happened to that guy last night?"

"The creep? Vanished, I guess. Maybe he's the one who blew up the boat. I still say it was no accident. Anyway, he's gone, disappeared as fast as he showed up. But we have a new entry, another gaping spectator. Have you seen him? Divine. He's a little earthy for my taste but he's divine looking."

"Who?"

"The little mini-bull. He walks with his head down, like he's going to charge at you. I kept saying, *toro, toro,* but he wasn't having any. He probably doesn't speak Spanish. Maybe he's Italian or something. Haven't you seen him?"

Edgerton shook his head.

"He's in the bar dancing up a storm with Maryellen. Talk about Saturday night fever . . . this guy is a whole epidemic on Wednesday night." He turned to Edgerton's direction, pointed him toward the bar. "This you've got to see."

The jukebox was blasting. The draperies were drawn against the midafternoon sun, only slits of light at the edges penetrating the darkness of the room. There was the bleak, blue-white light of the fluorescent tube under the bar and the soft-mixing purple, pink, and blue lights of the Seeburg. The young Italian was stripped to the waist and barefoot, his sweat-covered torso reflecting the colored lights. Maryellen had taken off her bikini top, tied it into a turban around her head, also danced bare-breasted. She was unaware of the man, not following his movements or coordinating with his rhythm. She was in a world of her own, her entire being abandoned to music.

The bar was crowded. Couples huddled together in dark corners, groups filling all the tables. It was too dark to identify anyone. He groped along the upholstered bar rail to the center undercounter light. "Gin on ice," he said to the black woman tending the bar. He waited until she poured the drink, took a sip, pushed it back to her. "More ice, please." He drank half of it straight down and then continued to the end of the bar, steadying himself against the rail. His hand touched the soft leather bag placed on top of the Italian's discarded shirt. The hardness in it was a gun.

As a record was changing, a moment of silent relief, the Italian looked up, saw Edgerton and walked over to him. The woman kept dancing in the silence, her rhythm not changing when the music began again. They both watched her undulating body, writhing white skin, and staring brown nipples. "Crazy lady," the Italian said. "Crazy, crazy lady. No tits. No ass. But crazy."

"I thought you were flying back."

"I changed my mind." He inclined his head toward the dance floor. "I think maybe I stay and fuck the crazy lady." He shook his head. "She's too far gone for a good fuck."

"You got another joint?"

"Most of the time, it don't matter what I fuck. Fucking is fucking." He took the bag, unzipped it, extracted the paper and pouch, rolled the cigarette, lighted it, and handed it to Edgerton without first inhaling it. "But with all the ass around here," he said, "a man has choices."

For Edgerton, the one moment of truth had come and gone. He held the smoke in his mouth, swallowed some of it, and felt it being absorbed into the fiber of his body. There had been that instant when he could have overpowered the pilot and become the one-man army. But once that instant was over, any chance for action was gone. He was again the man he had always been: impassive, not in his own control, a man waiting for something to happen to him. Callender would find him. Key West would send a replacement contact. It would all happen in time and now this drugged time was stretching minutes into hours and eternity was in reachable view. He was an instrument again, an instrument for other men's action. He took a deep drag again before he handed the joint back to the Italian.

The other man smoked with a quick, popping action. His eyes did not flinch or waver as he stared at Edgerton. "You don't look like no five-hundred-dollar hustler to me."

"What do I look like?"

"Crazy. You look like if it was the right time and the right person, you could do crazy things. Maybe you don't even know how crazy. Maybe it takes a crazy man like me to turn it on."

Edgerton did not answer.

"You want to dance?"

The thin veil of the marijuana was on the edge of becoming a denser cloud covering his consciousness; he knew the pattern of his own sensitivity to the drug. In the few remaining moments before moments became hours, he made the professional appraisals. Guido held the key to the time and place of the Cuban invasion. There was no doubt of that: it was number one priority, the only priority. Everything else was secondary to a sworn commitment to the United States government. At this moment he had no personal life, no personal values, no personal integrities beyond his professional dedication to doing his job. If his person, his convictions, his ethic had to be violated in the process, there would be time later for vengeance against the outrages.

He took another deep mouthful of smoke, held it, and then swallowed it.

"How about it?" the Italian asked.

The stimuli were all sensual now; the incessant beat of the disco music, the animal heat of the Italian man beside him, the vibrating flesh machine of the woman on the dance floor, his own body feeling heavier, more powerful, straining to burst out of the confines of his skin. Without saying anything, Edgerton made the long walk of a few steps to the dance floor, turned around and waited. The Italian had taken his shirt, was drying off his body with it, then raised his arms one at a time, patted his armpits dry. He took a deep, last drag from the cigarette, pinched off the lighted end, left it on the bar, started dancing in position, his head slightly down, and then danced forward keeping beat to the music until he was on the dance floor and in body contact with Edgerton. Then Edgerton broke down, succumbed to the stimuli, his body supercharged, unleashed into a rhythmic fury. His mind was a diminishing entity to the vanishing point. There were two men with the same faces and bodies. He was both of them. One man was standing aside watching the same man crazy on the dance floor, a controlled robot watching a fluid animal. Then there was only the animal.

He couldn't be sure if it was real or an apparition, Monica's horror-stricken face watching the animal on the dance floor, the sweating and half-stoned man dancing opposite and responding to the rhythm of another man. Her face seemed to appear, disappear, and appear again. Edgerton was too far gone, too far committed, to find her, to try to explain.

Ceaselessly, the music beat on; Edgerton with it, his body gyrating, undulating, controlled by this other mechanism.

1978
AUGUST

10

THURSDAY

SAN ANDROS BEACH CLUB, ANDROS ISLAND, BAHAMAS, WEST INDIES

Edgerton's eyes were open before he awakened; he wondered if they had ever been closed. His right hand was clenched in a tight fist: he could not direct his physical power to open it. He was aware of surroundings but his eyes could not focus, saw only a darkish blur. He remembered darkness. Now there was blinding daylight. Not able to lift his head from the pillow, his eyes rotated first left and then right. He forced himself to concentrate, forced his vision to delineate the blur into defined objects. *Andros Island. This room. His room.* The bed next to him was empty, not slept in. *The Italian. Monica's face.*

If he sat up, swung his legs over the side of the bed, put his feet on the floor, raised his body, put foot in front of the other, he could walk between the beds and turn to the left and then to the left again and he would be in the bathroom. One step at a time. He sat up, waited until the dizziness passed, and then swung his legs over the side of the bed. He felt the carpet against his feet but did not seem able to put his feet firmly on the floor. He pressed down with great effort until he felt the hardness underneath the carpet.

He looked at his clenched fist. With his free hand, finger by finger, he forced it open. He saw the gold cock ring in the palm of his hand. His hand closed over the ring, became a hard fist again. He was beginning to remember.

Still clutching the ring, he groped his way to the bathroom, ran his free hand in a circular motion on the wall until he made contact with the light switch, turned it on. His eyes closed automatically at the increase in brightness. Using great effort, he raised his eyelids, concentrated on keeping them fully open. He stumbled on the low curb getting into the shower, leaned against the cold tile, and was aware of the labor of his breathing, did not move until his pulse rate subsided. He was remembering more and more.

He turned on the cold water full-force, stood face-up, mouth open under the hard spray, and let it pummel him until what had happened, and the sequence of what had happened, took definition in his consciousness. He opened his hand, took the cock ring, clenched it between his teeth, reached for the soap, and lathered himself while he prodded his memory.

Port-au-Prince. Tuesday. That was what he had to remember. *Port-au-Prince on Tuesday.* He was going to meet the Italian on Tuesday in Port-au-Prince.

Monica's horror-stricken face.

Still soapy, he took the gold ring, slipped it over his scrotum, forced his penis through the circle and pushed it back toward the base until it stopped binding him. He turned on the hot water, rinsed his body, stepped out of the shower, dried himself as well as he could with the soggy towel, dressed quickly, left the room, and walked outside toward the clubhouse.

The door to the manager's office was locked but a clerk behind the registration desk unlocked it for him. "I'm making a private call," he explained. "Don't unlock the door for anyone. Okay?" The clerk nodded.

202-657-0798.

While he waited for the call to go through, he tried to remember the rest of it. *Tuesday. Port-au-Prince.* But where? He had told him where in Port-au-Prince but he could not remember it. The name of a man? The name of a place? The name of a hotel? Where in Port-au-Prince?

He picked up the phone before it stopped ringing. The operator informed him there was no answer.

Monica's horror-stricken face.

He slammed the door of the office, held up his arm to shield his sensitive eyes from the light. All channels of communication were closed. No new contact with Key West had appeared and Callender still did not answer his phone. He finally had discovered the one big key besides the installation on Great Guana; *Port-au-Prince, Tuesday.*

Maybe today, he thought, when the new photographic crew arrived, there would be a replacement for Herbie with them, a liaison with control.

Lindsay was on her way into the office, stopped when she saw him. "Christ, if I thought you looked lousy yesterday. . . . Lived it up a little too much last night?" Edgerton made a noncommittal gesture with his shoulders. "You and that Italian certainly cut a number on the dance floor. Didn't think you were the type. Well, you can never tell by looking, can you?"

"Grass and gin are a fairly deadly combination."

"If you think you were a surprise last night, you should see Miss Goody-Two-Shoes today."

"Monica?"

"Guess what? She not only took off her little white gloves, she has taken off the top of her bikini and is letting her little white tits hang out. As a matter of fact, they're not so little. Peck and Peck can disfigure a lady, hide a lot of curves. Take a look for yourself. She's down on the beach. You may have to fight your way through the gaping spectators, but it's worth the trip." She started past him, turned. "Stay available will you, Edge? We may get some shooting in later this afternoon. The new gang is due in about noon. And for Christ's sake, do something about getting your eyes and your blood running again. You look awful."

Russell Langston and Jody, the other male model, were sitting on the sand about twenty yards from where Monica was stretched out, face down, bare-assed, reading a book. Some native fishermen were keeping a respectable distance on the other side, laughing to each other and jabbing each other in the ribs at their own jokes as they stared at her. Edgerton's body cast a shadow on the pages of the book. She turned, saw him standing there, reached for her cover-up, changed her mind, and started to read again. He lay beside her, close enough so that he would whisper. "What the hell are you trying to prove?"

"That I have a great ass and great boobs. You had me thinking there was something wrong."

"Okay, you proved it. Now put something on."

"And spoil the boys' fun? No way. They're loving it. It's a change for them from all those skinny models. They seem to be enjoying a real female."

"I take it that this whole exhibition is because you're pissed off at me."

"Don't flatter yourself. I've just learned to join the group. When in Rome . . ." She turned the page, continued reading.

He reached across her, took the robe, and covered her. She pulled it off, threw it on the sand. "There's no way I can explain about last night," he began.

"Don't even try. It was obvious. As a matter of fact, I'm glad it happened. It restored my self-confidence. I didn't turn you off the other night because I was me. I turned you off because I'm a girl. It isn't just me, it's all women. No wonder you didn't stay married."

"I told you the truth. I told you why my marriage broke up."

"You told me you weren't a homosexual."

"I'm not."

"Do you always dance with men in bars?"

"I can't explain that. You have to go on blind faith sometimes."

"I'm not buying that again, Mr. Polo. I try to never make the same mistake twice."

He rolled over on his back, covered his eyes with his arms. "If it's any consolation," he said, "you do have a great ass and great tits." He heard her moving beside him. When he took his arm away, she was standing up, putting on her robe. She stuffed the two parts of her bikini in the pocket, kept her finger between the pages of the book, cut across the beach, and walked toward her room.

WASHINGTON, D.C., AND
NEW YORK, NEW YORK

Farnsworth had not left Callender's office since he had talked to the undersecretary the morning before. All hell had broken loose in the department. When he tried to find Callender, warn him of the developments, the undersecretary was not in his apartment at the hotel nor at any of the alternate telephone contacts. No one had seen him or heard from him.

When he heard Callender's voice, a cold sweat broke out on his body and tears came into his eyes. Until he felt the inadvertent tears, tried to talk and no words would come out, Farnsworth had not been totally aware of the depths of his own feelings or the intensity of the stress he had been under. Callender hammered the name again. "Farnsworth! Farnsworth, are you there?"

He managed then to answer. "Yes, sir. I'm here."

"Well, speak up, for God's sake. I don't have much time."

"Are you okay? I mean, you're all right, aren't you?"

"Of course I'm all right. Why shouldn't I be? What's the matter with you, Farnsworth? Are you sick?"

"No, sir. I'm not sick." He stood up, straightened his body, cradled the phone between his chin and shoulder, tightened his belt. "Where are you?"

Callender hesitated before answering. "It's probably just as well that you don't know," he answered. "Have you had a lot of heat there?"

Holding the phone again, he wiped his cheeks with his free hand, slumped in Callender's chair, put his feet up on Callender's desk. "The weather is okay. The heat has been tremendous."

"Talk fast, Farnsworth. What's been happening?"

"I don't think we ought to talk on the phone. Even this line is probably bugged."

"Can you scramble?"

"Not on this line. Your office has had a major overhaul of the communication systems. It seems the lines are suddenly overloaded. There have been repairmen working around the clock. All of this happened yesterday after I spoke to you. I guess the Oval Office had trouble getting through and reported the difficulty to the telephone company. They responded instantly, if you know what I mean. Very efficient. The repairmen are even armed."

"Bad as all that?"

"Worse. Besides the President, Jud Wheeler, and Vance's hatchet men, we have the D.C. police, the FBI, and four hundred departments of the CIA." Farnsworth laughed to reassure himself. "The last number is an exaggeration. But it's been wild. Telephone bingo."

"Is there a tail on you?"

"I don't know. I haven't been out of this office in three days. I had to call a friend to feed my cat and water my plants."

"That bad?"

Farnsworth confirmed it. "That bad," he said. "I've had to use your shower and borrow two shirts and a pair of socks. I hope it's okay."

"It's okay." Callender was silent for a moment. "We have to take a gamble, Farnsworth. If this line isn't secure, we'll have it risk it anyway. There are certain things I need to know. Don't explain anything, just answer negative or positive. Is that clear?"

"Go ahead."

"STINGRAY?"

"Negative."

"BARRACUDA?"

"Questionable."

"SAILFISH?"

"Negative."

"YELLOWJACK?"

"Negative."

"MARLIN?"

"Negative."

"WAHOO?"

"Questionable. Scratch. Positive."

There was a silence while Callender appraised the information. "Plan D," he said. "Are you up to it?"

"Yes, sir. I'll try."

"Borrow another shirt if you have to. Good luck."

It was exactly three hours and twenty-seven minutes later that Farnsworth stood outside the door of suite 1749 of the Sherry Netherland Hotel in New York. He released the button on his watch, the numerals disappeared, and there was the blank red glow of the face. He turned the lapel of his jacket, unfastened the single key he had pinned there, opened the door, stepped into the vestibule, saw the small suitcase on the floor, refastened the key, used the deadbolt to double-lock the door, took a deep breath of air-conditioned air, bolstering his courage with the intake. He released his tension with the expungence and then was finally ready to face Lowell Callender.

It seemed to Farnsworth that he was more sunburned than the last time he had seen him, a bronze coating, almost like makeup covered Callender's face. When he stood close to him, he could see shadows under the coating, remnants of bruises. He questioned again the complexity of his relationship to this man, the farrago of emotional reactions which he could not sort out or separate to examine. He set down his attaché case on the coffee table, took off his jacket slowly, giving himself time to define the exhilaration he was feeling, aware only that what had been a hollow void was void no longer.

Callender's voice was gentle. "Were you followed?"

"I don't think so. I took every precaution. I'm not professional at this. I'm not experienced enough to know for certain if anyone followed me. Nothing . . . no one looked suspicious. On the other hand, everyone did. Do you know what I mean?"

"It doesn't matter. It's done now. Whatever will happen will happen. It was a necessary risk." He sat on the sofa, took the brief-case which Farnsworth had brought, fumbled with the combination lock, and then used a small key to release each side lock. Quickly he thumbed through the documents in the case, speed-reading the contents, hesitating only once to reread a paragraph. He looked up. "All right. I know what's in here. Now tell me what is not in here."

Farnsworth pulled up a chair, sat opposite the undersecretary, started, then hesitated, and finally put his feet up on the table. "There is more that is not in there than is."

"Don't play cute, Farnsworth. There may not be time. Be explicit."

He took his feet off the table. "The President for one thing. He's hot. You know how he gets. Once he got on the phone personally and ate my ass out because I didn't know where you were. The Secretary of State did it eyeball to eyeball, had me on the carpet, and really laid it on me, said I could be convicted of traitorous activity against the United States government. He sure lost his cool." He smiled. "Nobody has paid this much attention to me since I played high school basketball."

"How tall are you, Farnsworth? I've always meant to ask you."

"Six five and a quarter."

"Any clues why everyone was suddenly so hot to find me?"

"The secret is high up. None of it has hit the ladies' powder room yet. I've had my usual Tampax network in operation. Not a hint. But all hell is breaking loose somewhere."

"Wasn't Cy due to go to Israel?"

Farnsworth nodded. "That whole section flew out there. It took the heat off a little bit." He added, "But not enough."

"Anything else unusual?"

"I almost forgot. The District Police have also been hot to find you."

"What for? Do you know?"

"They're a little easier to handle than the FBI and CIA. They weren't hard to smoke out. It seems they're investigating Laurie Golding's murder. They know you were friends. They told me that it was a routine investigation, questioning all the people who had known her, even casual acquaintances. That's going to take forever. They just want to talk to you off the record. They think maybe you can fill in some holes in their information. I gave them the diplomatic immunity schtick, told them you were too involved in solving the problems of the world to solve a crime of passion."

"Who said it was a crime of passion?"

He smiled. "That information does come from the Tampax network. It seems the lady was fucked to death. The strangling was only a formality."

"Do the police have any clues?"

"Not from what I can pick up from the newspapers or the newscasts. Not a clue in the world. Everyone is as nervous as hell. She seems to have slept around a bit. Most of her scoops were pillow talk. Lots of nervous cocksmiths in high-up places around Washington. Her television network isn't going to let up on this. They're trying to make it a combination of Elizabeth Ray and Watergate." He looked around the suite. "Anything to drink up here?"

Callender shook his head. "Call room service."

"Do you want anything?"

"See if they have diet Dr Pepper."

Farnsworth walked to the back of the room, picked up the phone, dialed the room-service number. "What if they don't have diet Dr Pepper?"

"Iced tea."

"You look like you could use booze."

Callender rubbed his face, stopped when he felt the pain from the bruises. "Have them send up a bottle of Jack Daniel's. I guess I'll need it before this is all over."

"Room 1749," Farnsworth was saying. "Send up a bottle of Jack Daniel's, four Cokes, and do you have diet Dr Pepper?" He held his hand over the mouthpiece. "What name do you use here?"

"Kunz," Callender said. "Luis Kunz."

Farnsworth repeated the number into the phone, hung up, sat opposite Callender again. "You look dead on your feet. Why don't you sack out for an hour. Everything has waited this long, it can wait for another hour."

"No way. Time is vital. First things first. The job has to be done first." He put the back cushion of the sofa against the arm, stretched out, kicked off his shoes. "How do you read it, Farnsworth?"

"It could be BARRACUDA. It could be YELLOWJACK. It could be both; two prongs. My money would be on YELLOWJACK."

"Did you talk to Edgerton personally?"

"Yes. I talked to him but he wouldn't talk to me. He kept repeating the distress code. He kept saying the word over and over again and getting madder than hell. I could tell from his voice. There was no way to get back to him. I tried to get some information out of the Agency. That was like talking to a dead horse."

"Good for Edgerton. He learned well. Good man. I knew he would be."

"All hell broke loose in BARRACUDA. You know that girl we thought would be as tough as nails? It turns out that she cries like other girls. I guess those sharks got three of the crew. She was half-hysterical telling me about it. We may have to scrap that whole unit, start over. Whatever is happening down there, I don't think that she will be able to handle it. Was it an accident?"

"I don't believe any of these things are accidental. Did anyone from the Agency corroborate these findings?"

"I told you that no one would talk to me. But they were calling every other minute. They must have known what was happening in Cozumel. Maybe they've gone in there to straighten it out." Farnsworth fidgeted in the chair. "Fulsome in BARRACUDA would tell me very little, only that there was trouble. If we ever do this kind of thing again, you have to wire me into the chain of authority." Callender's eyes were closed, his face impassive. "Sir," Farnsworth said, then repeated it. "Sir."

"Don't get paranoid, Farnsworth. I'm hearing every word."

"It's not that, sir." He cleared his throat. "Where does a man pee in this place?"

Without opening his eyes, Callender inclined his head toward the opened bedroom door. Farnsworth loped through the room and into the bathroom, hesitated, and then turned the thumb lock. While he was urinating, he noticed a false moustache on the sink, a small bottle of fixative. With the edge of his fingers he opened the medicine cabinet. There was the usual shaving gear, a comb and brush, toothpaste, but also a bottle of liquid makeup and a tube of Aramis Bronzing Gel. He closed the cabinet, flushed the toilet, zipped up his pants, and then studied himself in the mirror, not seeing anything.

He shook Callender awake. "Sir," he said. "There's a personal thing. I didn't enter it anywhere in any of the records." He shrugged his shoulders. "I don't know whether or not this is the time to bother you with it."

"What is it?"

"Your wife. She called maybe six times. The last time she called she sounded a bit tipsy." He spread his hand, rocked it back and forth. "Not drunk exactly but not like she usually sounds."

"What did she want?"

"The sum and substance, sir, was that she was going back to New Orleans and filing for a divorce."

"You're not telling me the whole thing, Farnsworth."

"She said that if you didn't like it . . . well, she said if you didn't like it, to go fuck yourself."

Callender smiled. "If my wife said that, she was drunk. My wife is a lady, Farnsworth. Even under the most trying of circumstances, my wife is usually every inch a lady."

"Somehow, sir, even when she said it, she made it sound like an invitation to a tea party."

"Good observation, Farnsworth. You have just capsuled my marriage into a one-liner."

"I'm sorry, Mr. Callender."

"Don't be sorry. She won't file for a divorce. My wife has been under a great deal of stress. My being in public life has been too much for her to cope with. She lived through it all once and hated it. She is Senator Longchamps' daughter, you know."

"Yes, sir, I did know that. But you would think that because of her father she would understand the pressure of public life."

"Maybe she understands it all too well." The buzzer at the front door sounded. "Never mind. She's a proper Southern lady and in the final analysis, she'll behave the way proper Southern ladies should behave." He jumped up from the sofa, recharged with unknown sources of energy. "Let me get behind that closed door before you let the waiter in."

Farnsworth signed the check with his own name, locked the door again, poured a double shot of Jack Daniel's and a Coke for himself. He rapped on the closed bedroom door. "Bring it in." Callender was stretched out on one of the beds. He took the glass, put it on the night table without tasting it. "It's awkward for me to show emotion, Farnsworth." He took the glass again, held it but still did not drink. "I was brought up in a certain way. My grandfather was the biggest influence in my life. He was an old pirate, a tough, old bird. Maybe my father was just as big an influence. My father is a very gentle man. Weak in many ways." He thought for a moment. "I guess strong in some ways that I don't appreciate. But either way, I was brought up to believe that exposing any chinks in an armor is unmanly, not acceptable in the ethical code of conduct. Children aren't raised like that anymore. My generation is the last of that line. Maintaining an armor is a terrible burden sometimes, exhausting both physically and mentally. My generation is trapped: too old to change and not really old enough to believe that a man's armor is all that important." He put the glass down again, swirling the ice cubes in the glass. "All of this wisdom, Farnsworth, is a way of saying that I understand that this has been difficult for you. You have done a good job of holding down the fort: you haven't gone to pieces under pressure. I am grateful to you." He smiled. "Now that wasn't so hard for me to say, was it?"

Farnsworth shifted from one foot to another, felt a blush of blood in his face, was aware of an intimacy which had never existed between them before. He looked away, sat on the edge of the other bed, hesitated a moment, and then took Callender's bourbon, drank half of it, and laid back on the bed. "I believe in what you're doing, sir. I believe that this country needs bold, decisive action against our enemies. I've been in the State Department for six years. I've seen everyone pussyfoot around problems, not having the guts to meet them head on. I know how much personal sacrifice you have made to do your job. It takes courage and devotion." He looked across to the other bed. "I wish I had your kind of guts."

"There's an excitement that I can't explain to you. I cannot even explain it to myself. There's a physical excitement involved as well as a mental and moral exhilaration. My body feels it and my mind feels it all at once."

"Like fucking when you're in love," Farnsworth said.

Callender sat up, finished the bourbon, and then got off the bed.

Farnsworth started to rise; Callender motioned him back. "Get some shut-eye. You need it. I think it's time for one country boy to communicate with another country boy."

"Won't the White House be able to trace the call?"

"It doesn't matter. When I tell the President what I have to tell him, he will have no alternative but to do things my way." He smiled, straightened up, the weariness gone from his posture. "You're right, Farnsworth, it is like that: it's like fucking when you're in love."

PALM BEACH, FLORIDA

"The President is pissed at you, Lowell. Mighty pissed. He's been cussing and you know that it's not like him to cuss a lot. He was very cantankerous about your disappearance. Lucky I was there to intercept when you called this morning. A man in public trust can't just be wiped off the face of the earth even for three days. A man has to be somewhere."

"I was working."

"Well, you were working in the wrong place then. All hell broke loose in the Caribbean. All kinds of freak accidents were happening to the CIA teams down there. Too many accidents to be accidental. Pendleton's boys got caught with their pants down. Just plain incompetence. The President understands that Pendleton is a new appointee but the CIA has been around a while. The President feels they ought to know their business. He said to me, 'Jud, the only man who can solve our problems down there is Lowell Callender. He put his finger on this trouble almost before the trouble started.' That's what the President said, Lowell; his very words. He instructed me to circumvent the CIA. 'We've got to depend on Lowell,' he tells me. Now how can we depend on Lowell when we can't find him? That's not the way a diplomat behaves."

The young man talking to Callender was Judson Wheeler. His

title was Special Administrative Assistant to the President. In practice he was the can-do and get-done arm of the Chief Executive. He kept a low profile in the White House, was almost unknown to the press, and made no public appearances in an official capacity. But his access to the Oval Office was instant, his electronic communication direct.

They were sitting side-by-side on lawn chairs at the edge of the water. The grass at one time had been velvet-smooth, geometrically manicured. But since the government had inherited this Palm Beach estate in legal procedure, maintenance was minimal. The old, stucco building was crumbling, the red tile roof partially destroyed by storms. The government used it as a retreat for high-level government officials and sometimes for clandestine meetings.

"The President knew," Callender said, "when he gave me this job that I am not a diplomat. He gave me the job because he knew I'm a hard-nosed businessman who knows how to get a job done."

"It don't pay to be hard-nosed with the hand that feeds you." The President's special assistant smiled, ran his hand through his unruly hair. "I keep forgetting that you make your own bread, Lowell." He stretched his legs, concentrated on a fishing boat cutting through the water. "If I had your kind of bread, I wouldn't put up with all this shit. No, sir. I'd get me a yacht like the one out there and live the good life. That's what I'd do for sure."

"You've learned the administration's technique well, Jud. You've even managed to get rural-looking, cracker up your way of speaking. A man could easily mistake you from right off the farm. Nobody would guess that you're fourth generation Atlanta gentry, third generation Harvard Law School. Your pappy must be mighty confused about the change in his youngun'. How does he explain you to his law partners and his friends at the Piedmont Driving Club?"

"A man is entitled to return to his roots, Lowell." He clasped his hands behind his head, leaned back in the chair. "A man does what he has to do to make out in this world. He plays the other man's game until it's his turn to call the shots. Then the others play his game." He looked over at Callender, used his boyish grin. "I learned that at my pappy's knee." He added, "Right under that big walnut desk on that antique Persian rug." His face became serious. He sat up straight. "Where did you learn your philosophy of survival, Lowell? Whose knee? Rasputin? Metternich? Robespierre? Or maybe it was Aaron Burr." He thought for a moment. "More likely it was John Dillinger."

"Come to the point, Jud."

"The point is that you have the President over a barrel. At the moment he has no alternatives. We've made so damn many laws and regulations that the CIA is tied up in them, can't move fast enough in an emergency situation like this. After what's happened in the last few days, the President now acknowledges that you were correct in your appraisal. You know what he said, Lowell? He said, 'It would appear as though that son of a bitch Callender wrote the script.' The President is a very perceptive man, don't you think?"

"You're telling me that he has agreed to my terms?"

Reluctantly he nodded. "You've got the whole damned Army, Navy, Coast Guard, and Marine Corps or any part thereof available if and when you need them. He did mention that I should apologize for his taking the liberty of excluding nuclear weapons. You can manage without nuclear weapons, can't you, Lowell?"

"Whom do I contact to push the buttons when I need action?"

"Me, Lowell. You just mention to me what you need. This little boy has all those colored telephones at easy access. You just tell me and all the hell you want will break loose."

Callender stood up, picked up his jacket from the lawn. "I'll be in touch, Jud, and tell the President that I am grateful for his confidence in what I am doing and for his trust in me."

"He doesn't trust you one little inch, Lowell. I thought I made that clear. He's forced to accept your terms. He understands pragmatically that under these very specific conditions, you are probably the most qualified mentality in the country to avert what could be a world disaster. I agree with him. No one knows that fourth world out there better than you do. And no one can make things happen out there like you can. Your credentials are overwhelming. They're frightening but overwhelming nonetheless." Although the words stopped, his voice seemed to be in the middle of a sentence.

"Finish it, Jud. Say it all."

"I was just going to mention that when this is all over, no matter how it comes out, the President is going to have your ass, Lowell. And if he doesn't, I will."

Callender picked up his slim attaché case.

"There's a hook, Mr. Secretary. The President of the United

States has attached a condition to his acceptance of your terms."

"I told you on the phone that my terms were not negotiable. No ringers. No concessions."

"You get what you want. You've even got more than you wanted. You get company, someone to talk to, and someone to help you."

"One of my conditions was no surveillance."

"Now you know, Lowell, that we can agree to that with one side of our mouth and put some very special operatives on your tail by talking out of the other side of our mouth to the Secret Service. You'd probably never know. If the operatives were good enough, you'd never know." He twisted his mouth to one side. "We agree to no surveillance." He straightened his mouth. "This friend who's going to accompany you from now on is not there to spy on you. He's going to be there to implement you, Lowell. He's going to help you in any way he can."

Callender's decision and opportunistic acquiescence was instant. "Who is it?"

"Let's say his name is John Fowler. That's a reasonable sounding name."

"What are his qualifications?"

"Judgment. Reason. Loyalty. Super backgammon player." He smiled. "What more do you need, Lowell?"

"Can he handle a gun?"

"Shoot the pecker off a mosquito."

"Good enough. Where do I pick him up?"

"You already picked him up, Lowell. You just didn't notice."

"You?"

"Little old me. The country boy." He stood up. You ready to get moving? I am."

Callender hesitated, assessed this development. As though he was reading his mind, Wheeler said, "I reckon it this way, Lowell: We eliminate the middleman by having me by your side. Everything will go lickety-split. No red tape." He touched Callender's shoulder, applied slight pressure to move him forward. "You're going to have to be a big-daddy to me, make certain that I don't get lost. If you lose me, there's no way you can get to the President. It's like the buddy system: we're looking out for each other. Maybe we ought to hold hands."

"Like Cain and Abel?"

GREAT GUANA CAY, EXHUMA CHAIN, BAHAMAS, WEST INDIES

Because of his mangled fingertips, Hotdog Schwartz handled the card awkwardly. "Gin," he said, spreading his cards on the table. "With the kind of luck I'm playing on tonight, I ought to go right to Vegas, play my hot streak. I should be at a crap table, not fucking around with nickel and dime rummy."

Aldo Rinaldi counted his hand automatically, wondered why Guido was not back from Andros yet. Did it mean trouble? The man in the plane yesterday, the model from Andros, appeared to be what Roger said he was: a high-priced hustler. Rinaldi had checked the intelligence on the magazine group photographing on the island. There was nothing circumspect. But he had sent Guido back with the man there to double-check, to make sure that he was not an agent. The young Italian had an instinct for danger. He would trust Guido's gut reaction. They were too close now to take any chances of an accidental foul-up. "Sixteen plus gin." He looked over the score. "Does that put you out on the second game?"

Schwartz nodded, shuffled the cards. "And you're on a blitz on the third game."

"Do you think we ought to go through procedure again, take it step by step?"

"I know it like the back of my hand." He began dealing. "I don't even need those two guys that you're sending with me. I've rehearsed this so many times in my mind, I could recover that money blindfolded. Besides, I didn't bury the stuff that deep. I don't know what all the shit about the shovels is. If I had my fingernails back, I could scratch it up with my bare hands."

"It's been seventeen years. There could have been a ground shift, shrubbery grown over it. You might not find it the first time."

"I know the tree. I marked it good. I'll find it."

Rinaldi arranged his cards, cocked his ear as he thought he heard the sound of an airplane in the distance. He looked out the window. There was still enough light for the plane to land. In fifteen minutes it would be too late. Holding his cards, he went out onto the pool deck. The tip of the sun appeared over the water at the horizon. There was a horizontal band of pink-orange light. Then darkness above it. He looked away, closed his eyes, strained his audio senses. The sound was definitely a plane. He searched the sky until he saw the speck of moving light coming closer and he could identify it. He went back into the room, sat at the card table. "We'll have to make this the last hand, Hotdog. The plane is coming in."

"That Guido is something else, isn't he? Victor sure seems high on him. I don't figure how Victor can trust him. That kid fucks anything that moves. In my day, I would never have trusted a guy like that. Fucking comes first with him. Business second."

"Victor knows what he's doing."

"Maybe. But I remember what it was like before Victor took over. Those were real men. Smart. Tough. None of this Switzerland shit. There was this island off Miami, built like a fucking fortress. Poker games and broads. The times we used to have. But business came first." He rocked his head back and forth, smiled at his own memories. "I knock on four."

Rinaldi turned over his cards, looked out the window. The plane was low over the water, coming in slowly. Schwartz had counted the exposed hand. "You're blitzed on the third game."

"Add it up."

Schwartz moved his head up and down the columns, calculated silently. "Sixty-eight dollars."

From his wallet he started to count out United States currency, put it back, and paid off Schwartz in Canadian dollars. "Why can't you pay me in U.S. dollars?" Rinaldi shook his head. "This is crazy. Why do I have to come in from Montreal anyway? Why can't I come in with the other guys?"

"I've explained it. The cover is very important. You need the disguise. People in Havana may still remember you. Besides, you have to go in first, get set up."

"I don't look like no agricultural expert. Neither do those mugs going with me. We're going to stick out like sore thumbs on the tour of hicks." He took the Canadian passport from his pocket, placed the money in it, looked at his picture. "Who's going to believe that a face like that could be named Paul Prideux?"

"You worry too much, Hotdog. This has all been planned very carefully. We've planned it for a long time."

Schwartz rubbed his fingers against the palms of his hand. "Not as long as I've been planning it. I've been planning it since the day they did this to me. I always promised myself that I'd get the money back and kill that bastard Castro." He looked at his picture again in the passport. "Do you know who Jack Ruby was?"

"No," Rinaldi answered.

"He was a little guy . . . a two-bit hoodlum like me. But big balls. The little guy is dying of cancer. He knows it. But he wants to do one big thing before he dies. One thing that shows he's a big-ball guy, not a punk."

"I remember now."

"I'm going to be like that. I don't have cancer or anything. God forbid. But everybody has always laughed at me, made fun of me. I'm a two-bit punk. I know that. The money don't mean nothing to me. I'll take my cut. Those bodyguards you got for me can stand right there while I count it out. But that's not the numero-uno reason that I'm in on this. After I get the dough, that's when the punk is going big-time. I'm going to be like Jack Ruby, do the one big thing in my life."

Rinaldi knew the script, knew that Hotdog Schwartz was not destined for his moment of greatness. Whether the money was recovered or not, the mercenaries would be Schwartz's assassins. They would substitute a U.S. passport for the Canadian one, stuff it with the forged documents, starting a trail which would eventually link Julius Schwartz to the CIA. The little, scarred body would be left under the tree for Castro's police to find, the evidence to incriminate the United States, put a stop to the normalization process between the two countries. He put his arm around Schwartz's shoulders, hugged him. "Don't be a hero, Hotdog. Take care of yourself. I want to get you back alive. I want to win my sixty-eight dollars back."

"I'll pay you off in Canadian dollars. See how you like it."

The refrigerator door was open. Guido had a can of beer in one hand, an apple and a piece of cheese in his other. He hit the door with his hip to close it.

"Well?"

"Nothing. Like Roger said, there's nothing on Andros but these crazy people, stoned out of their minds. Lots of puss, lots of action."

"What about the boat that blew up? Did you find out anything?"

"Nothing. It was an accident like Roger said."

"No one takes into account the fact that Castro may have agents looking for us . . . looking for something. It all seems to be going too smoothly."

"You guys do the thinking, not me. I do the fucking and the killing." He sat down at the center table, took his leather bag off the other chair, felt the weight of the gun, the outline of the cartridge with the recording of the Laurie Golding tape. "You worry too much, Aldo. Sit down and relax."

"Victor didn't tell me until the night before last that I was going to be directly involved in the actual military operation."

"I'm going to be like Victor some day. Smart like that."

"I believe you."

"You really haven't got the balls for it, have you, Aldo? You're used to planning everything and letting someone else get blood on his hands. This is too close for comfort, isn't it?" Rinaldi did not answer. "When are you going to tell me that it's my job to finish off Roger?"

"I wish that there was another way."

"How do I do it?" He bit into the apple. "When do I do it?"

"At the last minute. After the money is recovered. The scuba team will bring in two extra wet suits and equipment. After you get the steel boxes and pass them on to the underwater team, make sure that Roger puts on his equipment." Rinaldi put his hands over his eyes, rubbed them. "Do it then. Leave him on shore. Before we leave Port-au-Prince, I will give you some documents. They must be found on his body. You understand?"

Guido nodded. "Is your wife in on this?"

"No."

"She doesn't know that any of this is happening?"

"No."

"She going to get her share?"

He nodded. "She won't know where it came from."

"She can read, can't she? She's going to read in the newspapers that her son was killed on the Cuban coast. That lady is no dummy. She'll know."

"Perhaps."

"She'll want in on it. I wonder how Victor has that one figured? He's thought of it, all right. He thinks of everything. I wonder how he's going to handle her when she wants a big cut of the take."

"I'll handle it."

"How are you going to handle it when she accuses you of being in on the murder of her son?"

"She'll never know it."

"What if I tell her?"

Aldo smiled. "I'll kill you first."

"Big talk, Aldo. You don't have the stomach for it. You know what's going to really happen? You and me are going to wind up being partners . . . business partners. That's more your style. Making a deal is a more aristocratic way of doing things. Bloody hands are for peasants."

"Everyone has a hero. Hotdog wants to be Jack Ruby and you want to be Victor Castle."

"Who's Jack Ruby?"

"A two-bit hoodlum."

"Why the hell does Hotdog want to be like a two-bit hoodlum?"

"Someday, if you're alive that long, you will understand."

There was a slight, cool undercurrent in the night air. Roger Ramirez did not turn around when he heard the footsteps behind him or the sound of a chair being dragged across the roof deck. They sat side-by-side without speaking until Aldo pointed up to the sky. "A shooting star. Did you see it?"

"You're with them . . . against me."

"You know that I have no choice."

"If you did have a choice, what would you do?"

"It's dreaming, Roger. Thirty years ago, I had a choice. Not now. Not anymore."

"Pretend, Aldo. If you had a choice right now, what would you do, would you still be against me?"

"No."

"Why not? I am not your son. I am Carlos Ramirez's son, not yours. Why would you not be against me?"

He thought before he answered. "I love your mother very much."

Ramirez jumped at the words. "You love my mother, not me."

"Let me finish, Roger. Let me, this one time, say what is in my heart." He waited. Ramirez was silent. "I love your mother very much but I know her weaknesses. I know the things about her which are not to love. Your mother should have been born a princess. If she had been born a princess she would not have had to fight and scratch and dig and work to be what she is today. She needed to love herself more than anything in the world to become what she is. She loves herself more than you . . . more than me."

"That's not an excuse."

"No, it is not an excuse. It is an explanation."

"It does not explain why, if *you* had a choice, you would not be against me."

"I was brought up in a house of much love. I know what it is for a son to love his mother, to love his father, and to have that love returned. When I married your mother, that love was cut off by my parents; not given to me anymore because they did not approve of divorce or the woman I married. To this day, they do not acknowledge your mother as my wife. They hardly acknowledge me as their son."

"I don't want to hear about your mother or my mother. I want you to answer my question . . . if you had a choice, would you help me?"

"Have we stopped pretending? Are you telling me that I do have a choice?"

"Yes."

"How?"

"Can I trust you?" He faced him directly, waited for an answer.

Rinaldi thought for a moment. "No," he said, "I am too deeply committed. I don't trust myself. In the end, I will take the easy way, the safe way."

"I need your help."

"Don't ask me to pit myself against Victor Castle."

"There is enough in those steel boxes so that you'll never need Victor Castle again."

"He won't let me live."

"I can protect you. I have a plan."

Rinaldi jumped up, put his hands on his ears. "I don't want to hear anything. Please. Don't tell me anything." He lowered his hands. "I told you not to trust me. Don't trust anyone here."

"I trust you, Aldo. You're the only one. I trust you more than you trust yourself." He walked to the railing, looked down to the deck below, turning his back to his stepfather. He heard no sound behind him. He did not know if Aldo was still there or if he had gone.

The seed was planted.

In no position could Rinaldi fall asleep. He lay with his eyes open, his lips immobile, praying to a God who no longer accepted him and in the language of a church which had excommunicated him. It had been a shock when Victor Castle had told him that he was to go to Great Guana Cay, take over the direction of the final stages of preparation, and to participate directly in the operation. "This operation may be worth eighty million. Big chip stuff," Castle had explained, "and the mission for the Russians is touchy. It needs your hand, Aldo. I need someone on the spot who I can trust completely, make on-the-spot decisions. You are the only one who knows the total plan for the invasion." No one ever argued with Castle or with his instincts for survival.

There were soft, whispered words below his window. He got out of bed, checked his watch on the night table, walked to the window. The mercenaries stood a twenty-four hour guard on the cay. It was two o'clock in the morning. A new shift was coming on duty. The four men were together on the pool deck. Rinaldi strained to hear their conversation but their voices were low and their language an idiomatic soldier's shorthand which he could not understand. Three of the men laughed at the other man. None of their movements was intense or frantic. No trouble. It was a peaceful night, a bright half-moon, the constellations of stars clearly defined in the night.

Yesterday, when he had come back to Great Guana and seen the holocaust the soldiers had made of the house, he had fought with the leader, was adamant in insisting that the entire force be put on cleanup detail to restore the villa and grounds to some semblance of order. He personally had cleaned up his wife's room which Roger was using, changing the linens on the bed and washing down the marble walls of the bathroom with a strong disinfectant. It had been necessary, and again he had fought eye-to-eye with the mercenary commander, to rebillet the three men who were bunked in his own bedroom. He had gone through the house carrying back the furniture which had been dispersed in other areas until his own room was in its original condition, precise and uncluttered.

His white silk pajamas were placed neatly on the bench at the foot of the bed. He put them on now, slipped his feet into the leather, Gucci encrested mules, put on a monogrammed, white silk robe, and went downstairs.

There were two men on duty in the command post. One was stationed at the communication center, the other was half-asleep, his feet up on the makeshift desk. Both men straightened up when Rinaldi came in: neither of them spoke to him. "Are you in contact with the yacht?"

"On schedule." The radio operator moved the headset away from his ears. "It's a good night for it. They're running clean, should be here at daybreak, anchored in the harbor by six-fifteen or six-thirty."

"How many miles is it from Nassau?"

"Seventy-five statute, give or take. Sixty-three nautical."

Rinaldi turned, studied the huge tactical map, put his finger on Nassau. "How many knots can she make?"

"Full power . . . maybe eighteen or nineteen. But they're not running her full. It's supposed to look like a moonlight cruise."

Since he had been back at Guana, Rinaldi had memorized the charts, knew the displacement of all the units, the timetable of action by rote. He had a new respect for Roger Ramirez, for the military organization his twisted mind had created. Although the professionals had refined it and supplemented it under Castle's direction for an expanded two-prong operation, the basic concept was Roger's plan: clever, imaginative, and battle-sound. If there had not been a Castro, Rinaldi was thinking, had Carlos Ramirez lived to pass on a heritage, Roger would probably have become a military leader in Cuba. Actually, properly directed and sufficiently motivated, he could have been a successor to Batista. Rinaldi's finger, as his thoughts were wandering, traced the line from Nassau to Great Guana and then beyond it, southeast to the Caicos Island, his finger stopping at Providenciales where the mark of the brigantine was indicated on the charts with the symbol of a square rig drawn in red. There was a dotted line from Caicos through the Windward Passage, passing the tip of Haiti, running between Jamaica and Santiago de Cuba, stopping at an X marked on the Great Cayman Island and then continuing through the Caribbean with another X indicated at Cozumel and continuing through the Yucatan channel, turning back east and finally stopping at Havana. "What about the brigantine? Are you in contact?" It was the one phase of the operation which worried Rinaldi. The brigantine was not solely dependent on the wind—auxiliary engines had been installed. But it was still a risk factor. The operation could be accomplished without the sailing vessel but it was the decoy action which would give the raid the necessary cover and create the military diversion.

"She made good time last night," the radio operator said. The storm helped her, put her a little ahead of schedule."

"Does she report any surveillance?"

"A couple of Cuban MIGs out of Santiago, diving to take a close look. Nothing after that."

"Nothing out of Guantanamo?"

"Nothing. But that doesn't mean anything. The U.S. base looks like it's doing nothing, but they have some sophisticated equipment. They keep a low profile, but they have it thick behind the ears."

"Have you contacted Panama? Have there been any inquiries checking the brigantine's registry?"

The man at the other desk spoke for the first time. "Harry handles that."

Rinaldi walked over to the desk. "Please wake up Harry and ask him."

The man hesitated, started to get up, leaned back, saw the set of Rinaldi's jaw and the intent in his eyes, and finally stood up, walked slowly from the command post.

Rinaldi sat where the man had been sitting, checked the count-down schedule taped to the top of the desk. The timetable began with the arrival of the yacht, *Valkyrie,* from Nassau at seven in the morning. He read it again, step by step, testing the fallibility of the progression. But his attention kept wandering. He was wondering about Roger, no longer underestimating the brilliance-quotient of his cunning mentality. He wondered if he had allowed Roger to trust him, what would Roger have told him. His mentality was capable of inserting fail-safes into the plan. He was capable of protecting himself. He looked at his hands. Where did his loyalties lie?

THE ISLAND OF COZUMEL

It was eleven o'clock at night. Hernando grabbed the long handle of the paella pan with both hands, feeling the heat of the skillet through the asbestos pot holder, wondering, as he breathed in the aroma of the steaming pan, if he had added too much pepper sauce. He carried it from the open oven through the tiny waterfront restaurant and into the courtyard where there were three groups finishing dinner, plus the two men who had come in late. They were sitting in the isolated plaza, elevated around the old Mexican well he had found on the island years ago, when he had first built the restaurant. It was a table which, during the tourist season, he reserved for honeymooners or for his regular customers. The view of the Caribbean from the plaza was breathtaking. He would sit there himself during the early hours, before the customers arrived, eat his own dinner, never tiring of the vista, always fascinated by the ever-changing colors and the motion of the sea. He signaled to one of the white-coated busboys who quickly wheeled a cart to the table. Hernando set down the pan, stood back, and waited for his work to be admired.

The shorter, dark-haired, moustached man stood up to look at the paella, leaned over it to smell it. In Spanish he said, "You never loose your touch, do you, Hernando? Beautiful. It looks like a painting and smells like a poem." As he sat down, he spoke in unaccented English to the man next to him. "I have been eating Hernando's paella since I was a little boy. Since we were both little boys, right, Hernando?" The man nodded, began arranging the two dinner plates. "His father had the best restaurant in Havana. My grandfather used to take me there. It was a long time ago. In the good old days, right, Hernando?"

The owner set the food in front of each man, pulled up the empty chair, sat opposite them, his back to the water. "These days are better days than the old days." He nodded at the plates. "Eat before it gets cold." He turned around to look behind him. "As long as I can watch the water, I do not miss the old days." He explained in English to the taller man, "When we first had to leave Havana, my father came to Mexico City to open his restaurant there." He clutched his throat. "A man born by the sea cannot breathe in Mexico City. The air is thin and polluted with all the stinking Mexicans and their stinking machines." He stopped, watched the men's faces as they ate the first bite of the paella. Too much pepper for the gringo: perfect for his old friend. "So, when I am twenty years old, I come here. This island is nothing then. Maybe only two thousand people on the whole island. Not more. I open this place by myself. I fuck Indian girls, cook and live in the clean air and the clean water. It is enough for a man."

Two of the tables at the end of the courtyard had paid their checks, were getting up to leave. Hernando went over to them.

"Lowell," Wheeler said, "you've got to have a cast-iron stomach to eat this stuff. It's hot."

"Drink your beer, Jud. It goes down easier with beer."

"How come you can't come right out and ask him what the hell is going on here? You're the one who keeps talking about urgency and not playing games. Why do we have to pussyfoot around with this man? Why can't we come right to the point?"

Callender noticed that in the party of three men leaving, one of them had a withered arm, a patch over one eye. The other two he did not recognize.

"Hernando knows why I'm here. He knows what information I want." He removed a small chicken bone from his mouth, put it on the side of his plate. "He also knows when it is safe to talk and when it is not."

"I can't get used to you looking the way you do." He smiled. "It's kind of like Superman and Clark Kent: your whole personality changes. You look like a tough bastard now. It don't come as such a surprise that you're a mean son of a bitch."

The party of three had gotten into a Jeep, headed north toward the harbor and the Caribe Cozumel, the hotel at the far end of the island. Hernando was back at the table, filled Callender's plate again, shook his head at Wheeler's still half-full plate.

"Pretty good crowd for this time of year," Callender said. "Funny time of year for tourists."

"More and more they come all year round. Where else is there water like this? It's maybe the best scuba diving water in the world. Those three men are businessmen looking for property. Condominiums. Everybody is crazy with condominiums."

"It's good for business, Hernando."

He shook his head, shrugged his shoulders. "How much business do I need to be happy? Very little."

"Are they Mexican investors?"

"Two of them are. They were here once before. Now, they've brought the other man with the bad arm and one eye. He's not Mexican. He's probably got all the money and needs Mexican partners."

"What else is happening lately?"

Hernando automatically began to answer in Spanish. Callender interrupted him. "Talk in English. My friend does not understand Spanish."

"There was a bad accident the other day." He rolled his head sadly. "Very bad. Not good public relations for Cozumel."

"What happened?"

"At the Hotel El Presidente there is this group of young people . . . maybe fifteen or sixteen people. Three sharks come from nowhere . . . like someone had set them loose. Tragic."

"I read about that," Callender said. "Did the group clear out?"

"Young people. What do they know about fear? They're still there, still scuba diving every day. Fortunately, no more sharks. You stay at the El Presidente, no?" Callender nodded. "You'll see them tomorrow. They line up on the pier early, waiting for the Cozumel boats."

"Any of them come in here to eat?"

"Not much. It's a packaged tour . . . meals included at the El Presidente. One girl comes sometimes with a local man. Indian man. Pretty girl. Long blonde hair. The Indian has plenty of money. I don't know from where, but he's got plenty of money. He fucks her, I think. What does it mean anymore? I would like to fuck her but she laughs at me." He shrugged his shoulders. "American girls . . . who understands them? Now, the French girls are different."

"French girls?"

"At the Caribe Cozumel. Plenty of French girls. They're making an underwater film there."

"Who?"

"Who knows who. Some film company. All day they rehearse underwater. They stay to themselves, don't mix with the natives or the other tourists. No one talks Spanish or English. Only French."

"What kind of film, do you know?"

"It must be about a war under water. They have all kinds of underwater weapons. They could kill a whale with all their guns."

"The French are crazy about water films," Callender said. "Jacques Cousteau is a national hero. Are you sure that it isn't some kind of scientific film? What kind of equipment do they have?"

"An old submarine," Hernando said. "Maybe from World War Two. A little one."

"Anything else?"

"Not much. You'd think they would have more camera equipment. I've seen underwater photography being shot here before. You never saw that much equipment. But not these people. Very little photographic equipment." Hernando noticed the last couple getting up to leave. He went over to their table.

Wheeler asked, "What does it mean?"

"Pieces of a puzzle." He shrugged his shoulders. "I don't know yet. None of it is fitting together."

"This French film outfit . . . they could do it, couldn't they?"

Callender nodded. "Part of it anyway. When we get back to the hotel, we'll check it out, see what the CIA has on the group."

"How do we do that?"

"The scuba tour at the El Presidente," Callender explained. "CIA."

"Son of a bitch," Wheeler said.

At one thirty in the morning, they were still sitting on the pier behind the El Presidente, their shoes off, their bare feet in the warm, gentle water. "Look down there, Lowell. You can see fish." Glittery reflections moved under the surface. "You sure don't get much sleep in this job, do you? I thought we kept rough hours in the White House . . . not like this."

"Go to bed. I'm not even sure that Hernando was able to contact the girl. She may not even know I'm here."

"You just going to wait here all night?"

Callender nodded.

"There's fifteen or sixteen of them, or were before the sharks hit. Let's wake up one of them, ask someone else what's going on."

"My contact is only with this one girl. No one else will talk to us or even acknowledge why they're here. Go to bed. If anything happens, I'll wake you. Either way, we have to be out of here at daybreak."

Wheeler stood up, stretched his arms over his head. "No tricks?"

"If I had wanted to shake you, Jud, I could have lost you before we took off from Palm Beach. But like you said, I need you. I need your finger to push the button when I say push. You've done a clever job setting this up. You've made yourself almost indispensable to me."

"It would be a terrible thing, Lowell, if you and me began to have mutual respect for each other. You can't tell where a thing like that could end up. We may even get to like each other." He touched Callender's shoulder. "I'm easy to wake up. You just have to blow in my ear."

At two thirty in the morning, when he thought it was safe, Callender began phoning from the lobby of the hotel. On the third call,

he reached the man he tried first in Bogota and then in Panama City.
"I've found him," Callender said, without identifying himself.

"San Marco?"

"Yes."

"Where?"

He explained he had seen San Marco at the restaurant in Cozumel. "I need him alive."

"But you said before that . . ."

"Never mind what I said before. He is worth more money to me alive than dead. Do you understand?"

"Very clearly."

"Do not lose him. Watch him every moment. When the time comes, I will tell you and then he must be taken instantly."

"If he returns to Cuba, it will not be so simple."

"You told me before that you can handle things inside Cuba."

"It is not simple. It can be handled but it is not simple."

"I will depend on you."

"The other thing . . . it went well, did it not?"

"You killed six people unnecessarily."

"Killing is not always an exact science."

"You have people here in Cozumel who can act quickly?"

"It is not to worry, Luis," he said.

It was four-fifteen in the morning when the girl finally appeared. Callender had moved off the pier by then, set up a sun chaise under a cluster of palms, and lay in the darkness.

"That Indian," she said, "fucks like it's going out of style."

"Make it fast." He looked at his watch.

"Those sharks were no accident. Somehow somebody let them loose, straight at us."

"Old news," Callender said. "What about the French filming up at the Caribe Cozumel?"

"That's where the Indian comes in. He's a technical consultant on underwater stuff. You should see that bastard operate underwater . . . I don't mean fuck, I mean swim. He probably fucks under water, too. He's done this before, acted as a consultant to underwater films. He says this group are real pros. They don't need stand-ins or stunt men to do their scuba stuff. As far as I can tell, they're doing a kind of submarine *Star Wars*. Underwater in outer space. I can hardly wait for the movie to be released."

"Who's in charge?"

"I can't get close enough to find out. They have two toughs keeping the tourists away. The Indian doesn't talk French. They all communicate with him in a kind of sign language so he really only knows what he sees, not what they tell him or say to each other."

"Any sign of their winding up, moving out?"

"I can't tell. The hotel says that they're booked for the whole month."

"What do they do exactly?"

"As far as I can tell, the shots they're doing here involved a unisex army defending something from someone. I cannot tell whether they are fighting fish or people or little gnomes from Mars."

Callender stood up. "Okay. If anything breaks, if they show any sign of closing up or moving out, let me know instantly."

"The same number?"

"Yes. If I'm not there, give the information to Farnsworth."

"Is he the one I talked to the last time?" Callender nodded. "He must think I'm hysterical. I was in shock after the accident."

"It wasn't an accident. Remember that and the next time you won't go into shock."

"What about my CIA contact here? Do I give him any information?"

"Does he know why you're fucking the Indian?"

"No."

"Does he suspect the French film company?"

"I'm not sure. The guy is beautiful but he doesn't talk much. He asks me a few questions and that's it."

"Don't tell him anything important. Tell me or Farnsworth first, then wait for instructions."

At five-ten in the morning, Callender shook Wheeler awake. The man bolted up, looked at Callender. "You scared me, man. I told you to blow in my ear." He saw that the bed beside him had not been slept in. "Did you get any sleep at all?"

"No."

"Did she show?"

"Yes."

"What did you learn?"

"Not much more. Nothing definite. It still looks possible. Part of the invasion could come from under water. It's good commando tactics. Maybe air overhead used as a distraction from the main thrust coming from underwater."

"What are you going to do?"

"At the moment, nothing. But you're going to do something right now."

"What's that?" Wheeler had sat up on the edge of the bed, leaning forward like an anxious boy.

"First off, Jud, I was brought up never to trust a man who sleeps in his socks and shorts."

Wheeler looked down at himself. "Shit, Lowell, give me a chance to shape up. I'm new at this. And stop making fun of me and tell me what you want me to do."

"Hot-line to the Chief of Naval Intelligence. I want him and whoever is in charge of their porpoise training program at my house in New Orleans in three hours."

"Porpoise training?"

"The Navy has been training porpoises as man killers as well as other underwater war functions."

"No shit."

"Jud, I wish you'd put your clothes on." He smiled. "Sitting there like that you look just as human and as vulnerable as anyone else. Put on your pin-stripe armor. We have to get going." Callender took off his jacket. "Call Naval Intelligence. They'll give you the run around. They don't want to admit to the porpoise training program. Don't let them stall you."

"I'm the honcho headcracker in this administration, Lowell. I would reckon that my reputation precedes me."

"While you're cracking heads, try the submarine base on Andros Island."

"What submarine base? Where the hell is Andros Island?"

"Talk to your friends in the Navy. Get the in-charge man at Andros to my place by noon."

"You sure you don't need an aircraft carrier or two?"

"I might, before this is over. You'd better get on the phone. I'm going to take a shower."

Before he could get to the bathroom, Wheeler called to him. "Lowell?"

"What?"

"Where do you live in New Orleans?"

"Belle Rivage Plantation. Anyone in New Orleans will know where it is."

Wheeler had picked up the phone but called to Callender again. "Now what?"

"I'm not really such a bad guy. Neither are you. We're a lot alike. People don't understand us. We know what it takes to get a job done and we do it."

Callender did not answer. Properly motivated, properly trained, Wheeler could become an effective arm for him in the future.

SAN ANDROS BEACH CLUB, ANDROS ISLAND, BAHAMAS, WEST INDIES

Edgerton waited until midnight. The new crew had been late arriving on Andros, summer storms delaying them in Miami. There was a photographer, a middle-aged man who had an upset stomach from the bumpy flight, an assistant about the same age as the photographer, and a young black girl who functioned as a go-for. As soon as they arrived, Edgerton introduced himself, kept himself visible all evening. Key West had to know about the explosion of the *Playgirl* catamaran. One of these people had to be a replacement agent. After dinner, all three of them had gone to bed. Edgerton waited in his room but no contact was made.

Before he went into the office to try Callender's number again, he looked in the bar. It was jammed with townspeople, dancing and drinking. Monica was at a table with three natives, dazzlingly white among the shining blacks. She was laughing and talking. While Edgerton watched, she took one of the men's hands, dragged him to the dance floor. The jukebox was playing "Chattanooga Choo-Choo" to a disco beat. Edgerton started in, decided not to, went to place his call.

This time there was an answer: not Callender's voice.

Edgerton did not respond to the hello, was aware that he was breathing deeply, the sound of the breathing being transmitted to Washington.

"Don't hang up," the voice said. "Mr. Callender is not here but I'm taking his calls. This is Farnsworth, his assistant."

Time was desperate. Edgerton took the risk. "Name a fish."

"BARRACUDA."

"Another."

"STINGRAY."

"Another."

"YELLOWJACK."

"Mayday," Edgerton said.

"Stay there. Is that clear? Acknowledge."

"Mayday."

"Stay put."

Edgerton hung up, repeated the distress out loud. "Mayday."

1978
AUGUST

11

FRIDAY

BELLE RIVAGE PLANTATION, NEW ORLEANS, LOUISIANA

Wheeler asked, "How much does your wife know, Lowell?"

"My wife is a senator's daughter. She was brought up on politics and government services."

"What's that supposed to explain?"

"She knows enough not to ask questions and to forget what she overhears."

"Does she know that you're sometimes this other man, this Luis Kunz?"

Callender shook his head.

The chauffeured Buick turned off the expressway, followed the clover leaf onto the westbound highway. They passed a large shopping center, Belle Rivage Mall. Wheeler turned back to look at the sign. "That's the same name as your place." Ahead was a tall building, a large sign identifying it as the Belle Rivage Tower. "Did all this land used to belong to your folks?"

"Still does," Callender said. "We've developed some of the land around the plantation."

"How much you got left to live on?"

"Must be down to eighteen hundred acres."

Wheeler smiled. "A man can hardly get by on that little bit, can he?"

"We manage."

"You got kids?"

Callender nodded. "Two. A boy and a girl. They're both away at school."

"It must be mighty lonely for your wife. Living alone most of the time on those eighteen hundred acres."

"She manages."

"It sure was a shocker about that televison lady, Laurie Golding, wasn't it? The scuttlebutt around the White House is that you two were close friends."

"I read about the murder. Do the District police have any leads?"

"They've got a list a mile long of people who wanted to get rid of her. She kept a vault full of tapes. They were all stolen. Seems like every guy with a zipper on his fly is a nervous wreck. That Nixon tapeworm syndrome can be mighty contagious once it gets lodged somewhere. Lots of the boys have a bad case of nerves." He grabbed the side strap, pulled himself up slightly, moved closer to the window. "You nervous, Lowell?"

"We both have zippers on our flies, Jud."

"That's the truth. It's one thing I learned in this job. There's not a man in this world, I don't care how high and mighty, who hasn't had his zipper down at the wrong time or his hand in the till. Not a living one of us."

They turned off on a gravel road lined on both sides with scraggly grassland. A mile ahead there was a wall of green trees grown high and thick behind a brick wall. A small, polished, brass sign shined on one of the gateposts. Belle Rivage. The chauffeur took a remote device from the glove compartment, pressed it, and waited as the iron gates swung open, then drove through. The road surface changed to old paving bricks set in a herringbone pattern, edged with a triple, straight-stacked border on each side. Spanish moss hung draped between the huge gnarled trees, filtering out the sunlight.

"Nothing like this left in Atlanta," Wheeler said. "Everything's been subdivided, broken up."

"Portman's paradise," Callender said.

"That's the truth. Everything is round and tall, made out of glass and has a big hole in the middle of it. Progress, Lowell. It's hard for a man to feel his roots anymore. Not like this. A man can feel his roots in a place like this, know damn well what being a Southerner is all about."

They drove the remaining two miles to the house in silence.

There were periodic openings between the trees, glimpses of long lawns, gazebos on high points of slopes, a white, fenced corral, and a stable which was a miniature replica of the main house. Wheeler looked from side to side, sometimes turning all the way around to see out the back window.

Callender leaned forward toward the driver. "Take the cutoff road, Bill. I want to go in through the side entrance."

Wheeler touched the armrest between them, rubbed the upholstery. "It's been a long time since I've been in the backseat of a Buick. A man has to be mighty rich to drive around in the backseat of a Buick. Folks have to know that a man can afford a fleet of Cadillacs and a couple of Rolls-Royces before he can be seen riding around in the backseat of a Buick."

"You're nervous, aren't you, Jud?"

He hesitated. "Some," he said. "You're right. I don't usually rattle on like this."

"Career admirals are just like other people. Their heads crack, too."

"You've got a lot of cool, Lowell. I admire that."

Dense shrubbery screened the side entrance from the front of the house. There was a flagstone path to the pillared portico surrounding the brick building and a pair of insignificant looking doors leading into the house.

The cold air in the side entrance hall was not manufactured. It was held there by the quality of the ancient construction; thick walls and high ceilings, whirling fans circulating the air. Callender held Wheeler back, put his index finger to his lips to indicate silence. He opened a polished mahogany door to his right, motioned for Wheeler to precede him. The room was dark, the windows shuttered against the hot day. Callender pressed the double-button light switch. Dim lamps went on, inadequate to fully illuminate the room. The overhead fan made a grinding sound as the blades began to rotate slowly. Callender pulled a long, needlepoint bell cord suspended on the wall next to the fireplace.

"How come you don't just drive up in front, walk through your own front doors, and holler that the lord and master is home?"

"The servants know I'm here." He looked at his watch, back to Wheeler. "Sit down, Jud. We may have a long wait."

"I told them to be here by noon at the latest. Those guys have every kind of jet at their beck and call. They ought to be here pretty soon."

A black man in a white coat came silently into the room, smiled at Callender. "Welcome home, Mr. Lowell."

"Thank you. Is Mrs. Callender here?"

"Yes, sir. Upstairs."

"Would you ask her to come down, please."

The servant hesitated. "Miss Adele has not been well. I think she's still to her bed."

"I'll go up. Thank you, Lowell." He started to leave. "I'm expecting some other gentlemen. Show them into the library when they come. They may want a drink." Callender turned to Wheeler. "What about you, Jud? Do you want a drink?"

"Iced tea would handle me just fine."

"Bring Mr. Wheeler's drink in here, Lowell."

Wheeler waited until the man closed the door. "His name is Lowell, too?"

"Lots of the people around here are named Lowell." He nodded at the telephone. "I think you ought to call Pendleton at the CIA, get caught up with what they know, what reports they have had from all the missions." He pointed to the table. "Open that drawer and press the third button from the left after you have dialed. It will record the call. I need as much detail as I can get. Little pieces of the puzzle are important."

"He isn't going to like talking to me. We're not exactly on the best of terms. The President gave me the ass-chewing job on Pendleton when all those things began happening in the Caribbean. If you think he was pissed at you, you should have heard him on the subject of the CIA. He was pissed at you because you knew too much. He was pissed at Pendleton because he didn't know anything. If it hadn't been for you, Pendleton would have no idea that this Cuban invasion plan was going on. It doesn't speak well for the Agency, does it?"

"Pendleton ought to realize the urgency by now. He's lost personnel in this action. That alone should convince him that this is not a figment of my imagination."

"It is the official position of the President that you and the CIA should be interrelating, trading information. Pendleton is going to tell me what he knows and then he's going to turn around and ask me questions, like: What's new with Lowell Callender?" He smiled,

"Maybe I just say that he's alive and well and living high off the hog in New Orleans."

"You might get good at this, Jud."

"What if they're on to something hot, do I let them go full steam or tell them to cool it?"

"If they're on to something hot, I doubt if they'll tell you. They do things in their own way and in their own time. They have a well defined procedure for fending off high-level questions and outside pressure. They've had a lot of practice at it. They'll do to you what they do at a Congressional investigation; throw you a few crumbs of documented information which they think is irrelevant to their main thrust. But I need every crumb I can get."

"You don't have to settle for crumbs. This country boy may get you a whole loaf of bread. Honcho headcracker. Remember?" He opened the drawer under the telephone, peered down, and pressed the third button from the left. "What do these other buttons do?"

"Various things."

"Like this red one." He held his finger over the button. "What does this do?"

"It rings the stable. Nothing more sinister than that."

While Wheeler was beginning to dial, Callender left the room, went upstairs to his own room, locked the door. The drawer in his desk had the same set of buttons which were under the telephone in the room downstairs. Callender dialed the number, then pressed the red button to scramble the call.

Farnsworth answered on the first ring.

"What happening?"

"Edgerton. We've finally heard from Edgerton."

"What?"

"Mayday. That's all I know."

"When?"

"He called last night, a little after midnight."

"He must be on to something big. Wouldn't he tell you anything else?"

"Only that he's still on Andros."

"If he gave the mayday signal, it's happening fast."

"What are you going to do?"

"I'll get to him."

"How?"

"Personally."

"Isn't that dangerous?"

"I'll have to take the risk." Callender thought for a moment. "Did you tell him to sit tight?"

"Yes."

"Did you hear from BARRACUDA?"

"No."

"Anything else?"

"Why is the heat off? What's happened? I mean the telephone isn't ringing every minute with somebody screaming at me. Why did it all calm down suddenly?"

"I made a deal. I'll tell you about it later." He hung up, released the red button, dialed Butler aviation, waited while his personal pilot was paged. "Do some homework," he instructed him. "We're going into Nicollstown, Andros Island. See if the jet will go in. If not, make arrangements to switch to a prop in Miami or Palm Beach. I'll be back to you in fifteen minutes. Make all the arrangements. Be ready to go in an hour."

He dialed another number, pushed the red button. "I need cover for two men to go into Andros Island. Fake passports. The works. Me and a man ten years younger than I. Make it good. Our lives may depend upon it. I'll be back to you in ten minutes."

From the window he could see that one limousine was already parked in front of the house and that another was just coming into the courtyard. It was almost noon. In his closet, hidden by clothes, was a panel which he slid back. He got down on his knees and worked the combination lock. There were four different guns on the bottom shelf. He took the smallest, put it in his inside pocket, started to close the safe, then opened it again, took another revolver, checked the chamber, and put it in his side pocket.

In front of the mirror, as he was straightening his tie and brushing his hair, he noticed the bulge the revolver made, tried unbuttoning his suit jacket, but the lump still showed in his pocket. He searched the bottom drawers of his desk, then the top drawer of the highboy at the other end of the room, finally found the shoulder holster, wadded and dusty. He took it in the bathroom, used a clean towel to wipe it off, put the revolver in it to make sure it fit and went back through his room.

His wife was waiting outside the bedroom door. In his hurry to get downstairs he bumped into her. She saw the gun. "Were you coming to kill me, Lowell?" She walked by him, into his room. He followed her, closed the door. It was the first time he had ever seen her unkempt, slatternly looking. And she seemed older to him, deep lines marring her complexion and puffy bags under her eyes. "Haven't you killed anyone since . . . when was it, Lowell? Last Tuesday. That's right. You killed that Golding woman Tuesday night. Haven't you killed anyone since then?"

"You're drunk."

"Southern ladies are never drunk. Tipsy. Southern ladies get tipsy."

"Get hold of yourself. Don't let yourself go like this."

"Why? What plans am I fouling up for you? There have been alcoholic first ladies in the White House before. I'll sober up long enough for the inauguration. I'll wear black. Widow's black. Maybe I'll go down in history as another Mrs. Lincoln. Didn't she wear black all the time as though she knew that her son would die and that Mr. Lincoln would be assassinated?"

"If you don't care about me, care enough about yourself to snap out of this."

She snapped her fingers weakly. "Is it that easy, Lowell?" She tried snapping her fingers again, made no sound as she did it. "I've lived a whole life that I've hated. Barren. Everything has been barren. Why should I care about myself? Who cares if I care about myself?" She sat on his bed, her back to him, her fingers tight around the carved bedpost. "I told Ralph that I wasn't afraid of you anymore, that I would divorce you and marry him. It scared him away. He never really wanted to marry me. I was just a convenient lay." She fell forward on the bed, still clutching the post and sobbed, her face burrowed into the soft quilt.

Callender looked up from his watch, started toward the door, reversed direction, and sat on the bed next to her, lifting her and holding her in his arms, his body absorbing the shock of her wracking. Slowly, the torment subsided. The tears stopped. She released her grip on his back, pulled slightly away from him, wiped her eyes, and brushed back her hair. She stood up, straightened her gown, and tied the robe tighter around her body. "I have arranged for sandwiches and fruit to be served in the library. There wasn't time for Bessie to bake cookies." At the door she turned back to him. "How many will there be for dinner?"

He forced her into his arms, tried to put his mouth over her mouth. She turned her head away. Callender backed off. "We'll all be leaving within an hour." He walked back to the bed, picked up the gun and holster. When he turned around she was already gone. He made two telephone calls and went downstairs.

The two admirals, wearing civilian clothing, were seated side-by-side in straight chairs. The stuffy parlor had an aura of death, the rigid naval officers as grim as mourners.

"Sorry to keep you waiting. I am Lowell Callender." He shook hands with each man.

The older man nodded his head. "Admiral Sorenson."

The younger man, about Callender's age, stood up, tried to smile, felt the gloom of the room. "Josh Wittaker."

"Didn't one of the servants offer you a drink?" He went to the side of the white marble fireplace, pulled a long bell cord. "It won't take much time, gentlemen. As you must know, there is an imminent crisis. Did the President make that clear?"

Admiral Sorenson said, "Our instructions were to communicate with you *and* with Mr. Wheeler. The President made *that* quite clear."

"Of course. Jud's here. He must be washing up." Noiselessly, the butler had appeared at the door. "Fix these gentlemen something cool, will you, Lowell?" He turned to the naval officers. "Does a planter's punch sound good? It's that kind of a day." Both men nodded. "On your way back to the kitchen, ask Mr. Wheeler to come in, please." Callender turned back to his guests. "Lunch will be ready in a few minutes. It will be perfectly safe to talk. The servants have been here since I was a boy. They've been trained not to listen."

Wheeler came in. Callender made the perfunctory introductions. "Do you want to start the ball rolling, Jud, or should I?"

"It's your show, Lowell. You tell the boys what you have in mind. I'd just like to say that I've been on the phone to the President, hung up a minute ago. He sends his regards and his thanks to you both for leaving your busy schedules to come here. The President has given this emergency top priority. He's pulling out all the stops." He gave the admirals his country-boy smile. "That's all the talking I'm going to do."

"The crisis," Callender began, "is in Cuba. To avert an international war I need both of your expertise and your strengths." He looked at the younger man. "Admiral Wittaker, I need your attack force of trained porpoises. How fast can you move them to Cuba?"

Wittaker looked from Callender to Sorenson and back again. "I know nothing about porpoises, Mr. Secretary."

"Come on, Admiral, it's an open secret that the Navy has been training porpoises for years to be man's enemy instead of his friend. There is going to be an underwater army invading Cuba. We must stop them. You can understand the danger. I need your porpoises with their spears attached to their backs to attack this army before it can land."

They were all silent as the butler returned with a silver tray with four tall drinks. When he was gone, Wittaker looked at Jud Wheeler. Wheeler nodded his head. "You've got them," the Admiral told Callender.

"Admiral Sorenson, I need a submarine from your base on Andros with an underwater fighting team as backup for this operation."

"I'm like Admiral Wittaker, Mr. Secretary. I don't know that we have a submarine base on Andros Island." He smiled at Callender's set jaw. "Tell me when and where."

"In time, gentlemen. We don't know the exact location of the invasion yet, nor the timing. I suggest, Admiral Wittaker, that you have your porpoises ready off Key West and that you, sir, have the submarine proceed to the west side of Andros; stand ready to move quickly either east or west when our intelligence information is complete." Callender looked at his watch, stood up. "Lunch will be ready by now. Please follow me. Bring your drinks."

SAN ANDROS BEACH CLUB, ANDROS ISLAND, BAHAMAS, WEST INDIES

It started out to be a wasted day. The new photographer's upset stomach turned out to be a twenty-four-hour virus. He stayed in his room, complaining, through his assistant, about the inadequacy of the Bahamian plumbing. The girl had come with them, carried an empty clipboard around, took random shots of people and the scenery with a Polaroid. Edgerton spent the morning on a remote part of the beach trying to even out his suntan. Every once in a while he stood up, monitoring the water, looking for another snorkel tip, another body to emerge from the sea and say, "YELLOWJACK." But there was no attempt to make contact with him. The man who had answered Callender's phone had instructed him to stay put. He lay on the hot sand thinking about Monica, cursing himself for behaving like an adolescent schoolboy, knowing that the future with her was impossible. He blamed himself for the hurt he had inflicted on her. An agent knew better than to get involved on an assignment. But seeing her naked in the moonlight, knowing how vulnerable and alone she was, had brought forward a buried network of emotional responses that he had mistaken for a renaissance of his sexuality. Then why had he gotten an erection during the storm?

The information that the young Italian was going to be in Port-au-Prince on Tuesday was crucial, the indicator of the timetable for the invasion plan. He closed his eyes and saw the map in his mind: the geographical position of the Hispaniola Island in relation to Cuba, the distance of Port-au-Prince from the Providenciales and the distance from the Providenciales to Great Guana Cay.

Monica was finishing lunch, a stack of yellow Teletype pages beside her. It was the first time Edgerton had seen her wearing glasses. She pushed them back up on her head when he came over, sat down. "Are those the questions for the interview?" She nodded. "When do you want to do it?"

"No hurry."

"This afternoon would be a good time. If the new photographer is back in shape, we're going to be busy as hell tomorrow."

"Any time."

"I'll come around to your room about four."

"I'll meet you in the bar."

She left the table. Edgerton munched on the potato chips she left on the plate, sipped the iced tea she had not finished. Lindsay stopped at the table on her way out. "It's back to work tomorrow. The word is that the new photographer's stomach flu is not terminal. His associate says the runs and whoopsing have stopped."

"Where are we going to photograph?"

"I'm not sure yet."

"Did you find out anything about that house we flew over the other day?"

She nodded. "L.A. put their supersleuths on it. The whole damn island belongs to some Italian count who lives in Milan. Wait. I wrote his name down." She fumbled in her pocket, went through three crumbled slips before she found the correct one. "Count Aldo Rinaldi. How do you like that monicker? Plenty classy. Someone in our Rome office is trying to track him down, see if we can rent the joint for a couple of days. In the meantime, we'll probably shoot around here tomorrow. We're so far behind now, I don't see how we'll ever make the deadline. We've decided to junk all the shots we took on the catamaran, scrap that whole layout. We'll probably hire one of those raunchy fishing boats with a stone-faced crew. I think that would be the ultimate chic, don't you? Bare ass and floaty chiffon against an authentic native background. What do you think?"

"It doesn't matter to me. My ass is out either way."

"And a mighty pretty ass it is, Marc Polo. Mighty pretty." She leaned over, kissed him on the cheek. "I wish to hell I understood men," she said.

He got to the bar early, ordered a Coke, looked around for an electrical outlet for Monica's tape recorder, found it next to the jukebox, moved a table and two chairs on the dance floor, dug in his pocket for a Bahamian coin, pressed some buttons, watched the colored lights of the machine begin to move, sat down, and waited for Monica.

Two men came into the bar. In the darkness at the far end of the room, Edgerton could not distinguish the faces. Both men were dressed in business suits. One carried a briefcase. When they got closer, he realized that the other man was Lowell Callender. His movements were casual, leisurely as he stood up, examined his watch in the light of the jukebox, and slowly walked toward the door. There was an instant firefly-light flash of memory. He was the nineteen-year-old boy again, walking toward the stern face of his father's business agent. Edgerton stopped. The men looked up at him. For a split second it was back with him, the trauma of that time of his life. Then he regained his professionalism and following safe procedure, did not acknowledge Callender, but kept walking. Monica was coming into the bar, the sheaf of papers in her hand, the tape recorder slung over her shoulder. "Wait for me inside," he said. "I have to pee."

He hesitated up ahead until he saw Callender and the other man leave the bar, then he followed the path around the club house, through the decaying, wooden fence, and stopped again outside the kitchen service door. When they turned the corner, Edgerton continued, circuiting to the left, cutting across the courtyard, taking cover at the side of the shed which housed the generator. The sound of the machine would muffle their conversation and the thicket of tall shrubs would screen them from the road and from the beach. He leaned against the wall, felt the vibration of the generator shaking the woodshed and wondered about the man with Callender: he had the demeanor of a harassed accountant, was probably CIA.

The two men squared off in front of him. Callender did not even smile, begin with a greeting, or introduce the other man. There was no indication of the one-to-one ambiance of their first meetings outside Washington and in Key West. There was none of the soft, seductive, Southern tone in the undersecretary's voice when he spoke. "Couldn't you have picked a better spot? We won't be able to hear ourselves think. Now, give it to me fast," Callender commanded, "and keep it in sequence. Don't leave out any detail whether you think it's important or not. I'll decide what's relevant. Is that clear?"

Edgerton started his report. For the last two days, when he had been out of communication with both Key West and Callender, Edgerton had rehearsed the recital of his findings, edited his information to be explicit, exact and in logical progression. He repeated it now to the audience of two men, the three of them huddled close together so that they could hear each other over the sound of the generator. Edgerton began with the aerial finding of the house on Great Guana Cay, then told the photographer's story of the brigantine, *Aventuro,* which had been on Cape Eleuthera and was on its way to the Caicos Islands by the time they went to hunt it down. He reported the appearance of the creep on Andros, described the explosion of the *Playgirl* catamaran but did not mention his effort to swim out to save any possible survivors. Callender was registering no emotion, seemed to be looking through Edgerton to the clapboard, driftwood siding. The other man's reactions were openfaced, hearing the words with concentrated interest and seeing the man beyond the words.

Edgerton went on the describe the flight to Nassau, the scene in the bank, and finally the landing on Great Guana. He detailed the topography of the island, the position of the house in relation to the harbor, and the installation of the communication tower and the network of wires over an empty swimming pool. He was meticulous in enumerating the contents of the hangar. Then he gave them a rundown of the people he had seen on the island: the ground mechanic, the pilot, the shadowy figure lurking under the eaves, the man who said he was the creep's father and had given him five hundred dollars as a pay-off, and finally a detailed description of the young Italian who had accompanied him back to Andros. In the same flat voice he used in reporting everything else, Edgerton explained how he had gotten the information from the Italian. He pulled the cock ring out of his pocket, let each man examine it, and then put it away. He finished by telling them the Italian wanted to meet him again. The time was Tuesday. The place was Port-au-Prince.

Then he stood back, waited for the approbation of the undersecretary, the applause at the end of the recital.

Edgerton was stunned by the unexpected violence of Callender's reaction, thrown off guard by the behavior of the undersecretary. He had been briefed and warned in Key West that Callender had a short fuse, lost his temper easily. Instead of approval and a pat on the back, there was the lash of unexpected furor. "You fucking coward. You had it all there, right in your hand, and you didn't have balls enough to do anything. You're like the rest of your generation. You'll carry banners and write letters to the editor but you won't get off your ass and use your bare hands." He was screaming now over the throbbing sound of the generator. "They said you were a killer. They said you had a record of bravery in Vietnam. And I believed in you. I thought you were more than they said. I thought you had both balls and brains. You have neither. You're nothing."

When the unexpected verbal blast began, Edgerton recoiled into an instant of no-feeling but then something triggered a release of his own emotions; the frustrations turned to anger and the anger into violence. Rage sluiced through his body. Fury was directing him. The words of Callender's tirade jackhammered in his mind. He lunged toward the undersecretary.

Jud Wheeler stepped forward, buffered his body between the two men, felt the heat and outrage in both of them. He could not understand the intensity of Callender's reaction. The agent, Edgerton, had sounded effective and professional. Wheeler questioned Callender's intent, wondered if the anger was real or a deliberately calculated tactic. The undersecretary was lethal, not explosive. Gently, he pushed Edgerton back, winked at him, communicated compassion.

Edgerton said nothing, felt everything.

"You had your chance to be a hero, Edgerton. One fucking chance to save the whole damn world and you blew it."

Callender and Edgerton pressed against Wheeler to get at each other. Wheeler said, "Take it easy, Lowell." He backed the men off. "I don't even see what he did wrong. What could he have done?"

"He was on the damn island. It was all there. Everything that's happening is being controlled from that island. He had the chance to destroy it."

"How could I? Even if I had knocked out the pilot, what then? I didn't have a gun. I didn't have any grenades. They told me in Key West I wasn't suppose to be a one-man army."

Callender shouted down Edgerton's next sentence. "And I told you that you were capable of independent thinking and independent action. I thought I got through to you that the CIA doesn't understand the importance of the action, doesn't understand the urgency. I thought I got through that pretty face and thick skull to make it clear that you were functioning as my special arm, a special agent."

"You told me to use my head. You told me to use my judgment. I used it. Son of a bitch, I'd do the same thing all over again. There was no way I could get off that island alive if I knocked out the pilot. You think I didn't examine the possibility? I used my head. You wanted the setup. I got you your information. I almost got fucked to get you the information."

Callender's voice was normal again, the lowered volume almost drowned out by the repetitive machinations of the generator. "You probably enjoyed it."

This time the force of Edgerton's charge knocked both Wheeler and Callender to the ground. Wheeler's body shielded Callender, did not yield when Edgerton tried to pull him off. Edgerton backed off, breathed heavily as the two men got up from the ground. Callender's glasses had fallen off. He cleaned them with the end of his tie. "They're the enemy, Edgerton, not I."

Wheeler was brushing the dust and sand from his gray suit. "You're both behaving like a couple of kids. I don't understand you, Lowell. I don't see why you're so pissed."

"You don't have the guerrilla mentality."

"I'm a country lawyer trying to prevent a damned world war. I have the mentality to understand that this man did his job, that we now have the information to go in and blow this thing wide open. And he got it for us."

"What's your suggestion, Jud? You going to send the United States Navy in to bomb that little speck of ground in the middle of the Bahamian Republic? Talk about starting another war!"

"There has to be a way, Lowell. You know where the control point is. It seems to me that you just go in there and destroy it."

Callender's finger accused Edgerton. "He could have done that. He had the perfect chance." He lowered his hand; his shoulders dropped in disgust. "This must be a commando action by an un- identified group. If we do anything officially, we defeat our own purpose. This is an exercise to keep the United States government *un*involved."

"Where are we going to get unidentified commandos?" Wheeler asked. "Should I get on the horn to Pendleton?"

"Too late for that. By the time the CIA gets its act together, it will all be over."

"What are we going to do?"

"Play it out," Callender decided. "Let it run its course."

"I don't concur."

"You're not here to concur. Your function is to implement."

"I'm not going to implement anything that I think could be done a less dangerous way."

"Give me an alternative, Jud."

"Give me an hour to think about it."

"There are no hours left, only minutes." He started toward the clubhouse. "Come on, Jud. We're going to track down that brigan- tine."

Edgerton said, "The photographer and the assistant art director were going to fly into the Caicos and see if they could use the islands for some fashion shots."

"Too late. We won't be able to fly into the Caicos after dark. That ship may be the key. I can't wait for the information. I need it now."

He followed behind them, finally asked, "Do I go with you?"

Callender turned around, looked him up and down. "What good would you do? You stay here with your fly open. That's all you're good for." Then he softened slightly. "If I'm not back tonight, I'll be back early in the morning."

"What if you don't come back?"

"Go get fucked in Port-au-Prince."

Darkness had come. Callender and the other man had not returned. Edgerton heard a plane coming in to land just before dark. He thought it might be Callender, but it was the *Playgirl* crew returning from their scouting mission. He went back to his room, kept alert for the sound of another plane. When he was certain that it would be too late for Callender to land, Edgerton relaxed his vigilance, reconstructed the meeting with Lowell Callender and the nameless man. He heard word for word replays of what he had said and what Callender had said. It was a broken record that would not stop. He relived the scene on the landing strip at Guana, fantasized what would have happened if he had knocked out the pilot, had become a one-man commando unit. But each time he replayed that scene, any way he relived it, he would always come out a dead hero. Not even a hero, he decided. The internal dialogues went on in his mind long past midnight. He tossed and turned, tried every position to sleep. The air conditioning of the room was not powerful enough to cool his furor or confusion. He sweated heavily, writhed on the bed. Finally, exhaustion fought the dialectic, overpowering it slowly. He lay on the edge of consciousness, did not hear sounds in the room, only subliminally aware of a pressure beside him, the contact of another body against his, a repetitive stroking against his groin. In the daze between sleep and waking, he was not able to distinguish the reality from the dream. But at the wet contact of a mouth over his mouth, he started up, felt the scrape of a stubble of beard against his own face. The first reaction was physical, uncontrolled. He shoved the intrusion away, saw the body disappear between the beds, heard the impact of it as it fell to the floor. There was a thin line of blood at the corner of Russell Langston's mouth as his face appeared over the edge of the mattress.

"We're playing rough tonight?" He wiped his mouth, blood stayed on his hand. "I can handle that."

"What the fuck do you think you're doing?"

"Don't play cute, Edgerton. Don't play the outraged virgin with me. I saw you and that little wop last night. You don't think I believed all that shit about you being straight, do you? I want a piece of your ass and I'm going to have it." He stood up, breathing hard, his body sweating, the blood still running from the corner of his mouth. "You like to play rough? I can play rough." Like a cat, he sprung from a standing position, landed on top of Edgerton who, momentarily taken off-guard, submitted to the impact and then struggled free of the other man's weight. Langston caught him and they grappled in the bed, wrestling each other to the floor. The bodies pitted against each other for physical supremacy, rolling around the floor, knocking one of the beds off its frame, toppling a chair and a standing lamp in a seesaw battle of alternating manifestations of equal strengths. Langston's was the larger body, the greater weight. He finally pinioned Edgerton to the floor, his force holding Edgerton spread eagle on his back. Edgerton was immobilized by Langston's dead weight on top of him. There was a momentary submission, then Edgerton recovered, played the submission as feint, permitting the fighter to weaken into a lover and in this unguarded position, using all his strength, pulled himself free. Langston was thrown off balance long enough for Edgerton to chop at the base of his skull, stunning him unconscious. Langston's body went limp. The combined sweat of the two bodies was the emollient that let Edgerton slip loose from under the dead weight. He stood up slowly, waited while his heart rate subsided and the stun of the attack was over, then picked up the body, carried it across the room, set it gently on the bed. He took Langston's inert hand, pressed his fingers against the wrist, felt the pulse beat, counted the cadence of it. Satisfied, he let it drop back to the bed. His mind started back to a memory in Vietnam. He shook his head, pounded his own ear to throttle the emerging image.

Edgerton made no attempt to muffle the sound as he turned the knob of Monica's door, tried to force it open. He had put on his cut-offs, not bothered to wash the sweat from his body and raced across the crescent to her room. When the door did not yield, he ran around to the pool side of her room, raised the handle of the sliding glass door, juggled it, heard the lock disengage, opened the door, went into the room, found the light switch, turned it on, and stared back at the woman sitting up in bed watching him, without fright, covering herself with the edge of the sheet.

The recording machine was on the floor. He put it on the table next to her bed, knelt on the floor to find a plug, and then connected it. He brought over her folder of notes and questions, threw them on the bed and turned on the machine, activating the tape.

"Start asking your fucking questions."

She dropped the cover of the sheet. Her taut nipples were another pair of eyes staring at him, mocking him.

Without touching the folder beside her, and without wavering the fix of her stare, she groped on the table, clutched the tiny hand microphone, held it in front of her mouth. When she spoke there was no fear in her voice, her hand did not tremble.

PLAYGIRL: When did you turn butch?

Edgerton gripped the sides of the chair, restrained the unexpended furor still in his body. "Ask the questions in the folder."

Inexplicably, the brown points of her breasts distended, became soft undefended discs.

PLAYGIRL: You are returning to films, starting a new career in a generation of macho box-office stars . . . men with rugged looks and Italian names. Do you think the women of the world will respond to your boy-next-door image?

The nipples contracted again.

MARC POLO: Do you?

In the periphery of the fix of his vision, he saw her legs rise, kick off the cover of the sheet. Then her body was still, her legs slightly spread. Edgerton's eyes lowered, focused on the confluence between her legs, the pink edge of moist flesh. One by one, he directed his fingers to release their grip on the chair. His hands were free. Still he sat there. With his right hand, he unbuttoned the metal buttons of his cut-offs, pushed them down, let his erect penis spring free.

There was time to examine the genesis of his erection. It was not necessary. It existed. The target for it was the moist anterior lips below the defined triangle of hair. Straddling her body, he thrust himself into her, impaling her immediately without a foreplay of words or caresses.

At last it was back, like no other feeling: the contracting cunt expanding to urge him into it, vise-tight as he drew back. And the sound of the back-and-forth movement, like no other sound. He was aware only of his own sensation, the perfection of the pumping mechanism of a round object into a round orifice, lubricated with natural juices. Like no other feeling, no other sound.

The orgasm came quickly with a shattering force gushing into the fragile body beneath him. For a moment, he collapsed; dead weight on top of her. Then he hoisted his body up, drew out of her slowly, fighting the taut muscles trying to hold him in, feeling the wakes of orgasm as he eased out. He fell back beside her, breathing deeply. The long ordeal of emptiness was over; the man power was back, bludgeoning with brutal force.

Quietly, Monica raised herself on one elbow, looked down into his face, touched his cheek with the tip of her fingers. "Haven't you ever loved anyone?" she said. "Haven't you ever been in love? Hasn't anyone ever loved you?" She put her lips against his, not hungrily seeking but soothing, reassuring. She kissed each eye to remove the edge of tears. He put his arms around her gently, saw again how blue her eyes were, felt the soft touch of her breasts graze him as he guided her on top of him. "I'm going to teach you how to love," she whispered. "I'm going to teach you what love is."

And what began as a ravage, a militant proving of self, became a long night of many acts of love, involving whole beings, whole persons. For the first time, Edgerton learned that his entire body could be made erogenous by love and that loving was an interchange of sensations. Rage had yielded to gentleness and gentleness had become tenderness.

There were no pictures from the past in his mind.

VICTOR CASTLE'S VILLA, GENEVA, SWITZERLAND

After dinner, she went into the powder room, examined herself in the full-length mirror, adjusted her jewelry, pushed up her breasts so that they were more exposed in the low-cut gown. She had dressed with even more than her usual attention to perfection for this meeting with Victor Castle. He had always admired her; she knew that. During dinner she was amused that his eyes had been undressing her, never looking at the food he ate. There was a certain honor, an unwritten standard of conduct that men like Castle and Rinaldi had for their own kind. It explained why Victor had never approached her. He was waiting for her now in the library. Was he imagining—because Aldo was out of the country—that she had arranged this meeting as a tryst? Of course he did. There had been candlelight at dinner and delicate wines. His young cocotte had been shunted off somewhere. Except for the servants they were quite alone. The countess smiled at her own reflection in the mirror. Poor dear. Victor Castle was in for a surprise.

As though a film director had blocked out her movements, she reentered the library, walked over to Castle, touched his cheek with the tips of her fingers, moved away before he could reach out for her, continued on to the fireplace, waited for a count of four, then turned around to face him. "Victor, most men—even brilliant men —are deceived by beautiful women." The words were the words of an obscure film writer. She had played this scene before. "Men underestimate a woman's instinct for survival . . . her resources for survival." In the script, the actor opposite her was not supposed to be smiling, not appear amused. Victor Castle was about to laugh. She went on with the script. "Women are not endowed with physical strength. We are not like female animals in the . . ." He was laughing openly now. "What's so fucking funny?" the countess asked.

"I'm not afraid of any man. Not anymore."

"But you're afraid of me?"

Still smiling, he nodded. "I only know how to handle beautiful, dumb broads who want a piece of jewelry or a thousand-dollar bill to tuck into the front of their dress. I don't know how to handle famous movie stars and high-class countesses, particularly beautiful women with gorgeous tits who have balls like a man."

"I want in, Victor. Not just a little piece. I want in all the way."

"In on what?"

"Don't play games. I know what's going on. I'm not blind. I've watched this develop. My son and my husband made the mistake of underestimating me. They never said a word. They told me nothing. But I have eyes. I know."

"In a business deal, when a man wants in on the deal, that man has a commodity to trade. He has something we need or he has some protection we can't get any other way. We don't cut anybody

into a deal for no reason. What's your reason? What do you have
to sell?"

"Let's make the assumption that what I have to sell will make the
difference between success and failure. What then?"

"Are you telling me that you know something we don't know?"
The countess had come across the room, sat down opposite Castle
as he asked the question. "Are you telling me that if we know what
you know, we win and if we don't know, we lose?"

"Exactly."

"I don't believe you." Castle's face was grim now. "You're
bluffing."

"No one is ever sure about bluff until it's called."

Castle said, "I'm calling it."

She looked at the empty table between them. "Where are the
chips?"

"What are the stakes?"

"According to Carlos Ramirez's last will and testament, half was
for the widow and half was for the son. You can have half of Roger's
share. The rest of it is mine."

"What about Aldo?"

"You take care of him out of your twenty-five percent."

"And your son?"

"I am not naive enough to believe that he will come out of this
alive."

He seemed puzzled. "You have no feelings for your own kid?"

"He made the commitment. He made it without consulting me.
It's too late. Nothing I can do will save him now."

"If you could, would you?"

"Are you offering me that trade?"

He leaned back, released his tensions. "You're one tough tomato,
Countess." He locked his fingers together, decided her fate, won-
dered if there was time to get Guido back and forth to do the job.
"I don't think I want to do business with you."

"You have no choice. I told you that without my information, your
plan will fail."

Castle had already examined the alternatives, guessed that she
was bluffing but it did not matter. The high stakes were the Russian
money. She had no way of knowing that. Rinaldi would never have
told her. Castle understood Rinaldi's love for his wife, that he would
never give her information which would endanger her life. And

Castle never doubted Rinaldi's loyalty to the organization. "If we fail, we fail," he said. "If we lose, we lose it all. But if we win, we win it all. I like those odds."

"You'll regret it if you turn me down."

He shrugged his shoulders. "There's no such thing as a sure bet. When you gamble for high stakes, you win or lose big." He stood up. "You want some brandy or something?"

Losing to Victor Castle had not been a consideration in her plan. It had all seemed so simple to her when she plotted it out. She wondered if Castle thought she was bluffing. How much could she tell him without exposing her whole hand? "I wasn't foolish enough to give my son Carlos Ramirez's map without keeping a copy."

"Maybe it would look good framed on your wall."

"It might be interesting to compare what Roger gave you to the original map."

"What's that supposed to mean?"

She stood up, smoothed out her gown, held her head high. "You can think about it overnight. Maybe you can figure out the meaning. I don't fly back to Nice until the ten o'clock flight tomorrow morning."

"Listen, if you think that . . ."

She cut him off. "Be a dear, will you, and ring for your chauffeur. I suddenly have a splitting headache." She went over to him, kissed him on the cheek. "The dinner was divine, Victor. Swiss chefs are really the best, don't you think? Except for, perhaps, the Chinese. We have a Chinese chef . . ."

The hard slap across the face stopped the words. Under the impact, an earring fell to the floor. She stared at Victor Castle until he broke out in a smile, leaned over, picked it up, and handed it to her.

"If your husband had your balls," he said, "he'd be where I am."

The Countess Rinaldi was fastening her earring as she walked out of the library.

THE THIRD TURTLE INN, CAICOS ISLANDS, BRITISH WEST INDIES

Again Callender fed all the information through the computer of his mind. Disconnected fragments were beginning to fit together into a defined pattern of action. But there were still intelligence voids which needed filling in before he had detailed enough data to fine-tune and then activate his counterattack. Timing was the most important factor; their timing and his. He had to know the exact schedule. There were two indicators: the charted course of the brigantine and the meeting of Edgerton with the young Italian in Port-au-Prince. Jud Wheeler had alerted the Navy, was waiting for an intelligence report on the brigantine and an estimation of the sailing time to Cozumel. Callender guessed that it would not be a non-stop run, that the ship would probably stop for provisions at one of the Cayman Islands, a little more than halfway to Cozumel. Earlier, when he had gotten through to Farnsworth in Washington, he had given instructions to alert Stingray to keep constant surveillance for the *Aventuro*. Farnsworth had relayed the report from Cozumel: the underwater filming had stopped; the entire crew was still on the island but were confined to the hotel with their equipment packed and ready to leave on an instant's notice.

Although the patterns of action were taking form and the battle lines taking definition, Callender still had no clue as to the motivation of the impending attack or any identification of the motivators. Julio San Marco, in the interview with Laurie Golding, had assumed that the plot was created by Cuban Nationals living in Florida and was directed at Havana, possibly at Castro himself. From the deployment of the installations on Cozumel and Great Guana, Callender now believed that San Marco had been right; the main thrust of the raid would be at the capital. Castro's security was reputed to be impenetrable. Callender made a mental note to get a schedule of Castro's agenda of public appearances during the next week.

The British owner of the Third Turtle Inn clapped his hands together loudly. One of the native waiters appeared from the bar. Callender put his hand over his drink indicating that he did not want another. "What about your friend, will he want the same thing?"

Wheeler had been called to the telephone ten minutes before, was still upstairs in the communication room.

"You'd better wait until he gets back," Callender said. "I don't know what's taking him so long."

The owner shook his head at the waiter. "Our telephone system is an unpredictable phenomenon. You learn patience in the islands."

They were sitting on a stone-floored veranda between the bar and the dining room. There was a clear view from here to the harbor and the ceiling above was the darkened sky, the stars just beginning to show brilliance.

Conway Greshman continued with the story he told every guest; how he chucked everything in London, found his paradise on the Caicos islands and recounted the long tribulation of building the Third Turtle Inn. Callender was nodding and smiling at the right intervals, only the edge of his awareness hearing the man.

The function of the brigantine was defined, clear in his mind. But Edgerton's meeting in Haiti was more obscure. He had been too abrupt with Edgerton, had handled him wrong. Callender could not account to himself for his own violent reaction to Edgerton, his undisciplined behavior. In retrospect, Edgerton had done the prudent thing. Callender realized he was identifying too closely with Edgerton, expecting Edgerton to be motivated the way he would have been motivated in the same situation. He should have taken the time and had the patience to debrief Edgerton completely, put him through a series of interrogations. There were details in Edgerton's unconscious that were important, more fragments to fill the void. He decided that there would be time enough tomorrow when they flew back to Andros at daybreak.

Wheeler had returned, tried to politely listen to Conway Greshman's continuing story but kept looking at Callender, the tenseness of his body communicating the urgency of the information he had received.

When Greshman stopped to sip his rum punch, Callender smiled slowly. "We have all had romantic dreams. You made yours come true. I admire you for that. But it's different today. Young men aren't waiting until they're too old to live their dreams. That brigantine you were telling us about . . . young men, weren't they?"

"Girls too. The love of sailing seemed to be the common denominator. Gender didn't seem to matter to them. They were all sailors."

"Mostly Americans?"

Greshman shook his head. "All kinds. I told my wife it was like a floating United Nations."

"You went on board?"

"Scrubbed and shining to the nines. Beautiful sight."

"Did they do a restoration job below?"

"Never got down there. I expect they considered me an old fuddy-duddy, that I wouldn't understand that they all berthed together. Young people have limited vision. They think they invented sexual freedom."

"Did they even restore the old cannons?"

"They have that iron as shiny as the day it was mounted."

"Funny that they would just sail off in the night."

Greshman was remembering something from his own past. "Leaving a stack of unpaid bills and bar chips is as close as they can come to being pirates. Young people don't have the stout heart of my generation." He stood up. "I had better check out the kitchen." He looked at this watch. "We eat late here. You have about an hour to drink. There are only six other guests. But I can't complain. That's more than we usually have at this time of year."

When the owner was out of hearing range, Wheeler said, "What an old windbag." He moved his chair closer to Callender. "Count Aldo Rinaldi is the black sheep of the family. His people have been goldsmiths since the de Medicis, still have big jewelry stores in Rome, Florence, and Milan." He waited for Callender to react. "How come you don't ask me why he's the black sheep?" He did not wait for the reply. "It seems Rinaldi divorced a respectable Italian lady to marry a movie star . . . an American movie star. Did you ever hear of Marla Worth?" Callender nodded. "She must have been a little before my time. We only had one picture show where I lived." He studied Callender. "Are you way ahead of me, Lowell?"

"Marla Worth was married to Carlos Ramirez. She had to flee Cuba when Castro moved in. Ramirez was the number-two man under Batista. She made a dramatic escape with her son. It was a famous story in all the newspapers and motion-picture magazines."

"It begins to make some sense, doesn't it? Son of a gun." He slapped his knee. "I might get to like this kind of work."

"Most of Batista's crowd lived in the Miramar section right outside Havana. Get on the horn back to Washington. Pendleton is going to be the shortest distance between two points on this one. Get a fix on where Carlos Ramirez lived . . . I want it exact. See if they can find out what happened to the house, if it's still standing and if it is, what it is being used for now. Is that all clear?"

Excited, Wheeler stood up quickly, knocked over the chair he had been sitting in. "That creep that Edgerton told us about . . ."

Callender nodded, had already fed this new data into the machine of his mind. The total picture was less fragmented now.

Wheeler started from the table, turned around. "I forgot to tell you about Rinaldi." He touched Callender's shoulder. "Lowell, are you listening to me?"

"What about Rinaldi?"

"Not clean. Not dirty either. The FBI has been staking out the Mafia don, Victor Castle, for some time. Their files show that Rinaldi appears to have business dealings with Castle from time to time. That Castle must be some operator. In all this time, they've never been able to nail him with a definite criminal offense that will stand up in court. Rinaldi either. The FBI doesn't have the foggiest idea what kind of business dealings they have with each other."

"You're about to spend another night without sleep, Jud. Get moving."

The information about Victor Castle explained how the invasion plan was being funded. It also was an indicator of the huge amounts of money which must be involved.

Rinaldi's timetable was still the main missing ingredient. There were minor mysteries: how were the planes on Great Guana Cay going to be used, how were the mercenaries going to infiltrate Cuba? Callender decided he could handle that tactically if necessary. But the main thing he had to learn was the exact schedule. He would use Edgerton for that. The key to it had to be in Port-au-Prince. Once he had that information, he would be able to put his own counteraction in operation.

He would have to escape the surveillance of Wheeler long enough to contact Bogota as soon as possible. It was time to take Julio San Marco into custody.

Then Callender considered the best way to eliminate Wheeler, tried to decide when the timing for that would be exactly right.

Uncontrolled, a picture of his wife came into his mind. They were in one of the rooms at Belle Rivage. She was telling him about Ralph. All the details of this room he had slept in since he was a boy were in clear focus; the big dark wood bed, the worn geometric carpeting, the age-yellowed Rough-Rider poster on the wall— Theodore Roosevelt charging at San Juan Hill.

1978
AUGUST

12

SATURDAY

BARRANQUILLA, COLOMBIA

The immigration official studied the photograph in the passport and compared it to the face of the impatient man waiting across the counter. Under normal conditions, a private plane arriving this early in the morning would have to wait for clearance until ten o'clock when the immigration and custom stations officially opened. But at five A.M. a telephone call had come in from Bogota to the in-charge Barranquilla officer. When the head of the Bureau made a demand, there was no questioning compliance to it. The official wondered what was so special about an insignificant looking man named Luis Kunz. The passport was Panamanian, the occupation of the bearer listed as merchant. With all the confusion in Panama, and because the request had come from so high up, the man was probably a spy. But then he wondered, why would a spy go through the routine of official clearance into the country? The rubber entry stamp was at his fingertips but there was no point in making his job appear unimportant and routine. He thumbed through the other pages of the Kunz passport, noted on a form the last date of entry into Colombia, saw that the man had traveled extensively to European and Mideast capitals in the last six months.

He looked up from his pad, studied the face again. Beyond Kunz, blocked off by the glass barricade, he recognized the solitary man who had appeared there and was waiting, an impatient scowl on his face. The official quickly stamped the passport, smiled at Kunz. "Welcome to Colombia," he said.

Carrying no baggage, Kunz walked through the Customs counter without looking up. The officer there, who had also been pressed into opening early, decided to exert his authority, stepped over the counter, was about to put a restraining hand on Kunz's shoulder when he recognized the face of the man behind the glass barricade. He reached beyond Kunz and respectfully held the door for him.

"Trouble?" Kunz asked.

"Possible. We cannot talk here."

A mouse-gray Chevrolet, the engine running, waited outside the airport entrance. Kunz and the other man bent their heads and slid quickly into the backseat. As soon as the door was closed, the car gunned down the road. "Did you get San Marco?"

"We have him now. It better be worth it to you."

"What happened?"

"I told you that if San Marco was in Cuba it would be difficult. It is not easy to work directly inside Cuba." He rubbed his eyes. "We lost a man, shot by a guard. But worse than that, Castro knows that San Marco was kidnapped."

"I told you to make it appear as though San Marco defected again."

"I know. But I thought you understood that I could not guarantee this. I explained the difficulty." He was silent for a moment. "Our man was wounded in the escape. I could not leave him there for Castro to interrogate. It was necessary that we kill our own man."

"I'm sorry, Miguel. But in our work, it can happen to any of us, at any time."

"The price keeps going up, Luis. The more danger, the more the price. You understand that?"

"I have never questioned the cost."

"It is what makes us wonder about you sometimes." He leaned back, crossed his legs. "You are not an innocent, Luis. You understand that these things which I do are not accomplished alone, they are not put into action without help." When Kunz started to answer, Miguel silenced him with a hand gesture. "I do not speak of my men . . . I do not speak of the men under me. You must know that there are men over me, men to whom I am responsible."

"I am aware of this."

He seemed surprised. "We have never discussed it. You have

never, in all these years, indicated that you knew that other men were involved."

"It was not important. The dealings were between you and me. How you accomplished your missions was your own business."

"No longer. There has been a change. A man died. Natural causes. His sons have taken over. You know how it is when a son takes over for the father. It was like that with you and your grandfather. You and I were much younger then, full of young ideas. We considered men at the age we are now too old for this kind of work. We thought that their ideas and methods were obsolete. You remember those days, Luis?"

"I remember."

"It is like that again but now *we* are the old ones with brains and bodies not to be trusted."

"But that is not true. We have not even reached our prime."

"Look at us with twenty-five-year-old eyes, Luis."

They rode in silence for a few miles. Kunz noticed that the driver had taken a cutoff that bypassed the city and was headed toward the sea in a direction which would put them east of Barranquilla.

"You are taking me directly to San Marco?"

Miguel shook his head. "You understand that this is no longer my decision. I have direct instructions. The young sons want to flex their muscles, test their power. They wish to speak to you directly."

"Time is crucial. I must see San Marco first."

"I have no choice. It will be the way I am instructed."

Kunz waited, rephrased the words several times in his mind before he spoke them. "Considerable sums of money are involved, Miguel. Up to this time, I have always taken your word, accepted that word as final. There is no man in the world whom I trust more than you. In the past, I have wondered about the men above you but there was never reason except curiosity to know their identities." He paused, looked ahead into the sun low in the sky. "Who are these men?"

Miguel shook his head. "They will tell you what they want you to know."

"Are you allowed to tell me about San Marco?"

"It depends on what you want to know."

"Has he been injured?"

"No."

"Does he know who has kidnapped him?"

"He thinks Cuban Nationals from Florida. I think he believes that he is back in Florida. I warn you, there has been a change in San Marco. He has become the man he used to be. Again, he and Fidel are like brothers."

"That's good," Kunz said, and did not explain further.

The lobby of the luxury hotel was empty at this hour. Miguel led Kunz to the elevator, pressed the top-floor button. On the twenty-second floor they got off and walked around the corner of the corridor where Miguel inserted a key into a call signal for a private elevator. They waited for it to come down, got in, and as soon as the door closed, the elevator started up. It opened directly into a foyer of a large penthouse apartment, a clear shot through the long living room out to the Caribbean. Miguel hung back, motioned for Kunz to go ahead.

He identified the dead father from the faces of the two young men in swimming trunks having breakfast on the terrace. They were taller than the father had been and their skin was fairer, bodies slimmer and less hirsute. The Nordic genes of their mother had refined the coarseness of the father's features and diluted to zero the last traces of the Eurasian lineage. Only the eyes were the same as the father: sparkling black with the slightly viscous film over the eyeballs. It was clear now why Miguel's connection could accomplish any mission in any part of the world.

Both young men stood up when he stepped out on the terrace. One of them pulled back an empty chair. "Sit down, Mr. Secretary. Please join us for breakfast." They spoke English with the crisp definition of British public schooling.

Kunz sat down, considered the alternatives, played it straight, and became Lowell Callender again.

One of the men poured the thick, syrupy coffee. The other passed a native basket filled with hot breads.

"Good trip?"

Callender nodded, sipped the hot coffee, liked the sweet taste of it.

The brother on Callender's right said, "Our father always told us that the best working hours are those before anyone else is awake." He reached over, took a muffin, broke it in half, and began buttering it. "Our father always spoke highly of a man he never met, named Luis Kunz, didn't he, Ted?" The brother smiled. "He often spoke of a legacy of trust in a man named Luis Kunz." He munched on the muffin, wiped the corner of his mouth. "He didn't say anything about a man named Lowell Callender."

"I'm not aware that I knew your father. My dealings have always been with Miguel."

"The initial contact with our firm . . . how was it made?"

"My grandfather," Callender explained. "He evidently did business with your organization. Perhaps he knew your father or your grandfather. I wasn't aware until now that yours was a family business."

The brother who had been called Ted, answered, "It's very definitely a family business." Then he explained, "It's a large family . . . one drop of our blood is all that's required."

"There was never a need to go beyond Miguel. My grandfather taught me never to question or try to dissect another man's success. My long dealings with Miguel have always been successful. That is all I needed to know."

"It's been mutually beneficial, Mr. Secretary. My brother and I have been going through the accounts. Our relationship with you has been a long and profitable one . . . evidently for you as well."

Callender pushed back his chair, put his napkin on the table, crossed his legs. "Why don't we leave it as it is, continue on faith."

"The reason Ted and I wanted to see you was to tell you just that. As much faith as we have always had in Luis Kunz, we are prepared to have even more faith in Lowell Callender."

The other brother picked up the conversation, carried it further. "We think that, potentially, Lowell Callender will be an even bigger account than Luis Kunz. The way we see it, with a few political breaks, with the proper funding, a man like Lowell Callender could go on to become President of the United States. We're sure that you have considered the possibility. You have, haven't you?"

The meaning of the conversation was clear to Callender. No matter what he did, these two boyish-looking men were going to be his partners. Through them, he would be connected to the single greatest subliminal power force in the world. In the end, he would be their puppet but the most powerful puppet in the world. He had no alternatives. The commitment had been made years ago. They held the evidence which could destroy any public ambition he had. But political success for him would be financial success for them. That meaning was also implicit in the conversation. Callender made the pragmatic transfer of allegiance. They meant to use him when the time would come. Callender did not arbitrate the fairness of the trade, he accepted it as a reality.

"What happens in the future," Callender explained, "depends on the imminent situation. The timing here is critical."

The brother, Phil, pressed his point. "With all respect, Mr. Secretary, we need to talk straight out, have a direct verbal commitment. I realize that you and Miguel, because you have worked together for so long, can communicate with each other in a kind of shorthand." He grinned to show naiveté. "But, in a sense, this is the first time out for Ted and me. We need direct reassurances. We need your word or a handshake. Later, when we get to know each other better, we'll establish our own kind of shorthand. Right now we need assurance that we are both talking about the same thing."

Supplementing his brother, Ted explained, "You see, Mr. Secretary, we have done some research on this current project of yours, tried to put some pieces together to understand what's happening and particularly what your personal motivations are. Up to now, dealing only with Miguel, your contact with our organization has been limited to a very confined geographical area of our interests. I think it's clear to you that our resources are global and our information pool probably the most complete and the most sophisticated in the world."

"Including major powers," Phil added.

"We understand from the United States' standpoint how awkward a commando raid into Cuba would be at this point. With Castro flexing his muscles all over the world, it would be embarrassing for your government if it appeared as though you were trying to interfere with Cuban politics either domestically or geopolitically. Our guess is the same as yours: Whoever is masterminding this plan is going to make it look as if your CIA is behind it, implementing it with CIA brains and CIA guns. Phil and I talked about this a lot, tried to get into the head of the perpetrators. From the Russian standpoint, the ideal situation would be to have this raid happen, have Castro assassinated and have the United States take the blame. Isn't that about the way you see it?"

Callender nodded.

"Then we looked at it from inside Castro's head. If the raid were to happen and there was an unsuccessful assassination attempt, his global position would strengthen immeasurably. His license for

ideological imperalism would be validated in every country; there
would be no stopping him. Castro is capable of creating this operation himself. It's a very definite possibility, don't you agree?"

Again, Callender nodded but said nothing.

"Officially and diplomatically, it is in the best interest of your
government to abort the raid before it happens, hush up the whole
thing. Your country has the most to gain by making it appear that
none of this exists or ever existed. The maximum success your
country can hope to achieve is another white paper buried in the
vaults at Langley."

"From what Ted and I have been able to learn . . . and we admit
we have only bits and pieces to go on . . . your personal plan is
somewhat different than your official plan as undersecretary. Not
different, perhaps, but it goes beyond the official counterplan. It is
this element of personal gain that interests Ted and me: we can see
the long range advantages to both of us." He handed the basket of
hot breads to Callender who took one, broke it in half, buttered it
slowly. "From what we can see at this point, we believe that you
probably have enough information and enough resources to thwart
the raid now. But it appears that you have a plan beyond that
. . . or why kidnap San Marco? He knows nothing. We've questioned
him thoroughly. Why this meeting with Miguel? There can only be
one answer: You need some military capacity in addition to your
CIA paramilitary forces, or perhaps to combat your own paramilitary forces. There are lots of unanswered questions."

"And we haven't talked about the Cuban Nationals living in
Florida. They've become a very interesting economic and political
force in your country. Did you know that they have had you under
surveillance? Don't underestimate the Cuban Nationals. They may
all appear to be waiters in Miami hotels but they are very well
organized; some keen minds are directing them. The only press they
get is from the fanatics in the movement. The fanatics make good
cover for the real power of the Nationals. We have definite evidence
that they have direct dealings with Castro, are undercover partners
with him in various operations around the world. They represent
considerable wealth."

"They don't know Luis Kunz," Callender said, "unless there has
been a leak at this end. But I doubt that. I trust Miguel completely."

"Nevertheless, Mr. Secretary, I would use great caution. You're
a good target for the Nationals. As undersecretary, you represent

normalization with the Castro government. We understand that they have already made an attempt on your President's life."

"How much," Callender asked, "do you know about the invasion plan?"

Both brothers shrugged their shoulders. Ted said, "We're not sure. It's our gut feeling that they're following you because they think you're the secret liaison between the United States and Castro in the normalization dealings. They know that you and Castro have done business in the past. You're the logical man to be working on this. They have already put out the contract on San Marco because of his apparent defection; they want to make a case out of him."

"I must talk to San Marco right away," Callender said. "He may be able to give me some of the timing information I need."

"It's possible that he'll talk to you, tell you things he would not tell us. But first we must clarify our understanding." Phil turned to his brother. "I'd say that at this moment, the key issue is Mr. Callender's personal plan, wouldn't you, Ted?"

Callender turned from one alike face to the other. "It seems to me that you boys have read that rather well."

The brothers exchanged glances that congratulated each other on their perception and concurred their mutual support for Callender.

Phil said, "What do you need, Mr. Secretary?"

"Let me talk this over with Miguel. Why change a successful organization?" Callender continued. "I will give Miguel the instructions as I always have."

The brother, Ted, shook his head. "Before, we have helped you in straight financial endeavors. The politics have only been means to an end."

Callender leveled his eyes at Ted and then at his brother. "Is it different now?"

"There is a philosophical question here, Mr. Secretary. What is the end product? Is it power or money? We have talked about that a lot between the two of us. Does a man want power to accumulate money or does he want money to accumulate power?" He grinned. Callender thought of a toothpaste commercial on television. "My brother and I don't see eye-to-eye on that. We can't resolve the philosophical question. So we have developed a very practical solution. Phil will handle the problem of money as a means to accumu-

late power and I will handle power as means to accumulate money."
Playfully, he snapped a napkin at his brother, a practiced gesture
from boyhood. "With the two of us covering opposing positions, it
would seem that we have all bases covered."

"My brother is the family intellectual, Mr. Callender. He compli-
cates action with ideas and concepts. What he is trying to explain
to you is that we see enough potential in this situation to handle it
personally."

"If timing is crucial, Mr. Secretary, I suggest that you start enumerating the items on your requisition."

"My immediate needs are dependent on what I can learn from
Julio San Marco." Callender set his jaw. "I must see him first."

"San Marco is in the hotel. The meeting with him will happen
quickly once my brother and I understand your plans. But first, we
would appreciate knowing the general scope of your needs."

"I need a group of approximately fifty trained guerrilla fighters
of various nationalities to begin infiltrating Cuba at once and structured so that they can be assembled into a fighting unit, equipped
with weapons, on two-hour call."

"Where do you want them assembled?" He grinned again. "San
Juan Hill?"

Callender controlled his temper. "I need the men within a fifty-
mile radius of Havana. I do not have all the details. I must talk to
San Marco first."

The brother called Phil stood up, stretched in the warmth of the
beginning sun. "These fifty men . . . how do they get out of Cuba?"

"I can handle it through another source or you can arrange it
yourself."

He looked at his brother. "What do you think, Ted?"

"We pay widow's benefits. We've already lost a man getting San
Marco. We'd better let Miguel and Arnold figure it out." He turned
to Callender. "We'll handle it."

"What else, Mr. Secretary? It can't be all that simple."

"I will probably need a small jet which can land in Havana without
suspicion."

"We assume you're going in as Luis Kunz?"

Callender nodded.

"What else?"

"Until I interrogate Julio San Marco, I am not certain."

Ted asked, "What are the risks?" When Callender seemed puzzled, he clarified, saying, "I'm not talking about personal risks. What are the geopolitical risks?"

"It depends," Callender replied, "on what your nationality is."

"Neat point, Mr. Secretary." He looked at his brother and winked. "Any more questions at this moment, Phil?"

"The banker mentality applies here. Old customer. Good record. Current statement solid." He shrugged his shoulders. "The collateral is okay, isn't it?"

"Payment will be made through the usual channels," Callender said. "That's still the way you want it?"

"Same way."

"The only thing, Ted, is that when an old account is going into a new business, when the diversification is lateral . . . it's usually a good idea to get the concept of the new venture."

"It seems to me"—Callender kept straight-faced—"that you understand the concept of the new venture very well." He stood up. The brothers closed on each side of him and they walked three abreast into the living room.

"Miguel." There was no answer. He called again, raised the volume of his voice. "Miguel!" They waited but the man did not appear. The inner alarm sounded in the three simultaneously. Following Ted, they ran through the hall and into the kitchen. Miguel was sitting at the kitchen table, his head bent too far over the morning newspaper. The hilt of a knife protruded from the base of his skull, thrust into the man with extraordinary strength. There was a door from the kitchen to the back stairs. Ted opened it; the three men held their breaths listening for sounds as they ran down. There was nothing.

"San Marco," Callender warned.

They took the elevator down to the floor below. Again following Ted, they ran in a line down the hotel corridor. Two men guarding a door at the far end of the hall stood up, drew guns. When they recognized the brothers, they put them back in their holsters.

"Have you seen anyone?"

The men looked at each other. The taller man answered. "There has been no one, nothing."

"Give me the key."

Quietly, he turned the key in the lock and silently cracked the door open enough so that he could see in, then closed the door

soundlessly. "Everything seems okay. We'd better get back up."
They started running toward the elevator, stopped when they realized that Callender wasn't following them. They looked at each
other, silently agreed. Phil called back to the guards. "Let him in."

The lock turned behind Callender. San Marco was on the bed. His
head moved in Callender's direction. Callender put his finger to his
lips to indicate silence. He knew that the room would be bugged.
When San Marco's head turned further, Callender saw the hilt of the
knife sticking out of the socket where San Marco's good eye had
been. He gagged and heaved, the sticky, sweet coffee erupting from
his mouth, cascading onto the carpet. When he recovered enough,
he went over to San Marco, just in time to hear a death sound fill
the room and see Marco's good arm drop over the side of the bed,
his whole body as inert now as his battleworn arm.

Callender tried the door, found it locked. Neither of the guards
opened it. With the flat of both hands, he beat against the polished
wood. The guards had fled. No one was there to hear him. At the
opposite end of the room, he fumbled with the double set of draperies to get them open, finally ripped them down, opened the lock
and safety catch on the glass slide wall leading to the balcony. He
looked down in time to see the two guards running out of the
entrance and into a waiting car. The revving wheels stirred a spray
of dust. When it settled down, the car was gone. There was no
doorman to call to. He could see no sign of life in the hotel parking
lot or on the jungle-lush grounds. He looked up toward the penthouse terrace. One of the brothers was running out to investigate
the screeching sound of the escape car. Callender cupped his hands
in the shape of a megaphone.

The man who turned around was Ted. Using the side of his hand,
Callender made a cutting gesture across his throat. It took a moment for the signal to register and then he ran off the terrace.
Callender went back into the room, did not look at the body on the
bed, stepped around the spot of vomited coffee, and waited at the
door.

The cold Coke seemed to settle his stomach. Miguel's body was
in the process of being removed from the kitchen. Ted was giving
instructions in Spanish to two unidentified men. "Ask your brother
to come in, please. Something must be done before San Marco's
body is disposed of. It's important."

He went to the kitchen door, signaled his brother, and they both came back into the living room.

"Strip the body," Callender instructed them. "I need every piece of his clothing and identification. Don't forget the eye patch and the arm sling. Strip the body clean."

Ted returned to the kitchen.

"You'd better tell us what you have in mind, Mr. Callender."

Callender peeled off the black wig, carefully removed the moustache, and placed both objects on the table next to him. "It would seem to me, on the basis of what has happened, that you and your brother are still in the learning process."

"We did bungle it a bit, didn't we?"

"Your ineptness cost you the most important man in this part of the world. And I have lost a valued and trusted friend." He rubbed his eyes. "You have also endangered a very sensitive situation by allowing San Marco to be killed."

Eating from a carton of yogurt, Ted came back into the living room. "Has Mr. Callender been giving us a dressing down?"

"I don't understand what we did wrong." Phil looked at Callender. "I know that you aren't going to believe this but whatever security mistake was made, wherever this went amuck, the blame has to fall on Miguel. The kidnapping and the escape from Cuba were all his plan. The personnel, including the two guards, were Miguel's men. Ted and I have simply been observers. Wouldn't that be the way to put it, Ted?"

"We have had indications from time to time," Ted explained, "that Miguel was becoming slack. Rather too old for the job. I would say that this bungling substantiates our information."

Deliberately, Callender feigned patience. "Miguel was the single most effective man at this work of any man I have ever known in my whole life."

"It doesn't accomplish anything by stewing around about a deed done, does it?" Ted pulled a chair next to his brother, sat down. "It's rather like a Euclidian problem. One ought to take a geometric approach. Given that two sides of a triangle are equal . . . I should think that kind of mentality is required at this point. Miguel is dead. San Marco is dead. What do we do now?"

Phil asked Callender, "Would it help to know who killed them?"

"In my equation," Callender explained, "if they were killed by Castro's Cubans, one set of circumstances apply. If they were killed by anti-Castro Cubans, which is the most likely explanation, different options exist. If they were killed by some other group or power structure, another set of alternatives is available to me."

"Us, Mr. Callender. Three people make a plural."

The undersecretary ignored the interruption. "I am going to assume that San Marco and Miguel were not killed by Castro. The motivation for Castro would be against Miguel but certainly not against San Marco. At least I can see no reason for him to want to kill San Marco. Both Miguel and San Marco were killed by the same man. There can't be two men in the world who wield that deadly a knife."

"Castro would be motivated if he thought San Marco had defected again."

Callender could not understand the source of the brothers' information, the depth of intelligence information at their fingertips. Miguel had known none of the details of the Kunz plan, had never questioned motivations or details unless they were specific to the tactical execution of his part of the mission. And who would know about the poster in his bedroom—Theodore Roosevelt leading the charge on San Juan Hill? "I am going to take the calculated risk that Miguel and San Marco were murdered by Cuban Nationalists. They are the only ones with sufficient cause to eliminate San Marco. They must have known that he was back with Castro and they would consider that defection a traitorous act to the Nationalists' movement." Callender saw again the picture of the dagger plunged into the eye socket, felt the nausea return. "The punishment fits the crime from the Nationalists' standpoint."

"What if you're wrong? What if Castro *does* know that San Marco is dead?"

"In order for me to proceed, I must go under the assumption that Castro thinks that San Marco is still alive." He thought for a moment. "There is a way to test that." He looked at Phil. "Put your machinery in motion. Put through a ransom demand to Castro, ask a million-dollar ransom for the return of Julio San Marco."

"Castro will laugh. San Marco isn't worth that kind of money to Castro."

"Exactly," Callender said. "If he negotiates the price, then we can assume that he believes that San Marco is still alive."

The brothers exchanged glances. "It's worth a try," Ted said.

"Meanwhile," Callender continued, "I will need a man to impersonate San Marco. We have all his clothing. We need a man about the same general size and stature. The lame arm and missing eye can be faked."

"I think we ought to know more details of your plan, Mr. Callender."

The undersecretary's smile was indulgent, paternal. "I can understand your enthusiasm for wanting to be seasoned in the field but not at my expense, not where my life is at stake and my future is on the line."

Ted said, "Are you saying, play it your way . . . or else?"

Callender nodded.

"We'll play it your way, Mr. Secretary, but we would like to go on record that the decision is based on the exigency of time, the imminence of danger. We are temporarily deferring to your age and to your experience." The soft smile on his face turned into set-jaw determination, the diffident tone of his voice changed to hard words, harshly spoken. "This is the last time you're going to power play with us. Understand that clearly. We are not spirited boys who have just broken a window playing baseball and are standing like soldiers to receive punishment. You are still face-to-face with the largest, single, private power structure in the world, including the organization known as the Mafia. Without us, you accomplish nothing. Without our power, you have no strength. You need us, Mr. Secretary, we don't need you." He looked the older man up and down, a hauteur of disgust. "We keep a tremendous inventory of men like you, men who will sell their souls to feed their ambition. If we don't use you, there is someone else available to suit our purposes."

In a counterplay of attitudes, speaking in a less threatening voice, Phil said, "What my brother is trying to point out to you, Mr. Callender, is that our deference to you is temporary. Pragmatic. Father always taught us to be pragmatic, didn't he, Ted?"

GREAT GUANA CAY, EXHUMA CHAIN, BAHAMAS, WEST INDIES

Guido said, "You get jet lag on this job. One fucking airplane after another. The jet lag is more dangerous than someone taking a shot at you." He was throwing clothes into a small duffel bag. "I can't figure out what's so important that Victor Castle needs me in Europe. Doesn't this shoot the timetable to hell? I mean, what does this have to do with our schedule? I'm supposed to go to Haiti with Roger."

"I've worked it out," Rinaldi said, compulsively folding Guido's clothes before the Italian mashed them into the suitcase. "Whatever it is that Victor wants you to do, he said it won't take long. It sounds like an in-and-out job. You can fly back directly to Port-au-Prince. That will save time. There will be no point in your coming here, we'll be gone by then."

"It doesn't sound right to me. It doesn't make any sense. It doesn't sound like Castle." He started to say something, changed his mind.

"Victor knows the timetable. He wouldn't take any risks. He says you can be back and forth easily."

"I need travel money," Guido said. "I need a lot."

Rinaldi counted out three thousand American dollars. Guido zipped up his bag, counted the money. "When I get to Miami, I'm going to call Victor in Switzerland." He studied Rinaldi, waited for a reaction. "Don't you care that I'm going over your head to contact Victor directly?"

"Why should I?"

"Because I think maybe you're lying to me, making up this story about Victor having a job for me to do in Europe. I figure if I were you, I'd want me out of the way for a lot of reasons." He squared up to the older man. "You know that I'm going to kill Roger. I don't figure you for the kind of man who is going to stand back and let his wife's son get killed." Rinaldi looked away, did not answer. "And maybe besides saving Roger's life, you figure to do a number on Victor, cheat him maybe."

"You're a crazy kid, Guido. We both swore an oath. I know the priorities of my loyalties, I know my obligation." Rinaldi's smile was indulgent when he looked back at Guido. "If I wanted to get you out of the way, there would be an easier way. I would not have to involve Victor Castle."

"In the end, Aldo, you and I will be partners; we will need each other. Victor Castle is old. He will not live forever. I am like a son to him. Do you understand?"

"Maybe some day, Guido. Who knows? I've seen your kind come and go. Victor Castle was like you in the beginning but he survived. He was smart enough and tough enough . . . and lucky enough not to get killed."

"Not luck. Instinct. Don't think it's luck, Aldo. Don't make that mistake. Men like Victor and me can smell danger, feel it coming, know where it's hiding."

"Like animals."

Guido smiled, left the room.

Leaning against the side of the house, shadowed by the overhang of the roof, Rinaldi watched the little plane take off, head for Miami. One day, he was thinking, there would be a Guido . . . possibly this Guido . . . who would claw and scratch and maraud his way to the top. It had happened before and it would happen again—as certain as the natural circular structure of an acivilized jungle, the progression of lions, the supremacy of the bull elephant. The only real survivors were those who did not challenge, who could adapt to a new cycle of power evolution. Rinaldi realized that he lived in a civilization of lions and like a cub reared by humans and then turned loose into a natural habitat, his instincts were not fully developed, not honed sharply enough to kill and survive. There was not even the instinctive reaction to protect a cub.

One of the mercenaries touched his arm, brought him back to the reality of this particular instance of survival. "Harry wants to see you." Rinaldi followed the man around the house, through the chain-link gate and into the control room.

"They're nibbling at the line," Harry said.

"I don't understand."

"The brigantine. Our connection in Panama radioed in. There have been three inquiries into the registry of the *Aventuro.*"

"Any details?"

"One from the Third Turtle Inn at the Providenciales. The *Aventuro* was anchored there for two days. The English owner of the inn complained that the crew left a stack of unpaid bills. He wants to find the owner of the ship, collect his money."

"Who else?"

"The United States Navy, no less. That inquiry must have come through Guantanamo. The third request came from Santiago de Cuba. Official. The Cuban government made that inquiry."

Rinaldi was at the big map, tracing the course of the brigantine. "It will take weeks to unravel the tangle of the Panamanian registry. They will learn nothing." He smiled at the mercenary. "Everything so far is working perfectly: the fish are nibbling at the bait."

The man called Harry walked close to Rinaldi, talked in a low voice. "In the beginning, I thought this was the craziest operation I'd ever heard of. If it hadn't been for the big money, I'd still be in Africa where everything is fucked up but understandable. In Africa you expect everything to be fucked up . . . it's normal there. This thing looked crazy to me . . . not do-able: a commando raid into Cuba was crazy and then when I began to know the specific plans it seemed even crazier." He shook his head. "I have to confess, I thought Roger Ramirez was insane. Maybe he is but he sure knows how to plan an operation. Professional military minds couldn't plan this as well. Maybe you have to be crazy. Maybe Hannibal and Alexander were crazy. Maybe Napoleon was a raving maniac."

"You're a student of military history?"

He put his finger on the course of the brigantine. "Enough to know that the *Aventuro* is a wooden horse."

Rinaldi laughed, patted the man's shoulder. "You have all underestimated my son."

Harry hesitated. "We've had our orders; you know that. I'm sorry if we've given him a bad time but . . . well, orders are orders. You understand?" Rinaldi nodded. "I didn't know that he was your son. It was my understanding that Roger is your wife's son."

In the animal kingdom, Rinaldi reasoned, it is the female lion who protects the cub, kills to feed it. "And if the lioness doesn't?"

"If the lioness doesn't . . . what?"

He was not aware that he had asked the question out loud. He turned, walked away without answering Harry's question or his own.

1978
AUGUST

13

SUNDAY

THE GRAND HOTEL OLAFFSON'S, PORT-AU-PRINCE, HAITI

In the half-light of the darkness descending, the gingerbread architectural details were white silhouettes against the darkening sky. Olaffson's Hotel was like the picture of Dorian Gray aging into a deformed, depraved monster in a hidden corner of an attic. What it had once been, the postcard beauty of fanciful Victorian architecture in a lush tropical setting, was scarcely discernible now. The white paint was gray and peeling, the green shutters broken, some off the hinges and hanging at oblique angles, the iron railings rusted and missing sections, the jigsawed fretwork broken and never replaced; an old face missing teeth. The vegetation had grown unchecked into macro-sized leaves and tentacles, green prehistoric forms slowly consuming the building.

Edgerton and Jud Wheeler stood at the street level, looking up at the building on the hill. "Are you sure that this is the right place?"

"The Italian gave me the name of the place to meet him. I'd forgotten it but when I checked the hotel directory at the airport, it came back to me."

"It looks like a flophouse to me." A black, native woman approached them, teetering on spike-heeled, high-platform shoes. She stood in front of them, raised her arms, and turned slowly to exhibit her body. Wheeler blushed, looked away, wiped the palms of his hands against his trousers, looked over to Edgerton, and then back to the woman. "I don't think this is the right place," he said.

The woman curled her tongue, darted it in and out of her mouth.

Edgerton pushed her away. She wavered, unsteadily off-balance, then walked on. "You can do what you want. I'm going up there." He picked up his suitcase, started up the uneven brick surface of the semicircular driveway, not looking back to see if Wheeler was following him.

It was a calculated risk, letting Wheeler accompany him to Port-au-Prince. When Lowell Callender had not reappeared on Andros and no contact had materialized to reestablish communication with Key West, Edgerton had examined the alternatives, went through the painful process of determining prescribed procedure, effective action. As a professional agent, there was no question that he should proceed to Haiti, learn what he could, abort the action if possible, become a one-man army if necessary in spite of the warning from Key West. That was clearly what he was paid to do. But his thinking was diverted and dissembled by his personal problems, this decision crucial to the rest of his life. Two pictures stayed in his mind: the very real picture of Carroll Coulter, a man broken now beyond repair, nowhere to go but down, a declining future. Edgerton equated himself to Coulter: saw a similiar pattern of future decay. Then there was the fantasy picture of Edgerton the star holding out his arms to the man who had fathered him.

The *Playgirl* story, which was real to him only as a cover identity, was more than that to the *Playgirl* staff. They all saw it as a chance for him to recapture a film career, a new start. All dreams were possible if that miracle happened, if that success came. Carroll Coulter would reascend with him; neither would end derelict. And he could meet his father, man-to-man, star-to-star, and finally, son-to-father.

Monica was another complication. She had started as an hostile object, taunting his masculinity and his masculinity had resurged as a potent weapon to counterattack the threatening object. After that, they had become two people capable of the physical act of loving and of being loved by each other. A tenderness developed and now existed between them, a beginning of a total relationship.

Disappearing from Andros, abandoning the *Playgirl* assignment before it was completed, rejecting Monica and the potential that relationship offered, was consistent with Edgerton the agent, the compulsive loser. Those were the words of the funny psychiatrist ... compulsive loser. The question remained unanswered in his own mind—was that label for the man, or the label of the covert identity of the man?

In the end, Jud Wheeler had made the decision for him. Wheeler had come back to Andros raving mad, looking for Callender, who had slipped away from him. It was Wheeler who waved the United States flag at Edgerton, filled him in with enough details of the Cuban operation to convince him of the importance of the interception of it to world peace. It was Wheeler who put the first doubt in his mind about Callender's loyalty, the allegiance of Callender's objectives. Edgerton had taken Wheeler's credentials at face, aware that the man could be an enemy agent, could be trying to subvert the interception rather than implement it. Accepting Wheeler's identity as real was a calculated risk but Wheeler's arguments were convincing and he offered transportation to Port-au-Prince. With one telephone call, he had been able to make a small unidentified plane materialize at the Nicollstown airstrip that flew them first to Cap Hatien and then through the high mountains, across the island, past the Citadel, and finally landing at Port-au-Prince.

During the flight to Haiti, they had sat crammed together in the middle row of seats. Wheeler had used Edgerton as a sounding board, talking and asking questions aimed to sort out his own thinking, not to enlighten Edgerton. "I'm a student of political history," he explained. "From Machiavelli on, I've studied the power strategy of the movers and shakers of the world: how they grasped power, how they held on to it, and what mistakes they made, why they lost it. Good guys and bad guys use the same disciplines, the same tricks. In the beginning, when they make their first moves, it's sometimes hard to predict which are the black hats and which are the white hats. Some of the bad guys do a lot of good in their initial power-play moves. It's a feint and a deception for their ultimate objectives. The smart ones aren't all bad, that's why they're smart. Amin isn't smart. In the beginning, Nixon was. Nixon was really little league compared to the big guys, more of an opportunist. Trouble with him was that he didn't aim high enough.

"Huey Long was like that. So was McCarthy," he went on. "They had the right kind of cunning but basically they were small potato guys, weren't really big shooters."

"You think Lowell Callender is like that?"

Wheeler nodded. "I think he's a big shooter, plenty smart. It looks to me as though he's using the Teddy Roosevelt game plan, going to create a whole fucking war to catapult himself into the limelight, make himself a hero to gain political power."

"I thought Teddy Roosevelt was a good guy."

"The myth continues," Wheeler said. "In the end, maybe he was. He needed to be a bad guy to become a good guy. There have been others like that. But they all start the same. Do you see my point?" He asked the question but did not look over for the answer. "In the beginning they have the greed, have the dream and the vision to make that dream come true. It's an historical pattern of ascendance to power. Strip off the time of history and the place in history, make an outline of their early moves. It's all the same. Alexander. Caesar. Napoleon. Hitler. Castro. Name them all and you'll find a pre-scribed methodology. You need a war if times are good. Or you need the oppression of bad times to overthrow existing power.

"But, in the beginning, you need to assemble a palace guard, a hard core of honchos, tough enough to make it happen, keep the ball bouncing. That was Nixon's problem. The guys who ringed him were inept. Like I said, small-potato mentalities. If I had been where Ehrlichman was . . ." His voice trailed off.

"Isn't that where you are now?"

"But the man has no dream. He's got the greed and diligence. But not the big dream. You need the big dream."

They had flown the rest of the way to Cap Hatien in silence. Edgerton understood that Wheeler was dreaming with his eyes open.

Edgerton climbed the steep, decaying staircase to the porch which surrounded both levels of the hotel, looked back and watched Wheeler chugging uncertainly up the driveway, reluctantly putting one foot in front of the other, a man walking to gallows. All that Edgerton could see inside the lobby were a few pink shaded lights, white-coated natives shuffling noiselessly through the rooms. There was the mechanical sound of a player piano.

Wheeler was breathing heavily when he came alongside Edger-ton. "How do we handle this?"

"Register separately. Two rooms. Use a phony name."

"Won't they ask for my passport?"

"I doubt it. Bluff your way."

"What about you?"

"I'll use my own name. I want them to find me."

There was a maze of rooms on the first floor, accumulations of furniture from all over the world. The first room seemed to have been cribbed from a Moorish palace, a huge bird cage sitting on the center of an octagonal banquette, a stuffed, dusty red macaw permanently perched on a swing. Beyond it was a small room, a huge, littered table in the center of it, a slowly rotating ceiling fan over the table; the walls studded with framed photographs, taped-up snapshots, out-of-date calendars, irrelevant theatrical posters, and faded dust jackets of books.

The fat man was sitting in a large, peacock-shaped, rattan chair behind the table wearing a large, white, straw hat, his shirt sleeves rolled up, a black-string tie hanging askew from his rumpled collar. He did not look up as Wheeler stood in front of him, was absorbed in reading a postcard. "Reservation?"

Edgerton answered. "No. We need two rooms."

He took a large yellowing paged ledger, opened it, flicked through the pages. "What is the date today?"

"August thirteenth."

The man found the page with that date. Edgerton tried to read the list of names on the registry but they were written in a small, illegible hand and there were many cross-outs and insertions. "Very busy for this time of the year. Very busy." He was American, his voice flat, midwestern sounding. "Seems that we're full up. Not usually full this time of year." His hand smashed against a call bell on the table and for the first time he looked up. "You boys from Guantanamo?" He shook his head in answer to his own question. "Too old. Most of the boys that come over from Guantanamo are just kids. Unless you're specialists. Lots of specialists come over from Guantanamo." He hit the call bell again, studied the reservation list. "None of the regulars come at this time of the year. We get writers mostly. Did you know that? Harold Pinter and Lady Antonia just left. We get some actors. New York mostly. Not phoney enough for the Hollywood crowd." He looked up at one of the white-coated natives. He spoke to him in a pidgin French, speaking very quickly. Edgerton caught a word or two, could not follow the conversation.

While they were talking, Edgerton happened to look up, saw three men coming down the stairs. The man in the middle was Roger Ramirez. He saw Edgerton, gave no signal of recognition. The three men crowded into the small room, one of them threw two keys on the cluttered table. The owner interrupted his conversation, switched back to English. "No point in leaving your keys. The locks on the doors aren't worth a damn. I won't be around by the time you finish dinner anyway. There won't be anyone to give the keys back to you. You can just leave them lie here if you want but some of those damn beggars might get to them."

There was time, while the man rambled, for the men with Ramirez to study Edgerton and Wheeler closely. They had positioned their bodies as a protective cordon around Ramirez. Edgerton assumed that they were part of the mercenary group based on Great Guana but the odds were against their recognizing him from the brief stopover on the island. He had been visible only on his walk from the plane to the hangar and back again. Ramirez continued to play out the bluff, looking at Edgerton directly, a stranger examining a stranger. Ramirez walked out before the other two men. They looked at each other, quickly picked up the keys and followed Ramirez. Edgerton could not determine from their behavior if the two men were in custody control of Ramirez or were bodyguards under Ramirez's direction. Wheeler had no way of identifying Ramirez. Edgerton decided to play it that way: tell Wheeler nothing.

The owner and the white-coated native picked up their pidgin conversation, examining the ledger book, turning back and forward to examine the reservation lists. In English, he asked, "How many nights?" He was looking at Wheeler when he asked the question; Wheeler looked back to Edgerton.

"Two or three," Edgerton said. "It depends on the weather."

"Always beautiful. Irving Stone used to love Haiti in the summer. So did Hemingway." He pointed vaguely toward the walls. "You can see from the photographs on the walls what kind of people we get here." He slammed the book closed. "I have one lousy room upstairs . . . all the way at the end of the building. This was a Marine Corps hospital once, many years ago. Did you know that?" He was not interested in their answer. "The only other thing available is the Sidney Sheldon suite down by the swimming pool. It used to be the Graham Greene suite but I changed the name for political reasons. There's plenty of room for both of you in there."

"We'll take the two rooms," Edgerton said.

"I'm warning you that the single room is small, not one of our best."

"It's okay."

"You boys going to flip a coin for the suite?"

"Not necessary," Edgerton said quickly. "Mr. Judson might not be staying as long as I am."

"You pay for breakfast and dinner whether you eat them or not. We have good food; the best this side of Pietonville. Breakfast from seven until ten, lunch from twelve through three, dinner from eight until eleven." He looked up. "You pay in advance." He stood up, belched, pulled up his wrinkled white trousers over his bulging stomach. "Marcel here," he nodded at the native, "will figure up how much money and show you where your rooms are." As an afterthought, he said, "Have a nice stay."

When the owner left and Marcel had gone to get their suitcases, Wheeler said, "How come I get the shitty room?"

"Remember why we're here. I may have an Italian roommate. I want to be able to entertain him properly."

Wheeler cocked his head toward the bar. "Those were three suspicious-looking guys."

"In this kind of an operation, everyone begins to look suspicious. You don't trust your own mother after a while."

"I still think I ought to contact the CIA. There must be agents in Haiti who can give us some reinforcement if we need it. The least it would do is give us some channel of communication back to Langley."

"You try anything funny, Jud, and you lose me. My instructions are explicit. I wait to be contacted; I never initiate a contact. Sometimes, your faith runs out, you think everyone has forgotten that you're alive. But eventually, the contact comes." Edgerton had retrieved the ledger, opened it casually, studied the names on the reservation lists. None of them meant anything to him. The names were a mixture of French, German, Spanish, and American. Some of them probably no more real than Irving Judson. "Let me explain something about my training," Edgerton said. His voice was just above a whisper. "I have official authority to kill to accomplish an assignment. It's a special designation. The CIA spent a lot of money teaching me how to kill, all the different methods of killing, sharpening my instincts to know when to kill. My discipline is to eliminate any obstacles." He smiled. "What if there is a man named Irving Judson and he becomes an obstacle?" He waited while Wheeler understood him. "I eliminate him, right? That's my job. How do I know that Irving Judson is really a special assistant to the President? What way would I have of knowing?" He closed the ledger and put it back in position. "I'd be an agent doing his job."

"You know something, Edge? You make Lowell Callender look like one of the Hardy boys."

Edgerton sat alone at the bar, dressed in cut-offs and a tank top. He was barefoot. He had purposely used too much musk oil, did not like the overwhelming smell of it. He had taken the time to add bleach to his hair, blow-drying it carefully into perfect shape. He was the bait again.

From where he was sitting, by looking into the mirror behind the bar, he could keep surveillance on the dining room behind him. Ramirez sat alone. The two men who had been with him earlier were eating together at another table. There was a group of five men around a circular table, a black man with a young, blonde, white girl, two middle-aged women at a small table, another nondescript man eating alone and a trio of young men whispering secrets and then giggling loudly at each other's comments. They had seen Edgerton walk into the bar and from the way they looked over at him while they were talking, it was evident that they were appraising him.

Wheeler, disgruntled by his accommodations, angry at being shunted out of the way and alternately belligerent and subdued by Edgerton's threats, had taken a cab and gone up to a restaurant in Pietonville to have dinner, understanding that for Edgerton to be effective he had to appear to be alone and unencumbered.

There was no sign of Guido. The appearance of Ramirez was not a surprise to Edgerton. Whatever was beginning here in Port-au-Prince would involve them all.

Through the mirror, Edgerton saw Ramirez stand up, take his demitasse of coffee, and walk toward the bar. He set the cup next to Edgerton, then hoisted himself on to the barstool. The men in the dining room watched every move.

"We will talk as strangers," Ramirez said, "and then I will say my name and you will say your name and we will shake hands. Do not talk loud and pretend to flirt with me. Do you understand?" Edgerton threw his head back and laughed. Ramirez said his name, held out his hand. Edgerton repeated the deception, felt the clammy moistness of the handshake. "It is not accidental that you are here," Ramirez said, no question in the inflection of his voice. "You are American intelligence. There is no other possible explanation."

"I could be crazy about your body," Edgerton said. "Or your money. That's a possible explanation. You passed me off to your

father and that young Italian as a hustler. You look like you have
enough bread to make the hustle worthwhile. How do you know that
I'm not just another hustler?"

Ramirez put his hand on Edgerton's shoulder and then on his
neck. "They will think you are a hustler." He indicated the men at
the other table. "They will expect me to try to pick you up." With
his thumb he flicked the lobe of Edgerton's ear. "Play the game with
me. I will make it worth your while." He put his hand down, drank
the rest of his coffee, slapped his hand against the bar top, waited
until the bartender appeared, and then ordered two rum punches.
His voice muffled by the sound of the blender, Ramirez continued
talking. "You must understand that whatever you are—whether
you're CIA or just a hustler—it will be worth your while. Is that
clear?"

Edgerton waited to answer until the bartender had put the drinks
in front of them and disappeared into the room behind the bar. "I
listen a lot," Edgerton said. "Keep talking."

"How much do you already know?"

"I told you that I'm a good listener, Ramirez. I was never a man
to talk very much."

The Cuban turned away, lowered his head, looked down into the
rum punch. "There is no one to trust. I must trust you. I know that
you will not tell me the truth. If you are a CIA agent, you will not
admit it. I understand that. But there is no other explanation for
your being here now. I have examined all the possibilities which
could explain why you are here. There is the only logical explanation. I hope you are CIA. I think that there is danger to your country. By helping me, you will be helping the United States. I must
make you believe that."

"How?"

"By telling you the truth, by telling you the whole story."

"Start at the beginning."

Both at once, through the mirror, saw the two men coming toward them from the dining room. Ramirez whispered, "I will come
to your room later." He touched Edgerton's cheek and then took
out a wad of bills, counted out fifty dollars, tucked them into the
front of Edgerton's tank top. "They will expect me to come to your
room later. It will be all right."

"By the pool," Edgerton said. "The suite by the pool."

He watched the reflection of the two men form a shoulder-to-shoulder wedge on either side of Ramirez, lead him off toward the staircase. Then the trio of giggly men who had left the dining room now surrounded him, their perfume as potent as his. He slipped through them without looking at them, sauntered back into the dining room to have dinner, heard one of the men mutter the word "bitch."

Later, after Ramirez had left his room, Edgerton drew from memory an outline map of Cuba on a piece of toilet paper, marking Havana with an X. In the lower right-hand corner, he sketched the shape of Haiti, guessing at the width of the Windward Passage which separated it from Cuba. He Xed in the two approximate points of Cozumel and Key West. When he had completed the crude drawing, studied it, he crumpled it and flushed it down the toilet. Taking a long streamer off the toilet paper roll, he sat down and blocked out the timetable Ramirez had given him.

TODAY:
    HOTDOG SCHWARTZ IN CUBA.
    MERCENARIES BEGIN INFILTRATION.
    RINALDI, ON HIRED YACHT EN ROUTE
    TO POSITION BETWEEN HAVANA AND
    KEY WEST.

WEDNESDAY:
    GUIDO ARRIVES PORT-AU-PRINCE FROM
    WHERE?
    AVENTURO ARRIVES COZUMEL, LOADS
    EXPLOSIVES
    UNDERWATER ARMY BOARDS SUBMARINE
    OFF COZUMEL.

THURSDAY:
    RAMIREZ AND GUIDO LEAVE PORT-AU-
    PRINCE WITH 4 MERCENARIES. FLY
    PORT-AU-PRINCE TO KINGSTON TO
    HAVANA.
    RINALDI DOCKS PALM BAY CLUB, MIAMI-
    TAKES PROVISIONS - PROCEEDS.

AVENTURO DEPARTS COZUMEL – FULL
SPEED TO RENDEZVOUS POINT
OFF CUBA.
SUB FOLLOWS IN AVENTURO WAKE.

FRIDAY:
 ZERO HOUR (NINE P.M.)
 AIRCRAFT FROM GREAT GUANA
 FEINT ATTACK ON SANTIAGO AND ISLE
 OF PINES SIMULTANEOUSLY.
 GUIDO AND RAMIREZ AT COAST
 POSITION WHERE JEWELS AND MONEY
 HIDDEN.
 UNDERSEA ARMY ARRIVES RENDEZVOUS
 POINT WITH EXPLOSIVES AND
 EQUIPMENT.
 AVENTURO EXPLODES
 RINALDI COMES IN BEHIND
 TERRITORIAL LIMIT TO PICK UP
 SURVIVORS
 UNDERSEA ARMY IN POSSESSION OF
 JEWELS AND MONEY – GIVE OUTFITS
 TO GUIDO AND RAMIREZ WITH TANKS
 AND EQUIPMENT. ALL RACE TO
 RAMIREZ YACHT.
 ZERO HOUR PLUS ONE (TEN P.M.)

ALL SAFELY ABOARD YACHT – PROCEEDS
 BACK TO GREAT GUANA.

Ramirez had been unclear about the exact details of the plan involving Hotdog Schwartz. Ramirez was not sure if Schwartz's role was to recover money or to assassinate Castro. He was obviously motivated and capable of doing both. Whatever arrangements were made for Schwartz to get out of Cuba were unknown to Ramirez. Again, using guesswork, he thought the overall plan was for Schwartz to be apprehended either before or after the assassination attempt.

There had been an unstated empathy between the two men as Ramirez told Edgerton about the father he had never really known, a man whose picture he had never even seen, a legend of a man nurtured in Ramirez's own mind. Ramirez was no longer the creep. Edgerton understood how the childhood anguish had matured into adult vengeance and had respect now for the twisted brilliance and keen perception of Ramirez's mind. There was that bond between them.

"What about Rinaldi?" Edgerton asked. "He seems to care about you."

"Rinaldi is in on it. He knows that they plan to kill me. He is powerless in the organization to stop it even if he wanted to." His face softened for a moment. "In his own way, Aldo has feelings for me . . . he feels responsible that my mother does not love me, can't stand the sight of me. Since I have lived with them, he has tried to compensate for my mother. I am more realistic about her than he is." He shrugged his shoulders, the gesture of a man abandoning a dream. "No matter what is in Aldo's heart, in the final analysis, he will do as Victor Castle directs him. They will all do exactly as Victor Castle directs them. Even Guido. In the beginning, I thought Guido was an ally."

"Who is Guido?"

"An Italian I picked up in a bar in Rome." Ramirez shook his head. "Now I can see that they planted Guido in the bar. Guido is paid by them, is part of their plan to get my money and destroy me. Guido will do it. Guido will kill me. He loves and kills with the same intensity."

Unconsciously, Edgerton's hand went into his pocket, touched the cold circle of the snake ring.

"Guido and I will go into Cuba together. The plan is for me to lead Guido to the exact location of my father's money. It is then that Guido will kill me. I will be more useful as a corpse. They will leave my body on the rocks for Castro to discover and to use the name Ramirez again as a symbol of greed against all the Cuban nationalists and loyalists to remind the world of the Batista corruption. He will use my dead body to reinforce his revolution. Castro will make it appear as though I have been financed by the United States, that I am an agent of your government. It is Castro's pattern. He knows how to make it work."

All the pieces of the briefings in Colorado came together in Edgerton's awareness. There were no longer alternative courses of action, no time or places for personal introspection, psychological indulgences. The commitment was clear, unavoidable.

"If you know that it's certain death," he had asked, "why do you go? Why don't you just disappear, wait for another time?"

Quietly, a smile coming on his face, Ramirez said, "Because I am more clever than they think. It does not have to be certain death. My plan will still work in spite of them." He zeroed his attention straight on to Edgerton. "You must help me. If you help me, if we do this together, we can both live and both be very rich."

"How?"

"First you must kill Guido. Before it is time to go to Cuba, you must kill Guido and take his place. I cannot do this alone. You will become Guido."

"How can I get away with that? What about those men with you? How are you going to lose them?"

"They will have to be eliminated first."

"Say that could happen." He leaned closer to Ramirez. "Say that one way or another we get rid of the two mercenaries and Guido. We're still out there bare-assed with all of Castro's forces aiming at us."

"The map," Ramirez said. "I have the real map. I told you that I protected myself against this. I built in a fail-safe factor. The map which I gave to Aldo and which Aldo gave to Castle is fake. I faked the real map which my father left for me. The location of the cliffs is a mile west of where their map shows. There are only two copies of the real map. I have one and my mother has one in her jewelry vault at Cap Ferrat." He leaned back, straightened his body, smiled at his own cunning. "They forgot that I am Carlos Ramirez's son."

"What you are telling me is that this whole commando strike, all the action is keyed to the wrong place?" Ramirez nodded. "The real treasure is a mile away?"

"Exactly. It was my safety device. If everything had gone according to plan, if everyone had not tried to double-cross me, I would have changed the coordinates at the last minute, directed the strike to the correct place."

"Say that I believe you. Say that we get there and find the vaults, the brigantine and the planes and Rinaldi's yacht were all methods of getting you and the vaults out of Cuba. "How are you going to do it without them?"

"That is the risk. Together we must carry the contents of the vault across the country, traveling at night, hiding by day. It will be dangerous. But if we can get to Santiago, there will be relatives there who will help me. They will be able to get a boat and take us across to Haiti again."

"And Victor Castle? What are you going to do about him?"

"There will be a way. With money, there is always a way."

Edgerton had left Ramirez hanging. Although he made the commitment in his own mind, he had not verbalized it to the Cuban. In the final analysis, he would kill Guido and the two mercenaries if necessary, act out the plot with Ramirez, wait for tactical opportunities to accomplish his own mission: avert the invasion, intercept Hotdog Schwartz, and get Ramirez out of Cuba with or without the treasure of the vaults. The maximum effectiveness he could accomplish would be to make everything appear as though nothing had happened, no invasion attempted, no undercover diplomatic communications disrupted.

Then there was the X factor of Lowell Callender.

The heat of the night became cloying. Edgerton stripped off his clothes. Guido's cock ring fell to the floor. Edgerton picked it up, manipulated himself into it, went into the shower, soaped himself slowly, thinking about many things, many people.

1978
AUGUST

14

MONDAY

ON THE PORCH, THE GRAND HOTEL OLAFFSON'S, PORT-AU-PRINCE, HAITI

Edgerton watched the three men get out of the native taxi. He was having breakfast on the porch of the hotel. There had been no sign yet of Ramirez or his captors nor had Guido appeared. Wheeler had taken an early morning swim, gone back to his room to change clothes. He had been able to convince Wheeler that nothing had happened the night before. He still kept Ramirez's identity a secret. In the end, he might be forced to use Wheeler, either directly or having him contact the CIA. He would not be able to single-handedly abort both the Schwartz and Ramirez actions if they were scheduled simultaneously.

It took a moment for the identity of one of the men climbing the steps to register. Edgerton remembered the photograph which Callender had shown him that night in the garden at Key West. Patch over the eye. Arm in a sling. Julio San Marco.

Callender had given him no explanation for San Marco, only the warning to call the telephone number if he saw him anywhere at any time. He wondered about the other men with San Marco. One of them appeared to be an Arab but, under closer scrutiny, his skin was too fair, almost a pink-cheek quality, and his eyes were a very light, transparent hazel. The third man was shorter, stockier, a more typical South American with bushy black hair, a full moustache, and a slight stoop to his walk. They passed by Edgerton without looking over.

When Wheeler joined Edgerton, fresh looking and scrubbed after a shower, he sat down, grabbed his coffee cup for support. "Son of a bitch. Lowell Callender is here."

"Callender?"

"He must have just walked in with two other men. I saw them registering at the desk when I was coming down the stairs." He tasted the steaming coffee, made a sour face. "Now what?"

"I saw those men," Edgerton began, then realized that the shorter man with the moustache was built like Callender. His mind stripped off the bushy hair and moustache, pressed out the rumpled suit, and straightened up the stooped walk. He echoed Wheeler's words. "Son of a bitch."

"How do you like those bananas? The Undersecretary of State runs around the world in disguise. Great diplomacy, right?" Sad and bewildered, he shook his head. "I have to be losing my mind to watch all this happen and not press the panic button."

"Did he see you?"

"I don't think so," Wheeler answered, "but that bastard has some kind of built-in radar. He probably knows that I'm here."

"He must have seen me. They walked right by here."

"He goes by the name of Luis Kunz." He looked back inside the building. The men had gone.

"The men with him," Edgerton asked, "have you ever seen them before?"

"No."

The digits of the telephone number Callender had given him in Key West were clear in Edgerton's mind. There was a temptation to call those numbers, give the San Marco report, and test the reaction. But that would be pointless. He needed a stronger test of Callender's loyalty, an intelligence probe of Callender's motivations, conclusive evidence of the man's intentions. "You've spent time with Callender. How do you read him?"

Wheeler thought before he answered. "Never the same. He's more than he appears to be at any one given time. Mostly people get hung up on his abrasiveness, pick it as the hard-line, hard-drive pompousness, don't see beyond it. I've seen the other sides of him, too. I've seen a good guy, gentle in some ways. I play golf with men like that. Old friends. And I've seen him be a bastard and I've heard him talking about geopolitics, economic and military balances of world powers, and emerging powers that left me feeling like a kid on the first day at school. I watched him snow the Navy department into an unprecedented action by being a brilliant, classical military mind." He rubbed his eyes, rotated his shoulders to loosen up his muscles. "I don't know how the hell I read him. I don't know if I'm watching World War Three start or World War Three be averted. I don't know if Lowell Callender is my best friend or my worst enemy." He stood up. "I know how I read myself. I'm a horse's ass to be playing I Spy with you guys. I ought to be on the horn right now talking to my boss, telling the President that all hell is breaking loose and that he ought to call out the Marines."

"I'd wait if I were you."

"Wait for what?"

"Wait for the answers to the questions that the President will ask you."

"Like what?"

"Like when is it going to happen? Is there still time to call out the Marines? Questions like, do Callender and I have it under control? Do we represent the minimum risk?"

He sat down again. "Look, Edgerton . . . no offense . . . you seem like a nice enough guy. I don't question your loyalty. But what am I going to say when the President asks me if I think one undercover agent and one schizoid undersecretary can save the world?"

"Tell him yes, Jud."

Wheeler sat down again. "There's a lot that you're not telling me, isn't there, Edge?"

"I'm suggesting that you wait to push the panic button. Talk to Callender first, find out what he's up to. Let me talk to him too. By noon you should have enough additional information to make an intelligent decision. One thing I warn you. If you do call the President, don't do it from the hotel. Make the contact from our embassy here, go through channels."

"Are you telling me that this flea bag is full of Russian spies?"

"I'm suggesting that you use caution." This time Edgerton stood up, leaving Wheeler at the table. "I'm going to the pool, keep myself visible. The Italian is supposed to show up this morning. He's still the immediate objective for me."

"Are you going to get fucked again?"

"If necessary," Edgerton said.

THE HEMINGWAY SUITE,
THE GRAND HOTEL OLAFFSON'S,
PORT-AU-PRINCE, HAITI

A living room connected the two bedrooms of the suite, long French doors at the far end of the room were opened to the screened porch. When Lowell Callender came out of one of the bedrooms, wrapped in a bath towel and drying his hair with a smaller towel, he motioned for Ted to come in. "Ever been in Haiti before?"

"No. We have considerable interests on the other end of the island. We've been assisting the Dominican Republic in some tourist developments. As a matter of fact we're into land rather heavily over there. I wish that there was time to go over to Santo Domingo and check out a few things."

Callender shook his head. "There won't be time. You'd better get on to Miami, set things up there. I spoke to Farnsworth in my office. He's bringing down the public relations people. They'll meet you in Miami tomorrow."

"You still don't know the timetable, do you?"

"Edgerton and Wheeler are both here. I'll check them out, see if they're on to anything."

Phil came in from the other bedroom, freshly showered, wearing a long caftan. "I never realized what a fright it is to be blind in one eye and paralyzed in one arm. Poor San Marco. Maybe it's just as well that he's out of his misery."

Callender said, "You'd better get your San Marco clothes right back on. I want to make sure that everyone around here sees you. I don't know what the direct lines are back to Castro but we can't afford to overlook anyone. I would suspect that some of the employees of this hotel are on Castro's payroll. They get a cross section of the world here under various guises."

Phil looked at his watch. "Castro should have the ransom demand by now. I'll check with Bogota about noon to see if anyone has risen to the bait."

"The man with Edgerton," Ted asked, "is he your President's assistant?"

"That's Jud Wheeler. I'm going to have to mend my fences with

him fast. He can still cut off the Navy and the paramilitary force. I'll
have to do a selling job on him."

"How do you intend to do that?"

"It's occurred to me that I might tell him the truth," Callender
said.

"Everything?"

Callender nodded. "Wheeler understands power structure. He's
addicted to it, as a matter of fact. By telling him the truth, I think
I can feed his habit enough to keep him hooked."

"Do you think he'll understand?"

"Wheeler is basically a hatchet man," Callender explained.
"Right now he's a hatchet for a man who prefers to use soft
soap. Wheeler likes behind-the-scenes power. Properly trained,
he could have run Hitler's gestapo. Subliminally, I think he real-
izes that I represent his chance to be the greatest head-cracker
in the world. I've played him to hook him. I think it's time to set
that hook!"

"All the president's men," Ted said, did not explain it.

Phil said, "Greed is an interesting philosophical concept. Remember, we talked about that, Ted. I mean, is a man greedy for the
object of his greed or is greed an end-product in itself?"

Callender went back into his bedroom to get dressed as Luis Kunz
again. The brothers were discussing greed.

THE IRVING STONE SUITE,
THE GRAND HOTEL OLAFFSON'S,
PORT-AU-PRINCE, HAITI

The disguise was putting Callender at a disadvantage with Edgerton. Although he knew his real identity, Edgerton was reacting
to Callender as a stranger. Callender could not rekindle the climate of their first meeting with Jack Kelly nor the strained intimacy which had existed between them in the courtyard in Key
West. He tried prodding Edgerton to recreate the fury of their

run-in on Andros. But Edgerton stayed calm and aloof, answering questions with a yes or no, sometimes avoiding any answer at all. There was a clear view from the pool area into Edgerton's room but Callender took the risk, removed his moustache and wig, pocketed the dark glasses he was wearing, walked toward the back of the room, sat on the end of the bed where Edgerton was stretched out, staring at the ceiling.

"I'm about done in," Callender said. "I don't think I've had eight hours sleep in the last four days." He put his hand on Edgerton's bare ankle. "How about you? You couldn't have had much sleep either."

"We do what we have to do."

"More. We do more, Edge. More than most men do for their country. We take chances. We put our lives on the line."

"I get paid for it. That's my job."

"Nothing more than that, just a job?" He smiled, drew his hand away. "I don't believe that. You're more committed than that."

So far they had told each other nothing, shared no information. It was unlikely that Callender would recognize Ramirez from the casual description Edgerton had given him on Andros. As far as Callender knew, Edgerton was waiting for the Italian, waiting to get whatever information he could on the timetable. "What if the Italian doesn't show?" Edgerton asked. "What happens then?"

"We guess. Take chances. We calculate the risks, play the best odds."

"Where did you go when you gave Wheeler the slip on Providenciales?"

Callender had indexed Edgerton in a puppet position, squelched his first reaction to what, in that frame of reference, was an impertinent question of an underling to a superior. "What has Wheeler been telling you?"

"Where did you find San Marco? Why did you bring him here?"

Something about the change in Edgerton made Callender back off from lashing out at him. He felt a reversal of roles, a new strength in Edgerton which could only be based on information which he was not sharing. The information which Edgerton was holding was more important than saving face or maintaining authority. "I need to get to Castro directly. I think San Marco can accomplish this for me." There was no purpose in telling Edgerton that San Marco was dead or explicate the impersonation.

"What kind of a deal are you going to make with Castro?"

"What's the matter, Edge? Why this turnaround? They're the enemy, not I."

"What kind of a deal are you going to make with Castro?"

"Give him a chance to save face, intercept the invasion with his own forces."

"At what price?"

"Clean bill of health for the United States. No U.S. or CIA implication. The maximum diplomatic advantage to our country is to come out of this with a clean slate, completely disassociated with it. From Castro's standpoint, the best thing that can happen is for nothing to happen, no word of this to get beyond his ears. If we supply the information to make that happen for Castro, he owes us one. We're that much closer to diplomatic normalization."

"What do you get out of it?"

"We're very much alike, Edge. We both get paid to do a job; we both do it the best way we know how."

Edgerton got up from the bed, walked toward the window, looked down at the pool. Julio San Marco was sitting in the shade. Several other people were stretched out in the sun. Two children were splashing at each other in the shallow end of the pool. He turned back to Callender. "Zero hour is nine o'clock P.M. on Friday," he began. "The coordinates of the point of attack are twenty-three point thirty Latitude by eighty-two point forty Longitude. If you do not get to Castro, if you don't make a deal with him, we must have an alternate plan of interception." Edgerton walked to the round table in the middle of the room. "Sit down here and I'll show you how I've worked it out."

When the explication was over, Callender smiled, seemed more relaxed. "You've changed, haven't you, Edge? You're not the same man that you were in Key West or even a couple of days ago on Andros."

"You're confusing the covert identity with the actual man."

"Is that what you are now . . . the actual man?" Edgerton did not answer. "I like the actual man, I like the power in the actual man. That kind of man could go far . . ." The soft, Southern sound of the undersecretary's voice trailed off. Edgerton recognized the bait being dangled in front of his eyes, watched it warily, said nothing. "I owe you an apology," Callender said.

"Forget it."

"I don't want to forget it. This Cuban assignment isn't the end of the line for you and me; only the beginning. I misread you that day on Andros, underestimated your professionalism. What you did on Great Guana was the professional thing to do. It paid off." He touched the pages of Edgerton's notes outlining the Ramirez plan. "If it weren't for you, the information you got, we'd still be nowhere. We're going to come out of this on top . . . a great diplomatic coup for the United States. It's going to change the history of the world. You did it, you're responsible for the success."

"There's a long way to go. There's an invasion to defeat."

"Tactical," Callender said. "I know how to work that. The important thing is that you've come up with the information so that I know what to do. In two days, God willing, we're both going to be different men."

Edgerton considered the question and then asked it. "What are you going to be?"

"The United States, in order to survive in a world of predators, needs a power structure of men . . . not naive do-gooders with one hand on the Bible. Think of what you could do, for example, if you were head of the CIA or the FBI. Think of what you could do with that kind of power."

"Not for sale," Edgerton said.

"Every man has his price." Callender smiled, stretched his arms, then put a hand on Edgerton's shoulder.

THE SWIMMING POOL, THE GRAND HOTEL OLAFFSON'S, PORT-AU-PRINCE, HAITI

What began as kinky sex games in the swimming pool, ended in murder. Edgerton assassinated Guido with a karate chop which stunned the Italian long enough to allow Edgerton to hold his head underwater until the noiseless drowning was accomplished.

This happened shortly before two o'clock in the morning. By daybreak the body was gone, the swimming pool blue and tranquil in the rising sunlight. Through clandestine connections, Callender had prearranged for the removal and disposition of the body. Guido no longer existed.

The sense of loss was a bewildering emotion to Edgerton. He at first confused this emotion with the legal/ethical question of murder authorized, sanctioned, or executed by a United States agent in performance of duty involving interference in the domestic affairs of a foreign country. That question was being examined by Congressional committees, legal scholars, and theoretical academicians. Edgerton's real loss was a loss of valor, an unexpunged vengeance against the outrage he had endured in the acting out of his function as an agent. He had murdered Guido as a professional; cleanly, quickly, and without emotion. There had been no catharsis in the killing; all of the outrage was still blocked inside him, left there to turn bitter and sour.

But he was still wearing Guido's cock ring. This sentimental gesture both confounded and clarified his confusion.

VERADERO BEACH, CUBA

Under the cover of the cloudy night, nine men were huddled in a cavernous cleft in the rocky coast behind the beach, instructed not to speak, moving as little as possible, not allowed to smoke or light a match in the darkness. The man in charge occasionally pressed the pinhead protrusion on his digital watch to illuminate the dial, check the time to the second. Like the dead man he had succeeded, his name was also Miguel, differentiated from the older man by being known as Little Miguel, although he was over six feet tall and powerfully built. Hugging the cliff, he moved from this circle of men to another natural shelter fifty yards away. There were four people hidden here: a single man trussed in a network of the straps of his cameras and photographic equipment, sitting apart from a crew of three, protecting a TV minicam, lighting and sound equipment. A huge cable had been snaked into a fissure in the cliff leading up the bluff to a camouflaged van hidden in the density of pine trees.

Little Miguel again illuminated the watch face, exchanged glances with the four men, smiled a signal of all-is-well, moved out, and noiselessly made his way back to the other group. His instructions had been explicit and precise; he had followed them meticulously. Of the eight men he commanded, four of them were black, dressed in Cuban Army, olive-drab, fatigue coveralls, insignia patches obviously removed, the cloth showing cleaner in those areas. The other four men were distinctly Nordic types, blond or sandy-haired, three of them with blue eyes. From a laundry in Havana, Little Miguel had arranged to steal enough clothing from Russian Air Force pilots and crews to outfit these four men. He had hired a barber in Havana to trim and cut their hair in the style of the Russians. The watches and rings they were wearing were of Russian manufacture.

Again he checked his watch. In forty-two seconds the alert would begin. If nothing happened within thirty minutes after that, he was instructed to disperse the crews, destroy any evidence, and proceed back to Bogota.

At nineteen minutes after the alert, he saw the small boat appear offshore. Without running lights it was hardly visible in the dark night and against the black water. It kept moving while a raft was lowered from it to the water. A large bag dropped overboard and one by one three men hung to the rail and then dropped into the sea. Little Miguel took the pencil-thin flashlight from his pocket, signaled his position. All the men had turned toward the boat. One of the black men crawled forward to the edge of the rocks where the sand of the beach began, crouched in the ready position of a foot racer before the gun. When the raft was fifty feet from the beach, Little Miguel touched the runner's shoulder and still crouched, he streaked across the sand, guided the raft onto the beach, destroyed it while the other three men who had been in it raced toward the blinking light of Little Miguel's signal.

The three drenched men were Lowell Callender, Jud Wheeler, and Phil. Callender moved immediately into action. Both Wheeler and Phil moved to the side, stripped off their wet clothing, shared a towel which had been packed in the waterproof bag, dressed again in dry clothes.

Callender stayed wet. It was part of his script.

The drama that was acted out on the beach was done without words and without direction, performed by actors well rehearsed in the pantomime script. Callender, as Callender, was grabbed by two of the men, his arms locked behind him, his face twisted in pain. Another man tore at his clothes, ripping his coat and shirt. One of the big, blond men aimed a machine gun at him. Little Miguel took catsup from a bottle, smeared the red at one corner of Callender's mouth and over his eye. The entire group, their guns drawn, surrounded him. The minicamera crew turned on their lights and began rolling the film. The still photographer darted around, getting shots of the action from various vantage points. Then the two men threw Callender to the ground; each one, with a heavily booted foot, pinning Callender's arms to the ground. The big blond man turned his machine gun around, rammed it stock first at Callender's face. The narrow miss was not recorded by the camera. In every shot, the minicam panned enough to record the faces of the men surrounding the brutality, identify their weapons and clothing.

The entire performance took exactly ten minutes.

When it was over, the eight men dispersed in various directions. The photographer and the minicam crew climbed a rope ladder which had been lowered to the beach, disappeared into the darkness of trees there. Only Callender, Phil and Little Miguel and Wheeler were left on the beach. Sheltered in the cave, Callender undressed, wiped the mock blood from his face and in the dark, assisted sporadically by Little Miguel's penlight, became Luis Kunz again. The waterproof bag they had brought ashore also contained Julio San Marco's clothing, his eye patch, and black sling. While Callender was transforming himself into Luis Kunz, Phil became Julio San Marco. Little Miguel turned the bag inside out to make sure that nothing was left there. An envelope fell out. He opened it, checked the inside of the passports, handed one to Luis Kunz and the other to Julio San Marco. Then he buried the bag under a formation of rocks.

They dared speak for the first time when they were on the road in the ancient Chevrolet, heading up the hills to a prearranged hideout. "You did well, Miguel," Phil said. "It went off without a hitch."

"Big Miguel at his best," Callender said, "could not have done it better."

Little Miguel acknowledged the praise with a simple smile, pleased most of all that Phil had called him Miguel without the diminutive adjective added.

The hideout was a thatched-roof farmhouse off a dirt road. There was no electricity here, the one big room inside lighted by kerosene lamps which attracted buzzing clouds of insects and emitted a rank odor. A portable radio command post was set up in the center of the room. Two Cubans who sat around it stood up when Callender, Wheeler, and Phil came in.

Miguel spoke first. "All went well." He went to the radio, studied the scribbles on the yellow legal pad next to it. He spoke in Spanish to the two Cubans, then spoke to Phil. "Contact has been made, the terms agreed."

"All our terms?" Callender asked.

"Our terms and their terms," Miguel explained. "Castro will come only after an advance group comes first to make sure that this is not a trap and that Julio San Marco is still alive. When they signal that everything is in order, then Castro will himself come to the house."

"Look here, Lowell," Wheeler said, "if Castro himself is coming up here, then I think that I should be the one to negotiate with him. I have direct authority from the President. He's going to think that you're just another hothead. I wouldn't be surprised at all if he takes out a gun and guns us all down. He doesn't care any more about human life than I do about those damn mosquitoes." He swatted an insect on his arm. "You're not dealing at the Geneva conference table. This island, as far as I can see, is an uncivilized jungle. When Castro learns who I am, who I represent, he won't dare try any funny stuff."

"You're our ace in the hole, Jud. If everything else fails we'll let you try your head-cracking skills. But in the meantime, you're going to sit there quietly and not say a word to anyone. Do you understand? If they ask you questions, answer yes or no. For God's sakes, don't tell them who you are under any circumstances. You could start World War Three single-handed. If there were a way to get you out of here, if there was a way to hide you, I'd do it right now. But the risk is too great." He turned to Miguel. "Ask them if they know what time the advance party is coming."

"As agreed. Tomorrow night at six o'clock."

"That means that Castro should be here by seven. That gives us only two hours before the invasion."

Phil asked, "Isn't that cutting it a bit close?"

"It allows no margin for error, no stalling for time by Castro. I explained in the beginning that this was a gamble. If I had scheduled the meeting earlier, it would give Castro time to create a counter-attack of his own. This way there won't be time. He will have to do it our way or else."

"Or else what?" Phil took off the eye patch, rubbed his eye.

"Or else the invasion proceeds unchecked. That, Castro can't risk."

Wheeler spoke up. "I think the whole plan is too dangerous. What assurance do we have that the advance party won't just storm in here and spray us all with their machine guns?"

"They have agreed to come unarmed."

"You don't really think that they intend to leave their guns out there on the field, do you? You're more naive than I thought, Lowell."

"If Castro wants San Marco alive, he will live up to his word."

Phil said, "And what happens to me if Castro decides he doesn't care whether San Marco is dead or alive, that all he cares about is killing the kidnappers? What will he do to me when he finds out I'm not San Marco?"

Turning from Wheeler to Phil and back again, Callender said, "Both of you pleaded to come along on this. Phil, I told you in Barranquilla that it was a risk for you to impersonate San Marco but you wanted to be part of this. If I remember, you explained to me that you wouldn't ask one of your men to do anything you wouldn't do yourself. I told you at the time that it was headstrong and foolish. Soldiers, by definition, are expendable. Death is inherent in the word soldier. You wanted to play soldier and you now have to take the soldier's consequences." Phil moved away from the glare of the kerosene lamp, stepped back in the shadows of the room. Callender swung on Wheeler. "You, too, Jud. You have no business in this kind of a situation. You have no training for it. You don't have the stomach for it. You blackmailed me to come along. You knew that I couldn't function without your contacts, without your clout. So you used it as blackmail so that you could puppy-dog along. Like Phil, you have to take the consequences."

Wheeler looked long and hard at Callender. "You son of a bitch. You're really not afraid, are you? You love every fucking minute of this. You should see your face: like a man having an orgasm. You're another kind of man, altogether, aren't you, Callender? Like the President said, you're a mean son of a bitch. But if I had you and him in a cock fight, I'd put my money on you."

1978
AUGUST

15

TUESDAY

MARINA, THE PALM BAY CLUB, MIAMI, FLORIDA

The yacht *Valkyrie* docked noiselessly in the early morning alongside the other luxury boats lining the long piers behind the Palm Bay Club. When Aldo Rinaldi appeared on the aft deck at nine o'clock, the crew had already been ashore for provisions. The breakfast table was set up for him, coffee in a gleaming chrome Thermos, a glass of freshly squeezed orange juice submerged in a bowl of crushed ice, and the Miami *Herald* neatly folded by the plate. He recognized her face even though only a corner of it was visible on the folded front page. He felt the disaster, knew the shock of loss, was rent apart with grief before he even touched the newspaper, confirmed his fears. He unfolded it slowly, tried to read the headline through the tears and the blinding rage. There were only big, black, unrelated letters emblazoned across the front page. He forced his eyes and his mind to relate the letters to each other until they formed words and the words formed a message.

FILM STAR MURDERED IN FRANCE

Marla Worth Strangled, Mutilated by Unknown Assailant in Riviera Villa

Blinded by tears, the small print of the story was illegible to Rinaldi but he knew the story without reading it, he knew why Victor Castle needed Guido in Europe. He had counted out three thousand dollars from his own pocket to send off a man to murder his wife. That picture would be with him forever. Nothing could ever be the same again.

Not ever.

It was only in the late afternoon when the *Valkyrie* was out at sea again, heading for the rendezvous point off Key West, that Rinaldi had recovered sufficiently enough to be able to read the whole story of his wife's murder. The attack had been brutal. The French Sûreté was quoted as saying that there was every evidence that the film star had been sexually assaulted both before and after the murder. Her personal safe containing jewels and private papers had been bombed open, the contents missing. Inside the newspaper there was a separate story of the life of Marla Worth, pictures of her when she was young, a picture of Rinaldi and a picture of Carlos Ramirez.

No one ever questioned Victor Castle's motives. Eventually his motivation became self-evident in the progression of his successes.

Rinaldi wondered how he could make it up to Roger. Was there a way that he could trade positions with him? Killing Guido or being killed by him would be a kind of bloodletting poetry, a semblance of a special kind of justice balancing one Judas against another.

There was still time to plot and still time to assemble enough courage to execute a plot.

He cried again. This time for himself.

ABOARD THE YACHT VALKYRIE, *SIX MILES OFF THE COAST OF CUBA*

Aldo Rinaldi debated in his own mind. His priority was vengeance. When the information came from Switzerland, instructions from Victor Castle to change the coordinates of the attack to a position two miles east, he understood why his wife's vault had been broken into, why Castle had designated her murder. She had kept one of the two original Ramirez maps in the same steel safety vault as her jewels. Rinaldi also realized now what Roger had been trying to tell him in Great Guana when he had hinted at the fail-safe device in his plan. Roger had protected himself by giving Castle a fake map.

Rinaldi's vengeance was directed at Guido, the instrument of murder, not at Castle, the source of the murder. His final decision was based on his own thirst for Guido's blood, his specific plan to castrate him.

In the radio control room of the *Valkyrie,* he relayed the change in coordinates to the submarine transporting the underwater combat team and to the control center on Great Guana in order to change the position of the equipment air drop to Roger. He made contact with the *Aventuro,* at that moment running full-sail and full-motor toward the rendezvous point, changing their destination.

At seven-twenty, he had the crew lower the high-speed motor launch from the mooring on the upper deck, equip it with water skis, flippers, goggles, and a wet suit. He secreted a gun and a knife in the zippered pockets of a dark blue waterproof jacket. He briefed the German captain of the *Valkyrie* on the new coordinates, warned him to be precisely on time for the pickup of the underwater team after the explosion. He rebuffed the captain's insistence on a member of the crew accompanying him on the launch. The small craft was equipped with a compass and a computer directional device. Rinaldi punched out the coordinates on the computer, checked the readout, started the high-power engines, signaled above for the line to be released. When he threw it into gear, the bow of the launch surged up and out of the water like the snout of an angry, attacking sea monster, then automatically changed direction, sped toward the shore.

FARMHOUSE OUTSIDE HAVANA, CUBA

Miguel, from his lookout position, saw the small, unmarked van turn up the dirt road leading to the farmhouse. He raised his hand to signal to the men in the room behind him, picked up the machine gun, sighted it on the predetermined position where the vehicle would stop. Four of his men were secreted behind trees and thickets of shrubs outside the farmhouse. He could not see them from the window but he trusted these men, knew they were deployed in place, their weapons aimed at the same predetermined position.

Lowell Callender, still disguised as Luis Kunz, gestured to Jud Wheeler who understood the signal, went into a small room, closed the door. The radio operator, his headset in place, his black face heavy with sweat, sat rigid in front of his equipment, guarded on each side by men with machine guns. In the corner, obscured by the darkness and shadows, the Julio San Marco surrogate was trussed to a chair, his good arm tied behind his back, his mouth gagged with heavy strips of black tape. The inert arm, cradled in a black sling, concealed a revolver, a last minute concession to Phil's fear. He was guarded by three armed men who were placed in a triangular cordon; one man directly in front of him, one on each side of him. The wall behind him completed the protective base.

The van stopped exactly at the prescribed mark. Quickly, two of Miguel's men got out of the front doors of the vehicle, stood at armed attention, facing back down the road. Each man counted slowly to sixty, alert for any movement on the road below. Convinced that they had not been followed, the driver signaled to the men in the van by hammering the stock of his automatic against the fender, a tiny thud in the quiet of the countryside. The two rear doors of the van opened at the signal, two more of Miguel's men jumped out, beaconed the area with their eyes and guns. Miguel stepped out of the cover of the house, stood on the porch, signaled with an incline of his head and then, moving backward, resumed his vigilance inside, glancing back quickly to reassure Callender.

Three blindfolded men were escorted off the van, lined up, and searched again for hidden weapons. They were dressed in civilian clothes. They were not young men. One of them had gray hair. All of them appeared to be in their sixties. Miguel motioned to Callender who came forward, stood behind Miguel, studied the three men who were rubbing their eyes, adjusting to the light after the blindfold. Without communicating in words, Callender and Miguel understood that Castro had sent expendable hostages as his advance party, had not risked the lives of young men with military capability. Callender calculated the Castro mentality, his own position if this was a trick, decided that there was no choice, nodded to

Miguel to proceed with the plan. Before Miguel could relay the go-ahead signal, the radio operator screamed Miguel's name. Turning his back to the window, Miguel saw the terror on the radio man's face. He ran over, pushed one of the guards to cover his position, took the headset the operator was holding out to him, pressed one side over his ear, heard the loud, strong pulse of a radar signal beaming their position. He ran to the window, shouted at his guards, who immediately began tearing the clothes off Castro's men.

Callender was beside Miguel. "What happened?"

"They've hidden a radar device on one of the men. It's signaling our position." He shoved his machine gun at Callender, ran outside shouting instructions. The men hidden on the grounds ran forward and, under Miguel's direction, searched the clothing as the men were being stripped, looking for the instrument source of the radar signal. The three men remained calm while Miguel's men tore at their clothes, submitted to the stripping as if they had been programmed for this to happen.

Behind him, Callender heard Phil trying to shout behind the gag of tape, struggling in the chair to free himself. Callender turned, instructed the guards to restrain him. When he looked back to the front of the farmhouse, it was already too late to shout a warning: the armored cars were coming up the road, the automatic weapons spraying the area. The two men on either side of the van were falling to the ground in a halo of blood. Miguel and his other men were safe only because of the protective cover of the van.

Miguel acted quickly, instinctively. He mumbled instructions. He and his men dropped their weapons to the ground, raised their hands over their heads. The naked men picked up the discarded guns, covered Miguel. One of these naked men lowered his head, stuck his finger down his throat, gagged himself until he vomited on the ground, repeated the process three times. Then he reached into the mound of his vomit, picked up a tiny metal disc, pressed it between his fingers to deactivate it.

While he watched the Cuban soldiers pour out of the armored vehicles, Callender estimated his own chances to escape, saw the men form an armed circle around the house, knew there was no way to escape. He peeled off his moustache, let it drop on the floor, took off his wig and dark glasses. From his back pocket, he took a handkerchief and wiped at the layer of bronze makeup on his face, smearing it enough to reveal the whiteness of his skin underneath.

Castro's soldiers had taken Miguel and his men and, using them as human shields in front of them, faced the house with their machine guns raised. Miguel, repeating instructions from the soldier he was shielding, called out for everyone inside the house to come outside one by one with their hands raised over their heads. Callender repeated the instructions to the three men guarding Phil and to the radio operator and the men with him. While they were lining up at the door, reluctant to go outside, Callender went into the room where Wheeler was hidden. Crouched under the bed, Wheeler saw that it was Callender, crawled forward, and stood up. "What happened?" He was breathing heavily, his metabolic rate racing with the pace of explosions of gunfire.

"It was a trick. One of Castro's men swallowed a radio beeper. They zeroed in on our position." There was a bowl of water on a stand, a tiny tin mirror over it. Callender used his handkerchief to wash off his face, then reached into his pocket for a comb. Wheeler grabbed at his arm. Callender pushed him away, combed his hair. "Keep cool," he said. "You didn't really expect Castro to be naive enough to walk into our trap?"

"What happens now?"

"Straighten your tie and try not to look like you just shit in your pants. We go outside with our hands over our heads."

"Then what?"

"Let me do the talking. Say nothing."

On their way back to the front door they passed Phil who had toppled the chair in his struggle to free himself, lay pinned under it. Callender instructed Wheeler, "Give me a hand." Together they righted Phil in the chair. Callender adjusted the eye patch over his eye, reinserted the revolver which had fallen to the floor into the arm sling. "Don't use it," Callender warned, "except as a very last resort." Pushing Wheeler in front of him, they moved to the door as the last of the men were going through. "Keep your hands over your head, Jud." He shoved him out on the porch, waited until he walked down the steps, then Callender put his hands up and walked out.

The soldier behind Miguel said, *"Esa es el ultimo hombre?"*

"The last man," Miguel said. *"El único que queda es Julio San Marco."*

At a signal, three of the soldiers dropped their hostages, threw them to the ground. One of the soldiers had taken a position at the front door, the other two were kicking in the glass of the windows on either side of the door. Guns raised, they burst into the big room simultaneously, each man monitoring a segment, saw only the man trussed helpless to the chair. While the center man maintained his position, moving his machine gun in a covering arc, the other men searched the farmhouse, kicking open doors, pulling down curtains, opening drawers, knocking over furniture which could hide a man.

Satisfied that the farmhouse was empty, the center man lowered his gun, went outside and indicated that everything was clear. Miguel, Callender, Wheeler, and the radio operator were led back into the house. The other men were herded into the rear of the van, jammed together inside, the door locked, the entire van surrounded by the Castro force.

Inside, their hands still above their heads, the four men were lined up facing a wall, their backs guarded by one of the soldiers. There was a sudden stillness; no sound of guns anymore or men shuffling against the wooden decks. The serenity of the countryside at dusk had returned, marred only by the deep breaths of men's fear.

By looking up at his outstretched arm, Callender could see his wristwatch. Seven-ten. The zero hour was nine o'clock. The Navy submarine with the crew of frogmen would be nearing the rendezvous point. The man-killer trained porpoises, deadly spears bound to their bodies, locked dorsally and protruding beyond their snouts, were ready in a huge underwater network cage, waiting for the shrill underwater siren to alert them to attack. The minutes moved like hours as they waited. Seven-twenty. The gamble was getting more desperate, the odds lessening with each minute.

Then there was the sound of heavy vehicles lumbering up the pot-holed road, the screech of tires being braked to a halt, car doors opening and slamming shut, the authoritative stomp of heavy-shod feet moving in a military cadence. Callender felt the impact vibrate the wooden floor under him. He smelled the heavy smoke of the cigar, looked up at his watch. Seven twenty-five. The long-shot gamble had paid off.

Fidel Castro said, "Turn around, Mr. Callender. It has been a long time that we do not see each other."

Callender lowered his arms to his side, turned around slowly, smiled at Castro. "A long time, Fidel."

"Men like us . . . one time we are friends and the next time we are enemies. Then friends again. Then enemies." He hooked the rung of the radio operator's chair with the toe of his boot, dragged it to him, sat straddling it, his arms folded over the back of it. To the man in charge of the soldiers, he said, *"Mata a los demás."*

Callender stepped forward in front of the raised automatic, took another chair, sat opposite Castro. "I suggest not," he said. "Tell your men not to shoot." Castro looked over at the soldier who then put his gun back into the hip holster.

"Do you think that I am a fool?" He looked over to the figure strapped to the chair. "Do you think that I believe that this man is Julio San Marco?" He spat on the floor. "In the years between the time we last saw each other, you have become the fool, Mr. Callender." He smiled as he stood up, kicked the chair out of his path, went over to Phil, tore the eye patch off his eye, ripped the tape from his mouth, leaving a band of blood across Phil's face. Callender held his breath as Castro reached for the black sling. The gun. He had forgotten that Phil still had the gun concealed in the sling. But as Castro grabbed at him, Phil pushed back with his feet, turned over in the chair and fell with it to the floor. Castro kicked him in the side, knocked him unconscious. "CIA. It is always the same. CIA." He strode over to Jud Wheeler who was still facing the wall. With strong physical force Castro spun him around, spat in his face. "More CIA." He sat down opposite Callender, mounting the chair, straddling it in the same position. "Twenty years almost. Twenty years all your CIA has tried to kill one man." He laughed, hit his hand against his knee. "Never, Mr. Callender. Never will you kill me."

"I suggest we talk alone," Callender said.

"You want to make a bargain, Mr. Callender? You want to make a bargain for your life?" He shook his head. "Years ago I bargained with you for the life of Cuba. I negotiated with you for the price of your guns. You thought you made the best bargain . . . five times what I should have paid, I was forced to pay you. But your guns won the revolution, Mr. Callender. A cheap price. You charged me five times too much but in the end it was a cheap price. I made the best bargain."

"I have come again to save Cuba," Callender said. "There is very little time. You must act at once."

"What is the price this time?"

"We must talk alone."

Castro sized up Callender carefully, sensed the controlled intensity, the calm self-assurance. He made a gesture to the leader of the soldiers. "Clear out the room. Wait outside. Give me your gun. I will be safe. This man and I are old friends." Herding Wheeler and Miguel, the soldiers left the room. At the last minute Wheeler pulled away, tried to get to Callender but one of the soldiers yanked at his arm, threw him through the door. Phil, overlooked by the soldiers, stayed motionless, tangled with the chair on the floor, only his free hand moving surreptitiously, working against the knots of the ropes restraining him.

"Laurie Golding," Castro said, "she told me that you knew about this. Why is she dead? Did you kill her?"

Callender ignored the question. "There will be a commando invasion of your country tonight. Nine o'clock." An automatic reflex made Castro look at his watch. "There is not enough time for you to find out where the attack will take place unless I tell you. And if I don't tell you, the raid will be successful."

"Who? Why? To kill me?"

"It doesn't matter now. What does matter is that if the raid is successful, you will become a fool in the eyes of the world. You have forces fighting four thousand miles away and yet you cannot defend your own country against attack. Not the Cuban Army and not the Russian Army can defend this island. How will it look to the world?"

He grabbed Callender, shook him in uncontrolled rage. "You will tell me. You will tell me." The gun slipped from Castro's hand, fell to the floor. Callender rocking with the buffeting, managed to kick the weapon out of immediate reach. Castro released his hold on Callender, started to lean toward the gun.

"Stay where you are, Mr. Castro." Both men turned to the sound of Phil's voice coming from the darkness, saw the unmistakable gleam of steel: the gun aimed at Castro. Phil was standing up. He took three long strides toward Callender and Castro, stopped before he would be in range of a shot fired through the broken window next to the door. "Mr. Callender is here to help you. We have a business proposition. Explain it to him, Lowell."

Castro assessed his position, took a fresh cigar from his pocket, struck a stick match against the floor, lighted the cigar. "You will never leave Cuba alive." He turned toward Phil. "Not you either."

"You have done business with me before," Callender said. "You know that I am thorough. You know that I would not face you without protection." He walked to the radio equipment, tilted back the metal box of the receiving equipment, pulled out a stack of photographs. "Let me have a match." Castro handed him a box of wooden matches: Callender lighted one of the kerosene lamps, handed Castro the photographs, waited while he examined each one slowly. When he was finished, Castro threw the photographs to the floor, looked up. The questions were in his eyes. He said nothing. "You will notice that in these photographs that there is a television camera recording my capture and torture by Cuban and Russian guerrilla forces. The television film and tapes are already in the United States." He pointed at the photographs on the floor. "The original negatives are also in the United States. If, for any reason, I do not return, the television tapes and the photographs will be released to the press all over the world. Not only you and Cuba but your Russian allies as well will be involved in the kidnapping, torture, and execution of a United States diplomat. The Russians will not risk a head-to-head confrontation with the United States over Cuba. We've called their bluff before. They are looking for an excuse to abandon you, Fidel; stop pouring money down this Cuban drain. This is the evidence they need to disassociate with you. Do you understand? You will be left alone here unsupported by the Russians and an official enemy of the United States. Who is going to come to your aid? Who will support you economically? Who will supply your military strength? Yemen? Angola? Ethiopia?" He picked Castro's gun up from the floor, tossed the weight of it in his hand, then held it out for Castro to retrieve. Castro looked at it, exhaled a cloud of dense cigar smoke, did not touch the gun.

"You have no choice." Callender looked at his watch. Seven-fifty. "You must play this my way." He pressed his advantage. "You must pay my price. Pull up a chair, Phil. And you can put that gun away. We won't need it now." Callender rubbed his hands together, turned back to Castro.

THE NORTH COAST OF CUBA, EAST OF HAVANA
The coordinates: 23.20 Latitude × 82.50 Longitude

Hiding in the darkness, camouflaged by a density of trees, Edgerton, his face blackened by a coating of mud, studied the Ramirez map, guiding a penlight over the yellowed paper. Roger Ramirez was stationed ten feet away. There was still an hour before the zero hour of attack. The reading of the map was perfunctory; he had already memorized it, could close his eyes and see every detail of it. He was using his focus on it as a physical diversion, while his mind assessed the tactical situation. Control in Key West had warned him not to try to be a one-man army. There was no choice. He was the only field commander, his gun the only artillery and he was the only foot soldier. It was Vietnam again, this cluster of trees a mini-jungle, but the odds were even more minuscule. The memory of leading Jack Kelly in the escape route from the POW camp diverted his attention from the immediate. He forced his mind back into concentration.

Priority One: Stop the invasion.

Because of the falsified map, both the raid and counter-raid would take place at the wrong coordinates, approximately two miles from this true position. Even if he risked the danger, tried to find Callender, apprise him of the actual situation, it would be futile. He had to go on the assumption that Roger Ramirez's secret was still a secret—the attack would take place at the false coordinates. If that was true, the attempt to abort it would have to be made at the same false coordinates. Young Ramirez had assured him that there had been only two copies of the real map. The other map was safely hidden in his mother's jewelry vault in Cap Ferrat and that his mother had probably forgotten by now that the map even existed.

Priority Two: Stop Callender.

The actual information on Callender's real motivations was fragmented bits of intelligence, not enough pieces of the puzzle to fit together into a total picture. Callender was dangerous; his gut told him that. In a vague way, the CIA chain of command had hinted at it. Wheeler had come right out and said it. Callender himself, back at Port-au-Prince when Edgerton had finally revealed the Ramirez plot, indicated that he controlled non-national paramilitary capabilities and had direct access to international networks of superpolitical power. Deliberately, the undersecretary had chinked his armor of secretiveness, given Edgerton a chimera of potential hegemony. It had been a mistake to turn on him at that point. Edgerton knew it at the time, did not have the discipline to control his need for emotional vengeance.

But the danger from him was not immediate. Whatever Callender's ultimate objectives were, at the moment his tactical position was the same as the United States government: stop the Cuban invasion.

Edgerton tabled Callender for future action.

Priority Three: Stop the murder of Hotdog Schwartz.

From what Ramirez had told him and from what he remembered of the CIA involvement with shadowy, underworld figures, Edgerton was certain that Schwartz's presence on Cuban soil was a threat of some kind. Ramirez did not know if Schwartz was still a United States citizen living in exile or if he had been stripped of his citizenship and was now a Moroccan national. Either way, if there had been CIA and Schwartz affiliation at one time, it was an even greater danger now. Dead or alive, Schwartz was potential dynamite.

Yet, he could not be in two places at the same time. Number three priority would have to wait for number one.

Priority Four: Protect Ramirez.

The Cuban ten feet away from him could bear witness to the truth. No matter what happened, Edgerton needed him alive to testify to the real source of the invasion. He was the one person who could unimplicate the United States if the plan succeeded. If his first three priorities failed, the testimony of Ramirez could avert world disaster.

But keeping Ramirez alive would be difficult. He had a suicidal compunction to recover the jewels and money.

Earlier in the day, they had reconnoitered the coast from the sea. Chartering a small fishing boat near Havana, they hugged the coastline to the approximate coordinates on Ramirez's map. All along this area, the land was a sheer, rocky drop-off to the water below: no beach. The incline to the land above was almost a straight ninety degrees. According to the map, the vaults were buried in the rocks approximately thirty feet below the edge of the cliff, forty feet above the sea. Ramirez had brought field glasses, located the building which had been the Ramirez mansion, studied rock formations below it, looked for some identifying tree stumps and roots his father had indicated as markers. But in twenty years, new vegetation had grown heavily and old growth had disintegrated or rotted away. Edgerton realized that there was no way the two men, working alone, hampered by the cover of the night, could scale the cliff and find the exact spot. It would take all the intricacies of Ramirez's original plan to recover the vaults: the underwater team, the metal detector, the explosives to loosen the rocks, the mountain climbing gear to enable them to scale the incline and the rope pulley to lower the vaults to the sea. He knew that Ramirez would insist on trying it alone and without the necessary equipment. It would be a futile exercise.

Later, back in hiding, they discussed the feasibility. "If we had radio equipment, could somehow signal the underwater team, give them the correct position, it could still work," Ramirez said. "But only Aldo, from the yacht, can redirect them. He's the only line of communication with the underwater team and with Great Guana. If only there was a way to get him." His body slacked with dejection. "Even if we could, he would not help. Aldo would not double-cross Victor Castle."

"The planes from Great Guana," Edgerton asked, "what time are they due to parachute the equipment down?"

"It is scheduled to happen simultaneously with the fire on the brigantine. The plan was to use the fire on the *Aventuro* as a divergence while the parachutes were being dropped. They are small chutes, black cloth. Everyone will be looking at the *Aventuro*. No one will notice them. You will see, the entire plan will work perfectly."

"But two miles away." Edgerton held up his hands. "What's the use?"

"We will try anyway."

"It's pointless, Roger. There's no way we can scale that cliff without equipment. All we have is a flashlight and our bare hands. There isn't a chance." He touched the other man's shoulder. "Look, Roger, there will be another time. You can try it again later. That stuff has been buried for almost twenty years. What's the difference if you wait another year or even two years? It'll still be there. You'll find another way, think of another plan."

"Tonight," Ramirez said. "We will do it tonight. If you are too frightened, I will do it alone."

"Trying to get down that cliff at night will be like committing suicide. Even if there are two of us, it will be like killing ourselves. It doesn't make any sense." Ramirez had stretched out on the hard ground, cradled his head in his arms, closed his eyes to try to sleep. "Maybe it's all working out for the best. If your original plan had gone through, Victor Castle would have had you killed by some means. He would have found a way to get those vaults and eliminate you. This way, you'll still be alive to try again."

"Do you think that Victor Castle will let me live? If I have no money, there will be no place for me to hide, no way to escape." He opened his eyes. "Do you really think that Victor Castle will let me live?"

Like most of the mansions along the coast, the Ramirez house had been converted into a public building housing governmental offices. It was deserted at this time of night, the structure kept dark in the energy crunch of the austere Cuban economy. In their hiding place, camouflaged by a thicket of shrubs and trees, Edgerton and Ramirez were able to whisper to each other. "You're sure that this is the house?"

"I am certain," Ramirez reassured Edgerton. "My mother described it to me many times. The bay window on the second floor used to be my mother's bedroom. It had pink curtains and flowers on the carpet. She always said it was the most beautiful room in the world."

"The night is too dark and we're too far away to see the *Aventuro* when she explodes."

"We will see the light from the fire. The sails will burn first before the explosion." Ramirez sat up again, looked toward the east where the *Aventuro* would be, started crawling on his hands and knees toward Edgerton.

The sound behind him, the telegraph of danger from Ramirez's eyes, happened simultaneously but too late for Edgerton to react. By the time Ramirez hollered the warning, Edgerton was already pinned on his back, rammed against the ground, motionless under the weight of an oil-slick body, everything black except the glint of the shiny steel knife touching his throat, the tip of it already puncturing his skin, drawing a circle of blood.

At first, when Rinaldi realized that this man under him was not Guido, he did not withdraw the pressure of the knife. With his free hand, he pushed the goggles off his eyes, still not believing what he saw; that this man was not Guido. His vision was blinded by tears of disappointment. He pressed the knife deeper, his rage so strong that any bloodletting would expunge it.

"Aldo."

When he heard Roger's voice in the background, bringing him back to the reality of the moment, Rinaldi's body went slack, the knife fell out of his hand, he rolled over on the ground. The tears became sobs at an ascending decibel, filling the quiet night with anguish. Edgerton recovered quickly, slapped hard at Rinaldi's face. When the sobbing did not stop, he silenced it by putting his hand over Rinaldi's mouth, applying increasing pressure until the man fought for breath, stopped sobbing, was at last quiet.

Ramirez whispered, "What are you doing here, Aldo?"

He had recovered enough to speak, "Warn you. Warn you, Roger. They have found your mother's map. They know the real coordinates. They will land here and kill you. Do you understand? They will kill you." His voice lowered, his grief surfaced again. "They will kill anyone who stands in their way." He put his hand out to touch Ramirez's shoulder. "They have killed your mother, they have murdered her to get the map." Rinaldi made the sign of the cross in the darkness, whispered the Latin words of the prayer. "I thought this man was Guido." He looked over at Edgerton, did not recognize him as the same man, the hustler in cut-offs on Great Guana.

"Guido is dead," Edgerton told him. "He got his."

Unexpectedly, Roger was crying without any sound, a hurt little boy, his face twisted in anguish, tears streaming down his cheeks. His tears triggered Rinaldi. The two men comforted each other.

Edgerton looked at his watch, estimated the time it would take to get to the false coordinates, warn Callender of the change. He did not consider the personal risks. It would be touch and go. It was unfamiliar ground to cover. He pulled Rinaldi away from Roger. "How did you get here?"

"The launch from the *Valkyrie.*"

"Where is it now?"

He pointed below to the cliff. "We can escape now, get back to the yacht."

Once more Edgerton checked the time. Trying to find Callender was too great a risk. He was unfamiliar with the terrain. It was possible to become lost and there would not be enough time to recover. Priority Four had to become Priority One. Keep Ramirez alive. The lesser risk was depending on Callender's counterattack force to be mobile enough to move the two miles in time to intercept the invasion in progress.

Coordinates: 23.30 Latitude × 82.30 Longitude

The white sails of the *Aventuro* glowed in the moonlight as the brigantine kept an even keel in the calm waters, proceeding at a steady speed two hundred yards off the shoreline, still almost a mile away. Castro handed the field glasses back to Callender. "I do not understand why they do not yet furl the sails."

Callender was dressed in Cuban battle fatigue, the famous Castro guerrilla cap on his head and a holster with two guns around his waist. He took off his glasses, adjusted the binoculars until the *Aventuro* came into sharp focus, the sails billowing in the following wind. He could not understand why the brigantine was not slowing down, why it was cutting through the water at full speed. It crossed his mind that Edgerton had lied to him, deliberately fabricated the story of the two Ramirez maps, two rendezvous points. In an effort to recruit Edgerton, turncoat his allegiance from the CIA, Callender realized that he might have told the agent too much. He had indicated that force would be met with force, given Edgerton a chance to join that force, be part of the nucleus of power. In his first assessment of Edgerton, he had tried to sound out that quality, the capability of Edgerton to switch loyalties. The exigencies of time had forced him to make a gut decision. He might have guessed that Edgerton was brainwashed enough by the Agency not to be able to make a midstream transition. But there was no way Edgerton would have been able to know or guess at any of the details. It took a big mind to shoot high enough to think of the Castro blackmailing plan, turning the Cuban leader into a puppet for his own purposes. Even Jud Wheeler had been flabbergasted. It was only the brothers in Bogota, Phil and Ted, who immediately saw that the impossible was possible. Their experience gave them ability to see that the Callender plan was feasible, that the giant dream could come true.

Callender leaned forward, handed the binoculars back to Castro who was sitting in the front seat. "There must be a change in the point of contact." Castro had one leg dangling over the side of the Russian command car. Quickly, he pulled it in, clenched the cigar between his teeth, turned back to Callender, who was checking his watch. It was twenty minutes before the nine o'clock zero hour. "Leave some men here and head east," Callender said. "Tell your men to watch the brigantine. When it stops, that's the point of invasion." Edgerton had not given Callender exact locations but had told him that the point where he and Ramirez would be was approximately two miles beyond the point of the invasion.

Castro shouted instructions into the darkness. Four soldiers materialized from the camouflage of shadows, carrying machine guns; two rode on the front fenders of the vehicle and two jumped on the back pushing Callender and the soldier next to him forward. They sped down the road, Castro standing up in the front seat, one hand on the windshield bracing himself steady, the other hand on the gun in the holster hanging from his hip. A tank and two armored troop carriers pulled in front of the command car, led the way, and another command car, this one jammed with television equipment and photographers joined the convoy. Following that were two more troop carriers and two additional tanks, side by side, protecting the rear.

The convoy drove down the broad boulevard, the same route Castro had taken when he had come down from the mountains twenty years before to make a triumphant entry into Havana. Passenger cars pulled to the side of the road and up on lawns to avoid the pincer cordon of military vehicles.

Castro, still standing up, saw it first. The flaming sails lighting up the night. He released his hold on the holster, picked up the walkie-talkie, shouted instructions to the lead tank which responded with an instant, sharp left turn, cutting across the wide park median and over lawns and shrubs, spearheading the convoy toward the sea. Callender looked up, heard the thin sounds of the piston aircraft, spotted the black parachutes drifting toward the ground. He stood up, having to brace himself against Castro's shoulder to avoid being knocked over by the jostling command car. He shouted over the noise of the engine. "Stop here." Castro looked back at him, puzzled. "Stop here. Tell the tank to stop." Castro mumbled the instructions into the radio. The noise of the first explosion aboard the *Aventuro* rocked the night, the fiery red mass making the sky even brighter as flames leaped up from the hold. His mouth against

Castro's ear, Callender said. "Give them five minutes to get in position." He pointed up to the sky at the last descending parachute, then held out his hand, his fingers spread. "Five minutes."

The soldiers from the troop carriers disembarked, fanned out across the area, crouching in position, ready for the signal from their commanders to advance to the cliff.

The two television crews were out of their vehicle, cameras focused alternately on Castro and Callender and then panning out to the scattered formations of soldiers crouching before the attack. Still photographers circled the command car like a swarm of fireflies, flashes of strobe lights illuminating the figures of Castro and Callender as the shutters clicked.

At the end of five minutes, Castro gave the attack signal. The semicircle of troops ran toward the rendezvous point and fifty yards away, their machine guns started firing, spraying a quarter mile of the coastline with deadly bullets.

Coordinates: 23.30 Latitude × 81.40 Longitude

Hotdog Schwartz had a wild animal intuition for danger, not an instinct for self-protection but a domesticated, acquired sense of loyalty sworn into his blood. It had been different in the old days of Luciano and Shransky: as long as a man stayed in line, did not try to double-cross authority, he would be protected. The old timers had a fierce devotion to taking care of their own. Victor Castle had been a punk then, a kid named Vittorio Casteleone who was hungry for power, clawing his way to the top, a cat going up a tree. Castle was a new kind of don, visible on Wall Street and Zurich as well as in the gambling casinos of the world. Schwartz did not trust him. In spite of the interchange of words of faith, Schwartz instinctively knew that he was being used by Castle, that the men who purported to protect him were really assassins.

There had been no trouble in locating the big ginko tree. The small dirt-farm had not changed in nineteen years. The house had the same thatched roof, in the same state of disrepair. There were fewer pigs sloughing at the trough, less regimented lines in the furrows of planting. The tree had seemed enormous the night he dug under it to stash the Mafia money. It was more enormous now, the girth even greater. Schwartz's mark still scarred the bark. His eyes followed the line to the ground where the old roots were partially exposed, growing above the powdery soil. A section of the root split in a V shape, the box was below the crook of this wishbone formation.

He dug quickly. The two men were behind him, their backs to him, their guns in position, their bodies beaconing the area in half-arcs . . . back and forth, slowly.

The shovel hit the hard steel. Schwartz turned to see if Castle's men had heard the sound. Evidently they had not. Their surveillance was steady, uninterrupted. Schwartz got down on his hands and knees, scratched at the ground with his mutilated fingers until the top of the box was free. He dug deeper at the sides, exposing the handles, saw the edge of the waterproof bag he had buried beside it. Slowly, he worked the bag loose, reached inside, and felt the cold steel of a gun, the sticky, thick oil of the grease protecting it.

His hand was shaking. The gun was slippery. He crooked his finger around the trigger, yanked it out of the bag, and aimed it at the back of one of the mercenaries. He pulled the trigger but it would not move. With all his strength he tried again but the mechanism was deadlocked.

The first bullet, muffled by the silencer, hit him in the shoulder, the impact flinging him against the ginko tree. Then the other mercenary fired, the same muffled sound, and a piercing pain as the bullet penetrated his throat, the trajectory stopped by the huge tree trunk behind him.

Schwartz was still conscious as the men kicked his body aside, pulled the steel box out of the grave. One of the men bent over him, took his papers from his pocket, substituted other papers, another passport. "I think this Yid is still alive." He looked to the other mercenary for instructions.

The last bullet ended the pictures in Hotdog Schwartz's mind. The revolutionaries were not torturing him anymore. They had at last stopped pulling out his fingernails one by one.

Coordinates: 23.30 Latitude × 82.30 Longitude

Edgerton fell to the ground at the first burst of machine-gun fire, rolled to the cover of a fallen tree, miraculously escaped the bullets. Rinaldi, who had been standing next to him, was shot down immediately, his body skipping across the ground under repetitive blasts of gunfire.

Ramirez and six mercenaries, roped together, about to begin their descent down the cliff, were caught in crossfire from the two segments, their bodies fragmenting under the double impact, pieces of bloody human meat spraying the sky.

Crawling on his stomach, Edgerton snaked through the brush to the edge of the cliff, rolled down a few yards, hung to a dead tree root protruding from the rocks, swung his body so that he could get a foothold in a deep fissure and was then able to brace his body against the rocks.

Below him, the black-suited underwater team tred water, looking up to the sounds of the machine guns, buoyed packages of explosives bobbing in the water between them. Edgerton spotted the herd of leaping porpoises streaking toward the shore, the spears attached to their backs, making strange silhouettes against the fiery light of the burning brigantine. In the three minutes, it was all over, nothing left on the surface of the water but the bobbing bundles of dynamite. The man-killer trained mammals had performed perfectly. Two minutes later, Edgerton spotted the herd surfacing in the distance, heading out to sea, responding to an underwater audio command calling them to their underwater network pen.

Out on the water, its white hull gleaming, the yacht *Valkyrie* was suddenly spotlighted from four sides by Cuban coastal-patrol boats which had surrounded it. The boats opened fire on the yacht simultaneously. It burst into flame, became the second burning hulk on the water.

The voices came from almost directly overhead. The two figures talking, pointing out to the burning vessels on the water, were illuminated by the bright lights of the television cameras. It was the victors: Castro and Callender.

Edgerton called out. "Lowell."

The answer was a single shot, narrowly missing him, ricocheting off the rocks.

"Damn it, Lowell, it's me . . . Edgerton." He looked up. It was Callender's gun that was drawn, the muzzle still smoking.

Callender took more careful aim.

Hanging on to the root, using all his strength, Edgerton swung his body in an arc, the jutting rocks grazing his body.

The bullet missed him.

When he caught footing again, looked up, there were two other men beside Callender. Fidel Castro was restraining Callender's arm, preventing him from firing the third shot. "Alive," Castro said. "I want the prisoners alive."

The edge of the cliff was in brightness as the lights of the television crew filmed Castro and Callender. Edgerton turned his head away, hiding his face as the camera was pointed down toward him, kept it hidden as three Cuban soldiers pulled him up to the safety of the level ground. Two of the soldiers twisted his strained arms behind his back, forced his head up, full face toward the camera. Another group had come forward, aimed their automatic weapons at him. The television cameras kept recording the rescue and capture.

"For Christ's sake, Callender, tell them who I am."

Castro signaled to the television crew. The lights went off, the sound of the cameras stopped. Castro turned to Callender. "You know this man?"

In the moment that Callender hesitated, Edgerton felt his insides empty out, his heart sink.

When the moment of decision was over, Callender said, "He's one of my men. I didn't recognize him in the dark."

1978
AUGUST

16

THURSDAY

CONCOURSE G, GATE 72, MIAMI INTERNATIONAL AIRPORT, MIAMI, FLORIDA

Edgerton saw her before she saw him, the trim, little figure in a neat linen suit and short white gloves. Her hair was pulled away from her face again, tied in back with a bright yellow ribbon. When she saw him standing in the center of the corridor, she hesitated and then ran to him. They kissed each other, clutched each other, soothed each other with silent caresses, oblivious to the people around them. When they separated, stood apart to examine each other, she touched his upper lip where the moustache had been, skimmed the bruises and cuts on his face.

"Are you all right?"

He nodded, afraid to talk, close to tears.

"I knew you'd come. I knew you'd call. That's why I waited for you on Andros."

"Blind faith?"

She nodded, biting her lip. "You've given me that." She lowered her head. "You've made me whole again."

They held each other tightly to avoid saying words with impossible implications. They both understood that what they felt for each other; although it was ended, it would endure for their lifetimes.

"What are you going to do after L.A.? Des Moines?"

"I don't think so. I'll stick it out for a while."

"Maybe . . ."

She put her fingers over his mouth to stop the words, shook her

head. "I used to be so afraid of the future. Somehow I'm not anymore."

The loudspeaker blared the final boarding call for National's
flight 867 to Los Angeles.

Without another word or another touch, she backed away from
him, half ran to the gate, stood at the end of the boarding line.
Edgerton watched her until she disappeared into the jetway, then
walked slowly down the passageway against the mainstream of
traffic.

The main terminal was jammed with confusion, people and police
preparing for the arrival of Fidel Castro's private plane bringing
Lowell Callender back from Havana to a hero's welcome in Miami.
Edgerton buffered his way through the crowd, went into the lobby
of the airport hotel, took the elevator up to his room, double-locked
the door, kicked off his shoes, turned on the television.

The media was dramatizing the parallel. The cliff at Miramar was
the new San Juan Hill; Lowell Callender the new Rough Rider hero
to a hero-hungry press. Side-by-side photographs of Lowell Callender and Theodore Roosevelt appeared on the inside pages of the
newspapers while the front pages blared the photographs of Castro
and Callender fighting off the commando raid against Cuba. For the
day and a half Edgerton had been back in Miami, every television
newscast reran the footage of Castro and Callender leading the
counterattack on the Miramar cliff so often that he finally kept the
tube blank most of the time.

None of the media seemed to question the sudden and instant
availability of background information, boyhood, and family photographs of the unknown, pedantic-looking undersecretary. Political
cartoonists came up with similiar concepts: Clark Kent into Superman, meek-appearing diplomat into fearless warrior. Worldwide
political analysis interpreted Castro's public statements of gratitude
to Lowell Callender as a giant leap forward in the acceleration of
normal diplomatic relations between the United States and Cuba as
well as being debilitating to Russian-Cuban détente. *Time* magazine,
working with a man named Farnsworth in Callender's Washington
office, was preparing a cover story. *Newsweek* was compiling questions to ask Callender on the Middle East on the theory that his
expertise could be expanded to deal with that crisis.

The excitement of the Callender story obliterated the smooth machinery backing up the serendipitous hero, directing the dissemination of information, organizing a hero's homecoming.

From the window of his hotel room, Edgerton looked out across the airport to the huge crowd gathered at the far end of the field, awaiting the arrival of Castro's plane. The same picture, close up, was repeated on the muted television screen. Edgerton ran his hand over his upper lip, felt naked without the moustache. He lay on the bed, watched the tube, saw the plane land, make the long taxi across the network of runways, stop in front of the cameras, and he waited with the world for the steps to be let down and for Lowell Callender to appear.

Edgerton kept the sound off. He was tired of hearing the lies unsuspecting news commentators repeated over and over.

Because of possible reprisal by Cuban Nationals living in Florida, this section of the airport was cordoned off by a solid line of United States Marine Corps elite. While there was a delay in opening the door of Castro's plane, the camera panned the faces of the guards: strong, young, American faces endorsing the hero.

Four Cuban soldiers got off the plane first, formed a guard midway and at the base of the steps. Jud Wheeler got off the plane first, smiling and waving, looking the part of an advance man for a presidential candidate. Finally Callender himself, back in the uniform of horn-rimmed glasses and seersucker suit, blinking in the sunlight, appearing to be overwhelmed by the hero's reception and appearing to be humble in the face of adulation.

An unsteady woman, supported by two bewildered young adults, was pushed toward him. Callender embraced them all as the camera recorded the family reunion.

One of the reception officials thrust a portable telephone into Callender's hands. The television screen split to Washington; the President, in one corner, smiling, saying toothy words. Callender in the other corner listening to the Presidential praises, mumbling modest thanks.

Edgerton turned off the television, faced the anonymity of another hotel, a future as blank as the television screen.

In the few minutes he had been alone with Callender in Havana, they had reached a standoff show of power, a balance of strength, equal nuclear capabilities. Edgerton related to Jack Kelly, knew the feeling of owing another man your life. Callender could have had Castro's men imprison and torture him, eventually kill him. He knew that he would never have broken, never revealed his CIA identity. He was trained for that. But at the last moment, Callender had saved his life. Why?

"We're going to need each other," Callender explained. "Some day, in some way, we're going to have to depend on each other."

"Or kill each other."

"Possibly."

"If you get out of line, Callender, turn from hero to tyrant, I promise you that I will personally gun you down. When you start fooling with the government, deceiving the people, remember that I'm out there somewhere with a loaded gun."

"Guns," Callender said, "fire in both directions."

Standoff.

Now this new period of waiting had begun, the short burst of action over until the next time. If the next time were ever to happen.

His cover identity was intact. He had run out on the *Playgirl* story and the project had collapsed without him. He was the compulsive loser again; the chance at another film career blown, a beginning of a relationship with Monica aborted almost before it began.

He looked down at himself, inexplicably erected: did not dissect the mechanism which had made him hard. It was enough to know that it was functioning again. He was left alone with the continuing confusion of self, with a loaded gun capable of shooting down a corrupt man who wanted to be President, and with a gold cock ring studded with emerald eyes.

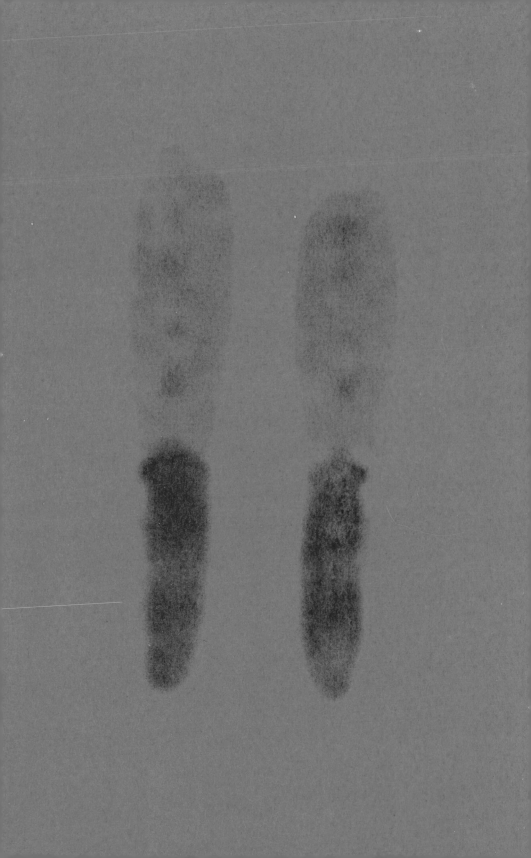

Himmel, R.
    Lions at night.

c. 3